North Harbor

Murder, Mayhem and Smuggling

on the Maine Coast

A Novel by Kennedy Hudner

Cover art by Jarmila Takac

Editing by Donald Kray

Disclaimer

Dedication-

To Jennifer – Who would have believed 43 years?

Not bad for two skinny kids who started out with twelve

dollars in the bank and a lot of dreams.

Other books by Kennedy Hudner:

Alarm of War

Alarm of War, Book II – The Other Side of Fear

Alarm of War, Book III – Desperate Measures

Riddle Me a Death

"The wind always blows a little colder in North Harbor."

--Luc Dumas, sculptor of *Last Charge of the Warrior*

Chapter 1

Fate of a Poacher

They had the anchor chain wrapped halfway around his body when he suddenly woke up and screamed. Scared the hell out of Jacques and Guy, who both backed up so fast that Guy lost his balance and sat down on a mound of baitfish.

"*Jesus Fucking Christ!*" Jacques screamed, which was a funny thing to say, since he'd been the one to shoot Mitchell with the AR-15, after all. It had been a tough shot, fired from the *Celeste* some two hundred yards across the moving Atlantic to Mitchell's lobster boat. In fact, Jacques had fired four shots and only hit Mitchell once, but that shot had grooved the top of Mitchell's head, smashing him to the deck.

A good shot.

They had thought he was dead.

Not quite, apparently.

Mitchell somehow struggled to his feet, screaming and tearing at the chain. Still in his frenzy, he saw the man at the pilot's wheel.

"For the love of God, Jean-Philippe!" Mitchell screamed in terror. "Don't let them kill me!" he implored. "It's just a lobster trap! Jean-Philippe! A fucking lobster trap! I'm begging you." He lurched to the side then, crashing up against the ship's low side rail, throwing out his arms to avoid falling overboard.

For any lobsterman in Maine, falling into the frigid Atlantic was the ultimate horror. Even a lobsterman who'd been shot in the head.

Jean-Philippe LeBlanc paused for a fleeting moment. Mitchell was the very worst thing a lobsterman could ever be: a *poacher,* but he had known him since grade school. They'd been altar boys together. But if Mitchell knew, if he *knew...* Fuck it. He glared at his younger brothers. "Don't just stand there, you morons, throw him over!" But Jacques and Guy stood frozen, repulsed and terrified at the sight in front of them.

Then there was a "BANG," followed by two more, and Mitchell's face blossomed into rose petals of gore. He toppled backwards over the railing and, with a last wail, vanished into the cold ocean depths, his body tumbling and turning as he sank. The end of the chain, still loosely wrapped around him, followed him over the side with a splash. Then there was an abrupt silence while the lobstermen looked at each other in shock at what they had done.

Bruno Banderas lowered his pistol. He looked at Jacques and Guy and spat contemptuously. *"Están pero si bien pendejos!"* he snarled. You are fucking idiots. Banderas was a barrel-chested, ugly bulldog of a man, with a jutting, pugnacious jaw and an angry expression that told everyone in sight he was just looking for an excuse to punch them.

He turned to Jean-Philippe. "Is it here?" he asked urgently. *"Is* it here?"

Jean-Philippe scanned the rear of Mitchell's boat, where the working deck was cluttered with lobster traps, buoys, coils of rope and buckets of baitfish. At one end stood a lobster trap that held a large waterproof sack, the size of a bag of fertilizer you might buy at Home Depot. Jean-Philippe sighed in relief. If it hadn't been here, he did not know what would happen. His brothers and he could hold their own in a bar fight, but Banderas...Banderas was a killer. More importantly, Banderas was the man sent by the Sinaloa Cartel to oversee drug smuggling through North Harbor into the rest of northern New England. He was not a Mexican, but was the leader of the Dominican gang in Massachusetts that worked with the Cartel. The gang's job was to make the "last mile" delivery of heroin produced in Mexico and smuggled into the United States.

Banderas was not a man to be trifled with. Or crossed.

"Right there," LeBlanc said, pointing. He worked to keep his voice steady. "I told you that he'd keep it."

Banderas opened the trap, pulled the bag out and cut it open with a knife, inspecting what was inside. He nodded once, looking relieved. He turned back to Jean-Philippe. He had very cold eyes. "Don't let this happen again, LeBlanc," he warned harshly.

"Me?" LeBlanc protested. "Shit, *I* didn't let anything happen. Mitchell stole one of my traps. It wasn't my fault, for Christ's sake."

Banderas shook his head in wonder. *Could the man really be that stupid?* "This is the Cartel you're dealing with. *Fault* does not matter, only failure. And if you fail, there is a price."

"What the..." But Jean-Philippe's voice trailed off as Banderas glared at him. And for the first time, Jean-Philippe LeBlanc understood, *really* understood, what he had gotten involved in.

They quickly set fires in the engine compartment and the main cabin of Mitchell's boat. Then, carrying the sack, they crossed back over to LeBlanc's lobster boat, the *Celeste.* Banderas clambered down the steps into the small cabin. He cut off the waterproof wrapping and took out two thick, plastic bags, which he placed next to a small scale. First, he weighed the larger bag, then the smaller, carefully noting their weight in a pocket notebook. Satisfied, he nodded. Thirteen kilos of some of the purest heroin in the world. About thirty pounds. The little bag had four kilos of fentanyl, just a bit under nine pounds. He took out a small, compact satellite phone and punched in a number. When the call connected, he spoke in rapid Spanish, nodding while he spoke. After a moment he held the receiver against his chest and looked at Jean-Philippe.

"They want to know when we'll arrive."

LeBlanc looked at his GPS unit, typing in a course that would not be a straight line from the scene of either Mitchell's murder or the pickup. He held up two fingers.

"*Dos horas*," Banderas said into the Sat phone. Two hours. He thumbed the phone off and packed it away. Folding his arms, he turned back to the table and the two bags. "We're payin' you twenty-five thousand dollars to get this to shore; good money for a few hours work." He looked LeBlanc in the eye. "So, you don't want to fuck this up, you understand?"

The *Celeste* motored westward towards the afternoon sun. Behind them, Mitchell's lobster boat was fully engulfed, with flames leaping twenty feet into the air, fanned by a wind that pushed it farther and farther out to sea.

There would be no evidence of who had been on board, or why.

———————

Already a mile behind them, and one hundred feet deep, the body of Henry Mitchell came to rest on a large rock outcropping. He landed on the side of a steep boulder and gently slid down its side, coming to a stop almost standing up. The chain had unwrapped and slid down his body until it just rested across his foot, still enough weight to keep him from floating up to the surface.

For now.

Chapter 2
North Harbor – Calvin

Calvin Finley quietly rolled out of bed. Across the room his older brother, Jacob, slept with the covers pulled over his head to ward off the morning chill. Calvin felt around until he found his swim trunks and pulled them on, then padded downstairs to the small kitchen.

Sunrise was still an hour away, but already the eastern sky glowed a warm blue, with long tendrils of gold caressing the sky. It was going to be a glorious sunrise. He put on a pot of coffee and began making a bowl of hot oatmeal, careful not to make any noise that would wake his parents in the bedroom above the kitchen. Then he pulled on a flannel shirt and a pair of sweatpants and stood in the large window that looked south across the mouth of North Harbor, which gave the town its name. To the east, Sheep Island sat a little more than half a mile out. Ten miles to the Northeast was Acadia National Park and the city of Bar Harbor, where the tourists flocked in the summer, eating ice cream and gawking at the seals. Just under five miles to the southeast – and a world away – was the Town of Stonington, famous for its lobster fleet, quaint stores and the rich folks who owned second homes there.

Calvin snorted under his breath. No rich folks in North Harbor. North Harbor was a hard-scrabble sort of town that made its living from the sea. It was as quaint as a Walmart parking lot. There was a mix of lobster and fishing boats, the Cadot Fishery, and the North Harbor Ship Yard that offered maintenance and repairs to the commercial boats that plied its waters, and the nets, traps, rope, fittings and spare parts they'd need in the normal course. North Harbor had two Catholic churches, an Episcopal church and a Baptist church.

The churches were thriving.

There were four bars, three small restaurants, a surprisingly good Hannaford's grocery store with a huge section that sold ships' supplies, Zedek's Funeral Home, Baxter's Drug Store and Goldsmith's Department Store, which sold bits and pieces of everything the other stores didn't.

The coffee was ready and he poured a mug, spooning in three sugars and topping it off with condensed milk. He was tall, lanky and dark haired like his mother, but with hard-earned swimmer's shoulders. He had a dreamer's smile and a toddler's belly laugh, which constantly embarrassed him. He sipped the coffee absently while he stirred the oatmeal, thinking about the physics exam he had to take that afternoon. It was his last year of high school and he still hadn't decided what he was going to do next year, lobstering or college, despite all the pressure from his parents to go to college and "stay on track." He had his eye on a twenty-four-foot Novi with a 4-stroke Suzuki 150 outboard. If he borrowed some money from Grandpa Dumas and sold his little boat, he could *maybe* buy the Novi. The owner wanted $30,000 for it, but Calvin figured he could get that down some. Calvin had $3,000 that he'd saved from part-time jobs and his lobstering, plus with luck he might get another $1,000 for his lobster skiff. With the Novi, he could carry more traps and could fish the coastal waters with no problem, though he'd be a fool to take it out to the deeper waters offshore. Once the lobsters migrated offshore in late fall, he could get a job as a sternsman on one of the big highliners and earn some pretty good money there. Two or three years and he could sell the Novi and get a bigger boat.

If the lobstering was good. *If* he didn't need any big repairs. *If* the price of lobsters didn't crash.

He sighed. Seemed like a lot of "ifs" and "maybes."

His oatmeal was ready. He took the hot pot to the table and put it on a trivet, then poured in raisins and sprinkled it with brown sugar. Outside the sky and the water were both creeping towards the "golden hour" that he loved so much. If his mother was awake, she'd be outside with her old Nikon, snapping pictures that she'd frame and sell in art shops in Ellsworth or Rockland. He glanced at his watch; he had to eat and get going. He wolfed down the hot oatmeal, put the dishes in the sink and checked the water temperature on his phone app: 53 F. Still pretty damn cold out there for the end of April, but he'd swum in cold ocean water almost every day for two years now, and he had the right gear. He went down to the basement, found his 7-mm wetsuit and began the laborious process of pulling it on. Suit, boots and hood, then gloves. He belted on an inflatable life belt and tested the strobe light he wore on the back of his hood. His grandfather had suggested the strobe light. "Won't keep you from drownin'," he'd said in his Down East accent, "but might make it easier to find the body. Be nice to give you a good Christian burial."

Lastly, he slipped a pair of goggles over his head, letting them rest on his forehead for the moment, then went out the back door and walked down the path past his Grandpa's house to the beach. No sandy beach here, it was a steep rock embankment that dropped thirty feet to a stone shingle. He walked down the stairs to the dock he'd built with his father and grandfather, keeping an eye out for any broken or sagging steps, then out onto the dock itself.

A cold northerly wind buffeted him as he walked out to the end of the dock, stirring up the waves. The water and the sky were golden now, shimmering and glowing with the approaching sun. Sunrise was no more than ten minutes away. Here in the local waters, thousands of lobster buoys bobbed in the morning breeze. In the distance he could hear the diesel rumble of the big lobster boats – the highliners – chugging their way past Grog Island and Bold Island, then past the rocky spire called The Shivers, and from there out into Jericho Bay itself.

It was all so beautiful. The sun, the salt tang in the air, the breeze in his face, the sound of the living ocean, and the golden glow of the morning. It filled him with a sudden, fierce exultation.

He nodded once, then lowered himself into the frigid, glimmering water, let his breathing settle, then took a deep breath and began to swim. Sheep Island, desolate and boggy, good for nothing except breeding prodigious quantities of mosquitoes and black flies, beckoned in the morning light of the day.

Calvin Finley swam towards it, like he always did, embracing the sea like a lover.

Frank Finley opened his eyes at 5:30 a.m. sharp and slipped from the bed. The floor was cold under his bare feet. He pulled on a heavy shirt and work pants, found a pair of wool socks and carried them downstairs to the kitchen. The light was on, as usual. An empty bowl of oatmeal, a partially empty cooking pot and a used coffee mug sat in the sink.

Finley grabbed the binoculars and walked out on the porch, which offered a clear view of the expanse between their little dock and Sheep Island. No fog this morning and the island stood out in dark silhouette to the rising sun. Focusing the binoculars, he first saw the strobe light Calvin wore, then located the fluorescent orange wetsuit Calvin used when the water was really cold, which was most of the time this far north. Calvin's mother, Danielle, was a nurse in the local clinic and ever mindful of simple, practical things that can be done to enhance safety. She'd insisted on the bright color, much to Calvin's dismay, but it made the boy stick out like a sore thumb. Which was the idea. He was swimming strongly, already reaching Sheep Island. Some days he turned around and just swam back, others he swam all the way around the island. He watched for another two minutes as Calvin rolled over and waved in his general direction, then began to swim back.

Finley checked his watch, then walked quietly back upstairs and shook Jacob awake. "You've got to get going or you'll be late again," he warned softly. "I'll get you some coffee you can drink on the way." Jacob muttered under his breath, but sat up and rubbed his face vigorously with his hands. "Why the hell did I take this job?" he groaned.

"But you did," his father replied, "and now you're going to do it well. Get going."

When he got back to the kitchen, Danielle was already there. She had brushed out her hair and it hung well below her shoulders, raven black against her pale skin. She was wrapped in a shawl over her nightgown to ward off the chill and her hands cupped a large bowl of steaming coffee.

She gestured to the binoculars that Finley still carried. "Where's our baby seal?"

"Just reached Sheep Island and is heading back. Should be here in fifteen minutes or so, depending on the current." He grinned. "That orange wetsuit does make him easier to spot."

She sipped her coffee and sighed. "I wish he wouldn't swim when the water is so cold." She didn't say it, but she recalled a boy in her high school class who had been swept off a fishing boat one winter day and died from exposure. The ocean was not forgiving.

Finley grinned ruefully. "So do I, but I'd rather have him swim where I can see him than sneak off somewhere. And he knows these waters now. Safer here than elsewhere."

"He's so pigheaded," she complained. She arched her eyebrows. "I wonder where he got that from?" she asked innocently.

"I think he'll be okay," Finley replied, ignoring her jibe. "With all the cold-water swimming he's been doing, he's put on a nice layer of subcutaneous fat that should protect him. Plus the wetsuit, of course."

Danielle giggled. "I shouldn't laugh, but he does look like a baby seal, all smooth and sleek."

A moment later Jacob shuffled into the kitchen, still half asleep. Danielle wordlessly handed him a cup of coffee while Finley buttered him some toast. She looked at him fondly, always struck by the attributes he inherited: his father's short stature, stolid features and innate wariness, broad chest and surprisingly broad shoulders – perhaps from lobstering for the last two years – and light brown hair that must have come from some ancestor on Frank's side of the family. Jacob lacked Calvin's spontaneous laughter and often seemed hesitant, as if waiting for something unpleasant to jump out of the closet. It always triggered Danielle's protective instincts. She sighed inwardly; how could the same parents have such different children?

"Don't get comfortable," Frank warned Jacob. "I'll run you down to the docks in just a minute. You'll just be in time."

Jacob grunted something unintelligible. Then Calvin came through the door, salt water dripping everywhere. His lips were blue, but he was smiling. Danielle shook her head and handed him a large mug of steaming hot chocolate. "You're pushing your luck, Calvin Finley," she scolded. "One of these days you're going to turn to ice out there and that will be that."

Jacob smirked. "When it happens, can I have your laptop?"

Calvin ignored them. "A pod of seals swam with me all the way out to Sheep Island. They kept circling me and barking!" He laughed. "It was the coolest thing; they were so funny."

"They'd never seen an insane human before," Jacob offered.

"Or some poor mother seal was looking for her long-lost pup," Danielle suggested.

Finley glanced at his watch and shook his head. "Jacob, time to go. Bring it in the car. Let's go." He kissed his wife and went outside to warm up the car. Even though it was already late April, there was a touch of frost in the grass.

After they left, Calvin sat in the kitchen, hunched over his hot cocoa. "Tease me all you want, but this sure as heck isn't Philadelphia."

Danielle smiled at him. The boys had complained mightily when their father had given up his job in the Philadelphia Police Department to come to Maine, but once here Calvin had been astonished at the beauty of the Maine Coast and the ocean. Philadelphia may have been a major port city, but you never felt connected to the water living there. Here, the ocean was with you almost every minute of every day. The boys had learned to sail on one of their grandfather's sailboats, had learned how to use a skiff, and Calvin had even started lobstering. Danielle was worried about the schools, but the boys seemed to be doing okay. Jacob graduated with solid marks, if not spectacular. Danielle wasn't pleased to see him decline college, opting instead for a job on a lobster boat, and let him know it on more than one occasion. All in vain. Jacob stubbornly refused to even consider more education. *You can lead a boy to water,* she thought, *but he might just stay there.*

Calvin was the stronger student, and Duke University was recruiting him for its swim team, but the pull of the ocean was strong and she wasn't surprised to see him thinking about full-time lobstering for a year or two. Dismayed, but not surprised. Sometimes she wanted to grab his shoulders and shake some sense into him.

Boys! she thought wryly. There were days she would have killed for one sensible, practical, future-minded daughter.

———

Finley pulled into a spot by the docks. Jacob wordlessly handed him the empty coffee mug and Finley put it into a brown paper bag to take back home at the end of the day. "Got everything?" he asked his son.

"Guess so," Jacob muttered.   He pushed open the car door and walked over to the picnic bench where the crews for the LeBlanc boats were getting their assignments.   He wasn't the last one to show up, but he certainly wasn't the first, either.   There were six boats owned by the LeBlanc family, and crews were assigned to them at random each morning at 5:30 a.m. He dutifully stood in line, shuffling forward when it was his turn.

A hard-faced man with broad shoulders and the clipboard looked up, nodding once. "Wondered if you were going to make it today," he said.

"I'm here," Jacob said, trying to put a little defiance into his voice, despite the fact that this man scared the bejesus out of him.   This guy radiated a "Don't-fuck-with-me-or-I-will-kick-your-teeth-in" vibe that made Jacob very wary in his presence.   But this guy also controlled the hiring for six lobster boats, so Jacob smiled and waited to see if he was working today.

The big man studied his clipboard again. "Okay, Finley, you're on the *Petite Marie* today, working the immediate coast. See Captain Marc." The *Petite Marie* was the smallest lobster boat in the LeBlanc fleet and only worked the local waters.   It wasn't fast enough to work the deeper waters twenty miles out.   It meant lots of stops and starts, hauling up one or two traps at a time instead of a trawl line of twenty or so.   Jacob would be the only sternsman.   It would be a hard day's work.

"Thank you," he said and began walking down the pier to where the *Petite Marie* was tied up.

Behind him, Jean-Philippe LeBlanc stared at the Finley boy for a long moment.   Jacob Finley was the son of a cop.   LeBlanc pursed his lips thoughtfully – that had so many risks...and such amazing possibilities.

Chapter 3
Six Months Earlier:
The Director of Puzzles

Wallace Charles Moore III was short, overweight, prematurely balding, sweated a lot and had few social graces.

He walked like a duck.

He also had a job that paid him $700,000, his own hacienda overlooking the bay, a butler, two lithe Mexican girls at his beck and call and a BMW M6 Gran Coupe, with driver. Wallace knew his driver was also a bodyguard, but he didn't know that the driver was under strict orders to kill him if it ever looked like he was going to be arrested.

This was simple prudence: Wallace knew *way* too much about the Sinaloa Cartel to be left in the hands of the authorities.

Just now, however, Wallace had a problem.

All up and down U.S. Highway I-95, his client's shipments of heroin and fentanyl were being intercepted at higher than usual rates. Much higher. And he didn't know why.

Wallace Charles Moore III came to the Sinaloa Cartel unconventionally. He wasn't Mexican, or Columbian, or even Dominican, the usual nationalities involved in big-time drug smuggling into the US. He was American, born and bred. For a boy who was overweight and walked funny, high school was a living nightmare best left behind. He survived it, barely, and left for college with a sense of relief.

In college he studied business operations and quickly realized that a company can have the best product in the world, but if it did not distribute it effectively into the marketplace, it was doomed. He focused on distribution systems: how they worked; what went wrong; who did it right and how. After college he first took a job with Fed Ex and stayed there for five years. It was a wonderful place to work and he learned something every day. He made some suggestions for improvements, most of which were implemented and worked. The bosses took note. He moved up fast, despite his woeful personality and physical appearance. Fed Ex respected talent, regardless of the package it came in.

But five years was enough to know he had learned most of what he could get out of Fed Ex. Wallace then looked around to see who was the undisputed master at fast, efficient delivery, then called Amazon and told them he had a way to save them three percent on every shipment.

Amazon respected talent, too. Within a week he had a job and within six months he got his first bonus, a 'thank you' from the employer who realized that Wallace had already saved it millions of dollars.

It was all good, but at the end of the day, he was still Wallace.

And he still walked like a duck.

His co-workers were polite enough, but he heard the snickers behind his back, heard the jokes. None of them were *friends*. When he asked women for a date, they still declined. It was all very polite, but he still had to buy sex. That was easy enough to do in Seattle, where catering to the needs of Amazon employees was a major industry, but even the prostitutes looked at him with derision.

Everything was okay, really. Except it wasn't.

He did not belong. He would *never* belong. Worse, he knew it.

So, he began to look for a new employer. An employer who could...*respect* him in all the ways he needed respect. An employer who had a great product, but chronic difficulty getting it to market. And so the next time Wallace bought cocaine, he told his dealer that he had something important to tell the supplier. The dealer recoiled in horror at the idea of taking anyone to see his supplier, let alone this fat, obnoxious white boy who might be a narc for all he knew, and turned him down flat.

Wallace was not put off; he had anticipated this. He wrote a succinct note, put it in an envelope and sealed it. "Give this to your supplier," he told the dealer. "If you don't, I'll make sure the supplier finds out and you will be in deep shit." The dealer didn't know whether to beat him, shoot him or obey him. Truth be told, the fat boy sort of creeped him out.

The following week, the dealer gave the note to his supplier.

The supplier read the note and started to throw it away, but paused and reread it.

"Who is this guy?" he asked the dealer.

"Some white guy works at Amazon. Fat."

"He smart?" the supplier probed.

The dealer shrugged, dipping into his very scant knowledge of the comparative pay rates offered by Seattle's high-tech industry. "Guess so, they payin' him good, far as I can see."

The supplier thought about it for another week, then flew to Los Angeles and gave the note to *his* supplier. This was the man who took the dope off the trucks, cars, boats and planes from Mexico. This was the man who dealt directly with the Sinaloa Cartel. The Big Boys.

The Big Supplier looked at the note and frowned. He read it two or three times, then pursed his lips. "Okay," he told the local supplier, "I'll take it from here."

Five weeks later, as Wallace was leaving work on Friday night, a car pulled up beside him and the rear window rolled down. The man inside waved the note out the window. "You write this note, Mr. Moore?" he asked pleasantly.

Wallace felt torn. This could be a cop. Or a Fed. Or...

Or this could be the chance of a lifetime.

He nodded.

The back door opened. "Get in, Mr. Moore, I am to take you to your job interview."

Wallace climbed into the car and his new life. Three hours later he flew out of the United States on a private plane to Mexico. After some lengthy interviews, three lie detector tests and four months of demonstrating what he could do, a tall, distinguished looking man with thick black hair walked into his office one day.

The man studied him curiously. "Do you know who I am?" he asked softly.

Wallace shook his head. "No, sir. I mean no offense, but I don't know who you are."

The man, one of the most powerful and feared men in Mexico, nodded, his face crinkling with amusement. The reports were right – this American was a lunatic. Brilliant, but a lunatic. "You have a job, Mr. Moore," he said warmly. "I think you will like the terms. We have only one rule that must be obeyed: Never, *ever* discuss our affairs with anyone outside of the organization, or you will be subject to...harsh penalties. Do you understand?"

Wallace nodded. Of course he understood. Did they think he was an idiot?

"Welcome to Sinaloa, Mr. Moore," the man said, shaking Wallace's moist hand. "I look forward to a mutually beneficial relationship." Then he left. Wallace eventually learned the man was Ismael Zambada García, the last surviving member of the original Sinaloa Cartel, a fugitive from every police agency in North and South America. His new boss.

Mexico was now his home. Forever. But there were compensations. That night, when he was taken to his new hacienda with a view of the bay, there was a slender, beautiful nineteen-year-old woman named Maria Elena waiting for him in his bed.

Wallace never looked back.

Smuggling drugs was traditionally a matter of flooding the smuggling route with as many couriers as possible and accepting there would be some losses. Bribing customs officials and local police helped, but still some five to seven percent of all the drugs smuggled across the border would be seized before they could reach the streets. That was just the cost of doing business.

Wallace took a more systematic, data-driven approach. He analyzed the data, identified the weakest methods of transport – big trucks carrying machine tools and other bulky items – and eliminated them. In their place he organized a series of hundreds of couriers carrying small amounts of heroin and, increasingly, fentanyl. Tourists returning from Mexico, Mexican-Americans traveling to Mexico to see family, businessmen, just about anyone with a good reason to travel from Mexico into the United States. He even arranged for the Cartel to intercept auto carriers bringing new cars into the U.S., but instead of hiding drugs in the cars, they hid it inside the tires of the auto carrier itself. In the first nine months, he reduced the amount of seizures from the customary five to seven percent down to three percent. This translated into tens of millions of additional dollars flowing into the Cartel's coffers.

There were problems, of course. Using the approach of many small shipments meant that instead of a few dozen people involved, there were hundreds, and in some years, thousands. People made mistakes. People got greedy, or stupid, or afraid. People got arrested, sometimes for something not at all related to drug smuggling. Once arrested, they often made deals and disappeared into witness protection programs. Then the Feds watched one of their networks and traced it from the drop point in, say, Maine, all the way down the line to the Mexican border.

Then, when the Feds were good and ready, the raids came and the Cartel lost hundreds of kilos of product. And, of course, the network, itself.

Wallace helped the Cartel stay one or two jumps ahead of the Feds and the State Police. First, he bribed a *lot* of people: drug enforcement agents at airports, TSA agents, State Police, freight handlers, pilots and local cops. Lots of local cops. Wallace thought of himself as an unofficial 401k for many a small-town police department. A Good Samaritan, as it were, helping underpaid government officials achieve financial security.

Second, he constantly investigated new routes. He even did trial runs. Often, he would not ship the real product at first. He would test the waters, so to speak. In one case, this saved him from immense embarrassment, and perhaps worse. When the Feds seized one of his trial shipments, they discovered that they had just confiscated one hundred and seventy-five pounds of Grade A pure...baking powder.

True to form, Wallace dropped that smuggling route and moved on.

But now DEA raids along Interstate 95, the Sinaloa Cartel's primary land route for smuggling drugs to New England, were having a disastrous effect. Losses were running fifteen percent and were rising each month. The Dominicans in Lawrence and Lowell were screaming for more product, and warning the Cartel that if they couldn't deliver, it was only a question of time before some other cartel moved in to fill the void. Wallace thought there must be an informer within the organization, but the Cartel's very efficient and ruthless counterintelligence guys couldn't find him.

The land route was compromised. Nothing lasts forever.

But, Wallace mused, if not by land, then perhaps by sea.

Wallace had never been to Maine, but he knew how to read a map. Now he stood in front of a large map of Maine and pondered. There were forty-four ports in Maine, but of those, only three were major cargo ports and Homeland Security infested every one of them like guard rats. Wallace was already smuggling dope by freighter up to Canada, but to get more dope into Maine, he needed something else. He tapped his finger against his lips and thought. Finally, he sat down at his computer and activated Google. Three minutes later he sat back. Maine had two hundred and twenty-eight miles of coastline, but that was measuring linearly from top to bottom. If you measured the actual *shoreline*, with all of its inlets, harbors, ports, bays and crenellations, it measured a whopping 3,478 miles.

In other words, a smuggler's paradise.

Wallace Moore smiled. He had already used lobster boats to smuggle small amounts of heroin and fentanyl into the state, just to see if it was viable. The total number of people involved had been less than a dozen and the report from the Dominicans had been favorable. Now all he had to do was scale it up.

It was just fitting together the pieces of a puzzle, and he was good at puzzles.

Chapter 4
Rumi in Arabic

Frank Finley had barely sat down before the Chief opened his door and bellowed for him. Finley suppressed a sigh and went into the Chief's office. Michael Corcoran eyed him balefully. Chief Corcoran had not been enthusiastic about hiring Finley, but the Town Manager had insisted. During the two years Finley had been on the force, Corcoran had quietly retaliated by making his life as miserable as possible. He was constantly assigned to the weekend and evening shifts and generally got as many of the shit assignments as Corcoran could muster.

"I've got a missing person complaint that I want you to look into," he told Finley without preamble. He pushed a thin file across the table. "And this afternoon I want you to transfer a prisoner down to Portland PD. He should be ready about 3 p.m."

Which really meant he would be ready around 4 p.m. It was a three-hour drive to Portland, which meant he wouldn't get home until 11 p.m. or so, if nothing went wrong.

"Who am I taking?" Finley asked.

There was the faintest hint of a smirk on Corcoran's face. "Ralph Harkins."

Inwardly, Finley groaned. Harkins was a nasty, mean thug, a member of one of the motorcycle gangs that sold heroin and cocaine up and down the coast. He was mean when he was drunk, and he was drunk most of the time. A big man – six-three or so – and surprisingly fast, he liked to beat up people just for the hell of it. He had been arrested last night after a brawl at a local bar where he'd beaten the tar out of one of the local high school jocks. Finley frowned. Normally, two officers would be assigned the task of transporting a prisoner as violent as Harkins.

"Who's going with me?" he asked.

Corcoran looked up from his desk, as if surprised to see him still there. "Nobody. Everybody's busy, Finley. But, hey, you're the big-shot cop from Philadelphia, are you tellin' me you can't handle a shackled prisoner?"

Finley stood up. Nothing more to say. He walked out.

"Get me a report on that missing person! Soon!" Corcoran called after him.

———

The missing person was one Henry Mitchell, a lobsterman out of North Harbor and one of a dozen or so Mitchell family members who made their living from the sea. He had gone out at 4 a.m. three days ago and hadn't come back. His wife had filed the report – Finley frowned – two days ago. Now that he thought about it, he vaguely recalled hearing that someone was missing, but hadn't paid much attention to it. From Portland up the coast to Bar Harbor, it was a rare week when some fisherman didn't go missing. Most turned up, but not all.

There was a notation that the Coast Guard had been notified, but there was no indication of any report back from them. There were two Coast Guard Stations near North Harbor, at Rockland and Southwest Harbor. A few calls confirmed that the matter was being handled by Rockland.

"We found some wreckage two days ago, sir," a young Ensign told him. "We've calculated that it started maybe fifteen to twenty miles off North Harbor and drifted east with the wind. It was burned down to the waterline, with only parts of the hull and superstructure still standing."

Finley frowned. "Wait, you said two days ago?"

"Yes, sir. We sent notices out to all the coastal police departments, inquiring about any ships reported missing or overdue."

"I see." Finley didn't see at all, but it was something to say. "Could you please just check to see who you sent the notice to in North Harbor?"

"Certainly, sir." There was a clatter of a keyboard. "Sir, I've got it here. We sent an email to Chief Corcoran at 6:13 p.m. on Tuesday."

Huh, so Corcoran sat on it for two days. Finley couldn't tell whether that meant anything or not. "Did you inspect the burnt-out ship?"

"Yes, sir, but you will have to speak to Commander Mello to get a copy of that report."

Finley thought about his schedule for the next few days. "Listen, Ensign, I have to transport a prisoner to Portland later today. Could I stop by late this afternoon? I'll need a secure room where I could leave the prisoner while I speak with Commander Mello."

The Ensign chuckled. "No problem with that, sir. We can babysit him for a few minutes."

"Okay, but fair warning, I could be there as late as 5 or 6 p.m. Does that work?"

This time the Ensign's chuckle was a little rueful. "Commander Mello works long hours, sir, and as long as he's here, I'm here."

They hung up and Finley thought about the time schedule. If he spent an hour with the Coast Guard, he wouldn't get to Portland until after eight. He'd be lucky to get home by midnight. He rubbed his chin in thought, then made a phone call.

———————————

Calvin Finley rounded the entrance into North Harbor and headed for the docks, as fast as his little lobstering skiff would go. Right after school he had taken the *She's Mine* out to collect his twenty-two pots, the amount dictated by the number of traps he could carry on the *She's Mine.* Now he was going to stop at the docks and sell his catch – seventeen hard-shelled lobsters that should go for $5.23 per pound. With a little luck, he'd get $133 or so for the batch of them. Course, he'd paid almost fifty cents per trap for the herring he used as bait, plus the cost of gas for the outboard. He'd net about $100. Still, not bad for a high school kid hustling around the islands for two hours after school. Whistling to himself, he piloted the *She's Mine* straight at the dock. Hot, engine screaming.

Standing on the dock, the Harbor Master stood, unmoving, arms folded, slowly shaking his head. Calvin waited until just the right moment, then spun the wheel to the right, then abruptly reversed course to the left and threw the engine into reverse. The little gasoline engine screamed in protest, but the propeller clawed determinedly at the water. As the skiff neared the heavy wooden pillars, it lurched sideways until it was parallel to the dock, then drifted to the right...and stopped a mere five inches from the ladder.

The Harbor Master stood on the dock five feet above him, gazing somberly. "Young Finley," he said gravely, "there will come the day when you misjudge that approach and reduce that little toy boat of yours to matchsticks. And I hope I am standing here to see it."

Calvin grinned, white teeth flashing. "Hi, Uncle Paul! Got a pretty good haul today, but I think some weather's coming in. Late tonight or tomorrow, I'd guess. After I sell my catch, I'm going to stop by and see Pépé Dumas."

Paul Dumas felt a twinge of guilt; he hadn't seen his parents in a few days. He'd have to stop by on the way home. "Tell you what, I'll send you with some lobsters and steamers. Tell them I'll stop by after work and we can have dinner together." Then he thought about what the boy had said and looked up at the sky. It was blue, but there was just the faintest touch of a milky haze creeping in from the northeast. Over the horizon there was a storm brewing.

Calvin followed his gaze. "Waves are startin' to come in from two or three directions, Uncle Paul, that's what keyed me in. Slapped me around in the skiff somethin' fierce."

"Yep," the Harbor Master agreed. "I think you're right. Wind always blows a little harder in North Harbor. Hand me up some of your catch and we'll get you off to Cadot's while they're still buying." Cadot's was the big lobster wholesaler that bought most of the lobstermen's catch at the "Boat Price" and sold it at a markup to retailers, grocery stores, lobster pounds and restaurants. It was part of Cadot Fisheries, which moved most of the fish and seafood caught in this part of Maine.

Calvin readily complied, then scrambled up onto the dock himself and tied off the *She's Mine*. Twenty minutes later, $100 in his pocket, a cold bottle of Coke in his hand and a bag of lobsters and steamers under his arm, he was back at the skiff, waving goodbye to his uncle and turning northeast, cutting across the harbor towards his Grandfather's dock. Pépé Dumas' dock was handcrafted wood, built just two years ago to replace a dilapidated metal dock that had come with the house. It was a dock befitting an artist, with figurines hand carved into the support piles and the railing, gargoyles squatting moodily on top of the pilings, and an eight-foot tall wooden statue of a warrior seagull, holding a spear and a shield, guarding the ramp that led down to the dock itself.

When he reached the dock, Calvin carefully tied up his skiff, putting two extra bumpers out to protect it when the storm hit that night. Then he jumped onto the dock and walked to his Grandfather's studio.

Luc Dumas sat in his favorite easy chair, staring intently at a twelve-foot-high block of marble that was sitting on a low car trailer. It had arrived a week earlier from a quarry high in the hills of Tuscany. The marble block was easily twenty feet long and the entire thing filled much of the workshop. Mounted on bulletin boards around the marble were a dozen black-and-white drawings of an Indian warrior on a galloping horse, spear raised high, ready to throw. On a large, flat table behind the easy chair, a variety of mallets, chisels, electric drills and saws lay in orderly rows, waiting.

Pépé Dumas looked like he stepped out of the Old Testament. Six-foot-four, he topped two hundred and fifty pounds, had a shaggy mane of white hair and an unruly beard that grew halfway down his chest. His face was weathered from thousands of hours on the ocean and served mostly as the launching pad for a large, bulbous nose, which jutted out aggressively and bespoke of Dumas' deep appreciation for wine. His hands, though, were his most arresting feature, thick and scarred from long years of swinging a mallet and holding an iron chisel. The fingers were calloused and lumpy, covered with countless white scars, each a reminder that he did not merely create art, but wrestled it out of living rock that sometimes fought back.

Strongly built, with a jutting jaw and huge shoulders, he radiated the physical presence of a bear and was marked by one obvious flaw: a four-inch scar that shone pale white against the back of his left hand. A reminder, he told his grandson, that one should never drink and sculpt at the same time.

Everyone in North Harbor knew Luc Dumas. He had an international reputation as a sculptor specializing in very large pieces. He was a prized possession of the little fishing town, recognized on sight by everyone over the age of ten. Famous for his artistic talent, his boyish sense of joy, his drinking binges, his politeness to everyone he met, the many sculptures he had created...and for the fact that he was believed to be the richest resident of North Harbor.

And for his legendary temper. One pissed off Luc Dumas at one's peril. One story recounted how Dumas had worked six months on a sculpture when three teenagers, drunk and hyped up on testosterone and crystal meth, broke into his studio and vandalized the art work. The statue was a half-finished winged Valkyrie destined for an athletic stadium in Sweden. They broke off the wings and spray-painted swastikas on the rest, apparently in the mistaken belief that Valkyries were of Jewish origin. (Calvin's grandmother had shaken her head in disgust and muttered, "There is no cure for *stupid*.")

The three young men were hangers-on of a local motorcycle gang that cruised around the central Maine coast. Pépé Dumas tracked them to a seedy bar in Belfast and, using two large rock hammers, reduced their motorcycles to scrap. When the three young men sought to intervene in this display of artistic deconstruction, he had smashed their knee caps and their collar bones and left them writhing on the pavement. The police had shown up, but when they found that all three of the men were illegally carrying pistols and heard the story of the destroyed Valkyrie, they determined on the spot that it was a clear case of self-defense. No charges were pressed. Threats were made by the motorcycle gang, but Pépé Dumas bought two shotguns, one for his studio and one for his house, and nothing more ever happened.

The Town of North Harbor could not have been prouder of its artist-in-residence.

Now the seventy-three-year-old Dumas sat in his easy chair, staring intently at the marble block. Calvin slipped in behind him and put the lobsters and steamers in the refrigerator, then sat down and waited. While he waited, he pulled out a book on Arabic and found where he had left off. There was a girl in his class, Gabrielle Poulin, and she liked to read Rumi's poems in the original Arabic. How she had learned it, Calvin had no idea, but if she liked Rumi in the original Arabic, then he would learn enough to recite them. Languages, fortunately, came easy to him, and he never doubted that he would be able to learn this one. It was tough at first, getting his mind around the different letters used in Arabic, but he'd gotten some help and found some books and it was coming along.

After several minutes, Pépé Dumas stood up, grunting, and stretched. "Calvin, get me some wine from the counter, would you, please?"

When Calvin returned, he found his grandfather glancing over his Arabic study guide.

"Have you seen it yet, Pépé?" Calvin asked as he handed him the glass. They both knew what the "it" was. Dumas was of the firm belief that the sculpture he planned was already part of the stone, already in position. Once he "saw" its position in the stone, he could start cutting away rock, but if he cut too early, without seeing the position of the finished object, he would ruin it.

Dumas shook his head. "It's in there, I can feel it moving around, but I can't see it yet. Don't know where to start."

"It will come, Pépé," Calvin reassured him. "It always does."

Dumas grunted again, taking a sip of his wine. "The casino insisted on a deadline, so it's not a question of whether I get this thing started, but if I can get it started in time."

Before Calvin could reply, the door to the studio opened and a tall, gangly man lurched into the room, arms swinging akimbo, legs and knees unnaturally bent. Stanley "Stan-the-Man" Curtis walked unevenly across the floor, carefully dodging bulletin boards, tools and tables. He was a forty-year-old man with the mind of a six-year-old, and the neurological disaster that had ruined his mind had ruined much of his body as well.

He was one of the happiest people Calvin had ever met.

"Hi, Mr. Dumas!" he shouted excitedly. He turned, eyeing Calvin. "Hi, hi, Calvin!"

Luc Dumas stood up and formally shook Stanley's hand. "Stanley, thank God you're here. There is so much work to be done. But I can't work until this place is properly cleaned up."

Stanley laughed and nodded, his whole head bobbing up and down. "Oh, oh, I can help you, Mr. Dumas! Let me get started." And with that he walked to the little closet in the corner and took out a broom and dustpan and began to meticulously sweep the work area.

It was the same thing – word for word – both men said every day Stanley came to the Dumas studio.

He had been coming for twenty-five years.

He couldn't drive, of course, and walking was exhausting for him, so he rode everywhere on an adult-sized Columbia tricycle – his "Big Moose," the love of his life – which he painted fire-engine red and polished obsessively. In the last few years, he was always accompanied by his brown and white beagle, Huckleberry, who rode in the basket with his tongue hanging out and a canine smile on his face. Jacob had once sniggered that Huckleberry was the smarter of the two. Pépé Dumas had picked Jacob up, carried him squawking and protesting to the end of the dock and tossed him into the ocean. When Jacob sputtered to the surface, Dumas had said, very softly, "Stanley would kill for *half* the gifts you were born with. Sometimes, Jacob, if you don't have anything nice to say, it is best to remain silent."

Now Huckleberry yawned, walked in a tight circle and lay down, his head on his paws, keeping one eye protectively on Stanley.

"I put some lobsters and steamers in the fridge from Uncle Paul. He said he'd try to stop by tonight," Calvin told him. Pépé Dumas was still walking around the marble block, which was huge.

His grandfather went to the counter and poured himself another glass of red wine. "Want a small glass?" he asked Calvin, waving the bottle.

"Thank you, Pépé, yes," Calvin replied. An offer of wine usually meant that Pépé Dumas wanted to talk for a while. It could be anything. Art, history, stories about Calvin's mother when she was a girl growing up in North Harbor. Whatever it was, it was always worth it...and Calvin liked the wine. Dumas sat back down in his easy chair and Calvin dragged a stool over to sit near him. They sipped their wine and stared at the huge block of marble, both of them willing the Indian warrior inside to reveal himself.

"Calvin, how many languages do you know?" his Grandfather asked.

Calvin frowned. "Three, Pépé, you know that."

His Grandfather sipped his wine. He had a fondness for California Pinot Noirs, Chilean Syrahs, French cabernets and...well, he liked wine. "English, of course, and French, of course, you learned those at your parent's knee. And German, right?"

"German, too," Calvin nodded.

"You take German in school?"

"No, Pépé, I taught myself because I wanted to be able to read the math journals."

"When did you do that?" His Grandfather's bushy eyebrows knitted together as he stared at Calvin.

Calvin squirmed. Where was this going? "I don't know; a while ago, I guess."

"I seem to remember getting you a book on German for Christmas when you were still in middle school," Dumas said matter-of-factly. "So, you would have been what, twelve years old?"

"I guess." Calvin gulped some of the wine.

"Sprichst du fließend deutsch?"

"Fluent? I wouldn't say fluent, but I can talk to Paul Schmidt's grandmother okay. I mean, she doesn't laugh at me or anything, but she says I have the weirdest accent she's ever heard."

They both sat for a moment, contemplating German spoken with a Downeast accent.

"And now Arabic?"

"What about Arabic?" Calvin frowned.

"You're teaching yourself Arabic, aren't you?" Dumas gestured to the Arabic guide Calvin had been studying.

Calvin shifted in his seat. "Yeah. I mean, Mr. Waterhouse is helping me at school. He learned Arabic in the Peace Corps. He gave me some books and stuff, and Mom bought me the Babbel app."

Pépé Dumas nodded. "Okay, why learn Arabic?"

"Well, mostly to learn how to read Rumi in the original Arabic."

"Rumi was Persian. He wrote in Persian," Pépé Dumas corrected him.

Calvin shrugged. "I know, but a ton of his stuff was translated into Arabic, and Gabrielle speaks Arabic a little and keeps saying how good Rumi is when you read it in Arabic, so..." his voice trailed off.

Pépé Dumas smiled broadly, delighted at this unexpected revelation. "Ah, now I understand. Gabrielle is a girl at school you're...friendly with?"

Calvin grinned, a little abashed, but not giving any ground. "I'd like to be *more* friendly with her."

"And you hope to impress her by learning Arabic. Perhaps so you can read her poems by Rumi?" Dumas teased.

"Well..." Now he did look embarrassed.

Dumas nodded. "So, how is the Arabic coming?"

Calvin brightened. "Oh, good, really good! Mr. Waterhouse says I've learned a bunch of vocabulary and syntax. We can talk together and everything." He smiled ruefully. "But I guess my accent sorta sucks."

Dumas tried to imagine someone reading Rumi in Arabic with a distinct Maine accent, but the image utterly defeated him. "Is this Gabrielle of yours a senior, too?"

"Yeah, she is," Calvin said proudly. "She'll be going to a little college outside of Philadelphia, Swarthmore. It's a school for real eggheads."

Dumas was impressed — Swarthmore *was* a school for real eggheads, one of those small treasures not very well known outside of academic circles. There was a lot more Dumas wanted to say to his grandson about college, but perhaps he had already said enough today. "Why don't you take the lobsters and steamers up to the house, Calvin," he told the boy. "Tell your *Mémè* I'll be along shortly, I just want to make sure Stanley is all set and on his way." Then he turned back to the block of marble.

After Calvin had collected the lobsters and steamers and left, Luc Dumas solemnly raised his wineglass in a toast. "To my grandson, who is learning Arabic so he can enchant some young lady with Rumi," he said, then boomed with laughter. Learning to read Rumi in Arabic for a chance to get laid. Maybe there was hope for this younger generation after all.

He swallowed the wine and poured some more. Then he walked forward, placing the palm of his hand on the block of marble.

"Are you in there?" he pleaded with the figure hidden deep in the marble.

But nothing happened.

––––––––––––

Frank Finley decided to leave a little early with the prisoner and stop at the Coast Guard Station on his way down to Portland. He went to see Sergeant Leroux. "What's the status on Ralph Harkins?"

Sergeant Leroux eyed him balefully. "Status? He's in jail."

Finley suppressed a sigh. Leroux was one of Chief Corcoran's "loyalists." Corcoran didn't like Finley, so Leroux didn't either. "Sergeant, I'm to transport Harkins to Portland this afternoon. The Chief asked me to stop along the way to make a missing person inquiry, so I'd like to get Harkins now and head out."

Leroux smirked. "Chief told me to turn him over to you at four o'clock."

"Is there any reason to wait until then?" Ralph Harkins was the only person being held in the North Harbor jail, so it was clear Leroux was just jerking him around.

Leroux frowned and looked at his desk, as if the answer might be there. "Well, the prisoner hasn't had lunch yet."

Finley nodded. The wall clock showed 1:30 p.m., so it was unlikely that Leroux had ever intended to get him lunch. That was one of Leroux's little quirks; he liked to keep his prisoners hungry.

"I'd be happy to arrange lunch on the way to Portland, Sergeant," Finley assured him.

Leroux set his jaw. "Chief said four o'clock."

"I understand, Sergeant, but that was before he asked me to look into this missing persons thing." Finley paused. "He said the missing persons matter is urgent, but I'll tell him I'll have to reschedule the meeting with the Coast Guard today if you want." He waited to see if the hook had sunk.

Leroux considered this, a sour expression creasing his face. "Tell Remy to release Harkins to you." Then he opened a file and began to read it.

"Thank you, Sergeant," Finley said. He went right to the holding cells, where Martin Remy sat at his desk.

"Frank!" Remy greeted him warmly. "You here for our boy?" Remy was the oldest serving officer in the North Harbor Police Department.

"Yeah, I'm taking him a little early."

Remy glanced around. "You taking him alone?" he asked, a touch of concern in his voice.

Finley shrugged.

Remy frowned. "Well, that ain't right. Harkins is mean as a rabid dog."

"Chief's orders." This confirmed it as far as Finley was concerned. Corcoran was setting him up to get hurt. Interesting.

"Well, I'll shackle him tight and proper," Remy assured him, "but you have a care. Ralph Harkins is trouble and he likes to hurt people, especially cops."

"Thanks, Marty, I will." He considered his options. "Listen, give me a minute to get my gear and I'll come back to help you get him into the shackles."

Remy waved him away. "Sure, sure, take your time."

At his locker, Finley considered his options, then checked to make sure his taser was fully charged and his pepper spray was on his belt. Then he took a second pair of handcuffs and, looking around to make sure he was unobserved, slipped a pair of brass knuckles into his pocket.

Back at holding, Remy looked at him worriedly. "Sure you don't want to wait to see if anybody is available to help you?" he asked in a low tone.

"I'm okay, Marty, but I appreciate it," Finley assured him.

Remy nodded. "Okay, but one thing – Harkins likes to head-butt. You can see the scars on his forehead. Always work him from the side or behind. Don't stand directly in front of him. And don't take any crap from him. He'll test you, try to feel you out. Shut him down hard and he'll think twice about giving you trouble."

"Thanks, Marty."

But Harkins gave them no trouble at all during the shackling process. He stuck his arms out to be cuffed and didn't move a muscle when they shackled his legs and put a waist chain around him, then connected the wrist cuffs to the waist chain.

"Hey, what about some lunch?" he demanded. "I'm fucking hungry. No dinner last night, no breakfast and now no lunch. What kind of shithole is this?"

"Shut your trap," Remy told him, and walked with Finley all the way to the squad car in the back of the building. "You be careful with this guy," he whispered to Finley, then went back inside.

Finley ran the holding chain through the metal loop and locked it. Now Harkins was unable to move more than three inches off the back of the seat, but that didn't prevent him from angrily kicking at the front seat like a little kid. "I'm hungry, goddammit! I got low blood sugar and I need some fuckin' food!"

"Why didn't they feed you this morning?" Finley asked him mildly.

"Ah, shit, you know Corcoran, that prick." Harkins looked away, suddenly quiet. Finley nodded to himself in understanding. Take a violent prisoner, then don't feed him to make him edgy and uncomfortable and pissed off, then aim him at your target.

They drove in silence for a time, Harkins strangely silent. Finley glanced over his shoulder once to see that the huge man was pale and sweating. Maybe he really did have hypoglycemia after all. He thought about that for a moment, then in the Town of Orland pulled over into a McDonald's. Harkins looked up, confused.

"I'm guessing you're a cheeseburger guy, right? Everything on it?" Finley asked.

Harkins nodded warily, as if waiting for the joke to be sprung on him.

"Okay, Ralph, you just sit tight. You make a lot of noise or try to smash the windows or pull any crap, I will come back and cheerfully beat the shit out of you, got it?" When the prisoner nodded, Finley got out of the car and carefully locked it. "I'll be back in ten minutes."

It took fifteen minutes, but he didn't think Harkins would really mind. He opened the back door, unlocked the chain that kept the handcuffs locked to a ring and dropped a large white bag on Harkin's lap. Harkins looked at him incredulously.

"There's three Big Macs with cheese, two bags of fries and two shakes," Finley told him. "I didn't know what kind you like, so I got one vanilla and one chocolate. The cuffs stay on, but you'll be able to eat fine."

Harkins stared at him, then tore into the bag. Finley got into the front seat and ate a chicken sandwich and a cup of coffee, tossed the empty bag onto the seat and resumed the drive to the Coast Guard Station. Harkins finished his food – all of it – in less than ten minutes, then promptly fell asleep as the sugar poured into his blood.

"Never underestimate the power of a Big Mac," Finley mused, smiling.

An hour later they pulled into the Coast Guard Station in Rockland. Finley showed his badge and drove to the Commander's office, where Ensign Kauders was waiting for him.

"Commander Mello is waiting for you inside, sir" Kauders told him, then glanced at the slumbering form of Ralph Harkins in the back seat. "This is your prisoner, I presume." He grinned. "Doesn't look too dangerous, I must say."

"Don't count on it," Finley warned.

"Oh, I don't," Ensign Kauders assured him, then called over his shoulder. "Gentlemen, I need you."

The door opened again and two thick-necked, barrel-chested Coast Guard petty officers stepped out. "Gentlemen, this is Officer Finley of the North Harbor Police Department. Officer, these fine specimens are Petty Officer First Class Josephs and Petty Officer First Class Santana. Although they are gentle creatures at heart and loathe violence in any form, I can assure you that they will secure your prisoner and that, try as he may, he will not harm them." Kauders grinned again. Josephs and Santana rolled their eyes, but they were apparently familiar with the Ensign's baroque humor and pulled Harkins from the car without comment.

"Don't worry, sir, we'll take good care of your boy," Petty Officer First Class Josephs promised. Only half awake after gorging on his lunch, Harkins meekly allowed himself to be taken to a holding room.

"Follow me, please," Ensign Kauders said and took Finley inside to the Commander's office.

Commander John Mello was tall, weathered and had squint lines from years of looking into the sun. He looked frankly at Finley, then exchanged a glance with the severe looking woman who sat in a chair beside his desk. Mello stood and offered his hand.

"Officer Finley, I rather hope we can help each other out on this. I understand you have a missing lobsterman."

Finley nodded. "Henry Mitchell, age sixty-two, a long-time resident of North Harbor and a local lobsterman since he was a kid. He went out as usual Monday and didn't come back. He owns a Duffy 42 named *High Stakes,* built by the Atlantic Boat Company in Brooklin."

"Please, have a seat," Commander Mello said. "Forgive my manners." The office door opened again and Ensign Kauders brought in a tray of coffee and pastries. Finley suppressed a smile; this didn't quite fit in with the spartan ambience of the Coast Guard Station. Commander Mello caught the look and chuckled.

"Yes, well," he said. "My very efficient Ensign here knows that I get a little sleepy in the afternoon and he is kind enough to prop me up with caffeine and sugar. Quite embarrassing, but I find comfort in the fact that I am doing my bit to delay the aging process."

Finley looked at the plate, heaped tall with buttery croissants, cream-filled éclairs and something else he didn't recognize, but which made his mouth water just looking at it. "It certainly looks medicinal to me," he offered diplomatically.

The Coast Guard Commander's face crinkled in amusement. "Exactly!"

Then the humor vanished and he was all business again. "This is Lieutenant Gloria Larsen, of the Criminal Investigations Division. She's an attorney in our JAG Corps and will be sitting in on this meeting because one of our cases may have overlapped with your missing lobsterman."

Lieutenant Larsen was an attractive looking woman, in a severe, Nordic sort of way, with dark blonde hair pulled back into a tight bun, light blue eyes and a distinctly no-nonsense air about her. Probably a terror in the court room, Finley thought.

"Usually Captain Mitchell would fish the local waters inshore" Finley told them. "But if he ran into trouble there, he almost certainly would have been seen by somebody. The inshore waters are crawling with boats of all kinds. Lots of eyes out there. The other possibility is that he went out to deep waters. About twenty miles due east of North Harbor, near the edge of the continental shelf, there is an area on the migration path of lobsters that some lobstermen like. We know Mitchell had some traps out there."

He looked from Larsen to Mello and back again. "I understand from Ensign Kauders that you found some burnt wreckage near there."

Commander Mello abruptly stood up. "Come with me, please, Officer Finley. I have something to show you."

They walked across the parking area to a large shed immediately off the dock. Commander Mello nodded to the guard, who opened the door and let them inside. On the floor in the middle of the shed there was a partially intact hull, approximately forty feet long. Much of it had been burned to the waterline, but there were large portions of the superstructure that were intact, including the very top arch of the cockpit. Finley studied it in silence a moment, then glanced at Mello and Larsen. If the Criminal Investigation Division was here, this was more than a burnt boat.

"Okay," Finley said. "Show me."

Commander Mello walked along the starboard side of the boat, or what was left of it. "When we found the wreckage, one of my men noticed two holes in the cockpit area, here and here," he said, pointing. "This area was singed, but not burnt through. Indeed, you can still see a part of the wheel and several of the cockpit controls."

Finley leaned over to study the holes more closely. He straightened. "Bullet holes?"

"Yes, Officer Finley, two bullet holes, very close to where the captain would have been standing," Mello confirmed. Behind him, Lieutenant Larsen nodded somberly.

"Makes you wonder, doesn't it?" Commander Mello asked.

"Wonder what?" Finley asked back.

"Makes you wonder if you find Henry Mitchell, will he have some bullets holes in him, too?"

Calvin opened the door to the main house. "Mémè? Mémè, I've got some supper for you from Uncle Paul."

Céline Dumas called from the back of the house. "In here, Calvin!" Calvin walked to the kitchen, which overlooked the harbor. He held up the bag of seafood. "Put it in the refrigerator, honey," she told him. "Does this mean that your *Oncle* Paul is coming to dinner?"

"That's what he said, Mémè."

Céline Dumas sniffed. "He'd better or I'll have his hide. He hasn't called or visited in a week, that scoundrel." She went to the window and craned her neck to see the studio. "Has he started the sculpture yet, Calvin?"

Calvin hesitated. Céline Dumas stood five feet one inch and weighed no more than one hundred pounds. Placed side-by-side with her oversized husband, they looked like exemplars from radically different species. But she was as fierce as a wolverine and was to be treated with respect...and caution.

"Not yet, Mémè, but he's working on it."

Céline made a rude noise. "I told him not to take the job on a fixed deadline, the old fool. It spooks him, stifles his imagination, and at his age, you can't count on having much left." She wheeled on Calvin. "He's just staring at it, isn't he? Waiting for the Indian war chief to 'show himself' so he can start chipping it out of the rock." She shook her head. "Fool! I told him, 'no more deadlines!'"

Then, abruptly, she smiled and touched his cheek. "I can't believe you're a senior now, about to go to college. And Duke! Goodness! You should be proud, Calvin, a very good school. Your mother must be thrilled!"

Calvin squirmed. "Mémè I don't know yet. There's a chance I might not go this year. I thought maybe I'll take some time off, maybe try lobstering for a year..."

Mémè frowned at him. "Don't talk foolishness, Calvin. Duke University! Of course you'll go. One grandson not using his God-given talents is more than enough." She peered at him anxiously. "There's nothing wrong, is there? You don't have some dreadful disease or something?"

Calvin laughed. "I'm fine, Mémè. I'm just not sure I'm ready to go yet."

She put her palms on his chest. "You look so much like a man, I forget you are still a boy. It's okay, Calvin, we all get nervous when we face something so new and different. It's a big change. Ask your mother how she felt when she left for college." The old woman laughed. "She called us twice a day, every day for the first month! God have mercy, the phone bills! But then she settled in and loved it. You will, too. Trust your Mémè on this." She patted him again, then turned to the window.

"Where is that old fool? It's almost dinner time."

Chapter 5
Straining to be Free

In the Atlantic, twenty miles off North Harbor and one hundred feet down, the body of Henry Mitchell slowly filled with decomposition gases, making him stand upright and strain at the chain that was draped across his foot. Attracted by the blood and the odor, small fish swarmed around the body, enjoying an unexpected feast.

Every once in a while, a vagrant current would rock the body. The chain over his foot would slip just a tiny, tiny fraction of an inch.

The body pulled at the chain, straining to be free.

Chapter 6
Pinching the Supply Line

Finley had almost reached Portland when he heard Ralph Harkins stir in the back seat. He didn't say anything, just looked at him through the rearview mirror. Harkins rubbed his eyes with the back of his hands like a young child, an incongruous gesture which made Finley smile.

"Where are we?" Harkins rasped.

"About five minutes to the Portland PD," Finley replied. Harkins grunted and lapsed back into silence. When the Police Department was finally in view, Harkins shifted in his seat.

"The food helped. I was feelin' poorly." It was grudging thanks, but it was a thanks nonetheless.

"No problem," Finley replied, astonished that Harkins had thanked him. "If it's any consolation, I hear the food at the Portland PD is pretty good."

"Hope so," Harkins grunted.

Finley got him out of the car and into the police station without incident. Harkins seemed subdued and preoccupied, almost docile. Then, as they walked down a long corridor to the Transfer Desk, Harkins lowered his head and spoke softly so no one else could hear.

"The food thing, I sorta owe you for that." He paused, then plunged on. "So, I'm tellin' you, watch the fuck out. You got people gunnin' for you." Then he fell silent. Finley glanced at him questioningly, but Harkins shook his head and refused to say anything more.

The paperwork took about forty minutes. When he was finished, Finley slipped into the Men's Room, locked himself in a stall and changed from his uniform into civilian clothes. As he walked down the steps to the parking lot, he glanced at his watch: 5:10 p.m. He took out his personal cell phone, dialed a number and waited for it to be answered.

"Yeah?" said the voice on the other end of the line.

"Where?" Finley asked.

"The Dock Side, in Falmouth. Maybe fifteen minutes from where you are."

Finley knew it. A very nice little restaurant nestled into a marsh, near the ocean. Finley hung up, carefully deleted the call from his phone and started out. Fifteen minutes later he was there, parking well in back so his car was not visible from the street. It may be an unmarked cruiser, but it still looked like a cop car.

Inside, he walked past the maître d' to the back and slid into a booth.

"Good to see you, Frank." The man across the table looked like a retired librarian gone slightly to seed. In his early seventies, a little stooped, with gray hair and tortoise-rimmed glasses, there was nothing to suggest that he was one of the Drug Enforcement Agency's most ruthless Division heads.

Howard Honeycutt studied Finley carefully, as he always did when they met. He had run countless undercover agents over the years...and had lost his share of them. But while some of his agents were discovered by the drug cartels and killed, most were lost simply because of the pressure. The day-to-day, unyielding, relentless, pernicious risk of discovery that sucked the souls from their bodies and left them joyless, cringing shells.

So now, sitting in a comfortable restaurant with a beautiful view, he studied Frank Finley for the subtle signs that the pressure of being undercover was grinding him down. If he saw it, then Honeycutt would have to make the hardest decision any Case Officer had to make: Do you jeopardize an operation by leaving a weak agent in place, knowing he might unravel at any moment, or do you jeopardize an operation by pulling the agent out, abandoning years of work? Honeycutt had made these decisions at different times, with varied outcomes. Still, he met with his agents whenever he could and studied them carefully.

A young waitress came over and the men both ordered beers, then spent a minute with their menus. She thought the older man looked like someone's nice old grandfather. Finally, orders taken, the men nodded to one another.

"Is it working?" Finley asked with a touch of urgency.

Honeycutt smiled. "Yes, I'd say it is."

"Finally!" Finley exclaimed.

"We've been hammering I-95 going north, from Washington D.C. all the way to Lowell and Lawrence in Massachusetts." Honeycutt smiled thinly. "Over the last eight weeks we've intercepted fifteen of their shipments, one of them two hundred pounds of Grade A heroin. We also arrested five handlers on one of their mule runs and seized three apartments they've been using as safe houses. Got maybe one hundred and fifty mules, forty trucks and some other vehicles. A very busy, productive two months."

These were major victories. The plan had been to disrupt the I-95 smuggling corridor from Florida all the way up to Massachusetts. This was the "Silk Road" the Sinaloa Cartel used to bring heroin, cocaine and fentanyl into northern New England. The drugs were brought by the Dominican gangs up to Massachusetts, then broken down to street level quantities, cut with something to stretch out the supply – fentanyl was preferred because it gave the user a quick, powerful high – and sold in the classic small glassine bags. The final leg of the distribution was usually done by motorcycle gangs or other local hoods. Several metric tons a year were smuggled into New England, most of it for consumption in New York and Massachusetts, but Vermont, New Hampshire and Maine were considered profit centers. Although there were fewer users, the Dominicans had a monopoly and charged as much as the market could bear. The volumes sold were relatively small, but the profit margin was huge. The big bosses in Sinaloa were happy, the Dominicans were happy, and the local biker gangs were happy. But the people in Maine, Vermont and New Hampshire were dying from overdoses in unprecedented numbers. The problem was the heroin was so pure that it was easy to overdose on that alone. Fentanyl made it worse. Much worse. Fentanyl is fifty times more powerful than heroin, so just a little too much in the mix is enough to kill a user within seconds. There were incidents of police searching the cars of dope dealers and accidentally touching some spilled fentanyl. Just a touch to the skin was enough to render them unconscious. If their partner happened to be carrying a naloxone injector, they lived. If not...

"So, any evidence that they've shifted their route?" Finley asked.

"Hmmm, I think so, yes," Honeycutt said. "Actually, you might already know about it. You've got a lobsterman missing up your way, correct?"

Finley sat up straighter. "Yes, a guy named Mitchell. The Coast Guard found his boat burned to hell three days ago, with two bullet holes in the cockpit area."

"Well," Honeycutt said gravely, "I can tell you that if you ever find his body, you'll discover he was shot with a rifle. We don't know the details, but our Confidential Informant tells us Mitchell somehow blundered into the middle of a big pickup offshore and may have actually tried to steal the drugs that were intended for someone else. We don't have any details, but a fair guess is that whoever was supposed to pick up the drugs shot Mitchell and recovered the drugs, then set fire to his boat."

"Jesus," Finley said. "It's really happening. Two goddamn years of waiting and it's finally happening."

Honeycutt knew three things governed – and limited – his law enforcement universe. First, the highway network in the United States was the largest, most complex of anywhere in the world. Second, the drug cartels had more money and resources than he did with which to conduct operations. Third, he could not inspect every car, truck and van coming into New England.

What he needed, above all else, were spies. Informants. Snitches. He did not care much about their motives; anyone who called in with operational information was welcome. That led to arrests, and arrests could lead to turning someone within the Cartel itself.

It had taken him years, but he had secured informants inside the roving motorcycle gangs that distributed the dope throughout northern New England. More importantly, he had one lone informant within the Dominican gang in Lowell, the Sons of Cristo Rey.

Three years earlier, Honeycutt had conceived of the plan to pinch the Cartel's land route for smuggling the drugs and force them to either bring in the dope by sea or by air. If they were brought in by air, Honeycutt had them covered. But if they brought them in by sea...well, that was more difficult. Rumors of corruption in small police departments on the Maine coast were rampant. Worse, it was very difficult to sneak a DEA agent into a local police department without anyone figuring it out.

Then he had come across Frank Finley working on a vice team in Philadelphia. Married to a native of North Harbor, Finley was perfect. Honeycutt checked him out very thoroughly to make sure Finley was not himself on the take, subjecting him to a series of polygraph tests. But he came out clean. Spotless. Strings were pulled and Finley was hired as North Harbor's newest police officer, over the strenuous objections of Chief Corcoran.

"Do you think Corcoran is dirty?" Honeycutt asked. "And is he on to you?"

Finley sipped his beer and thought about it. "He certainly doesn't like me. But is he dirty?" He shrugged. "Yeah, I think he is, but it could be he's just stealing money from the traffic tickets or blackmailing somebody he caught with a few ounces of weed. I dunno. I don't have anything that would connect him to any big-time drug smuggling by the Cartel, but I'm pretty sure that Corcoran's got something going on." He told Honeycutt about taking Ralph Harkins by himself to the Portland PD, and Harkins' warning that someone was gunning for him.

Honeycutt pursed his lips. "You think Corcoran wanted Harkins to beat you up?"

"Oh, yeah, that much for sure."

Honeycutt looked at him. "How did you handle Harkins? Did you have to rough him up?"

Finley chuckled. "I fed him three McDonald's Big Macs, fries and two milkshakes. Slept like a lamb."

Honeycutt laughed out loud, and mentally patted himself on the back once more for recruiting Finley. Then he sobered up. "Frank, take care of yourself. Keep your eyes open. And for God's sake, be discreet. We're close now. I don't want to scare them off by showing our hand too early."

"I'm okay so far, but if anything happens to me, look at Corcoran first. Like if I have a car accident or accidentally shoot myself while cleaning my service piece. Stuff like that. Corcoran is a mean bastard. If he's dirty and he finds out I really work for you, he'll come after me."

"Keep your eyes open," Honeycutt admonished him again. "Dead agents look bad on my annual performance review."

"Wouldn't want that," Finley said dryly. He sipped his beer. "What next?"

"The few times we know they used boats, the Cartel used the ports of Tampico and Altamira, both on the Gulf of Mexico. They're controlled by the Gulf Cartel and the Sinaloa Cartel has an arrangement with them to have the dope smuggled on board ships going to Canada." He gestured, palms up. "Problem is our confidential informant is not well placed to learn about shipments by boat." Honeycutt grimaced. "And we have to be careful working with the local Mexican authorities – too many leaks."

"When do you think they'll get a ship up here?"

Honeycutt shrugged. "I'm thinking it will take them a month to get a boat together and send it up to Saint John or somewhere like that. We'd like to get the transfer on film, if we can. I've got a LUNA drone at my disposal. It's pretty sweet: daytime and nighttime surveillance and can stay up for eight hours."

Finley frowned. "How we going to do this?"

"We'll put suspected ships under surveillance on this end, as they approach Massachusetts, Honeycutt said. "And when they try to off-load the drugs, we'll hunt them down and string them up by their balls."

Across the dining room, the waitress had been keeping an eye on the table in case either of them wanted something. As she watched, the older, grandfatherly man smiled at his dinner companion. It was a dreadful smile, cold and predatory. She shivered. Perhaps the grandfatherly man wasn't so nice after all.

Chapter 7
Contemplating a Problem

Wallace Moore sat at his desk in Mexico, surrounded by computer screens. The assault on his land route into northern New England continued and inventories in Maine, Vermont and New Hampshire were running low. Not a crisis yet, but soon.

Wallace had planned for this eventuality. He had an emergency stash hidden in the basement of a home outside of Portland, Maine. The home belonged to a retired couple who lived a quiet life, paid their taxes and kept a low profile. He had selected them from among his most trusted workers and bought them the house. Their job was to look normal, fit in, keep their mouths shut and protect the dope. In the basement was a fireproof vault with three hundred and twenty-five pounds of heroin, enough supply for a month for all of Maine and New Hampshire if it was cut properly.

Time enough to figure out how to get more product shipped in.

It was time for Plan B. There were four freighters leaving Altamira within the next two days, all headed for Canadian waters. The first ship out would be his "proof of concept" test. If it worked, all well and good. If not, then he would try Plan C.

Wallace was a man who liked having a backup plan.

Using a highly encrypted email, he carefully spelled out what he wanted the Dominicans to do and dispatched a messenger with the cash to cover their expenses.

Then he called his facilitator and told him he needed access to an oceanographer.

———

Meanwhile, in Maine, Jean-Philippe LeBlanc was contemplating his problem: Jacob Finley, son of a North Harbor police officer.

LeBlanc needed to either get rid of Jacob, or win him over. He could get rid of him by simply firing him, but if he did, he would lose access to whatever the kid might know – or could find out – about what his father was up to. Some key members of the North Harbor police were *not* getting paid off. They couldn't be trusted and would eventually have to be either shielded from the drug smuggling activities or…removed. Frank Finley was just a patrolman, but he had been with the Philadelphia police and that meant he had more training than the other North Harbor cops, probably a lot more. And now he was investigating the disappearance of Henry Mitchell. Corcoran had a made a mistake there. Having Finley poke around could be a problem.

"Jesus, just fire the kid," Bruno Banderas said impatiently. "Or if you can't fire him, kill him." The Dominican gang member was on his third beer and LeBlanc's moodiness offended him. There were simple solutions to simple problems. *This* was a simple problem.

"We can't just kill a cop's son, for Christ's sake," LeBlanc said irritably.

Banderas shrugged. "Sure we can. He's a young man. Young men die from stupid things every day. He gets drunk, then tries to drive home and hits a tree. Or a drug overdose. Or he falls off your boat and drowns. Plenty of options." He smiled like a cherub, happy at his work.

LeBlanc shook his head. "Bruno," he said patiently, "this isn't Mexico. Anyway, I can use this kid; I've just got to figure out how to win him over without him knowing he's being taken."

Banderas snorted. "For fuck's sake, he's a kid, right? What does every boy his age want? A little money, some drugs or booze to make him feel good, and a blowjob from a girl who is so hot he thought he'd never have a chance with her."

The two men looked at each other, then burst out laughing.

"I can arrange that," LeBlanc finally said.

It was simple, when you thought about it.

———

The girl was Katie Montgomery, and she looked exotic. She had an English father and a mother whose ancestry traced to French Guyana. Katie got the best of both their genes. She was tall, slender and leggy, with silky dark hair that tumbled past her shoulders and begged to be touched. She had light brown skin that turned soft gold under the summer sun and her eyes were a bottomless brown. Her parents met while her mother was in school in Canada. Katie was born ten months later. For a while they were poor but happy, but then her mother died when Katie was seven, and her father took her home to Stonington, Maine.

Her father, John Montgomery, was a dreamer. He dreamed of owning a fishing fleet, but the fact was he was a mediocre sailor and poor fisherman. While other skippers seemed to sense where the fish were and filled their nets, John always arrived too early or too late. The years came and went and he continued to barely scrape by. He borrowed money to pay his crew and the bank kept threatening to repossess his boat. John began to drink too much and one stormy night, as they returned to Stonington from a day of disappointing fishing, he put the boat up on a rock just outside the harbor entrance. He and his two-man crew scrambled into the life raft and made it to shore, but the boat was reduced to splinters. As were his dreams. After that, he turned to drink and lived on odd jobs.

His daughter, who never recovered from the death of her mother, sought numbness. In small town Maine, numbness meant opioids, and there were plenty to choose from. Katie Montgomery paid for them while she had money, and when she was out of money, paid for them with sex. She was a pretty girl and men were attracted to her. And sex was just sex. She didn't care, didn't hurt her none. And she got what she needed.

One day a hard-looking man knocked on her door and said to her, "I need you to do a little job for me. Nothing criminal, just taking care of a guy who's lonesome. You do this, and I'll give you enough White Lady you won't have to worry about nuthin' for three months. If the guy likes you and you stay with him, you'll get supplied for free for as long as you treat him right. Sometimes this guy might look to you for a little advice, and if he does, then you tell him what I tell you to tell him, got it?"

Katie Montgomery heard what the man said, but wasn't sure she really understood. "What's the matter with this guy, is he butt-ugly or something? Is he mean? Is he gonna beat on me?" She could take a little beating now and then and didn't really care if he was ugly, but a girl had her pride, after all.

The man laughed with real humor. "No, no, he's not ugly and as far as I know he doesn't get violent. He's shy, is all. He'd never meet up with anyone as pretty as you because he's shy around girls."

Katie mentally shrugged. One guy was pretty much like any other guy. They all liked to drink and fuck. "So, if I do this, can you get me some Dragon?" she asked, trying to sound casual, unaware of the voracious drug lust that was all over her face."

Jean-Philippe LeBlanc smiled inwardly. Everyone had a price. "Sure, we can do that," he assured her. Dragon was just heroin mixed with fentanyl – he had access to kilos of the stuff.

Katie Montgomery scrunched up her face. She still couldn't believe this was all happening and that she was going to get her dope for free just for fucking some guy. Had to be a trick of some sort.

"So, what is it you want me to do, exactly?" she asked nervously.

"Do?" LeBlanc replied. "Why, all you have to do is make this guy fall in love with you."

Katie felt a rush of relief. "That's all?"

Chapter 8
The Poacher's Children

Two days later, as the men gathered by the dock for their daily assignments, LeBlanc took Jacob aside. "I'm moving you to the *My Other Girl*, starting today. Marc tells me you've been doing a good job on the inshore boats and it's time you get some experience offshore as well. Okay?"

My Other Girl was one of four boats in the LeBlanc clan that went out twenty to thirty miles off-shore and laid down "trawls" of twenty or more traps on a line a mile long. Each boat usually carried the captain and two sternsmen. It was punishingly hard work, but when the lobsters were migrating through the area, the catches could be huge and very profitable. The lobster boats that went that far out were usually larger, forty-two to fifty feet long.

Jacob was stunned. He thought that only blood relatives of the LeBlancs ever got to go out on the highliners. It was a more prestigious, higher-paying job.

"Yeah, sure," he stammered. "Thanks, that's great."

"You'll get a percentage of the boat's take, just like the other sternsmen," LeBlanc told him, and gave him a figure. Jacob could hardly believe it. With that much money, he could finally buy the motorcycle he had been looking at.

"Thanks, Mr. LeBlanc," he gushed. "Thanks a lot."

"You've been working hard, Jacob," Jean-Philippe told him, clapping him on the shoulder. "We take care of our own."

Calvin had just reached Sheep Island when he became aware that there was a kayak paddling towards him. He stopped, treading water, upright in the water to see better. The pod of seals that were swimming with him all looked about excitedly, then dove underwater and disappeared. The sun was a bit over the horizon now and the golden light of early dawn had been replaced by a beautiful, shimmering light blue that sparkled on the waves. The kayak got within thirty feet of him, then stopped, the face of the paddler still in shadow from the morning sun.

"Excuse me, are you lost?" a woman's voice asked. "I'm assuming you were out jogging on this fine morning, but you should know that the road is about a mile behind you," she said, pointing vaguely towards shore. "However, if you are too tired to make it back, I could call you an Uber."

Calvin laughed. "How did you find me?"

Gabrielle Poulin put a puzzled look on her face. "Everybody is looking for the crazy tourist who plunged into the sea and started swimming towards his doom." She sniffed disdainfully. "At least we assume it is a tourist, for who else would be so *incredibly* stupid as to swim out to Sheep Island in April? Certainly not a local, certainly not someone who lives by the sea and respects its power." She shook her head in mock disgust. "No, it couldn't be one of us. Ergo, it must be a nutjob tourist, for as is well known, tourists are capable of doing just about *anything,* so long as it is foolish." She peered at him wide-eyed. "And you look like a foolish tourist to me."

Calvin laughed again. He and Gabrielle had been spending more time together for a few weeks now – not actually dating, but something – and it was exactly her flair for sassy boldness that made her so appealing. He rolled onto his back and began a slow backstroke. "I'm betting it was my grandfather."

Gabrielle smiled. "Close, it was your grandmother. I saw her at the grocery store and she told me all about your morning swims." She smiled and shook her head. "If I didn't know better, I'd think that your grandmother is trying some subtle matchmaking, though why I would be interested in someone who was a *baby seal* in a former life is beyond me."

Calvin abruptly flipped onto his stomach and began a hard, fast crawl towards the kayak, intentionally throwing up a lot of spray and water. Gabrielle shrieked and backpaddled furiously, staying just out of his reach. "Don't you dare, Calvin Finley!" she yelled. "This water is freezing and I'm not wearing one of your fancy wetsuits."

Calvin stopped swimming and put on a pained expression. "Aw, Gabs, I'm hurt that you think I'd try to get you wet, I really am."

Gabrielle snorted and smacked the paddle against the ocean surface, spraying him in the face, then prudently backpaddled a few more yards. "I'll see you ashore, Calvin. After I talked with your grandmother, your Mom invited me to come by for coffee after my kayaking this morning." She laughed, a nice laugh, warm and rich. "They're ganging up on us, Calvin. Good thing you're ugly or I might be swept off my feet!" And, smiling, she turned and began to paddle towards the Dumas' dock.

Calvin watched her go, then laughed when one of the seals popped its head out of the water and barked at him. "You got that right," he said, then began swimming home.

———————————

Frank Finley pulled into the driveway of Henry Mitchell's house a little after ten o'clock. There were already three cars in the driveway and several more parked in front. The Mitchell's extended family was large, he knew. Henry was the youngest of five brothers, all lobstermen, and there were a couple of sisters as well, plus aunts and uncles, and no doubt enough grandchildren to sink the Titanic.

A young woman answered the door and looked at him coolly. "Yes?" she asked.

Finley showed his badge. "I am here to speak with Mrs. Henry Mitchell," he said. "It's in regard to the missing person report she filed on her husband."

The woman studied him for a long moment, then turned and walked into the house. Taking that as an invitation, Finley followed.

In a small sitting room in the back of the house, a stout middle-aged woman sat in an overstuffed chair surrounded by two more women and five men. Small children could be heard playing in another room. The young woman who let him in knelt beside the older woman and said quietly, "Momma, this man is a police officer. He's here to talk to you about Dad."

Everyone in the room stopped what they were doing and looked at Finley. The five men were probably Mitchell's sons, he realized. All of them had the tough, weathered look of men who made their living from the sea. The other two women could be daughters or daughters-in-law.

The woman who let him in stood and extended her hand. "I am Katherine Mitchell Prescott," she told him. "I am the youngest daughter. I also practice criminal law out of Portland and if I think you are getting out of bounds, I will terminate this interview and kick you out so fast your head will spin. Do we understand each other, Officer?"

Mrs. Mitchell gasped and shook her head when she heard what her daughter said.   The five brothers grinned and shook their heads in amusement. Apparently, the youngest daughter was the she-lion in the family, and they had heard her roar before.

Finley nodded. "You don't have anything to worry about, Mrs. Prescott. Nor does your mother." He turned to Mrs. Mitchell and knelt down on one knee, so they would be on eye level. "Ma'am, I've reviewed the report you filed about Mr. Mitchell. I'm sorry to tell you that the Coast Guard found the burnt remains of a lobster boat some twenty miles off shore. The Coast Guard didn't find any people" – he refrained from saying 'bodies' – "but the timing is such that it could be your husband's boat."

Mrs. Mitchell gasped and put her hand to her face. Fresh tears rolled down her cheeks and her daughters huddled around her.

"I know this is hard, Mrs. Mitchell, but this is all I have right now," Finley said softly.

The sons looked at each other, then the oldest looking son leaned forward. "How long was the boat?" he asked.

"At the waterline, forty-two feet," Finley replied.

"And the beam?"

Finley pulled out a notebook and flipped to his notes. "Coast Guard said fourteen feet, six inches."

The sons exchanged looks again, and the older one sighed. "Could be a Duffy 42, like my Dad's boat." He rubbed one hand over his face. "Shit," he muttered.

"How did the fire start?" one of the other sons asked. Behind him, his mother's face had taken on the look of a terrible certainty finally come home to roost. She seemed to collapse in on herself. Katherine turned on her brothers in a fury. "Take it outside, you idiots! Can't you see what this is doing to her?"

The five men looked abashed and contrite. They meekly stood as one and motioned to Finley to go out on the front porch.

"We have reason to think the fire was set," Finley told them, once they were all outside. "It's circumstantial, but it looks intentional."

"Ah, Christ," one of them moaned, then made the sign of the cross.

Finley stood there for a moment, trying to figure out how to get the information he needed.

"Listen, fellas, there's no good way to ask some of these questions. I don't want to upset you or suggest any disrespect for your father, but I need some answers if I'm going to do my job right," Finley told them.

One of the younger brothers nodded, tears in his eyes. "Fuck it, just tell us what you need to know."

"Okay," Finley said slowly. "You guys knew your Dad pretty well, and you know the industry, know the informal rules lobstermen live by. So, I gotta ask this: Did your father do stuff that would make enemies? Did he poach traps, or cut buoys and lay traps where he knew he shouldn't? You guys are all lobstermen, you know the stuff I'm talking about."

The oldest brother bristled. "Hey, fuck you! Our father is a good man. He brought us up right; he wouldn't do any of that crap!" His face was red and his hands were balled into fists.

Finley just looked at him, then swung his gaze to the others. The other four looked at each other, then down to the ground, then at each other again.

Uh oh, Finley thought to himself.

After an awkward moment, the younger brother who had spoken up earlier sighed and shook his head. "Chris," he told the oldest brother, "that's not gonna help. We all know what Dad used to do, knew since we were kids."

Chris set his jaw stubbornly. "It's not right! If Dad is gone, Mom shouldn't have to live with any of this."

"Let him do his job, Chris," the younger brother said softly.

"I mean no disrespect, but if your father was up to something, I need to know so I can catch these guys," Finley said. "You can't share this with anyone, but we found two bullet holes in the top of the cabin. We can't tell how old they are, so if you guys can rule out foul play because those bullet holes have been there for years, that would help." This was bullshit, but he wanted to soften up what he was telling them.

The brothers looked at each other in varying degrees of realization, then Chris sat down heavily in one of the porch rocking chairs. "I told him," he said in a strangled voice. "I told him that someday he'd poach from the wrong guy and he'd be lucky if he didn't get shot."

"Your dad poached other people's traps?" Finley asked, as gently as he could.

"Goddammit!" Chris shouted, red with anger. Or, maybe, from embarrassment.

"Yeah, he did," the younger brother said. "We've all known since we were in middle school, working on the boat weekends and summers. He liked to empty the traps of some of the big guys who fish out twenty miles or so. Liked to jerk their chain. Sometimes he'd pull up an entire trawl and empty it, then leave early and get back to the docks ahead of them, sell their lobsters to Cadot's."

Finley nodded. "The lobstermen who owned the traps, did they know who was doing it?"

"Dad never told us he got caught or anything," one of the other brothers spoke up. "I think he would have. But catchin' him in the act and knownin' it was him are two different things."

Another brother chimed in. "People knew. They just knew. You're in this business for a few years and you get to know who the poachers are."

"Ah, Christ," the oldest brother sighed. "Ah, fuckin' Christ."

"Okay, but would somebody actually *kill* your dad over this? I mean, kill him?" Finley asked, even though he knew the answer. In Philadelphia, after all, a drug dealer would kill another dealer just for standing on the wrong corner.

The brothers just looked at him.

"Okay," Finley said. "Who else works out at the twenty-mile line?"

The brothers collectively shrugged. "Well," one said. "Bobby McDermott, he's been fishin' out there for years. He's got two boys."

"McDermott fishes out there, but his sons both stay close to shore," one of the others corrected. "But Todd Halpern's out there come October when the big migration hits. Greg Ryan. Jimmy Pelletier."

"And the LeBlancs," Chris, the oldest, said reluctantly, still resisting tarnishing his father's name. "Dad hated the LeBlancs; used to poach their traps a lot when he thought he could get away with it."

Finley looked from one to another of the five sons of Henry Mitchell. "Would the LeBlancs do something like this?"

The brothers shared another moment of silent communication, then nodded solemnly.

"Oh, yeah," Chris said. "They've got a whole section of the twenty-mile line that they treat as their private property." He rubbed his hand over his face again. "And they don't take kindly to trespassers, let alone poachers."

Now Finley was worried that he might have inadvertently started a range war, or whatever it would be called on the ocean. It wasn't exactly unheard of for a lobster boat to have a shotgun or a rifle.

"Okay, guys, listen up," he told them in his best 'I-am-not-shittin'-around' voice. "A lot of this is conjecture and wild guesses, so I don't want any of you going off half-cocked and doing something that will just land you in jail. We're not even sure it's your dad's boat yet and we certainly don't know who else might be involved."

"Hey, c'mon, we're not fuckin' vigilantes," one of the brothers protested.

Finley held up a hand to forestall him. "I'm not saying you are, but if something has happened to your dad, well, emotions run high. I'm just telling you, don't do anything stupid or I will put your ass in jail." He looked around at the five of them. "Are we good?"

They nodded, grudgingly, but they nodded.

"Good!" Finley said firmly. "I'll keep you informed if I hear anything." He paused, hesitating. "Listen, I noticed that none of you are in business with him. And the bullet holes we found in his boat? Is there any chance your dad was involved in drug smuggling? That would explain a lot."

The five sons of Henry Mitchell looked at him, stunned. This seemed to be a line they did not want to cross. "Good Christ, no!" Chris said emphatically. "Dad wasn't...wasn't...he wouldn't have the slightest idea how to even get involved in something like that."

The youngest son shook his head. "I think we would have known," he offered. "I mean, he could be pretty cocky about the lobsters, but hell, they were just *lobsters.* I just don't see him smuggling drugs. I just don't."

The other brothers nodded their agreement. Finley couldn't decide how much weight to give to this. Clearly, none of the sons wanted to think of their old man running dope.

And who could blame them?

"Okay, worth asking," Finley said by way of apology. "Listen, I hate to ask this, but in case we find somebody out there – a body, I mean – does your dad have any distinguishing marks? Tattoos, birth marks, something like that?"

The youngest son said, "On his left forearm he has a large tattoo of an anchor, with a mermaid riding it. You won't have trouble identifying him."

Finley knew that after several days in the ocean, there might not be much skin left, but kept that gruesome tidbit to himself. "Thank you for your cooperation. I mean it. I know this is a tough time for you."

And with that, he left the Mitchell house and drove back to the Police Station, all the while wondering if a man would really kill another man over a stolen lobster.

And knowing the answer.

Chapter 9
In Route

The freighter *Tampa Bay,* under a Panamanian registry, was off the coast of Delaware, steaming north at 12 knots.

Five more days to Saint John, New Brunswick.

Chapter 10
Homeward Bound

One hundred feet below the surface of the ocean, the body of Henry Mitchell gradually filled with more decomposition gases. A bluefish chasing a meal slammed into Mitchell's back, which made it rock forward. Just a little bit.

The chain over Mitchell's foot finally reached the rounded toe of the boot and surrendered its fragile hold on the remains of Henry Mitchell, father of five sons and three daughters, and grandfather of too many to count.

For a fraction of a moment, the body just hovered there, not moving at all. Then its hard-won buoyancy took hold and the body began to rise serenely to the surface far above him. There was no hurry, no sense of urgency. All that was past. The body was just an empty sleeve. Henry Mitchell had moved on.

As the lobsterman drifted to the surface, another force came into play. He could no longer feel it, of course, but he would have appreciated it.

The Eastern Maine Coastal Current took the fallen sailor into its gentle embrace...and so he began his final journey home.

Chapter 11
Buying a Fast Boat

It was late afternoon before Finley got back to the police station. Chief Corcoran was waiting for him. Corcoran looked at him and frowned, a puzzled look on his face.

"You take Harkins to Portland?" he demanded.

Finley tried to appear casual. "Sure, that's what you ordered me to do. I've got the paperwork here from Portland PD."

"No problems?" Corcoran asked suspiciously.

"Problems?" Finley shrugged. "No, went very smooth." He wondered if he was making life difficult for Harkins when he got back from Portland, then pushed that thought aside. First things first.

The Chief stared hard at him for a moment, then abruptly changed the subject. "What have you got on the missing guy, Mitchell?"

"Well, I think I know what happened," Finley replied.

Corcoran looked at him sharply. "Come into my office," he said abruptly. Corcoran sat behind his desk and Finley took one of the uncomfortable chairs that managers of all sorts seem to inflict on their subordinates.

"Tell me," Corcoran ordered.

"The Coast Guard found a boat about twenty miles out, an area that Mitchell liked to trap in. It was pretty badly burned, but they found two bullet holes in the pilot's cockpit."

Corcoran looked alarmed. "Bullet holes?"

Finley nodded. "No body, of course, but if Mitchell got shot and then dumped into the water, we'd be damned lucky to find him. I checked the marine weather for the day we think he disappeared. The wind was blowing out of the northwest. If he was floating in the water, the wind would have blown him right out into the Atlantic. Hell, if the Gulf Stream catches him, it could carry him half way to England."

"You said you had it figured out," Corcoran said. He sounded wary, like a patient asking his oncologist for the diagnosis, but fearing the worst.

Finley leaned back and crossed his legs. "Well, I asked around a bit. It seems our man Mitchell liked to poach lobster traps." When Corcoran didn't say anything, Finley added, "He was stealing lobsters from traps that belonged to other lobstermen."

Corcoran's face darkened. "I know what poaching traps is," he said testily. He sat back in his chair, glancing sideways to look out the window, then turned back. "So, you think somebody caught him red-handed and shot him?"

Finley shrugged. "Makes sense, doesn't it? You know some of these guys out there can get pretty rough if someone even comes into their territory. But poaching? Hell, poaching is the cardinal sin of lobstering. Worst thing you can do. Apparently, Mitchell has been doing this for years and a lot of people knew it, but never caught him at it." He shrugged again. "I think he got caught by the wrong guy and the guy popped him, then set his boat on fire to cover it as best he could."

Corcoran rocked his head slowly in thought, then nodded briskly. "Write it up," he ordered Finley.

"You want me to keep poking around to see if I can figure out who did it?"

Corcoran snorted. "To find them, you'll have to find the gun they used, and that gun is at the bottom of the ocean by now." He pursed his lips in thought. "Ask around for two more days, then report back to me and we'll see."

Finley stood up.

"Oh, and I need you to go up to Bangor today to get the transcript from the Coroner's Inquest in the Hadley case. They have it waiting for you at the Court House."

Finley stared at him for a moment. Corcoran stared back.

"Sir, you've just told me I only have two days to finish the murder investigation of Henry Mitchell, and now you want me to drive up to Bangor to fetch a transcript? Can't somebody else do that?"

"Fit it in, Finley," Corcoran told him sternly. "You're the newest man on the force, so you get the scut work. That's the way it is. Dismissed!"

Finley left the office. He should have been fuming, but he wasn't. He knew now, beyond all doubt, that Corcoran had been bought off.

———

Bruno Banderas had to go to Portland, Maine to find what he was looking for: a used Shockwave Magnitude 30, thirty feet long, with a 650-horsepower inboard. The owner swore it could do seventy miles per hour, which Banderas doubted. But maybe it could do sixty, which would be fast enough.

The asking price was $52,500.

"And if I paid in cash, now?" Banderas asked with a polite smile. Even his polite smile scared people. He unzipped the bag he was carrying and spilled wads of fifties and hundred-dollar bills onto the table. He knew he was announcing that he was in the drug trade, but he also saw the raw greed in the man's eyes.

They settled for $45,000, cash. The owner threw in the trailer and thirty minutes later, Banderas drove off with the go-fast boat. A day later it had been painted a matte black, the extra seats had been ripped out, the engine had been tuned, and a new GPS system had been installed.

The following day, Mateo, the boat pilot from the home country, took the Shockwave out for a shake-down spin. He came back three hours later, grinning ear to ear. *"Es muy rápido!"* he said enthusiastically. The boat had reached sixty-seven miles per hour, admittedly in calm waters.

Banderas nodded, satisfied. That damn boat would pay for itself in one night's work.

Chapter 12
Defending the Catch

Calvin steered the *She's Mine* into the dock. It had been a good haul, twenty lobsters in twenty-two traps. Helped make up for the days when he only got two lobsters in twenty-two traps, and God only knew there were enough of those. He kept out two lobsters for his grandparents and four for supper. He hesitated, then threw another into his bag. Just in case. He threw the rest of the lobsters into a second bag and tossed it up on the dock, finished tying off his skiff and climbed up the ladder, only to find himself facing three people he'd rather not.

Little Guy LeBlanc and his two cousins, Paul and Martin LaPierre, stood at the top of the ladder, smirking at him. Martin held Calvin's bag of lobsters. Calvin felt a little clutch in his stomach. Little Guy was the son of Guy LeBlanc, who was the younger brother of Jean-Philippe LeBlanc, the head of the LeBlanc clan and a big shot in North Harbor. Calvin's brother, Jacob, worked for Jean-Philippe.

Little Guy and the two LaPierre brothers were a year older than Calvin and they liked to hang around the docks, generally causing mischief that no one called them on, because nobody wanted to get on the wrong side of the LeBlanc clan.

"Hey, Calvin," Martin smirked. "Pretty impressive catch you got here, eh? Must be hard work bringing in a dozen lobsters. You got yourself a future in lobstering, yes, sir."

The other two snickered and Little Guy snatched the bag from his cousin. Without looking inside, he said, "I think all of these lobsters are too small. You should have thrown them back!" He raised the bag in one hand. "I am going to do my civic duty and return these illegal lobsters to the sea!"

Calvin had just spent two and a half hours pulling traps, rebaiting them and moving them out to rocky shallows surrounding Ram's Island. There might only be thirteen lobsters to sell, but they were hard-shelled and would probably bring him more than seventy bucks.

He smiled. "Yeah, yeah, Guy, but it's late and I've got to sell them and get home." He held out his hand for the bag.

Little Guy stepped back, his face suddenly crafty. It was too soon for the fun to stop. And besides, he didn't really like Calvin Finley, with his cop father and his fancy artist grandfather and his college pretensions. "Tell you what, Cal, I'd be willing to sell you these lobsters at a good discount and then you can sell 'em to Cadot's. Whadda you say, two bucks a lobster?"

Calvin considered. He really didn't want to take on Little Guy LeBlanc. For one thing, he was a big guy, running to fat, perhaps, but not to be underestimated. For another, the two cousins were with him and three-to-one odds always sucked. Besides, Calvin's dad would tell him not to break the law. His mother would say to turn the other cheek. And his grandfather...his grandfather... He *knew* what his grandfather would say.

"C'mon, Guy," he said, "I gotta get going. Let me have my lobsters."

Guy smiled, delighted. "No, no, Cal, I've got to protect these poor, undersized lobsters." He looked at his cousins. "What do you say, guys, shall we liberate them?" He held the bag out over the water, ready to tip it over and spill the lobsters into the harbor.

Okay, thought Calvin.

He took a diagonal step, not confronting Little Guy directly, but moving within arm's reach and positioning himself near Martin LaPierre, the smaller and lighter of the two cousins. Then he faced the second cousin and spoke.

"Listen, Paul, can't you talk some-"

Without finishing the sentence, he backhanded Little Guy across the nose with his left hand, then punched Martin hard in the sternum with his right. Little Guy's nose exploded in pain and his eyes flooded with tears. He staggered backwards, dropped the bag of lobsters to the dock and clutched his face with both hands. On his right, Martin stumbled back one step, then another...which was one step too far. With a wail, he fell ten feet into the oily harbor water.

Calvin looked at Paul, who hadn't moved. "Paul, I got nothing against you, but I've got to sell my catch and go home for supper."

Paul nodded slowly. "You shouldn't have hit Guy," he warned Calvin. He didn't say anything about his brother.

"Maybe," Calvin nodded agreeably. "Why don't you help your brother out of the water." Glancing warily at Little Guy, who was still clutching his nose, Calvin picked up the bag of lobsters and started down the dock, then thought better of leaving his boat untended once Little Guy got functional again. He walked back, jumped down to his skiff, untied it and motored all the way around to the other side where Cadot's was. The dock area was crowded with fishing boats and lobster boats a lot bigger than the *She's Mine,* but he squeezed in, tied her up under the dock where the larger boats wouldn't crush her, and then climbed the ladder.

He knew that he'd just made an enemy, but he was still too young to understand the unholy wrath of the Law of Unintended Consequences.

He would learn, soon enough.

Chapter 13
The Test Run

With Mateo at the wheel and Banderas riding shotgun, they took the Shockwave out to the drop point at night. Banderas sat with a chart of the surrounding waters and a GPS repeater in front of him. They took the boat out of Stonington and headed northeast, keeping their speed – and thus their noise – low as they crept past Russ Island, Camp Island and then the north side of Bold Island, avoiding the shallows and sandbars around The Shivers and Devil Island.

The radar showed dozens of small islands and large jutting rocks. As Banderas glanced repeatedly at the GPS, he saw that many islands did not have names. Looking up and peering into the darkness, he could see nothing. The boat chugged along. To Banderas – no seaman – it was like driving a car through a dark tunnel without headlights.

"Gets dark as all fuck out here," Jean-Philippe said, reading his mind. "And there is a goddamn current that passes through these little islands when the tide turns. If you're in the water, you'd better crawl up onto one of these dipshit islands, cause if you don't, you are on a one-way ticket into the North Atlantic. God help you, because no one else will, that's for sure."

They cleared the first mass of islands, crossed Jericho Bay and continued up and around Swans Island, then turned due east. The dark mass of Acadia National Park stood out under the stars on their port side. Two more miles and Mateo brought the thirty-foot Shockwave to a due north heading.

"Better put on your seatbelts," he said. "Might get a little rough!" Then he opened up the 650-horsepower, GT Performance engine and built up to full speed over a couple of minutes. The boat leaped ahead, engine growling with satisfaction. Mateo grinned wildly, nodding his head. *"Ella está muy bien, ¿sí?"*

"Si!" Banderas shouted happily as the wind snatched off his ball cap. It disappeared into the night behind them.

LeBlanc, who favored the stability of a forty-six-foot lobster boat, thought this plastic toy sailed like a cork bobbing in rough seas, but kept it to himself.

It was just about eighty miles across the Gulf of Maine to the drop point. Mateo kept the throttle down to fifty miles per hour and they reached their destination in an hour and forty minutes. He throttled back and the boat slowed grudgingly to a halt.

Banderas double-checked the GPS, then set a marker. Now they could find this spot again even in pitch darkness. He checked his watch: total time to get here was about two and a half hours.

"How's our fuel?" he asked.

"We're good," Mateo assured him. "Plenty to get back." He pointed northeast towards the point of Nova Scotia. "And there's land about ten miles that way, if we had to get off the water fast. Ten minutes or less at full throttle. No sweat."

LeBlanc shook his head. "It ain't the distance, for fuck's sake, it's the weather! Tonight is calm; the ocean's flat as the girl I took to the Senior Prom. But we get a lot of storms out here, and some of them come up real fast. The waves get up, six, eight, ten feet, easy. This boat is just a toy, she's not designed for big waves. If weather comes in, you'll have to slow way down to keep from getting swamped." He grinned evilly. "Then the Coast Guard will be all over your sorry ass. They got cutters, zodiacs and helicopters, all that shit."

Banderas did not like this big, loud lobsterman, but the man knew the sea, and he had a point. He suppressed a sigh. One more thing to worry about. It would be random chance whether the weather was calm on the night of the drop off.

They turned the Shockwave around and returned to Stonington, where they quietly moored the boat at a private buoy they had rented and rowed ashore in a little dinghy. Once they left the harbor again for the drug pickup, they would not return here. They would go to North Harbor, where they had an arrangement with the police, and once the drugs were offloaded, they'd sell the boat and buy another.

But first things first. When they got back to the condo where they were staying, Banderas called his contact at the Cartel and explained that any handover of the drugs could easily be foiled by weather. They needed a Plan B, Banderas explained to the voice of a person he had never met. The voice sounded American. He shrugged. Didn't matter. All that mattered was that the product got delivered.

———————————

In Sinaloa, Mexico, Wallace listened carefully, eyes closed. Of *course* the weather could be a problem. Banderas might be a very effective killer, but he was clearly no brain trust. Wallace Moore already had a Plan B in place, but that had its risks as well. First, they had to try the go-fast boat and if that proved unfeasible, then, and only then, would they go to Plan B.

After all, nobody in his right mind threw fifty pounds of pure heroin into the ocean if there was a safer way to deliver it. Christ, was he the only one who had ever heard of the scientific method?

He terminated the call with Banderas and called his man on the *Tampa Bay*. Quietly and efficiently, he gave the man very specific instructions. "Understand?" he asked when he was finished.

"*Sí, Sí,*" the man replied calmly. He was a good man, experienced and level headed. He had worked with Wallace before and understood the odd American was always nervous, but very smart. When the call terminated, the man went right to the workshop. There was much to do, and he wanted to get it done before his work shift started.

Chapter 14
The Warrior

Luc Dumas walked around the marble block for the fiftieth time, studying every feature, every blemish, every shadow.

Nothing.

He sipped his wine and tried to control his emotions, which were lurching up and down worse than an adolescent suffering through his first romantic obsession. The door opened and his wife came in carrying a plate of food.

"Even great artists have to eat," she said in mild reproof.

"What would I do without you?" he asked, kissing her cheek.

"Starve to death in dirty clothes," she said pointedly. "Hard to know which would kill you first."

"Now, now, no need to get snippy." He took a bite of the sandwich she'd brought, then washed it down with a glass of wine and poured himself another.

"You keep drinking like that, Luc Dumas, and your liver is going to jump right out of your body and hitchhike south to better weather."

"Just another way to lose weight," he said. "Don't be jealous."

Céline made a rude noise. Then the door opened and Stanley Curtis walked in, followed by Huckleberry.

"Hi, Mr. Dumas!" he shouted excitedly. He turned to Céline . "Hi, hi, Mrs. Céline!"

Luc Dumas stood up, formally shook Stanley's hand and said what he said every day: "Stanley, thank God you're here. There is so much work to be done. But I can't work until this place is properly cleaned up."

Stanley laughed and nodded, his whole head bobbing up and down. "Oh, oh, I can help you, Mr. Dumas! Let me get started." And with that he walked to the little closet in the corner and took out a broom and dustpan and began to meticulously sweep the work area.

Céline looked at the happy man-child as he busied himself with the broom. She smiled at her husband as a tear trickled down her cheek, then pulled him down to her and kissed him softly on the mouth. "You are a very good man, Luc," she whispered fiercely, "And I love you very much."

Dumas blinked in surprise. His wife of fifty-six years was many things, but demonstrative was not one of them. Céline, for her part, suddenly seemed to come to her senses. "I have work to do," she said brusquely, pushing him away. "Don't be late for dinner." But she didn't leave. Instead she looked at the huge block of marble, inspecting it critically, as one might study a hostile army arranged across the valley, ready to attack. She walked slowly around it, running her hand along the surface, feeling its grain and texture.

"It's good stone," she said.

Dumas nodded glumly.

"Where are your drawings?"

Dumas gestured to his work table and Céline bent over, studying the work drawings that he had prepared. They showed an Indian warrior on horseback, galloping forward, a spear raised in his hand, ready to throw. The horse's eyes were wide, nostrils flared, its ears flattened against its head, teeth showing as it charged down upon the enemy. The warrior's face, in contrast, was calm. Almost serene. And there was just the faintest hint of a smile at the corner of his mouth.

"Heavens!" she exclaimed. "Is he *smiling?*"

Dumas wagged his head back and forth. "I don't know yet."

She peered closer at the drawing. "Intriguing. Perhaps for him, it is not a fight to the death, eh? But doing what he loves." She looked up. "Does he even care about the outcome, or is it enough for him to simply *fight?*"

Dumas flapped his arms helplessly at the marble block. "Fight? Christ on a crutch, I'd be happy if he'd just peek out of the damn rock and say hello!"

Céline slipped her arm through his and tugged him towards the door. "Come on, you are marinating in your own anxiety. Let's go for a walk and clear your head. Stanley!" she called to the man-child. "We are going for a long walk to clear the cobwebs from Mr. Dumas' foggy brain. Are you okay here alone?"

Stanley paused in his sweeping. "Oh sure, sure, Mrs. Céline. And anyway, I'm not alone. I've got Huckleberry right here and Big Moose is just outside."

Céline smiled. Stanley's world was so rich that a living dog and an inanimate tricycle held equal prominence in his life. "Okay, Stanley, we leave the studio in your capable hands. If we are not back by the time you finish, just turn off the lights and shut the door."

"Okay, Mrs. Céline, you can count on me."

"We always do, Stanley, and you have never failed us." Stanley glowed at the compliment.

Dumas looked forlornly at the untouched block of marble waiting impatiently for him to start.

"Are you sure this is a good idea? I should really try to work on it."

"I'm sure," Céline replied. Then she shut the door and they left his disappointment behind.

Chapter 15
Setting the Hook

That night Jacob Finley stepped off the LeBlanc lobster boat *Celeste* and was immediately confronted by Little Guy LeBlanc, who had a seriously bandaged nose.

"Your fucking brother punched me in the nose!" he shouted, pushing Jacob hard in the chest.

Jacob had no idea what he was talking about, but he didn't like to be pushed, either. "Hey! Watch it! I have no fucking idea what you are talking about, but you push me again, Guy, you'll be sorry."

But Guy, who had been brooding for the last two hours, was beyond caring. "I was minding my own damn business and your brother punched me for no fucking reason!" he shouted, spraying spittle. Then he shoved Jacob hard a second time.

Jacob had been working hard for months and his arms and shoulders had thickened with muscle. He shoved Guy back, and the force of it pushed Little Guy directly into his father.

"What the hell's goin' on?" Guy LeBlanc yelled, grabbing both Little Guy and Jacob by the front of their shirts.

"He pushed me!" his son said, pointing at Jacob and trying in vain to break his father's hold on his shirt. Jacob, suddenly conscious that his job was on the line, stood still, content to let things calm down.

"You push my boy?" Guy LeBlanc snarled at Jacob.

"Mr. LeBlanc, I don't know what's going on here. As soon as I stepped on the dock, Guy started screaming at me something about my little brother, then he pushed me hard. I told him to back off and he pushed me a second time. I didn't hit him or anything, but I did push him back."

Guy LeBlanc stared at him suspiciously for a minute, then turned to his son. "That right, Guy? What he said?"

Little Guy seemed caught between conflicting impulses to fight or run. Eyes down, he muttered. "I ran into Calvin on the docks when he came in to sell his catch. He punched me in the nose." He glared at Jacob. "Punched me for no fucking reason!" he shouted.

Guy LeBlanc turned back to Jacob, who gestured helplessly. "I honestly have no idea what he's talking about, Mr. LeBlanc. Hell, I've been on this boat since 6 a.m. and just got off. Ask your brother."

"Ask me what?" a deep voice intruded.

Guy LeBlanc seemed to shrink back and grow smaller as Jean-Philippe LeBlanc stepped onto the dock. Little Guy cast his eyes back down to the dock.

"These boys got into a pushing match and-" Guy LeBlanc stopped abruptly at his brother's glare.

"Not you," Jean-Philippe snarled. "Him!" He pointed at Little Guy, who was now trembling.

"We was just funnin' with him," Little Guy blurted. "Me and Paul and Martin. We got his bag of lobsters and told him we'd sell them back to him. Then he just up and hit me for no good reason. I think he broke my nose!"

Guy LeBlanc looked disgusted. "You telling me that you took Calvin Finley's lobsters and tried to make him buy them back from you? And rather than pay you, he hit you and took them back?"

Little Guy stood there, a figure of shame, anger and terror. His father suddenly slapped the side of his head with one meaty hand. "That's for takin' somebody else's lobsters that they done worked for!" he shouted, then slapped Little Guy even harder on the head with his other hand. "And that's for being such a pussy that the *three* of you couldn't take one kid in a fight!" He gave Little Guy a shove down the dock. "Now get on home; I'll talk to you more when I get there."

He turned to Jacob. "We okay here?" he said brusquely.

"Sure, Mr. LeBlanc, everything's okay." Jacob might not be book-smart like his brother, but he knew when to concede gracefully.

"Okay, then." Guy LeBlanc nodded at his brother, then turned and walked away, his entire body stiff with anger. Or, perhaps, fear.

Never one to let an opportunity pass, Jean-Philippe took Jacob by the elbow. "Come on, let me buy you a drink." They walked to the bar – the Harbor Watch – just a few yards off the dock.

Jean-Philippe knew men, not that Jacob Finley was a hard man to read. He knew Jacob was afraid that somehow, he would be blamed for his brother's scuff-up with Little Guy and that it could cost him his job.

Fear was good.

Fear could be used.

"Listen, don't worry," he assured the young man. "I know Little Guy can be a jerk sometimes. He's impulsive and he's got a temper. But you're family now; you've got every right to stand up to him when he's being an asshole." He signaled the bartender for two beers and they took a table.

The barkeeper, who knew exactly how old Jacob was, decided that perhaps it was best if he did not ask Jacob Finley for any ID to verify he was of drinking age.

"So," LeBlanc continued amiably, "what are you going to do with the extra money you're earning?"

Jacob took a gulp of his beer. "First, I wanna get a motorcycle. Something used, I guess." He smiled slyly. "Unless you want to give me a big raise or something."

LeBlanc snorted in amusement. "Yeah, well, don't get ahead of yourself, Jake."

Jacob blinked. *Jake?* Nobody called him Jake. His family always called him Jacob, but he liked the sound of Jake. It sounded…more mature.

"Why a motorcycle?" LeBlanc asked casually.

"Oh, you know, getting around on my own. Don't have to depend on my Dad to give me a ride."

LeBlanc nodded. "Makes sense." Then he set the hook. "You've got a real job now. A man shouldn't have to depend on his parents to get to work in the morning."

That's for sure! Jacob thought. "I've been looking around at some used bikes, but no matter how you cut it, I'm gonna have to save up like three grand to afford one." Jacob took another gulp of his beer. "I should have enough by the end of July or so."

Sometimes it just falls into your lap, LeBlanc thought. "You know, I've owned a number of bikes over the years. Guess I've got three or four lying around. I could loan you one, a real sweet Honda Shadow, until you get your own bike."

Jacob could hardly believe it. "Really? That would be swell!"

LeBlanc suppressed a laugh. The kid had no idea. "Don't thank me too much. It's ten years old and needs a tune-up. And if I were you, I'd get a new rear tire; it's got some miles on it. But the engine is good and she rides well."

Jacob was delighted. "This is cool! Thanks, Mr. LeBlanc. Really, thanks a million."

"No problem." LeBlanc said. "I'll bring it here tomorrow afternoon after we get back in. You can have it then." He stood up. "Remember, tomorrow is a workday for you. Get some sleep and be ready for a hard day tomorrow. We'll be moving about three hundred traps to new spots, so we'll all be working our asses off. I expect you at the docks tomorrow at 5:30 a.m. sharp. Tomorrow's a short day, should be back around 3 p.m. or so, so you'll have plenty of time to take your bike for a spin and get a good feel for it. Make sure you wear a helmet! You're no good to me in the hospital with a busted head."

"Yes, sir, Mr. LeBlanc," Jacob promised.

As LeBlanc left the Harbor Watch, he saw Katie Montgomery standing outside. "Tomorrow afternoon I'm giving a motorcycle to Jake Finley," he told her softly. "When he's getting it ready, maybe you can introduce yourself or something. And be sure to call him Jake, not Jacob."

She looked at him with flat brown eyes, her face expressionless. "Yeah, okay," she said.

Chapter 16
Jacob and Calvin

Calvin was still at the breakfast table when Jacob walked into the kitchen. "Up early," he commented through a mouth full of oatmeal.

"Don't want to be late today. Boat's leavin' the dock at 5:30 a.m. sharp," Jacob replied through a yawn.

Calvin pursed his lips in thought – their father's alarm clock wouldn't go off until 5:30 a.m., too late to help Jacob. "Grab some food and I'll run you down in Mom's car," he said.

"What about your morning swim?" his brother asked.

"It's only five minutes down to the dock and five back. I'll still swim. You'd do it for me."

"Well, yeah," Jacob replied. "But that's because you are such a helpless dork."

Finley's alarm went off at 5:30 a.m., as always. He sat on the edge of the bed, shaking the remnants of sleep from his mind, then walked down the hallway to the boys' room. "Jacob-" he began, but stopped.

Both beds were empty.

Curious, he went downstairs to the kitchen. Calvin was still at the sink, rinsing his dishes. His hair was dry, so he hadn't been swimming yet. No sign of Jacob, but there was an extra plate and coffee mug in the sink – Jacob's spoor.

"Where's your brother?" Finley asked, rubbing his cheek to speed the wake-up process.

"Hi, Dad," Calvin said. "He had to be at the dock by 5:30 a.m., so I borrowed Mom's car and drove him down."

Finley blinked, digesting the news. "What about your morning swim?"

"Just about to go out. I'll do a short one today and still catch the bus for school."

Danielle wandered in, hair already combed and pulled tightly against her head. She kissed her husband's cheek and turned to the coffee pot.

"Jacob has already eaten and gone to work," Finley told her wonderingly. "Calvin drove him to the dock."

Danielle nodded. "I saw them leave in the Subaru." She turned to Calvin. "Keys?"

"In the basket, Mom," he told her, pointing to the little bamboo basket they used to hold all the car keys.

"Thank you," she said. She glanced at her husband and raised her eyebrows, silently communicating, *Our kids are growing up!*

Finley took a deep breath and let it out slowly, nodding back to her. *Who would have figured?*

Chapter 17
Should Have Married a Librarian

On Wednesday night, Finley got a call from Honeycutt. "Can we talk tonight?" he asked.

Finley glanced at the dinner table, where his family was waiting for him to join them. "Sure. Give me ninety minutes, just sitting down for supper with my family."

"Good," Honeycutt replied. "Usual place?"

They signed off and Finley sat back down at the table. Danielle looked at him from the corner of her eye and he nodded once by way of reply. Two years earlier, when Honeycutt had first approached him about moving to North Harbor and working undercover for the DEA, Finley had sat down with his wife and told her everything.

"Michael Corcoran is a snake," his wife had told him, "and whether or not he is involved in something criminal with the drug cartel, he *will* try to hurt you if he finds out you are an undercover agent placed in his police department."

"I'll be careful," Finley assured her.

"I'll go along with this on one condition," she said. "You have to keep me apprised about everything you're doing. I don't care if it's secret or not, you have to tell me. I need to know when you might be in danger. And one other thing." She paused, looking him in the eyes and reminding him so much of her ferocious mother that it scared him.

"What is it?" he asked.

"You have to buy me a gun and show me how to use it," she said bluntly. "Because if Michael Corcoran is dirty and decides that he has to get rid of you, he won't stop with you. He'll come for all of us."

"I won't let that happen," he promised her.

"Neither will I," she said firmly.

In the end, he purchased two guns for her, a pistol and a Sportical assault-style rifle. Once a week when the boys were in school, they went to a shooting range and she fired hundreds of rounds through them both. She would never qualify to be on a SWAT team, but she would be a nasty surprise for anyone coming into her home thinking she was nothing more than a housewife.

Now Finley and his wife exchanged a look, and with that look she knew that whatever it was that was happening, it was happening soon.

After dinner, Finley helped clear the dishes, then got his jacket and car keys. "I shouldn't be more than two hours," he told his wife softly.

"Are you armed?" she replied, kissing him on the cheek.

"Always."

"There are nights I dream I married a librarian," she said. "Fixed hours. No guns."

"You'd be bored to death in a week," he told her.

"Maybe," she conceded. "But what a week!"

The "usual place" was the Blue Hill Co-op coffee shop in Blue Hill, about a forty-minute drive away. Sometimes they met inside, sometimes they met in the parking lot. Tonight was a parking lot night. Honeycutt was there already, sitting in an inconspicuous Ford of indeterminate color. Finley was invisible in his black Ford Taurus. He got out and joined Honeycutt.

"You sure you're a big shot in the DEA?" Finley asked. "Whenever I see this car, I wonder if they are actually paying you a salary."

"Never draw attention to yourself. Ten minutes from now, not one person in this parking lot will be able to describe this car," Honeycutt replied smugly.

Finley made a show of studying Honeycutt's car. "What color is that thing, anyway?"

Honeycutt looked at him sideways. "It is a special color I picked out myself: 'Indiscernible.'"

"Yeah, well, I see why it's your favorite," Finley said. "What've you got?"

Honeycutt slipped into business mode. "Remember I told you I thought the Cartel would have a shipment here within a month? Well, I was wrong. We've been picking up a lot of satellite phone transmission from a small freighter called the *Tampa Bay,* bound for Saint John in New Brunswick. Listed cargo is fertilizer. Panamanian flag. But the interesting thing is that its last stop was Altamira, Mexico."

Finley could feel the vein pulse in his forehead. "And where were the satellite phone calls placed to?" He could barely suppress his excitement.

Honeycutt grinned. "Mazatlán, Sinaloa, Mexico."

"Goddamn!" Finley breathed.

"The calls were encrypted, but there were several of them. Although Mazatlán is a port, the *Tampa Bay* did not originate there or ever stop there. The calls have been traced to the warehouse district, but the boys and girls at NSA couldn't tell us more than that."

"Has to be drugs," Finley declared. "We know the Cartel ships out of Altamira and Tampico."

Honeycutt nodded. "Here's the thing, Frank. The *Tampa Bay* is somewhere off Maryland now, steaming at twelve knots. It will be going through the Gulf of Maine into the Bay of Fundy this time Friday night."

"But-"

Honeycutt held up a hand, palm out, to forestall him. "Relax, I've already got the Coast Guard shadowing the freighter. When it gets into Maine waters, the Rockland Coast Guard Station will take over. They'll have a 110-foot cutter that will be the base of operations. It carries three heavy machine guns and can launch a small, fast boat, which also carries a machine gun. But the real beauty is that they'll have a LUNA drone. It can constantly circle over the freighter and take pictures for about six to eight hours. Good cameras. They can zoom in tight and tell you the color of the guys' eyes."

"That will make a difference," Finley said dryly.

Honeycutt grunted. "Anyway, the LUNA will be able to see if they throw anything overboard and can mark the exact location. The Coasties can then sit back and wait to see who comes to pick it up."

"What can possibly go wrong?" Finley asked, raising his eyebrows.

"Yeah, yeah, I know," Honeycutt grimaced. "Plenty, and then some. One thing I am worried about: Henry Mitchell."

Finley frowned. "I'm pretty sure he is no longer an active player," he said sarcastically.

Honeycutt, a serious chess player, shook his head. "Mitchell went into the water three days ago. It's a long shot, but if the current carries his body down the coast, he could wash up around North Harbor any minute now. If someone finds him, and if he is full of bullet holes, there will be a big stink. Press coverage. Lots of noise."

Finley sighed. "And if that happens, the Cartel will almost certainly call off the drop Friday night." He should have thought of it himself. A very strong current ran from the mouth of the Bay of Fundy down the Maine coast. While the odds were slim that Mitchell's body would turn up, they weren't non-existent.

Honeycutt nodded. "If someone finds him, we'll have to try to keep it out of the news for a couple of days."

"It's not the news I'm worried about," Finley admitted. "We know some of the police departments in the area are dirty, we just don't know which ones. If the wrong police department finds him, they'll get word to the Cartel and whatever drugs are on that ship will just disappear."

Honeycutt held up his hands. "Like I said, it's a long shot. Just keep your ear to the ground. Let me know right away if you hear anything. As to the rest, Friday could be our big chance. Weather report is fair, with calm seas. High clouds, so the LUNA will be able to fly. And to top it off, we can get the Coast Guard helicopter from Rockland if we need it.

"The freighter can't run, not from the cutter," he continued. "Either they don't drop the drugs, in which case we've arranged for a search when they reach Saint John, or they do throw them over, in which case the Coast Guard keeps the drop point under surveillance." Honeycutt raised both hands, palms up. "I think we've got it covered."

"What about me?" Finley asked. "For once, I'm not on duty Friday night."

"Well, I am going to be sitting in the Command trailer, twelve miles north of you, in Brooklin. You're more than welcome to sit in and enjoy the show." The older agent smiled. "There's nothing like a good chase."

Finley got home before ten o'clock. Danielle was waiting for him in the kitchen. He smiled at her, then gestured with his chin, asking *'Where are the boys?'* She in turn pointed upstairs to their bedroom, where he could vaguely hear the sounds of a video game.

"Friday night," he said softly. "Things are moving"

She looked at him expectantly. "And?" she asked.

"And we'll catch them." He grinned wolfishly, reminding her once again that her loving husband and proud father of her children was also a predator.

Chapter 18
Thursday

The sun-kissed sky showed blue and gold. Waterfowl flew low over the flat water, and out by The Shivers seals slipped lithely into the ocean to find breakfast. In the distance there was the comforting rumble of a diesel-powered lobster boat heading out to tend its traps.

The water was streaked with gold and speckled with lobster buoys.

It was three minutes after sunrise, and it was glorious.

Paddling rhythmically, the two kayakers made their way past The Shivers and out towards Enchanted Island. They paddled in comfortable silence, neither one wanting to break the spell of the sunrise on the ocean. A seal surfaced near the lead kayak, barked quizzically, then dove under and disappeared. They went through a shallow area teeming with lobster buoys of various colors and shapes, then came out, facing an island about half a mile in front of them.

"That's Millet Island," Calvin said softly. "We'll go north around it, skirt past Saddleback Island and then Enchanted Island will be ten minutes further on. There are usually a lot of seals around there."

Gabrielle smothered a laugh. She had been kayaking in these waters since she was nine years old and knew every island within miles, but it pleased Calvin to be the tour guide, and she was content to let him enjoy it. Always treat a boy's fragile ego gently, her mother said. Not that Calvin's ego was that fragile, but still, it was the principle that counted.

They spoke little as they paddled, usually one commenting on something they'd seen. Countless seagulls, of course, but egrets and cormorants; two puffins sitting contentedly on a rock; once a Leach's Storm-Petrel, flashing its white blaze just above the tail feathers; a flock of black guillemots; and even a razorbill.

"They come to shore once a year to lay a single egg and incubate it," Gabrielle told him. "If something happens to that egg, that's it until next year. Scares me just to think about it."

Calvin nodded, but was taken by the thought that people were sort of like that, too.

Thirty minutes later they had passed Saddleback Island and swung south to land on the rocky skirt forming Enchanted Island's outer edge. The gulls screeched at them and grudgingly moved aside as they hauled the two kayaks out of the water. The sun was up now and the sky a cornflower blue. They flopped down on the rock, which was just beginning to warm under the morning sun. Calvin opened the rear storage compartment of his kayak and pulled out a Tupperware container of sliced cantaloupe, two energy bars, and a thermos.

"Lemon and ginger tea?" Gabrielle asked hopefully.

"Black coffee," he replied.

She wrinkled her nose. "At least it's hot."

They ate their breakfast quietly. They were still uncertain with one another, still feeling their way, aware that there was chemistry between them, but not knowing where it might lead. Both were also aware that in a few months they would be separated. Neither one of them knew what that would mean, but it added a frisson to their being together that was simultaneously distracting and delicious.

They were both thinking about sex, though neither would admit it.

After the cantaloupe and an energy bar, they shared a cup of coffee from the thermos' cup-top thingy. "Want the grand tour?" Calvin asked. Gabrielle looked around. Enchanted Island was a football field wide, slightly more in length, and was smoothly oval shaped, except for a pudgy little foot jutting out from the bottom side of the island.

"Is it big enough to have a *grand* tour?" She raised her eyebrows. "I think I've seen larger phone booths."

"Great views," he assured her. "And quiet."

"School's at eight," she reminded him. It was almost six-thirty now. "We will have to leave soon or we'll be late." She had no idea why she said that – school was the last thing on her mind today.

"We're seniors. We can be late. Not the end of the world."

She jumped up and took his hand. "Lay on, McDuff."

He smiled. "Not everyone gets that quote right."

They walked for a minute, each acutely conscious of the other's proximity.

"Have you decided about college yet?" she asked him.

Calvin grimaced and shook his head. "Just goin' round and round. I really want to go to college, but I can't imagine living somewhere else yet."

"Durham would be closer to Philadelphia," she offered casually.

Calvin sighed. "Yeah, that's sort of crept into the mix as well."

She squeezed his hand and then pointed to the far end of the island. "Beat you there!" And before he could respond, she was off, sprinting nimbly over the rocks. Calvin gaped at her for a moment, then sprinted after her. But Gabrielle was a soccer player, while he was a swimmer. Her muscular system was trained for running, while his was for swimming, and within a hundred feet he knew he'd never catch her.

Then she stopped.

She turned to him, her face stricken. He skidded to a stop beside her. "Gabrielle, what's wrong?" In response she pointed to the edge of the island a few feet away.

"I think it's a body," she choked out.

Frowning, Calvin dropped his hands from her shoulders and stepped around her. There, covered with seaweed, bobbing in the waves in the shallows, was...was...

As he watched, the body rolled over in the waves, revealing the man's face. Or what was left of it.

Calvin Finley, son of a cop and grandson of a Marine, lurched forward spasmodically and threw up everything he had ever eaten in his entire life. Then he collapsed to his knees and tried to do it again.

"Calvin! Calvin!" Gabrielle pulled him to his feet and turned him away from the terrible sight. "Calvin! It's okay, just don't look at it. Okay? Don't look." She hooked her arm around him and began to draw him away, but he straightened and stopped.

"Got to call my dad," he said. Then he looked at her, pale and shaken. "I'm sorry. I'm sorry. I don't know what happened. Once I saw it, I couldn't help myself." He looked miserable. He blew air out of his lips. "Christ, it's awful."

"Don't worry," she assured him. "Just a reaction..." Her voice trailed off.

Calvin pulled out his phone and dialed his father's mobile number. Then he closed his eyes, saw the face of the drowned man and began to retch again.

———————

Frank Finley's cell phone began to ring. He and his wife looked at each other. Phone calls at 6:30 a.m. did not foretell good things to come. He picked up the phone and turned it on to speaker mode.

"Yes?"

Over the small speaker he could hear retching and coughing.

"Calvin, is that you?" he said loudly. "Calvin?" There was the muffled sound of the phone being handled or dropped, then a woman's voice came on.

"Mr. Finley? Mr. Finley?" In the background he could hear someone groan loudly. What the hell was going on?

"Who is this?" he demanded.

"It's Gabrielle Poulin, Mr. Finley. I'm with Calvin on Enchanted Island."

Finley frowned. Who? Enchanted Island? What? "Where's Calvin? What's going on?"

Gabrielle sighed audibly into the phone. In the background, Finley heard Calvin's voice: "I'm okay. Give me the phone, Gabs."

More fumbling, then: "Dad?" His voice was shaky.

"Calvin, what's wrong?" Next to him, Danielle was looking at him with alarm.

"Dad, listen, we're at Enchanted Island."

"Enchanted Island? What are you doing there?" Finley asked. Danielle hit him on the arm. Hard. She glared at him and made a 'keep moving' gesture with her hands.

"Calvin, son? What is the problem?"

"Dad, we kayaked out here this morning." He paused, taking a deep breath. "There's a body washed up on the rocks here."

Finley froze. It was unusual to have bodies wash up in the island belt off of North Harbor and Stonington, but the Eastern Maine Coastal Current swept right through here. If... "Wait a minute, Calvin, hold on. I just need to check something. Hold on." He put the phone to his chest and walked quickly to the wall of their living room, where they had a large map of the area mounted under glass.

"Frank, what is going on? Is Calvin all right?" Danielle asked him.

"They found a body out on Enchanted Island. Cal is pretty shook up." He bent over the map, putting his finger over the area where they found Henry Mitchell's boat. Then he traced the flow of the Eastern Maine Coastal Current to Enchanted Island. "Shit," he muttered under his breath.

"What?" Danielle asked.

"I think Calvin may just have found the body of Henry Mitchell, but if the Cartel hears we've recovered him, they might get spooked and call off the drop tomorrow." He thought furiously, then raised the cell phone again. "Calvin?"

"Yeah, Dad, I'm here."

"Who is with you?" Finley asked

"What? Gabrielle, from school."

Finley covered the phone and turned to his wife. "Who is Gabrielle?"

Danielle sighed at his ignorance. "Gabrielle Poulin is a senior in high school with Calvin. They are interested in each other. You know her father, George. He works at Kennebec Savings in Ellsworth."

Finley considered. "Is she a solid kid or an airhead? Is she reliable?"

Danielle nodded. "Very solid. Very smart."

Finley went back to the phone. "Calvin, listen to me carefully. Is the body male or female?"

"Oh...oh, hold on," Calvin said.

Finley could hear voices through the phone. "He wants me to look at the body again to see if it's a man or a woman. I don't think..."

And then the girl's voice: "I'll look. Stay there." And a moment later. "It's a man. He's wearing waders like a fisherman."

"Dad," Calvin said. "It is a man and he's got clothing like you'd see on a fisherman or a lobsterman."

"Son, are you okay?" Finley asked with concern.

Calvin sighed deeply. "I got sick a couple of times after I looked at the body. Really got to me. Gabs' been helping. Sorry."

Finley frowned. This did not sound like the usual Calvin. "Calvin, can you put Gabrielle on, please?"

More fumbling and a muffled discussion, then: "Hello, Mr. Finley?"

"Yes, Gabrielle. Listen, first, are you and Calvin okay? Calvin sounds pretty shook."

"I think so. It was a bit of a shock, I have to tell you." She lowered her voice. "Calvin lost his breakfast and has been sick a couple of more times. He doesn't want to have to look at it again if he doesn't have to. Is there something I can do?"

Finley took a deep breath. Whoever Gabrielle was, she sounded solid as a brick wall. But they weren't out of the woods yet. "Gabrielle, I need you to look at the body, his arm. Got it? His left arm. Tell me if he has a tattoo of an anchor with a mermaid on it."

There was a moment of silence. The moment dragged on.

"Gabrielle? You there?" he asked.

"You said his left arm?" She did not sound very enthusiastic. Finley couldn't blame her.

"Yeah, left arm. An anchor with a mermaid sitting on it."

More silence. Then the crunching sound of someone walking on gravel and, increasingly, Gabrielle's breathing. The sound of walking stopped, but the sound of breathing increased. Finley could picture her bending over the body. A body, he reminded himself, that had been in salt water for close to three days. By now it would be in bad shape.

Then there was the sound of someone retching violently, followed by a cough and Gabrielle spitting. Then the sound of her panting for fresh air.

"Mr. Finley?" she sounded washed out and subdued.

"Yes, Gabrielle, I'm here." He spoke calmly, willing her to take strength from him.

"He's…he is badly eaten over much of his body; a lot of the skin on his arm is gone, but I can see the bottom part of an anchor tattoo and what might be part of a mermaid's tail. At least that's what I think it is." There was the sound of her gagging, then another cough. When she came back to the phone, her voice was weak.

"Mr. Finley, can you come and get us? Please? I don't think either one of us can kayak back right now."

"Gabrielle, you did great. Really great. Now listen, Gabrielle, okay, listen close. I'll be there within half an hour. Got it? Half an hour. I want you and Calvin to sit by your kayaks and wait for me. But listen, this is *real* important. If someone else comes before I get there, anybody at all, even if you know them, I want you and Calvin to get into your kayaks right away and paddle as hard as you can for shore."

There was another long silence. "Mr. Finley, I think the man was shot in the head."

"Why do you say that, Gabrielle?" Calmly, calmly. He waved frantically at his wife, then mouthed the words: *Get the boat ready!*

"The top of his head is gone, Mr. Finley." She sounded near tears now. "I saw it, that's what made me sick. Fish don't eat the head, do they?"

"Gabrielle, you and Calvin are going to be fine. I'm going to be there in just a few minutes and I'll take care of everything. I need you to be strong for just a little while longer. Can you do that, honey?"

A deep breath. "Yes, sir. And I'll take care of Calvin. But hurry, please, Mr. Finley."

"Gabrielle, put Calvin on the phone, will you, please?"

A pause, then Calvin's shaky voice: "Dad? Are you coming?"

"I'll be there in thirty minutes, son. But now listen very carefully. The body on the beach is a murder victim. If anyone gets to the island before I do, you and Gabrielle get into your kayaks and paddle like hell. If you can't head for shore, go to Saddleback and try to hide there. I'll be there as soon as I can. Is your boat gassed up?" But even as he asked, he realized it was going to be too small.

"Yeah, I filled it last night at Cadot's."

"How much battery life on your phone?" Finley asked.

"It's good, Dad. More than half."

"Okay, son. I'm sorry to get you involved in this. Go sit right next to your kayaks and wait for me. But if someone comes, run for it."

Calvin blew out a breath. "Okay, Dad."

"I love you, Calvin." Finley disconnected the call, then entered the number for Howard Honeycutt. Predictably, Honeycutt answered on the first ring.

"Frank?"

"Howard, we've found Mitchell's body. It looks like he was shot." Finley gave a short terse, report. "We need to get that body out of there, but quietly. Very quietly."

"Don't worry," Honeycutt assured him. "Enchanted Island isn't the crime scene, the boat was the crime scene. It's more important to keep this under wraps so they'll go through with the drop tomorrow night."

"Okay," Finley replied. "I've got to go. I've got two badly frightened kids out there and no way of knowing if someone is looking for Mitchell's body."

"What do you need from me?" Honeycutt asked.

"I need you here with a truck to take the body somewhere and put it on ice. Bring the truck right down to the little dock on my father-in-law's property."

"You got it. It will be waiting for you when you get back."

"Tell your guys to show their badges right away or I'll shoot them," Finley warned him. "And tell them not to wear their DEA jackets. This has to be low-profile."

"We've moved bodies before, Frank. Don't you worry."

They hung up and Finley turned to find his wife handing him his service pistol, plus the Sportical assault rifle they owned. "Let's go," she said.

"We need to borrow Luc's boat," Finley told her. "Calvin's is too small to hold the kayaks and four people." Plus the body, of course.

They were half way to the main house where Danielle's parents lived when Luc Dumas stepped out of his house. He looked at their taut faces, the rifle Finley was carrying and the pistol on his daughter's hip, then he grinned wolfishly.

"You guys need some help?"

Finley glanced at his wife, but she shook her head. "Dad," she addressed Luc, "we've got a situation and we need to get there fast. We need to take your boat. Is she gassed up?"

"We can be on the water in five minutes," he told them, including himself in their plan.

Husband and wife exchanged a look. Dumas' boat was an Ellis 36 Express Cruiser, designed after lobster boats. There would be plenty of room for Calvin and Gabrielle, three adults, two kayaks...and one body.

Danielle nodded.

"Okay, Luc," Finley said, "but we have to hurry. The kids are exposed out there and they're waiting for us."

Dumas stepped back into his house and came out half a minute later, dressed in a warm, waterproof jacket and carrying a shotgun. They walked briskly down the path to the gargoyle-festooned dock.

Finley gestured to the shotgun. "Luc, you know how to use that thing?"

"Son, I had the greatest teacher there ever was, the United States Marine Corps. That, plus a sunny, all-expenses paid year in the Republic of Vietnam, including the Battle of Khe Sanh. I have more than a passing acquaintance with shotguns."

"You never told me you were in that battle!" his daughter exclaimed.

"I never told you a lot of things," he retorted mildly. "Just like there are a lot of things you haven't told me. But let's save the intimate revelations until we finish this little mission of yours." He glanced at his son-in-law. "What are we going to fetch?"

"Calvin and his girlfriend, two kayaks and a body," Finley answered tersely.

Luc Dumas pursed his lips. "I've got some large plastic bags in the boat, will that do?"

"Yeah, I think so. But we've got to move fast here, Luc. There may be others interested in that body."

Dumas nodded, but inwardly he was smiling. *Great way to start the day!*

Four minutes later, they were backing off the dock and into North Harbor. Six minutes after that and they were out of the harbor and headed southeast into the maze of islands that would take them to Enchanted Island.

———

Calvin and Gabrielle sat on the rock shelf next to their kayaks, huddled together for warmth under a beach towel. They tentatively sipped the remainder of the coffee, their stomachs still too tender for any solid food.

"Well," Calvin said. "I told you we should do something a little different for our first date."

Gabrielle spluttered a mouthful of coffee. Calvin patted her on her back.

"You okay?" he asked in mock solicitude. "I mean, what could be better than a kayak trip at dawn, a beautiful sunrise, and an enchanted island complete with its own body?"

Gabrielle laughed, but the tears came as well. "Calvin, that poor man was shot! Murdered!"

Calvin sighed. "You know," he said tenderly. "I would have been perfectly happy to be here alone with you, just the two of us. We didn't need the body."

"Stop it!" she said, a small laugh escaping her, tears rolling down her cheeks. "It's horrible!" She leaned against him, head on his shoulder.

"It *was* horrible," he agreed. "No one's ever beaten me in a race before."

She elbowed him hard in the ribs. "Next time *you* can find the body first."

Suddenly serious, he put his arm around her. "Sorry about all of this, Gabs. I guess it wasn't much of a first date, after all."

"Memorable," she murmured. "But maybe therapy will help me forget. *Lots* of therapy."

He smiled. "I mean it. I am sorry for all of this."

Then he heard the boat.

———————

Finley spotted them through the binoculars. "There they are, north side of the island." He took out his phone and called Calvin's number.

"Dad?" Calvin sounded relieved and anxious, all at the same time.

"Calvin, I can see you. We are in your grandfather's boat. Where is the body?"

"On the other side of the island. South. Right at the water's edge."

"Okay, we are going to go there. Can you and Gabrielle paddle there and meet us?"

"Sure, easy."

"Calvin, while you were waiting for us, did anyone come nosing around?"

"No, Dad. We saw some lobster boats, but always at a distance and they just went out to drop their traps."

"Okay, son. Meet you on the south side in just a few minutes." Finley turned to his father-in-law. "Can you get us close in on the south side, Luc?"

Dumas nodded, but didn't speak. His Ellis 36 drew three feet, ten inches, but the area around the island was full of rocks. *Take it slow,* he told himself. *Slow and steady.* With one eye on the depth finder, he took the boat in at dead slow. "Danni," he called to his daughter, using her family nickname. "Go up in the bow and tell me if you see anything that can hurt us. If you suddenly see the bottom, call out. Remember, we draw four feet."

Danielle scampered to the bow.

"Frank, I want you on the starboard side. Same thing. Look for rocks sticking up or if the bottom suddenly appears."

They crept in, Dumas nudging the *Rock Head* ahead a foot at a time. Finally, about twenty feet from the shoreline, Danielle, shouted: "Rocks!"

Dumas throttled back, just slightly, and the boat stopped. "Okay, let's get two anchors out so she doesn't drift onto something nasty."

Danielle, meanwhile, was standing on the bow, turning slowly in a full circle. She waved to Gabrielle and Calvin, about a hundred yards away, then jumped lightly down into the cockpit. "No boats in sight, if you want to get the body on board without being seen."

Finley waved to the kids as well, then turned to his wife. "Danni, Calvin is used to seeing me with a pistol, but if he sees the rifle and his mother with a pistol strapped to her waist, he might freak out a little. Why don't you put the guns in the cabin, somewhere out of sight, but somewhere we can get at them if we need them." Danielle nodded and went below with the weapons.

The kids paddled up and began loading the kayaks onto the Ellis 36. Finley and Dumas, meanwhile, gingerly lowered themselves chest-deep into the freezing water and half-walked, half-swam to where the body lay, face upwards to the sun. The head was misshapen, whether from being shot or being immersed in water for several days, Finley didn't know.

Dumas leaned over for a better look. It had been almost fifty years, but bullet-ridden corpses were nothing new to him. "Huh," he grunted. "Look here. See, the very top of his head was shot, but the angle is very steep. The bullet just grooved the top of his skull." He frowned. "You know, he might have survived the shooting. Maybe, anyway."

Finley looked closer and suddenly felt his gorge rising. He hastily straightened and gulped several breaths of cool sea air, letting his stomach settle. Little wonder Calvin and Gabrielle were both sick: Mitchell's body and face were ruined. He shuddered. He didn't respect Henry Mitchell at all, the man was a weasel, but he wouldn't have wished this on him.

"Any other wounds?" he asked.

Dumas studied the body. "Three more gunshots. One to the chest, two to the face. And, of course, the fish got to him pretty good. Poor bastard, nobody deserves that."

They shook out the bag they'd brought along, but quickly found they could not stuff the body into it. They finally settled for rolling the body onto a tarp and tying it, both men losing their breakfast as more decomposition gases escaped from Mitchell's body. They dragged the body through the water, then tied a line to the winch and hoisted the body up and dropped it into the well of the *Rock Head.*

It made a nauseatingly wet *splat* when it landed. More gas escaped from the tarp. Everyone looked a little green.

"Oh, Christ, nothing like a rotting corpse in the morning," Dumas sighed. "Going to take a week to get rid of the smell." Then they pulled up the anchors and carefully backed into deeper water.

Finley got on the phone with Honeycutt. "I think we better change the meeting place to the northeast side of North Harbor, the town, not the harbor itself. You got a map?"

"Big GPS screen," Honeycutt answered.

"Okay, find Oceanville Road. You're going to take Fire Lane 33 north off of Oceanville Road. Take the fire lane all the way to the water. There is a small pier there. Don't worry about the house. It's a summer house and it will be empty now. And listen, you'll want to get Mitchell's body refrigerated as fast as you can or it's going to fall apart on you. Trust me."

Honeycutt chuckled unpleasantly. "Got it. Oceanville to Fire Lane 33. See you at the pier."

Danielle came out of the boat's cabin, walking gingerly around the tarp that held the body.

"How are the kids doing?" Finley asked her, wearing his 'Father' hat again.

"Drinking some hot chocolate. They're pretty subdued, but they are teasing each other, so they'll be okay." She wrinkled her nose. "No wonder they got sick. That thing stinks!"

That "thing," Finley reflected, was the father of eight kids. Even if he was an asshole, he didn't deserve this.

Thirty minutes later, they reached the end of the pier off Fire Lane 33. It wasn't much of a pier, but it didn't have to be. Honeycutt stood there, hands in his pockets, with three burly young men beside him.

"These your guys?" Dumas asked his son-in-law.

"Yeah," Finley assured him. "The older guy is my boss."

Dumas raised his eyebrows. Boss? But he said nothing.

The three younger men dragged a gurney out to the end of the pier, then hopped into the boat. The smell hit them almost immediately. "Jesus!" one of them complained, then reached into his pocket and brought out an air mask. The other two followed suit. They all put on thick rubber gloves. Within minutes the body was lifted from the boat onto the gurney and was rolled into the back of the truck.

Honeycutt stepped over to Finley. "Are you confident no one saw you moving the body, Frank?"

Finley nodded. "We were lucky. There were no other ships in the area."

Honeycutt looked relieved. "I was afraid something might have given it away. It wouldn't take much to make the Cartel call off the drop."

Finley nodded. "We're good, but I need your help with one other thing."

Honeycutt looked at him questioningly.

"I've got two teenagers in the boat. They found the body. One is my son, Calvin, the other is a girlfriend of his. Local girl from North Harbor. I had to warn them that someone might be hunting for the body, and to run if anyone stopped at the island. Now we need to tell them not to talk about this to anybody. I want you to do it."

Honeycutt made a sour expression. "Why me?"

"Because you're the big-shot Director of the New England Region and they both think I am nothing more than a local cop," Finley said patiently. "We want to keep it that way."

Honeycutt nodded in resignation.

The two kids were brought out and Honeycutt showed them both his credentials. They looked impressed by the badge.

"You guys have been great today. I mean it. I know that this has been a shock, but you handled it perfectly," he told them seriously. "I can't tell you what is going on, too many lives are at stake. But when this is over, I will come and tell you and your parents the vital role you played in this. Until then, you must not tell anyone. *Anyone.*"

"I can't tell my parents?" Gabrielle complained. "It's almost eight o'clock and I puked up all my breakfast. How do I explain why I'm going to miss school today?"

Honeycutt pursed his lips, gazing around at the assembly of Frank Finley, Danielle, Calvin and Luc Dumas. "You'll tell them you were late because Mr. Dumas had a heart arrhythmia and fell off a ladder in his studio. In fact, once you are back to his house, you will help take him to the hospital."

"How the hell do you know I have a ladder in my studio?" growled Luc Dumas.

Honeycutt ignored him.

"Mr. Finley will back you up on your story, but even other members of the Police Department will not know what happened. You cannot tell *anyone*. Am I clear?" He looked at them sternly.

The two teens looked at each other wordlessly, then nodded to Honeycutt.

"If you need to talk to me, or if something comes up, call Mr. Finley. He knows how to get ahold of me."

"What about the body?" Calvin asked earnestly. "Aren't you going to tell his family?"

Honeycutt mentally cursed bright, inquisitive children everywhere. "Not yet. I know the family is grieving, but more lives could be lost. Soon, very soon, I will be able to tell them everything."

He looked from Gabrielle to Calvin, then back again. "Are we okay on this?"

They nodded again, this time some of the drama and excitement seeping into their expressions.

One of the three younger men came back and whispered into Honeycutt's ear, "Sir, the goddamn stiff stinks like crazy. We need to get going or we are going to be puking our guts out all the way back to the office."

Honeycutt nodded judiciously, then turned back to the others. "I'm sorry, but there is something important I have to attend to, so I must leave now. Thank you again for your help...and your discretion." With that, he turned and walked briskly back up the pier and into the truck.

After the truck was out of sight, everyone deflated like a balloon. Calvin and Gabrielle looked spent, Finley felt like he needed a nap and a drink, not in that order, and even Danielle looked like she needed to just sit down for a while.

Luc Dumas had seen post-combat letdown before. "Back in the boat, everyone. Let's go home."

As they moved down the path, Luc Dumas turned to Gabrielle, "So, I understand you like Rumi in the original Arabic?"

Once on board the *Rock Head,* Danielle took the teenagers below to the cabin and began making another mug of cocoa for each of them. Gabrielle and Calvin oscillated back and forth, one minute nonchalant about discovering a dead body and the next minute shivering and pulling the blanket tighter around them.

Danielle got them settled with more cocoa and put her arm around Gabrielle. "Once we get back and Calvin's grandpa 'falls ill,' I will call your mother and tell her you've been through a bit of a shock and that I suggested you stay home from school today," she said. "But before we get into that, I just want to tell you that I am very impressed with the two of you. That was pretty rough back there and you both handled yourselves like adults. You should be proud."

Calvin and Gabrielle looked at each other, then Calvin grinned mischievously. "I thought I got sick to my stomach very nobly," he said, "showing great courage and fortitude."

Gabrielle nudged him with her elbow. "Maybe the first time, but the second and third times?" She made a face. "Not so much."

———————

Frank Finley and Luc Dumas stood in the pilothouse, neither of them saying much. The sun was higher now and promised a glorious Maine day, or, to be more accurate, one of those *rare* but glorious Maine days when Mother Nature showed her tender side. No fog. No rain. No storms. No heavy seas.

Dumas finally broke the silence. "So, the older guy is your boss."

Finley looked at him for a long moment, then nodded shortly.

"And he's with the DEA. Even though you're a cop with the North Harbor PD." He said it as a statement, not a question.

Finley sighed. "Look, Luc, I can't tell you anything about this."

Dumas idly scratched his chest. "Well, I take it that you're not running around with the DEA just because I've got a marijuana plant in my basement."

Finley smiled. "Actually, we've been watching you for years. We've got an entire task force dedicated to you and that scraggly-assed pot plant.

Dumas grunted. "Yeah, figures. My tax dollars at work." He looked closely at his son-in-law. "What *can* you tell me?"

Finley shrugged. "Not much, Luc. I'm sorry, but that's the way it is."

Dumas scowled. "Does Danni know? You're not keeping this secret from her, are you?"

"She knows," Finley assured him. "She knows everything."

"Hmm..." Dumas was not mollified. "Is it dangerous? I mean, we just off-loaded a dead body under what might be charitably described as 'suspicious circumstances.' And when we went out to fetch that body, you were carrying a small arsenal. Are you in danger?"

"Some," Finley admitted. "Hard to say how much, but I'm being careful."

Dumas took in a deep breath. "I'm going to go along with this, Frank, but sooner or later we are going to have a long talk. My only daughter and grandchildren are involved now. That doesn't make me very happy." He wrinkled his nose. "And to top it off, my boat stinks."

Chapter 19
Thursday Night

It was almost 5 p.m. when LeBlanc's *Celeste* pulled up to the Cadot dock. It was a great catch, some three hundred lobsters, most of them hard shell. It took the better part of an hour to off-load the catch and then Jacob and the other sternsman were left the task of washing out the boat. That took another hour, but by 6 p.m. Jacob was climbing the ladder to the dock.

"Hey, Jake, got something for you," LeBlanc called, and waved him over.

And there, parked at the dock entrance, was a well-worn Honda Shadow. LeBlanc climbed onto it, started it up and drove slowly around the parking lot. It was dinged, dirty and the engine smoked when he changed gears. It backfired when he shut it down.

Jacob thought it was beautiful.

"It needs a tune-up and a good cleaning," LeBlanc told him. He didn't tell him that the bike belonged to Martin LaPierre and that he had just taken it over LaPierre's objections. He reached into the side storage bin and took out a black helmet. "And for Christ's sake, wear this."

Jacob took the helmet reverently. "This is great, Mr. LeBlanc. I can't thank you enough."

LeBlanc snorted. "I want that bike back in one piece, Jake, and I want you in one piece while you're driving it. And drive slow until you're good and comfortable with it. See you tomorrow." He got back into his pickup and drove away, content in the knowledge that Jacob Finley was now deeply in his debt.

Jacob stood in front of the motorcycle, overwhelmed at his good fortune. This was the best thing that ever happened to him.

"Hey," a voice said behind him. "You really know how to ride that thing?"

He turned and saw a girl who looked like she stepped from a beauty magazine.

"Well?" she teased. "Do you?"

"Yeah, sure," he stuttered, feeling like he was fourteen again.

She nodded and ran the tip of her tongue over her lips in a way that gave Jacob an instant erection. "Good, 'cause I'm stuck here and I need a ride home." She stepped closer. "Could you give me a ride? Please?"

"Yeah, sure," Jacob said hurriedly, before she turned into smoke and disappeared.

She held out a hand. "I'm Katie." She smiled, and it lit up her entire face.

He took her hand in his. It was very warm to his touch. Something swelled in his chest.

"I'm Jake," he said.

Jacob got home late, after his parents had gone to bed. He and Katie had gone to a little diner in Ellsworth for burgers, then wandered through the Mall eyeing stuff that neither one of them could afford, and finally ended up getting ice cream cones in Blue Hill. The motorcycle had sputtered and smoked, but Jacob barely noticed. He had money in his pocket and a stunning-looking girl clinging to him as he roared along the Maine back roads.

He'd fix the bike. Later.

Right now he had more important things to think about.

Katie lived with her father in a double-wide trailer on a dirt lane off Airport Road in Stonington. This was the part of Stonington that the tourists never saw. And never wanted to.

Jake drove in carefully, mindful of the ruts.

"Better stop here," she told him, when they were one hundred feet from the trailer. "My dad goes to bed early and I don't want to wake him." She touched his cheek. Her hand was very warm. "I had a nice night, Jake. Thank you." Then she leaned forward and gave him a kiss that would keep him smiling for hours. A warm kiss, with a little tongue and lots of promise.

Then she was gone, with the door to the trailer closing behind her, leaving Jacob a little stunned and thoroughly smitten.

"Hot damn!" he muttered. He started his bike, slid it into low gear and, as quietly as possible, drove back to Airport Road.

Katie walked into the dimly lit kitchen. She could hear her father snoring softly in the master bedroom. She slipped into her tiny bedroom and carefully shut the door. Then she reached into her purse and withdrew one of the five glassine bags of Dragon – heroin laced with fentanyl – that LeBlanc had given her. She carefully tore it open, then packed the contents into a clay pipe. Then she lay on the bed with the lights off, put on some quiet, lonely, Spanish guitar music and lit the pipe.

She drew in a deep lungful of the lovely smoke, and released it very slowly. The music seemed written just for her, deliciously melancholy. She took in another breath, then another. Within minutes a wave of warm ecstasy rolled through her body, starting in her belly and spreading north and south. It moved slowly at first, but then, as the fentanyl kicked in, with deceptive speed. She felt it penetrate her core like a gentle lover, deeper and deeper and all-consuming. She sighed deeply and groaned in pleasure. The crest of molten ecstasy built higher and higher, then higher again, like a rogue wave towering over a tiny sloop in the far reaches of the ocean.

She had been craving this all day.

Her head sank back and her entire body softened. As she drifted off, a corner of her mind thought briefly of Jake. She genuinely had a wonderful time with him, which was a surprise because she hadn't expected to like him. But the thought was fleeting, ethereal. It detached and spun off into the roiling spume of the chemical tsunami that sped towards her.

The tsunami reached her brain, enveloping it. Devouring it.

She sank into delicious oblivion.

Nothing else mattered. Just this.

The Nothing.

Jake drove home slowly, reliving the taste of her kiss and the feel of her lips on his, blissfully unaware that he was the end result of a million years of human evolution, which assured he would fall head over heels with the first attractive female who showed sexual interest in him.

He rode west out Airport Road, turned south on Rte. 15 and then west again on Oceanville Road, which took him all the way into North Harbor. He killed the engine halfway down the last little hill leading to their house and rolled the bike silently into the driveway. He didn't have a chain to lock it up. Have to get one tomorrow.

Quietly, he crept into the dark house and up the stairs to the room he shared with Calvin. Calvin was still awake, reading some book in a foreign language.

"Somebody give you a ride home on a motorcycle tonight? Thought I heard one just before you came in."

Jacob smothered a grin. "Nope. That was me, on my new bike."

"What!" his brother exclaimed in a whisper "You got a motorcycle! Oh, God, Mom's gonna have a cow!"

"Shows you how little you know," Jacob teased. "Dad used to have one when they first met. Mom told me once they went everywhere on it."

Calvin crinkled his nose. "Mom and Dad riding around on a motorcycle? Hard to believe."

"Believe it, brother." Jacob undressed and slipped into his bed.

A grimace flickered across Calvin's face. "Jacob, I should have told you, I had a fight yesterday with Little Guy and the LaPierre brothers. Gave Guy a bloody nose and knocked Martin into the harbor. Watch yourself today; Guy's got a mean streak."

"Wish you'd told me last night," Jacob said ruefully. "He came after me when we docked at Cadot's, but it worked out all right in the end." He pointed a finger at Calvin. "I don't have to worry about Guy, but you sure do. He was really pissed, so watch yourself. And don't turn your back on him, he's a sucker-punching little weasel."

Calvin looked glum. "Yeah, I sort of figured."

Jacob tried for nonchalance, but couldn't quite pull it off. "Met a girl tonight."

Calvin grinned wickedly. "Blind girl, maybe? Can't see your ugly puss?"

Jacob made a rude gesture and Calvin laughed. "How'd you meet her?"

'Well-l-l-l, either she immediately recognized what an incredible stud I am, or she just needed a ride home," Jacob grinned.

"Is she nice?"

Jacob considered it. Katie was sexy as hell, and a little sad. But nice? "Yeah, I think so."

"Gonna try to see her again?" Calvin asked, grinning. It was fun to see his older brother gobsmacked.

Jacob grinned back. "Absolutely."

They talked inconsequentially for a few more minutes, then crawled into their beds and doused the lights, Calvin still reading by the light of his Kindle and Jacob staring at the ceiling, reliving his evening with Katie. Then Calvin put down the Kindle and propped his head up on one elbow.

"Hey, did you know that Pépé fought in Vietnam, at the battle of Khe San?"

Jacob rolled over to look at him. "Pépé? Mom told me he had been in the Marines, but I didn't know he was in any big battle. What was Khe San?"

Calvin, who had looked up the battle once he was home, told his brother all about it. The forward outpost, being surrounded, the shelling and the rushed attacks, the desperate hand-to-hand fighting. All of it. "Then today when we were coming back with the body, I heard Pépé and

Dad talking about it. Dad said something like, 'Well, I guess you do know how to use the shotgun.'"

Jacob sat up in his bed. "Wait! Back up! What body? And why did Pépé have his shotgun?"

Calvin looked at him, thinking furiously. That man, Mr. Honeycutt, had told them not to tell anyone about it, but this was Jacob! His brother. Family.

He took a deep breath. "This morning I was out kayaking with Gabrielle and we found a body washed up on Enchanted Island," he told his brother solemnly. "But you've got to keep this quiet. I promised the guy from the DEA."

DEA? Jacob wondered. "Of course I will," he said. "So tell me already!"

Calvin did. All of it.

Chapter 20
Friday

Calvin woke up at 5 a.m. sharp. To his surprise, Jacob got up at the same time and followed him downstairs to the kitchen. Calvin put on the coffee while Jacob washed up in the tiny bathroom. Jacob came out ten minutes later, drying his face with a towel.

"Forgot to shave, champ," Calvin told him.

"Growing a beard," Jacob grunted, making himself a bowl of oatmeal and pouring a tall glass of orange juice.

"Another early day?" Calvin said in a low voice, mindful of his parents' room above them.

"Yep, going out to the twenty-mile line again. Mr. LeBlanc's convinced the lobsters are coming into shore through there. Laid a bunch of traps couple of days ago."

"What's it like out there?" asked Calvin, who had never been farther than a few miles offshore.

"Big. No land in sight most of the time." Jacob drained his juice glass. "Little eerie, to tell you the truth. Get some big ocean rollers that lift the boat really high, then just set it down again in the trough. Don't think I'd enjoy being caught out there in a storm." He glanced at his younger brother. "You'd love it. Really pretty."

Calvin nodded thoughtfully. Jacob stood up, put his dirty dishes in the sink, then picked up his black motorcycle helmet and put it on, trying to look casual.

Calvin wasn't having it. "Darth Vader on a bender," he proclaimed.

"Up yours!" Jacob laughed, and was out the door. A moment later there was the sound of a motorcycle starting up and revving, then the sound receded.

Finley sat up at 5:30 a.m., rubbing at his eyes to force the sleep out of his mind. Tonight would be a late night, but first, breakfast and make sure Jacob got to work on time. He padded down the hallway, wooden floor cold underfoot, then peeked in the boys' room. Both beds empty, again.

He walked downstairs to the kitchen, but there was only a note from Calvin that he was swimming to Sheep Island, and two sets of dishes in the sink.

Danielle came down the steps wrapped in a bathrobe, her hair combed out and spilling over her shoulders.

"Jacob has already gotten up, had breakfast and gone," Finley said in wonder. "Two days in a row."

"Yes," she nodded, "and on his new motorcycle. I heard him start it up and leave the driveway."

Finley frowned in annoyance. "Motorcycle? Where the hell did he get the money for a motorcycle? And who gave him permission to buy one."

"Well, *I* don't know," she answered a little defensively. "I saw him drive off on it, but never had a chance to ask him about it."

"Dammit," Finley fumed. "I hope he had enough sense to get a helmet and some protective clothing. And insurance? Does he even have health insurance?"

Danielle pursed her lips. "Actually, he is still on our family health plan. And before we jump down his throat, let's at least find out what the facts are." She started to turn away, but then turned back. "And, yes, he does have a helmet. He was wearing it as he drove out. He may be nineteen, Frank, but he's not stupid."

"All nineteen-year-old boys are stupid. I was nineteen once; believe me, I know. A motorcycle! Christ, at work we must have to clean up after three motorcycle accidents a week. Dammit, what possessed him to get a motorcycle?"

She leaned into him seductively, hands warm on the skin of his chest. "Speaking of motorcycles, I seem to recall that we had a *lot* of fun on yours."

"I never gave him permission to buy a motorcycle!" Finley sputtered, feeling the argument turn against him, and not liking it. "He's only nineteen, for Christ's sake!"

"Almost twenty, old man," she reminded him. "And if memory serves, that first time you took me on your motorcycle down that trail under a full moon, weren't you just nineteen?" She made a look of surprise. "Why, my goodness, that made me just seventeen! And you, Frank Finley, you took my innocence and my precious virtue." She smiled as she thought of some of their teenage make-out sessions prior to the motorcycle ride. "Well, such as it was," she laughed.

Despite himself, Finley had to grin. They had been dating about two months when he had purchased that motorcycle. And he certainly did not have a helmet. Her parents would have had a fit if they had known he was giving her a ride on it, so she had to sneak out of the house. He had blasted down the highway under a full moon, with Danielle sitting behind him, her arms tight around his waist. Finally, she whispered — or perhaps had hollered — that she wanted to stop. In the glow of the moonlight, Danielle had looked bewitching as she dragged him off the bike and into the woods. They'd found a little clearing, threw the blanket on the ground and tore off their clothes in record time.

Every minute of it was burned indelibly into their memory.

"Loss of innocence? Is that what you're calling it? *Innocence?*" he asked dryly.

She leaned into him, cheek against the skin of his chest. Truth be told, the memory of that first erotic lovemaking with nineteen-year-old Frank Finley was turning her on a little. And if she was right, it was turning him on more than a little. She closed her eyes, savoring the sensation, then sighed — Calvin would walk in the door any minute now.

Suddenly, she laughed, a full-throated belly laugh. "Oh my God, do you remember the poison ivy?"

"It wasn't my fault the blanket had holes in it," he protested, wrapping his arms around her and pulling her close. "My mind was on other things."

"I had the most *embarrassing* case of poison ivy," she exclaimed. "Mom had to take me to Dr. Sweeney and I thought I'd die when he asked me how I got it. Dirty old man. How *else* could you get it there?"

Finley shook his head. "At least you didn't have to deal with your mother! When she saw me, she told me in no uncertain terms that they had a perfectly good, clean barn in the back of their property, and next time the two of us fell into heat we should use that, not copulate like wild animals in the bushes."

"She put me on birth control the next week," Danielle said. "No big lectures, no scolding. Just said that if I was old enough to be intimate, I was old enough to take precautions."

"Your mother is something else. We were lucky."

Danielle shrugged. "She knew you'd make a good husband. She used to tell me that nothing is certain in this world, but if the two of us stayed together, we'd be happy."

"Of course, now we've got a nineteen-year-old with a motorcycle," he reminder her, some of his former annoyance flaring up again.

His wife grinned up at him, eyes alight with mischief. "What do you think, should we give him a blanket as a present?"

Calvin walked in then, water dripping from his wetsuit onto the kitchen floor. He stopped when he saw his parents with their arms around each other.

"You guys hear Jacob's motorcycle?" he called out.

"Why, no," his mother answered, straight-faced. "Does he have one?"

Then they both burst out laughing.

Calvin looked at first one, then the other of his parents, mildly chagrined. "I'm sorry, but have I missed something?" he demanded.

They laughed harder. They were still laughing when he stomped upstairs to change for school.

Chapter 21
Friday Afternoon

Bruno Banderas met Mateo at the boat. "Be sure it's all gassed up and everything is running smoothly. I don't want anything to go wrong tonight."

Mateo nodded silently. He had already gone over the entire engine, cleaning it, tuning it and checking all the lines and hoses. But Banderas was a thorough man, and he meant well. So, he nodded.

"And the radio? I'm sending Pablo and Arturo with you, but I want to be in contact with you at all times, understood?" The radio was a military-grade encrypted, single-sideband, frequency-jumping radio that was bought from a Navy supply contractor. Amazingly, the sale was perfectly legal. America was wonderful.

Mateo nodded.

Banderas thought about what else he should tell him, but then saw Mateo's patient, bemused expression and realized there was nothing he could tell this man that he didn't already know. "Okay, my friend, you know what to do. The ship will be at the drop-off point at 9:20 p.m. It will be full dark, with no moon and a low cloud cover." Low clouds meant the Americans could not easily use their drones and helicopters.

Mateo nodded.

"Godspeed to you. No fuck-ups, eh?"

Mateo nodded.

———————

At his desk in North Harbor, Chief Corcoran contemplated how good it was to be in charge.

So many things come to the person in charge. Title and the automatic respect that goes with it. Responsibility, of course, but with that responsibility, power.

And with that power, opportunity.

And with that opportunity, money.

So *much* money.

Michael Corcoran had been a police officer all his life, rising slowly, slowly to this, the lofty pinnacle of his career: Chief of Police of a small, dirt-poor, grungy town in the armpit of Maine. He was fifty-eight years old, earned a pittance for a salary and reported to a Town Council made up of local businessmen whose biggest concern was how to make North Harbor more attractive to the tourists who flocked to neighboring Stonington.

Michael Corcoran had almost no savings and he was going to die poor unless he did something.

But what?

Then, one summer day one year earlier, a man had delivered an envelope to his house. A thick envelope, an envelope with some heft to it. When Corcoran opened it, $100 bills spilled out, one hundred of them. Ten Thousand Dollars on his kitchen table. Ten Thousand Dollars.

But why?

For three days, nothing. No one came to claim the money. No one called. Corcoran could have turned the money in, but to whom? *He* was the Police Chief, after all. He stuffed it back in the envelope and hid the envelope under the pots and pans in the kitchen.

Michael Corcoran may have been a small-town Police Chief, but he wasn't an idiot. He knew there would be a phone call. And he had a pretty good idea what the phone call would be about.

The call came on the third day. A modulated voice, smooth and unhurried. Oddly, an American voice, no trace of an accent.

"I trust you enjoyed our little present to you, Chief Corcoran?" the voice asked.

"Who are you?" Corcoran demanded.

"Someone who wants to be a friend. Someone who values people who are friends to us. Someone who shows appreciation when people do small favors for us."

"What sort of favors?" Corcoran was wary. Wary of a trick. Wary in case it was not a trick.

"Oh, this and that. Small favors for a man in your position."

"I'm listening," Corcoran said. And he was. Intently.

"A man will come to see you soon. With another little gift. No strings. The gift is simply to pay you for your time in listening to our...proposal."

"How do you know I won't just keep the money and throw your guy in jail for attempted bribery of a police officer?" Corcoran asked, half threatening, but partially out of genuine curiosity.

The man on the phone chuckled appreciatively. "Well, Chief, two reasons. If you do that, there will not be any more little presents. Ever. There are other police departments in Maine we can approach. And we know that your ex-wife lives in Burlington, Vermont. Such a beautiful woman. She lives in the brown house on Elm Street. Teaches at the middle school on Wilbur Lane, doesn't she? And your two daughters! You must be very proud of them. The older one, Cynthia, am I right? She's due to have a baby soon? That's a very special event for any family, Chief. And the younger one, Nancy? Getting her Master's degree in engineering at Rochester, correct? Lives in that cute little apartment on Maple Avenue, near the Mall. You are a lucky man to have daughters like those."

There was a long pause. Corcoran became aware he was breathing hard, as if he had just finished a race.

"We are businessmen," the voice continued. "We happily pay for valuable services. And if you don't want to provide those services, that is your choice. No harm, no foul. But *confidentiality*, Chief, confidentiality is important in life. Important to *us*. Were there to be a breach of confidentiality, well, the consequences would be dire, Chief. Very dire. It is important you understand that, Chief. Do you understand?"

"Yes," Corcoran rasped, his mouth dry. "I understand."

"Now that you understand the playing field and the, ah, rules of the game, shall we send a man to talk to you? If the answer is 'No,' why then you keep the money and we part ways civilly, so long as you remember your duty of confidentiality. "What do you say?"

Corcoran's lack of hesitation surprised even him. "Send your man."

"Excellent," Wallace Charles Moore III said. "I think you will find our proposal to your liking."

As it turned out, he did.

Now, sitting in his office, Chief Corcoran thought of what the night would bring. Once the drop-off date had been set, he had simply rearranged the Department duty roster to make sure his people were on duty that night. There was some grumbling, but most of the men usually on night shift found themselves working the Friday day shift for a change, or found they had an unexpected day off. And his men knew they were each going to receive a lot of money.

So, not too much grumbling.

One person who had questioned the changes was Jimmy McLeod, the senior lieutenant in the Police Department. Corcoran had dismissed him with a short reply. "Gotta shake things up every once in a while, Jimmy. Don't want people in a rut." McLeod had not looked convinced, but screw him. Corcoran grinned. He was going to make $30,000 for tonight's work. And each of his boys would make $5,000.

That was the essence of management: strong incentives and a win-win for everybody.

———————————

For Jacob Finley, Friday was a day of anticipation – tonight he would see Katie again.

The *Celeste* had pulled away from the dock at 5:30 a.m. sharp, Jean-Philippe LeBlanc at the wheel and Jacob and a man named Leo as sternsmen. Leo was a cousin or something of LeBlanc's and Jacob had seen him around the docks before. They cruised at fifteen knots and reached the area they had trapped within an hour and a half.

There were eight, one-mile trawls of twenty to twenty-five traps each, plus some areas where there were up to fifteen or twenty individual traps. They all had to be brought up from the bottom, pulled onto the boat, opened and emptied, then stacked for reuse wherever LeBlanc decided to place them. Meanwhile the seas were running five to eight feet, not crashing about or anything nasty, but enough to constantly lift and drop the boat like a cork. The work was hard, even with the winch, and you had to be careful to avoid crushed fingers or simply getting caught in the yards and yards of loose rope on the deck.

By lunch they had pulled five of the trawls. In one of them the catch was so good that LeBlanc immediately turned the *Celeste* around and they re-laid the trawl in the same location. Laying the traps was easy. You tied twenty traps together with roughly two hundred and fifty feet of line between them, lined them up like parachutists lining up for a jump, then kicked the first one off the open stern section. The first one hit the water and sank and, two hundred and fifty feet later, yanked the second trap off the boat, and so on until all twenty were off the boat in a line roughly a mile long.

A simple procedure, but not without its own risks.

Jacob never figured out what went wrong, but all of a sudden some rope coiled around his leg and he found himself flat on his back, getting dragged unceremoniously to the open stern as the traps were yanked off the boat one by one. He didn't even have time to scream.

About five feet from shooting off into the ocean, strong hands grabbed Jacob under the armpits and brought him to a jerking halt. Then the line tightened hard around his leg and he screamed in pain.

"Leo, get his leg free!" LeBlanc hollered as he fought to keep Jacob from being torn from his grasp. The *Celeste* was still moving forward and the drag of lobster pots threatened to dislocate Jacob's leg at the hip. "Leo!" LeBlanc called again. And then Leo was there, grunting and pulling at the rope to get a little slack, then reaching down with one gnarled hand to flip Jacob over and let the rope scrape over his leg.

Then Jacob was free, being pulled hastily out of the way of the next trap as it made its lemming run into the ocean. Jacob lay on the deck, laughing and sobbing, and then abruptly screaming, though whether in joy, anger, or pain, he wasn't sure. Jean-Philippe and Leo, who had both been in Jacob's position more than once, laughed and helped him to his feet.

"Jesus, Jake, this ain't no time to go swimming! We got work to do!" LeBlanc laughed and clapped him on the back.

Leo nodded somberly. "Water's damn cold, boy. Cold! Shrivel your balls! You don't want to go in that water, no." He grinned a thin smile. "But you slide real good. Fast! Thought you were going to outrun Jean-Philippe for sure."

"Jesus Christ," Jacob said weakly. LeBlanc disappeared into the cabin and came back with a pint of pear brandy. "Here, this will clear your head," he said, handing it to Jacob.

Jacob took a pull on the bottle and gasped as the liquid burned a molten path to his stomach. He coughed. "Jesus Christ!" he said again, and the two older men laughed and each took a swig. Meanwhile the last trap of the trawl pulled off the boat and sank to its appointed place on the bottom. LeBlanc took the tall, thin radar reflector and flag pole, which was tied to the last trap, and tossed it over as well. It would float upright and guide them to the trawl when they came to recover it.

"Christ Almighty, I thought my poor brother was going to have to deal with two dead bodies in two days," Jacob said shakily.

Jean-Philippe LeBlanc straightened slowly. "What's that?"

So, Jacob told him the story of the body of a dead lobsterman on Enchanted Island.

Chapter 22
Friday Afternoon

Katie was waiting on the dock in North Harbor when the *Celeste* pulled in to sell its catch to Cadot's. She was dressed in blue jeans with a soft white sleeveless blouse, setting off her *café au lait* skin. Her long hair blew in the afternoon wind.

Jacob Finley thought he had died and gone to heaven.

"Hey!" she said, all white teeth and brown eyes. "Fancy meeting you here."

Jacob was painfully conscious that he was sweaty, covered with salt and grime, and smelled like a boat bilge. He held up his arms helplessly. "Listen," he told her, "I've got to hang around for a few minutes to get paid, then I really need a shower and some clean clothes. Can I pick you up someplace in about an hour?"

Katie pouted, her lower lip thrust forward. "Well, you see, my daddy had to go to Boston for a meeting or something and – " she paused and smiled mischievously – "he won't be home until late tonight. S-o-o-o, if you want, maybe we could just get a pizza or something and maybe just have a bite to eat at my place." She smiled and raised her eyebrows. "Hmmm?"

Jacob felt a flush of hot blood race through his entire body. "That sounds...that sounds wonderful," he stammered. Then the smell of low tide and mud flats wafted into his nostrils. "But I really got to shower."

"I've got a shower," Katie said.

Jean-Philippe LeBlanc called the number for Bruno Banderas, but there was no answer. He frowned. He wanted to alert the Dominican that the police had found Henry Mitchell's body, and that by now they would know he had been murdered. He considered calling Corcoran, the Chief of Police, but thought better of it. What if the Police logged in all their calls? No, not worth the risk.

Besides, there wasn't anything going on that he knew about, so it wasn't as urgent as it might be otherwise. He put his phone away and went back to the dock to pay his crew.

The freighter, *Tampa Bay*, was eighty miles away from the drop point, steaming at fifteen knots. The Cartel's man stood in a small storage room near the stern and looked at the two packages, each weighing almost twenty-three kilos. One was wrapped in black plastic, the other was wrapped in white. It was very important not to mix them up. Not that he would; he was a very careful man.

He glanced outside the porthole and saw the cloud cover was thickening, then checked his watch. Just 4 p.m.

Everything was on schedule.

Chapter 23
Friday Night – Opening Moves

The sun was setting when Finley arrived at the trailer that Honeycutt was using as his Command post. The trailer was parked at the end of Naskeag Point in Brooklin, just where the asphalt road turned to dirt and disappeared further into the forest. In addition to the trailer, there were four unmarked cars. It looked, ironically, like a drug sale in action.

There were two tough-looking DEA guards standing outside, but Finley showed his credentials and they let him in. Honeycutt looked up and nodded as he entered.

"What's the status?" Finley asked.

Honeycutt motioned to the map of the Gulf of Maine. "Here is where the players are. Think of this like a chess game."

"First, this is the *Tampa Bay*, the freighter headed for Saint John. It is steaming at fifteen knots, about sixty miles from the Bay of Fundy, so figure four hours for it to reach the entrance. We have a Canadian Coast Guard patrol boat waiting just outside of Saint John, just in case everything goes wrong." Honeycutt always planned for failure.

"Second, here is the Coast Guard Cutter *Vigilant*, which has been shadowing the freighter for the last two days. Right now, the *Vigilant* is on the ocean side of the freighter, but the *Vigilant* can hit thirty knots and is only sixteen miles away. As the freighter closes in on the Bay of Fundy, we'll send it on a high-speed run west, towards the Maine coast. If we're right, that will put the *Vigilant* between the freighter and the Maine coast. It will also put her much closer to the freighter, shortening her time to respond to whatever the Cartel does.

"Third, the *Vigilant* has launched its LUNA drone, which is flying in a wide circle around the *Tampa Bay* and keeping an eye out for any other vessels that might approach it and take delivery of the drugs. So far, nothing, which makes sense. I think that whatever is going to happen, will happen after sunset. But if the drugs are handed off to another boat, we should have them. It's just a question of geometry, and we've got the angles covered."

"And if you see the drugs being picked up by another boat?" Finley queried.

Honeycutt shrugged. "Then we have to decide whether to follow them to shore or arrest them at the freighter's location."

"What if the pickup boat sees you and instead of running to shore, heads out into the ocean?"

Honeycutt smirked. "If they head into open ocean, we've got them. The Coast Guard cutter may be slower, but it has a *lot* more fuel. The go-fast boat will run out of gas within three to five hours. Once it does, the *Vigilant* will be all over it. We'll use the LUNA to track it so it won't be able to shake us off."

"Huh." Finley studied the map. "Weather is getting worse. How long can the LUNA stay up?"

Now Honeycutt grimaced. "That's the question, isn't it? Specs say it can stay up six to eight hours, depending on how much weight it's carrying. We decided not to arm it at all, too much weight. It's just carrying cameras. But it has to fly under the clouds and the wind is getting stronger. The Coasties say they can keep it up at least five more hours, but–" He shrugged again. "We'll see, I guess."

"And if they run?"

Honeycutt pursed his lips. "Well, the freighter is too slow to run. We've got that in the bag one way or another. If a go-fast boat comes alongside and picks up the package, then we can follow it with the LUNA and vector in the *Vigilant's* go-fast boat. It's got a heavy machine gun. If that doesn't work, we'll scramble the helicopter from the Coast Guard base in Rockland."

"So now what?"

Honeycutt sank back into his chair. "Now we wait."

Finley picked up the shopping bag he had carried in. "Anybody want a donut?"

———

Mateo and Pablo untied the lines holding the Shockwave to the pier. Mateo glanced at the sky, which was grey with thickening clouds. Good, the clouds would make it harder for the Yankees to mount aerial reconnaissance.

But not impossible. One thing the Yankees were very skilled at was finding you in the dark. But he had a little something up his sleeve that would help with that.

The engine started with a low rumble. Mateo went through his mental checklist. Food, fuel, water, GPS and maps, first aid kit, guns and spare ammo.

Just another day in Vacationland.

The Shockwave pulled away from the pier just as the last bit of the sun sank beneath the horizon. Mateo turned the boat north and increased power. He glanced west, admiring the sunset. He never passed up an opportunity to look at sunsets – you never knew when it would be your last.

―――――――――

On the *Tampa Bay,* Felipe Ochoa stood back and looked at his handiwork. The black bag had a flotation device wrapped around it. In addition, it was tied to a brightly colored orange float. No chance that it would sink beneath the waves and disappear.

The white bag was different. It had a precise depth gauge strapped to it, along with a small flotation device and some weights. They had experimented until they got it right. There was also an electronic device strapped to the bag with electrical lines running to two waterproof battery cases. The batteries were high-end lithium batteries, and he had them on a trickle charger until it was time.

He checked his satellite phone. Fully charged as well.

Satisfied, he lit a cigarette and sat down to wait. Maybe later there would be time to watch the football game tonight, Monterrey against Club Tijuana. They had already tied once this season, but Monterrey was the better team and should win.

―――――――――

Jacob took the motorcycle over the crest of the hill toward Stonington. Katie sat behind him, her arms around his waist. It was fully dark now, with stars brilliant above them, but clouds surging in from the northeast behind them. The downhill portion of the slope was straight and there were no cars coming. On impulse he turned off the engine and then flipped off the headlight.

The steep road in front of them vanished into darkness.

They rocketed down the hill in the dark. It was like a roller coaster ride through a tunnel, the wind howling in their faces and not being able to see a blessed thing in front of them. With only the sound of the wind, it was like flying at night in their own private universe, hurtling through space while the Milky Way galaxy hovered over them, so close they could reach up and touch it.

Their senses went into overdrive – their eyes told them they were barely moving, while their inner ears told them they were falling, falling through the blackness. Over the roar of the wind and his motorcycle, all Jacob could hear was Katie's laughter and, he thought, the sound of his own heart.

In front of them, the star-drenched sky was enormous.

Behind them, the storm-roiled sky was black upon black.

Katie screamed in delight and hugged him tighter, burying her head into his shoulder. "Oh my God, this is awesome!" she yelled in his ear. Her fingernails raked his chest and her thighs clamped tight against his.

A single, dim streetlight marked the bottom of the hill. Jacob braked slightly, restarted the engine and engaged the clutch, then flipped on the light just in time to make the turn onto Airport Road. His heart was beating wildly and he was grinning like a fool.

"You are the best!" Katie shouted over the engine noise, then ran her hands over his groin. "I am going to give you such a good time!"

———————

Mateo stopped in the lee of Clam Island and the three men set up the spray canopy, carefully tying it down to make sure that the wind would not rip it apart if they were running at speed. Pablo and Arturo checked their weapons and laid them out on the floor behind the seats. The ocean air was cool and the wind teased at their hair and clothes.

The spray canopy was their low-tech secret weapon to defeat the Coast Guard's infrared sensors. If the storm didn't hit them, or if the rain was not very heavy, they could use the spray canopy over the engine housing to mask the heat of the engine. It was an old trick, used by smugglers for years. And it worked, most of the time.

Then they were off again, the Shockwave punching through some of the growing waves, and hurtling off the tops of others. It was so noisy that the three men put on radio headsets with thick earmuffs so they could talk without shouting. Everyone put on their safety harnesses. It was rough now; it was going to get worse before the night was out.

Pablo activated his headset. "How fast?"

Mateo glanced at the speedometer. "Forty knots, except when we're airborne. Faster then."

The boat slammed down once more into a trough, then skimmed up the slope of another wave and went briefly airborne, only to slam down again.

"Can she take this pounding long enough to get there and back?" Pablo asked.

"We'll find out!" Mateo grinned.

"Are we going to make it in time?"

Mateo had his doubts, but he nodded. "I gave us plenty of time, don't worry."

The boat plunged down again, covering them with spray. Pablo grimaced. "I don't like this fucking water. Too cold!"

"Welcome to Vacationland, amigo!" Mateo laughed. "But if you fall in, kiss your balls goodbye!"

Arturo, reticent as always, said nothing.

They plowed on, staying in the lee of Swan Island, turning east to Great Duck Island, where Mateo stopped the boat and the three men checked all their gear, in particular the satellite phone, and fuel reserves, and looked over the boat to make sure nothing was broken or loose. Once they left the scant protection of Great Duck Island, they would be in open water all the way to the freighter and then back again. The Shockwave was a go-fast boat; now they would find out if she was a strong one as well.

Pablo checked the GPS unit again – still working, thank God – and used the measuring device to calculate the remaining distance to the rendezvous: 55.5 miles.

"We can make it, but it could take us two, maybe two and a half hours," Mateo said. Pablo broke out hot coffee and muffins – they would have all killed for a plate full of churros, but such delicacies were nowhere to be found on the uncivilized Maine coast – then Pablo gave each man two chocolate bars. On a night like this, calories would be important.

Beside them, Arturo picked up the PKMS machine gun and cradled it in his arms. Next to him, he had a tripod bolted to the floor. The large, night-vision scope on the PKMS was covered with a plastic sheath to protect it from the elements. Arturo could place half his shots in a four-inch circle at three hundred meters, albeit on dry land, but he was pretty sure that even with the high seas he could hit something as large as a Coast Guard cutter out to 1,000 meters. The only problem was visibility – the night scope was good, but whether it was good enough in the middle of an ocean storm was another thing altogether.

"Think you can hit anything with that when the boat's jumping around like a goat in heat?" Pablo teased him.

"Sí," Arturo grunted, then fell silent.

Another wave smashed the side of the boat. Pablo looked at Mateo and grinned. "Eh, this is going to be a fucking pig of a night!"

Mateo laughed and increased the throttle. Pablo sang a popular Dominican pop love song. Arturo stared stoically into the night. It began to rain.

The Shockwave surged out from behind the protection of the little island and plunged into the tender embrace of the dark, stormy Bay of Maine.

———————

Not far away, the *Tampa Bay* pushed stolidly through the waves, three hours from the rendezvous point.

Katie opened the door to her trailer and pushed Jacob inside. As the door slammed behind them, she flung her arms around his neck and kissed him hard on the mouth, hands pulling the shirt out of his pants and then tearing at the buttons.

Then she stopped. "Oh my God," she said, backing away a step and laughing. "You were right, you *do* need to shower." Laughing some more, she pushed him into the small bathroom. "Wash up, but hurry!"

Jacob, as aroused as he had ever been in his life, tore his clothes off and dropped them on the floor, then stepped into the shower and got the hot water going. "When did you say your dad is getting back?" he yelled through the door.

"The shower door opened and a very naked Katie pushed in. "Not until after midnight," she said breathlessly. She pushed her body against him and kissed him again, her hands roaming wantonly. "Plenty of time."

With his body ready to burst from desire, it never occurred to Jacob that all this was moving along a little too quickly.

In the cramped Command Center parked on Naskeag Point, it was like watching a slow-motion video game. *Very* slow motion.

The freighter *Tampa Bay* had reduced its speed to thirteen knots and was moving northwest towards the mouth of the Bay of Fundy. The Coast Guard Cutter *Vigilant* was now almost due south of the freighter, running on a course due west that would take it to a position between the freighter and the Maine coast. The LUNA drone had closed in to half a mile from the freighter due to the bad weather and was scanning the area with cameras and thermal sensors.

So far, nothing but rain and wind and more rain.

It was almost 9 p.m.

On board the *Tampa Bay,* Felipe Ochoa looked at his watch and cursed. They were running late. The freighter was supposed to be at the rendezvous point at 9:20 p.m., but the Captain had reduced speed and they would be at least thirty minutes late..

Did he dare a satellite phone call to alert the Cartel? The nervous American had said no calls until the pickup boat had arrived. He chewed on a fingernail and tried to decide what to do.

"Okay, we're here," Pablo's voice came through the headphones.

Mateo, who had been concentrating on the rough seas, looked up tiredly. The rain had lessened, but the storm clouds were still low. The storm wasn't through with them yet.

There was no sign of the *Tampa Bay*. "You sure we're in the right place?"

Pablo glanced at the GPS display. "Right on the money."

Mateo checked the time – they were five minutes late. Had the freighter already come by and was now steaming up the Bay of Fundy to Saint John? He didn't think so. In this shitty weather, it was more likely that the freighter was running behind schedule as well. "Pablo! Check the Marine Traffic site and see if you can get a fix on the *Tampa Bay.*"

Pablo complied. "Weather may be screwing it up, I can't tell. But it says the freighter is here right now."

Well, shit. They were about thirty miles south of Grand Manan Island, which sat like a sentry in the mouth of the Bay of Fundy. With the storm coming out of the northeast, the freighter would want to ride in the lee of Nova Scotia, but would be leery of getting too close to land in case the wind shifted. So...did the *Tampa Bay* turn to a more northerly course to cut the corner, or was it just running slower because of the storm?

"Pablo, I think there's a chance we got here first and the freighter is running late. They might cut north early to shave off some time. I want you to plot a course east-northeast for about five miles, then due south for four miles, then east-northeast again. Once you've got it plugged in, take the binoculars and keep scanning. *Entender?* Have Arturo help you with the other set of binoculars."

Pablo nodded and set to work. Two minutes later, he called out: "The course should be on your screen now. Just follow the path."

There was now a white line pulsating on Mateo's large navigation screen. He took another swig of hot coffee, then brought the boat about to the right heading and increased speed. He shook his head ruefully. Why was it so hard to find a six-hundred-foot freighter?

Honeycutt thumbed the mike: "Big Eyes, this is Gollum. Status report?"

Finley shot a glance at Honeycutt. "Big Eyes" was the Coast Guard Cutter *Vigilant,* which was controlling the LUNA drone. But Gollum? He knew Howard had an odd sense of humor, but his handle on this operation was *Gollum*? He glanced around the trailer. One or two of the operators were grinning, but most either didn't recognize the *Lord of the Rings* reference or were absorbed in their work.

It made Finley feel old.

Big Eyes: "Freighter is under observation and is moving slowly. No sign of any go-fast boats. Seas running five to ten feet and wind stiffening from the northeast. Weather advisory says storm will intensify over the next couple of hours."

Gollum: "Status of the LUNA?"

Big Eyes: "Still airborne, but fuel consumption is higher than forecasted. Winds are making it hard to stay on station and it has to get in close to get decent images of the freighter's deck. A good wind gust could slap it into the water."

In the Command Center, Honeycutt frowned. If they lost the drone, the night's work would be immeasurably harder. "Big Eyes, how long can the drone stay up?"

Big Eyes: "At this rate, maybe two and a half hours, max."

Gollum: "And how is your ride out there?"

Commander Diane O'Brien, Captain of the *Vigilant,* chuckled evilly. "Oh, this is just a walk in the park for us, Gollum. Except for the newbies of course; they aren't exactly happy right now."

Finley pictured half a dozen young sailors puking their guts out and winced. He was prone to sea sickness himself and did not envy them.

Gollum: "Thank you, Big Eyes. Please keep us informed."

Big Eyes: "Happy to oblige, Gollum; you are paying the bill, after all. Big Eyes out."

On the Shockwave, Mateo turned the boat south to stay on the plotted search path. The rain beat on them, making it hard to see much of anything. Also, the rain was playing hell with his headset, making it harder to talk to Pablo and Arturo.

They were running now with the seas following behind them, so they seemed to be going slower even though he knew they were going faster. The Shockwave yawed left and right, the steering sluggish. Mateo focused on keeping the boat from broaching sideways, which would be the death of them all. And a cold, fucking death it would be.

Then Arturo stood and pointed wordlessly over the starboard portion of the bow.

Mateo could have wept in relief.

Katie was clawing his back and screaming in his ear and Jacob was thrusting in her so hard the bed was bouncing off the thin carpet on the floor of the trailer. She kissed him, then bit his shoulder and arched her back to meet his thrusts and he could feel his climax building and building and then she cried out, "I'm coming! Oh, God, yes!" and her hands clutched his buttocks to pull him even deeper into her and he exploded inside her and collapsed, breath ragged and sweat pouring off his body.

And to his astonishment, Katie wrapped her arms around his neck, buried her face in his chest, and wept like a forlorn child.

On the stern of the *Tampa Bay,* Felipe Ochoa saw the Shockwave emerge from the storm immediately behind them. He got his flashlight up, a big, four-battery LED flash, and blinked out a simple code into the rain-swept darkness.

An answering blink came back almost immediately. Ochoa grunted, lifted the fifty-pound black bag as if it were no more than a bag of sugar, and hurled it overboard. The small boat darted in, the bag was hauled aboard, then two more flashes of light and it was off into the storm, headed for the coast of Maine.

Ochoa watched it go. Then there was a flash of lightning and clear against the dark clouds he sensed movement and saw a small, airplane-shaped object wheel overhead and turn in the direction of the receding go-fast boat.

"Aw, *joder!*," he muttered. Fuck! He pulled out his satellite phone and dialed the number for the American running the smuggling operation for the Sinaloa Cartel. He answered immediately.

"What is your status?" It was the same American voice.

"I have just given the parcel to the go-fast boat," Ochoa said, "but there is a problem. The Americans have a drone up. It saw the exchange and is following them."

There was a moment of silence. "Did they see your face?" the American asked in his nervous voice.

Ochoa was a not a fool. He would have lied if he had to, but there was no need. "We are in a storm, *jefe*. It is raining and it is very dark. The only way I saw the drone was because of a lightning strike. Also, I am wearing a hat and a hooded rain jacket. I tell you, they could not see my face."

The American pondered for a moment. "What is your exact position?"

Ochoa read it off the GPS.

Through the phone, Ochoa could hear the American rapidly entering the GPS position into a computer. There were a couple of more clicks, then a grunt of satisfaction and the American came back.

"Okay, you are still good. Throw the other package overboard now, Felipe. Right now! Then dispose of anything that might betray you to the Americans."

Ochoa grabbed the other bag – the white one – in one strong hand and heaved it over the stern railing. It struck the water with a splash and immediately sank from sight.

"*Realizado!*" he said into the phone. Then, realizing he did not know how fluent the American was, he translated: "Done!"

"Good," the American replied. "They will interrogate the entire crew when you reach Saint John. Be calm, Felipe. We take care of our own. Just be sure to throw overboard anything that might link you to us. You will be safe then."

"*Sí, señor.*" And surprisingly enough, Ochoa believed him.

He pulled his arm back and hurled the satellite phone and the GPS unit far into the ocean. Then he went below to his cabin to catch the rest of the soccer game.

Big Eyes: "Possible contact! I repeat, the drone may have something near the freighter!"

Gollum: "Something? What is '*something*'?"

Big Eyes: "Might be easier if I patch in the pilot of the drone. He can relay his camera image directly to you."

Gollum: "Isn't the pilot with you, Big Eyes?"

Big Eyes: "Are you kidding? He's at the Rockland Station, where he's not rolling around like a pinball and can concentrate on his flying. Patching you through now to Pilot Scott Kaeser."

Pilot: "I am circling the drone about three hundred yards off the *Tampa Bay*. Someone on the deck just dropped a large parcel to the ocean and a small boat moved in to pick it up. Boat has now departed, heading 300 degrees. Have lost visual contact with small boat, but am over freighter now. Orders?"

Gollum: "Pilot, track the go-fast boat. We know where the freighter is going."

Pilot: "Roger. Estimate ninety minutes of fuel before must return to base."

Gollum: "Find that boat!"

Big Eyes: "Command, we are west of the go-fast boat and it is heading in our general direction. We are turning to course of 90 degrees and will be searching for the go-fast boat using radar."

Gollum: "Understood. Good hunting."

———————

Mateo watched the fifty-pound package of heroin splash into the ocean. He blinked his flashlight twice at the small figure on the freighter's stern, then maneuvered the Shockwave in close to where the package landed. The Shockwave rolled and yawed in the waves and he feared broaching, but a death by drowning would be a blessing compared to what the Cartel would do to him if he failed to pick up this drop.

Then Pablo scrambled to the bow, armed with the long boat hook, and reached over the rail to grab the floating orange buoy. He brought up the rope, tossed down the hook and began to haul the package aboard. Another wave slapped the Shockwave hard on its port side, almost toppling him overboard, but he regained his balance and finally hauled a bulky, black, waterproof bag onto the deck.

He cupped both hands and shouted to Mateo, "Go! Go!"

Needing no urging, Mateo spun the wheel, advanced the throttle and the boat roared into the darkness, headed for North Harbor.

North Harbor, and safety.

———————

On the Coast Guard Cutter *Vigilant,* Captain O'Brien looked at the map in front of her. If the go-fast boat just picked up the drop from the freighter there – she marked the spot with a pin – and the *Vigilant was here* – another pin – and the drug smuggler's go-fast boat was on a course of 300 degrees – she drew a line that hit the coast just off the southern edge of Mt. Desert Island, between Tremont and Swans Island – well, then...then...

"Well, heck!" O'Brien exclaimed, "the idiots are coming right at us!" She grinned in delight. "Hooray for us!" She looked around the bridge. "Go to battle stations! We're going to nail these guys!"

––––––––––

Gollum: "Pilot, do you have a visual on the go-fast boat?"

Pilot: "Negative. I have switched to thermal, but the storm is so bad that whatever heat signature they've got is being masked. I can take the drone lower, but if I do there's a fair chance it will get slapped into the water by the wind or caught by spray." Depth perception through the cameras was notoriously tricky, especially at night, and in the rapidly moving storm the altimeter was almost worthless.

Big Eyes: "Pilot, be advised, winds are shifting to the north and increasing. Gusts are now over forty knots."

Gollum: "What's the strongest wind you can fly in?"

Pilot: "This is a small aircraft, sir. It only weighs ninety pounds. I shouldn't fly it in winds over 30 m.p.h. That's only 26 knots, sir. In this crap, there's a better than 50-50 chance we'll lose her."

Gollum: "Do we have another one available?"

[Voice of Commander Mello]: "This is Home Base in Rockland. We have another drone, but I won't authorize a launch in this weather. If absolutely necessary, I will launch a Jayhawk helicopter.

In the Command Center, Howard Honeycutt grimaced and looked at Finley. "Great, they're worrying about losing a $50,000 drone, so they're going to send a $17 Million helicopter to replace it. And the helicopter pilots will be *in* the copter, not sitting in some conference room watching a computer screen and eating doughnuts."

Gollum: "Home Base, will the copter be any better suited to handle this weather than the drone?"

Home Base: "Oh, hell yes! But that doesn't mean I like to risk it unnecessarily."

Pilot: "Hold on, I might have it! Getting some tickles on the thermal sensors."

Big Eyes: "What heading is he on, Pilot?"

KENNEDY HUDNER

Pilot: "Hold one."

Big Eyes: "Be advised that we are getting much stronger wind gusts here. Pilot, be sure to maintain a safe altitude or your bird is going to become a submarine."

Pilot: "Roger that." He had a floor of one hundred feet unless he received permission to go lower from Commander Mello.

Home Base: "Pilot, report your fuel status."

Pilot: "Maybe forty minutes. Fighting this wind is really sucking it dry."

Big Eyes: "Course heading on the go-fast boat?"

Pilot: "Thermal is fading in and out, but he has definitely turned north. Heading is now 350 degrees, almost directly into the wind."

Big Eyes: "Speed?"

Pilot: "Hard to tell. Slow, less than ten knots. Request permission to take her lower to try to get a better fix on the go-fast boat."

Home Base: "Risk factor to the drone?"

Pilot: "Very high, sir, but if I don't go lower I won't be able to pick her out from the storm spray and waves."

Gollum: "Do it, Pilot!"

Home Base: "That's not your call, dammit! That is a Coast Guard drone!"

Gollum: "And it is useless to us if it cannot locate the go-fast boat!"

In the Command Center, Honeycutt took a deep breath, considering what he could offer. And if he had the authority. Screw it, he thumbed the microphone toggle.

Gollum: "I will see to it that you are fully reimbursed if the drone is lost."

At the Rockland Coast Guard Station, Commander Mello drummed his fingers in thought. A good report from the DEA would look very good for this Station, he knew. Very good. And besides, the DEA had *oodles* of money.

Home Base: "Pilot, permission granted."

Mello turned to Ensign Kauders. "Tell the boys to get the Jayhawk ready. I want it ready to go on two-minute notice."

Pilot: "Crap, I lost him again. Taking the drone lower to regain fix on the target."

Chapter 24
Arturo's Big Mistake

The roar of the storm was so loud that Mateo couldn't hear the others, even with his headset on. The waves had grown another three feet and the thirty-foot Shockwave slammed around like a steer being herded through the gates at a slaughter house.

He had been running straight for the Maine coast, but got a bad scare when the Shockwave almost broached and rolled over as two large waves slammed into the boat's starboard side in quick succession. He turned into the waves, increasing throttle to power up their forward side and then reducing throttle once he was at the crest. So far, the wave incidence had not increased, but if it did, they were dead. The Shockwave just wasn't meant for this type of weather.

He ran north for a few minutes, more to settle his nerves than anything else, then decided to come around and run 270 degrees until he reached the Maine coastline, where he hoped the water would be calmer. From there he would hug the coastline, running southwest until he was in the lee of one of the larger islands, where he would get down on his knees and thank the Blessed Virgin Mary for bringing him through the storm.

He no longer cared how late they would arrive – he just wanted to survive.

"Pablo! Arturo!" he shouted until they looked up. "We're going to turn! I want one of you on each side of the boat to watch for waves. If you see a really big one coming down on us, tell me. Understand? Right away!"

The two men nodded. Mateo peered through the rain-streaked windshield. He would kill for some hot coffee, but the thermos had disappeared over the side an hour ago. He took the boat up two more waves, engine roaring on the steep face of each wave, then the entire boat falling down the backside while he reduced throttle and tried not to jam the bow into the face of the next wave. He was waiting for a slightly smaller wave to make his move, and finally got one. This one was more rounded, slightly less steep, without the dreaded, curling whitecap at its peak.

It was his only chance. He took it.

"Hold on!" he shouted, but had no idea if they could hear him or not. He goosed the throttle to climb up the face, then near the crest he reduced throttle, spun the wheel quickly to the left and, now sitting on top of the broad wave peak, brought the boat around until he was running back down and across its face, neatly reversing course from north to south. Their speed picked up rapidly and he ran through the trough of the wave and began to run up the back slope of the wave in front. He angled over so that they were going diagonally across the back slope on a heading of about 260 degrees, then when they reached the crest, he flicked the boat due south and they slid down the wave's face. Then he overtook the back of the next wave and again angled their ascent to 260 degrees, only to turn south again at the top.

In this way they slowly, laboriously sidestepped their way towards the coast of Maine.

And although they didn't know it, directly into the path of the oncoming Coast Guard Cutter *Vigilant.*

———————

On the *Vigilant,* Captain O'Brien peered through the dark night and wind-swept rain and saw...nothing. Grunting in frustration, she turned her head to the Petty Officer in charge of the radar.

"Elkin! What have you got?"

Petty Officer First Class Sanford Elkin sat back in his chair with a sigh. "Captain, I've good, solid returns from every wavetop within a mile in all directions. It looks like Grand Central Station at rush hour. If there's a small boat out there, it's hidden in all this garbage."

Captain O'Brien stepped behind him and peered at his large screen. It was one of the new blue ones, easier on the eyes than the older green models. White lines spiked in every direction and the background was a roiling fuzz. In the distance, there was a clean return from a large, metal object.

"That's the freighter, ma'am, heading toward Saint John. We think the small boat we're looking for is somewhere in this area," he said, pointing to the display showing wind-driven waves. "But even if it's there, most of the time it is in the trough of these waves, invisible to us. And there is so much wave, spray and rain activity that when it does appear, we'll only spot it for a moment or so."

"What are you telling me, Elkin?" O'Brien snapped.

"Captain, unless we spot that go-fast boat sitting on top of one of these waves within, oh, five-hundred yards of us, we aren't going to see 'em." Elkins looked apologetic and O'Brien clapped him on the shoulder.

"Keep at it, Mr. Elkins," she told him, but inwardly she seethed. It was a mighty big ocean and a damn dark night, and a five-hundred-yard net was pretty darn small. She sighed. Maybe the drone could locate the boat."

Then her Executive Officer touched her shoulder. "Ma'am?"

"What is it, Mr. Hillson?"

The XO shook his head. "It's the drone, ma'am. It's gone in."

Well, heck, Captain O'Brien fumed. *If that don't beat all.*

———————

Unaware of what was coming, Mateo gauged the waves and tried to generally head 270 degrees, due west. But the boat kept yawing so that sometimes he was headed 300 degrees and other times 230 degrees, with the result that he was weaving his way sluggishly westward. Fortunately, the waves seem slightly smaller as they moved west, nearer the coastline. He wondered if the storm winds were already shifting to come from the northwest, and so for now slightly flattening the waves that had originated from the northeast. Whatever it was, he was grateful.

At one point Pablo came to him, shouting in his ear: "We're taking on water in the cabin below. Must have sprung a leak from the waves."

Mateo felt a spike of panic. "How bad?" he shouted back.

"Not bad yet," Pablo assured him, clapping him on the shoulder. "Arturo and I are taking turns bailing. Have to keep an eye on it." He looked at his friend, whose face had aged ten years in the last few hours. "Want me to spell you for a few minutes?"

Mateo shook his head. "I've got a feel for it now. Keep your eyes peeled; that damn Coast Guard ship has to be out here somewhere." He didn't tell Pablo that he was worried they might run out of fuel before they could get back to port. Pablo started to turn away, but Mateo shouted after him. "You were right, one fucking pig of a night!"

Pablo flashed a grin and turned to watch the horizon.

Where, just off their port quarter, a large, white Coast Guard cutter burst from the gloom not one hundred feet away.

"Yankees!" Pablo screamed and pointed.

And despite the howling winds, Mateo could hear the piercing "WHOOOP WHOOOP" sound of the ship's battle stations siren.

———————

On the *Vigilant,* two things happened almost simultaneously.

First, the pilot lost control of the LUNA drone and it slammed into the ocean and sank. Captain O'Brien's hope of spotting the go-fast boat from the air sank with it.

Then, Petty Officer First Class Sanford Elkin sat bolt upright in his chair. "Contact! Contact, right on top of us!"

"Heading, Mr. Elkin! What's their heading?" O'Brien snapped.

"Uh, heading is 300 degrees, relative bearing is 120 degrees. Crossing right to left in front of us!"

"How far? How far is it?" she demanded, her eyes searching through the wrap-around windshield.

"Right in front of us! It's right in front, crossing under our bow!" Elkin shouted.

"What?" Captain O'Brien turned to the ship's pilot. "Hard left rudder! Full over! Emergency stop!" Then she had to brace herself as the twin screws jolted to an emergency stop, then changed direction and began to thrash at the water in reverse. She threw herself forward to look out of the wrap-around windshield, peering in vain to spot the tiny craft.

God help me, she raged inwardly. *All this work and I end up ramming the bastards!*

Not getting rammed was foremost on Mateo's mind. He turned the boat hard to the right, pointing them due north again, where he did not want to go. Fifty feet away he could see a figure crowded against the Coast Guard cutter's bridge windshield. Headed back into the waves now, but momentarily clear of the cutter, he waited until he was in the trough of the next wave and cut the wheel sharply to the left, bringing them back to a westerly course. Then he gunned the engines, intent on putting as much distance between them and the goddamned cutter as he could.

In the small cabin, Arturo had been pumping out water. When he heard Pablo scream, "Yankees!" he dropped the pump and ran back to the open deck. And there, so close he felt he could touch it, was a big white ship with a big red diagonal stripe down its bow.

The enemy.

Arturo picked up the PKMS machine gun and quickly locked it onto the tripod. He already had a 100-round ammo cannister fixed to the gun. The PKMS had an effective range of 1,000 meters, at one hundred feet he didn't even bother with the night-vision scope, he just aimed at the bridge over open sights and pulled the trigger. He walked the tracer rounds across the bridge as they passed directly in front of the cutter, but then the Shockwave turned away from the cutter and he lost the favorable angle. "Turn back!" he roared to Mateo.

Then the Coast Guard cutter was out of sight as the boat sank into a trough, but Arturo could feel the Shockwave turning left. He mounted another 100-round cannister and got ready, feet apart, bracing himself against the storm.

The next wave rolled under them, lifting them higher, higher, and there was the cutter again, parallel to them. Exposed and vulnerable.

Arturo opened fire with the PKMS, raking the cutter from bow to stern. Then he grabbed another 100-round cannister and, as the cutter began to pull astern of them, shot down the length of the boat, hoping that he might find a barrel of fuel or a window that he could shoot through and wreak havoc on those who hunted them.

He quickly ran out of ammunition and by the time he fitted in the next 100-round cannister, the *Vigilant* was disappearing into the night, a tongue of flame licking up the back of its superstructure.

Arturo laughed for the sheer joy of it.

―――――――――

On the *Vigilant,* the bridge windscreen imploded under the force of the heavy slugs from the PKMS. Captain O'Brien felt something slam into her shoulder, spin her around and smash her into the bulkhead. Stars and spots competed for control of her vision, but she gradually grew aware that she was staring at the ceiling.

And that people were screaming all around her.

Her left arm didn't work, so Captain O'Brien pushed herself up on her right. "Master Chief Ramirez, get on the Bushmaster and nail them!" She turned her head. "Pilot! Pilot, dammit, are you alive?"

Petty Officer First Class Cynthia Foster, shaken and pale, replied: "Yes. Yes, Captain."

"Well, turn us around, darn it! Get after that go-fast boat," O'Brien snapped. "Radar! Do we have them on radar?"

The ship's medic crouched down beside her. "Hold still, Captain, you're bleeding badly," he ordered, cutting away her uniform on her left shoulder.

"In a minute, darn it!" She pushed him away. "Where's the XO? Mr. Hillson!"

Lieutenant Commander Hillson appeared beside her. "Here, Captain."

"Are we tracking them on radar?" she demanded.

Hillson looked over at the radar station, where Petty Officer First Class Elkin's headless body sat at its station, still strapped in by the emergency harness. The radar display had two large bullet holes in it.

"No, ma'am," Hillson sighed. "We've lost them on radar."

O'Brien grunted with the effort of pulling herself up. "Master Chief, use the thermal imaging to find them!" The room spun for a moment. She thought she was going to throw up, but fought it off through sheer will.

Master Chief Petty Officer George Ramirez sat at the gunnery station and activated the chain-driven autocannon. The Bushmaster M242 autocannon was his baby. It could fire 200 rounds per minute and he could select from either armor-piercing or high explosive incendiary rounds. Both came with tracer rounds to help his aim. And they were heavy rounds, almost five and a half inches long, designed to kill small ships, unarmored vehicles and helicopters, with an effective range out to just under two miles, not that he could possibly see two miles in this crap. The cannon even came with a 10 kW spotting laser, the big brother to the red dot lasers used by police and special forces.

If he could see the damn go-fast boat, he could hit it.

The autocannon was mounted on the top of the superstructure to allow for a 360-degree firing arc. His computer screen had a large hole through it, so he slipped on the Galaxy View MX-72 virtual reality headset they had been experimenting with and turned it on. After a moment, the picture snapped into view and it was as if he was standing atop the *Vigilant*, peering through the storm. The rain had lessened for a moment, but the waves were still running eight to ten feet. The image was so real that he adjusted the VR controls to dampen the rolling motion of the ship. He turned in a complete circle, scanning for any sign of the drug runner's boat.

Nothing.

He flicked on the thermal imaging and did another circle. To the west, there was an intermittent smudge. Just a smudge. Then gone. He set the controls so the thermal sensor would alert him both visually and aurally. Then he took a deep breath and scanned the area again.

And again.

On the Shockwave, Arturo stacked four fresh cannisters of ammo next to him and lined up the thermal imager on where he thought the Yankee ship would be when they hit the top of the wave.

He put his finger lightly on the trigger.

At the wheel, Mateo suddenly realized that something was missing: the rain. It had stopped raining. This close to the Coast Guard cutter, it meant that they would stand out like a bonfire on the Yankee's thermal imaging sensors.

"Pablo!" he screamed. "Turn on the sprayer! Turn it on!"

Pablo understood immediately and leapt forward, slapping his hand against the switch. The electric pump chattered on and a fine mist suddenly rose over the engine compartment and blew backwards with the wind.

Mateo felt a wave lift them up and prayed that the cooling spray would mask them from the Yankee's thermal sensors.

As soon as they reached the crest, Mateo slammed the throttle forward and raced down the back of the wave, seeking concealment in the trough.

Master Chief Ramirez swept the thermal sights back and forth in a 60-degree arc. "C'mon, you bastards," he growled. "Come out and play." But before he could spot anything, a torrent of red tracers raked across the *Vigilant's* hull. There were a series of loud thuds as the rounds struck the ship squarely, and one round ZINNNGGGGEEEDD off the hull. The last of the tracers seemed to be coming right at him and Ramirez ducked involuntarily, then cursed as he belatedly remembered that he was wearing the VR helmet and he was on the bridge, not outside on the deck.

"Ayup," Captain O'Brien said, struggling to sound Down East despite the black spots that were rapidly crowding her field of vision. "That's the boat we're after. I would appreciate it, Master Chief, if you would show them the error of their ways."

The Master Chief quickly snapped his head back to where the tracers had originated. The Bushmaster swiveled with his head motions.

Nothing.

Temporarily hidden in the trough of another wave, Mateo turned on Arturo. "Arturo, you stupid son of a jackass whore!" he shouted angrily. "DO NOT SHOOT!"

Arturo glared at him, but lowered the barrel of the machine gun.

Mateo had only caught a glimpse of the Coast Guard cutter, but thought it was maybe 500 meters or more behind them. It would have to turn around in these waves, which would slow it down. He kept the throttles forward and steered slightly up the backside of a wave, then tried to maintain that position as they raced westward, but he kept sliding back into the trough and then onto the face of the advancing wave on his starboard side. He pushed the throttles harder, desperately seeking to increase the distance between his thin-skinned little boat and the Yankee warship.

He thought about all the men he had killed in his service to the Cartel, and wondered if they waited for him, arms extended to pull him beneath the storm-maddened waves.

He prayed the rain would return.

Inexorably, he felt the Shockwave begin to lift.

———————

Master Chief Ramirez waited, eyes straining. Then the left earpiece of his headset beeped once. Then again. Ramirez swiveled his head to the left. Both earpieces beeped at the same volume. Increasing the magnification of his headset, he finally detected a very faint smudge on a wavetop 700 meters to the west.

"Captain, I have a faint heat smudge at 700 meters, bearing 270 degrees," he reported.

"Well, dammit, shoot the smudge!" the Captain snapped.

He pressed the firing stud. The electric-driven chain engaged and sixty high-explosive incendiary rounds spat out, arced through the night sky and...flew just over the top of the go-fast boat.

Cursing, Ramirez corrected the targeting laser onto the smudge, then fired again. Thirty-four rounds sped through the night and hammered into the target, which immediately disappeared.

"Target is out of sight, but I hit it!" he said, trying to keep his voice calm.

Captain O'Brien angrily waved away the medic fussing over her. "Pilot, how is she doing with these waves?"

"Nothing we can't handle, ma'am," replied Petty Officer First Class Foster. "I'm getting eighteen knots out of her and could coax another knot or two if we need it."

"Maintain speed, but turn us to 270 degrees. They're running for the coast, perhaps to meet another boat. Let's keep the pressure up." O'Brien turned back to Master Chief Ramirez. "Master Chief, you are weapons free for the next fifteen minutes. If you get a clear view of them, take them." She shook a finger at him. "But don't you shoot up a lobster boat or some sorry-assed freighter trying to make port."

"Yes, ma'am," Ramirez replied, smiling.

———————

Arturo was gone.

One moment he was standing by his beloved machine gun, the next he was a blood-red mist blown away by the wind. The force of the shell that killed him was enough to rip him out of his boots, which were still on the deck where he had been standing.

Pablo was screaming and rolling around on the deck, blood pumping out of the bloody stump where his right arm had been. Mateo looked down at his own chest and saw several large splinters sticking into him like knives, and as he looked the pain hit him and blood suddenly flowed down his chest. Panic flared up for a moment, but he pushed it aside. They were still an hour to the coast and then another half hour or more to the small cove where they would off-load the drugs.

Gritting his teeth against the pain, he turned back to the wheel and, throttles to the stops, ran the Shockwave westward as fast as he could, praying to the Blessed Virgin to keep him alive a little while longer.

He never noticed that the spray system had been shot away and that the heat from his 650-horsepower engine clung to the boat like original sin.

———

Master Chief Ramirez kept his eyes on the west. God alone knew how much damage he did to the smuggler's boat with his last burst. The drug smugglers would run for it now, he felt. He kept the Bushmaster up and ready, watching for any sign.

For several minutes, there was nothing. The rain still held off, but the dark clouds scuttered low against the sky and Ramirez knew the rain would return. And when it did, it would mask the thermal signature of the smuggler's go-fast boat.

He watched. He waited. He desperately wanted to itch the itch in the middle of his back, but he knew – he *knew*– that if he took his finger off the Bushmaster's trigger for even a second, the damn go-fast boat would appear and then disappear for good.

And then it was there, on top of a steep wave 2500 meters away, the engine cowling glowing red in his thermal sights.

He mashed down the trigger. The autocannon spat out forty rounds, then another forty, then twenty more.

The smuggler's boat vanished from sight.

"Hit on target!" he called out excitedly.

But no one replied. He looked around and for the first time saw that while he had been focused on the drug boat, people were gathered around the Captain and lifting her onto a crash cart. The medic was performing CPR on her and screaming for someone to get the goddamned defibrillator and some blood expander from sickbay.

"Master Chief!" the XO's voice rose above the din. "Do you have a fix on the target?"

"No sir," Master Chief Ramirez answered.

The XO turned to the Pilot. "I am terminating the mission. Get us back to shore the quickest way possible! Move!"

In all the commotion, Master Chief Ramirez didn't even think to get back to the autocannon and hunt for the smugglers until it was far too late.

The heavy Bushmaster slugs tore through the Shockwave's fiberglass hull as if it were tissue paper. One round caught Pablo as he was struggling to his feet. The round went through his chest and then punched through the control panel and traveled most of the way to the bow before it stopped. A second round hit something metallic; exploding and spraying splinters through the open cockpit and peppering Mateo's face, neck and chest, knocking him to the deck. He sprawled on top of Pablo, whose dead eyes stared at him reproachfully.

Mateo struggled to his feet and caught the steering wheel, screaming as he tried to hold the wheel with his right hand, which had a six-inch splinter stuck through his thumb. Somehow, he managed to turn the boat, preventing it from broaching before the oncoming wave. Despite the carnage, the GPS unit was still working and he brought the Shockwave about to a heading of 260 degrees. He didn't know how far away the Coast Guard cutter was, but he knew the only thing that might save him was distance. Distance and rain.

"Pablo?" he called to his childhood friend. "Eh, Pablo?"

But Pablo just lolled in a puddle of water stained with blood.

Mateo shook his head in resignation. "A fucking pig of a night, man," he whispered. The rain started again, heavy and thick, cold enough to mask his engine's thermal signature. He advanced the throttles a notch and continued westward.

West, to safety. West, to fulfill his duty to the Cartel and bury his friend.

From the command trailer, Finley listened as the Executive Officer of the *Vigilant* reported in to the Rockland Coast Guard Station.

"We have one dead and two injured, including Captain O'Brien," Lt. Commander Hillson reported. "We need to have a medivac helicopter waiting at the dock. The Captain has lost a lot of blood. Our medic has put an Israeli field bandage on it and is giving her blood and plasma intravenously, but her blood pressure is low and irregular. The medic thinks there is probably internal bleeding."

"Big Eyes, this is Home Base, should we send a copter to pick up the Captain at sea?"

The XO grimaced. "Negative, Home Base. The sea state is terrible with high winds, heavy rain and bad seas. I think the risk is too great. Our medic advises she is in critical condition, but as stable as he can make her. We think we can be in North Harbor in ninety minutes or less."

"Mr. Hillson, this is Commander Mello. We can land a chopper at the Bass Harbor ferry landing, which is a bit closer to you and is on the mainland. We can land the chopper in the parking lot and pick up Captain O'Brien, then fly her directly to Blue Hill Memorial or, if she is stable enough, to Eastern Maine Medical Center in Bangor. EMMC has a good trauma unit if we can get her there."

The XO checked the charts. Bass Harbor was much closer and had the advantage of being on the mainland. If the weather closed in and the copter couldn't fly, they could take Captain O'Brien by ambulance. "Sir, that sounds good. We will proceed to Bass Harbor and meet you at the ferry landing. Advise to have an ambulance on hand in case the weather closes in."

"I am scrambling the Jayhawk with a medical team now," Mello said. "It will be waiting for you at the ferry landing. Home Base out."

In the command van, Honeycutt turned to Finley. "What the hell happened out there?"

Finley shook his head.

Honeycutt frowned. "What do you think, do we drive over there and talk to the XO when the boat arrives?"

Finley thought about it. "It's a ninety-minute drive from here in good weather, but we can ask the *Vigilant* to wait for us. We should notify the police departments on the coast to keep an eye out for the go-fast boat. They've got to put in somewhere."

Ten minutes later, they were in a four-wheel drive Ford Interceptor, lights and siren on, speeding along Rte. 175 north.

Chapter 25
Home From the Sea

At Elm Tree Cove, just where Rte. 15 passed between Elm Tree Cove on the north and Holt Pond on the south, Chief of Police Michael Corcoran sat in his squad car, sipping coffee and listening to the rain hammer on the roof. He had four men with him in two other cars: Higgins, Burrows, Wolf and Alisberg. They were handpicked men, all trustworthy, all hungry for some cash and not fussy about what they had to do to get it.

He also had Bruno Banderas, sitting in the front seat beside him, scanning the night with a pair of very expensive Generation 4 ATN night-vision goggles.

"Relax for Christ's sake," Corcoran told him. "It's too soon for him to be here yet."

"What if the Coast Guard got them?" Banderas asked.

Corcoran shook his head. "If they'd gotten the boat, we would have heard about it." He squirmed in his seat to get more comfortable. "No, they're out there, still playing hide-and-seek. Besides, this weather sucks; it's going to slow them down for sure."

"They haven't radioed in," Banderas said. Corcoran had never seen him so nervous.

"And if they're smart, they won't. Coast Guard and DEA will be monitoring all radio signals in this area. If the boat calls in, they'll nail it." He glanced at Banderas. "We've just got to wait. They'll come."

They sat in silence for a few minutes. Corcoran sighed. "Listen, I gotta tell you, they shot up the Coast Guard ship, killed one of the sailors and fucked up some others. Every swinging dick for one hundred miles around is going to be hunting your boys. That's bad, real bad. Bad for you, bad for me. Very bad for your bosses in Mexico."

Banderas shrugged noncommittally. It was a tough business; these things happened.

"When your guys finally come in tonight, they have to disappear, understand?" Corcoran continued. "You have to get them across the border into New Hampshire and take them somewhere they can't be found. *Absolutely* can't be found."

Banderas said nothing. Corcoran was telling him what he already knew, but this wasn't what the real message was, and both men knew it. The *real* message was that if the men were wounded and couldn't be moved, or if they needed a doctor or, God forbid, a hospital, well... The bosses had to be protected.

It was a tough business.

––––––––––

At one point, Mateo crossed only a mile behind the Coast Guard Cutter *Vigilant*, but neither ship saw the other. The *Vigilant* turned due north to reach Bass Harbor and care for its wounded, while Mateo turned the Shockwave due west to weave his way through the islands to Elm Tree Cove, in North Harbor.

Barely able to stand, weak from blood loss and in intense pain, Mateo carefully guided the go-fast boat south of Black Island, then Johns Island and a little further south of Lazygut Island, then northwest around Whitmore Neck and finally turning into Inner Harbor and the welcome calm of Elm Tree Cove.

There was a little beach on the north side of Rte. 15, where the bridge divided Holt Pond from the Cove. Mateo slowly brought the boat around and, too exhausted to do any fancy maneuvering, just ran it onto the beach. The engine sputtered for a moment, then coughed and died. He just stood there, bloody, numb, and spent, the captain of a dead ship and its dead crew.

He had given all he had to give, there was nothing left.

There were three cars in the parking lot. Men climbed out of the cars and stood there, looking at him, but not approaching. Then Banderas got out of one of the police cars and slowly approached.

"Eh, Mateo," Banderas called.

Mateo looked at him, not really understanding.

"Bruno?" he asked hoarsely.

"*Sí, amigo*. Mateo, where are Pablo and Arturo?"

Mateo looked at him with stricken eyes. "Pablo is dead," he whispered. "They shot his arm off. Arturo...Arturo is gone. The Yankees blew him up with their cannon. He's gone."

Banderas blinked, but his expression did not change. He still had his job to do. "*Mateo, ¿tienes el paquete?*" Do you have the package?

Bruno was closer to him now and could see the splinters sticking out of his body. He was covered with them. Some were six inches long and looked like spikes that had been hammered deep into his flesh.

Mateo considered the question for a long moment, struggling to remember. Then he nodded haltingly. "We have it, Bruno. *Hicimos nuestro .*" We did our duty.

Bruno looked at him sadly. "I know you did, brother. I know you did."

Tears began to cover Mateo's cheeks. "They killed us, Bruno. Couldn't get away from them. They have this big gun." He turned his face up to the night sky, letting the rain cleanse his tears. "They just killed us."

Bruno began to draw his pistol, but a shot rang out, then three others and Mateo's chest blossomed in red and he spun to the ground.

Enraged, Bruno spun around to confront Michael Corcoran.

"Wouldn't work for you to shoot him, Bruno," Corcoran explained calmly, not pointing his gun at the man, but not pointing it away, either. "Forensics. They will perform an autopsy on your man. It has to be a police bullet that killed him, or it wouldn't look right."

Corcoran motioned to his men. "Find a gun on board and put it next to this guy, and get the bag of dope. We just caught a boat load of smugglers trying to bring heroin into the State of Maine and we'd better have some proof." His men scrambled on board the Shockwave.

Banderas once again turned to Corcoran, who shook his head.

"We've got to take it, Bruno," the Police Chief told him flatly. "We've got a shot-up smugglers boat and two shot-up smugglers. If we don't seize the dope, there'll be questions. Questions I don't have answers for. Count your blessings, my friend. All the witnesses who could link this to you or your bosses are dead. You'll just have to find another way to get the dope into Maine."

———————————

Not far from where Mateo picked up the bag of dope from the freighter, a white, fifty-pound package hovered twenty feet below the surface of the water. It hung there motionless for a time, then it was caught by the Eastern Maine Coastal Current, which began to drag it slowly southwest.

Towards North Harbor.

Chapter 26
Saturday

The smuggler's go-fast boat looked like it had been through a war.

Which, in a manner of speaking, it had.

Huge chunks of the cabin area were missing, blown away by the force of the Bushmaster's shells. The radar was gone, as was the radio mast. Half of the windshield was torn off – not simply splintered, but completely torn away. A body had been found on the deck of the pilot area, missing an arm. The arm was nowhere to be seen. A pair of sea boots belonging to the third smuggler were found, but the seaman was gone. Blood splattered the entire inside of the boat. Most of the instrument panel did not work, dials shattered and inoperative.

Finley nodded to himself. "Do not fuck with the U.S. Coast Guard," he murmured.

He was standing in a vehicle shed used by the Police Department to store trucks. The storm had passed and the sun was shining. As far as he knew, Police Chief Corcoran did not know that he had spent the previous evening in the DEA command trailer, monitoring the Coast Guard's search for the smugglers through the night.

He had been with Honeycutt in the trailer when Corcoran's voice came over the radio, alerting all of the law enforcement in the area that the North Harbor Police Department had intercepted the smugglers as they tried to come ashore in Elm Tree Cove. There had been a gunfight; the only surviving smuggler had been killed. A large bag of dope had been seized.

Finley and Honeycutt had exchanged an incredulous glance and Honeycutt had left to go to Elm Tree Cove. Finley, who wasn't supposed to be on duty, let alone with the DEA, had gone home to preserve his cover.

Saturday morning, he had gotten calls from two other police officers, both excitedly telling him what had gone down the evening before. Both of them essentially said the same thing: "Can you believe it? In North Harbor? Nothing ever happens here!"

All that was left intact of the smuggler's boat was the GPS, the steering wheel and the engine. When they started the engine, it chugged for two minutes, then ran out of gas and stalled. It was a remarkable feat of seamanship that the last smuggler had managed to elude the Coast Guard and reach Maine, then actually find the Elm Tree Cove in pitch darkness, during a storm, when there were at least four dozen other inlets, coves, nooks and crannies in the immediate area.

Finley pursed his lips. It was even more remarkable that Chief Corcoran and his four men had been waiting at the Cove when the smuggler brought his boat in. What were the odds of that?

Why shoot the smuggler who had reached shore? He'd have to check with Honeycutt to see if the guy had been badly wounded. He was still trying to work it out when he heard footsteps and looked up to see Chief Corcoran walk into the shed.

"Finley! What are you doing here?" Corcoran barked, looking annoyed.

"Just wanted to see what was going on, Chief. Must have been quite an exciting night."

"Well, you are not on the investigation, Finley, so get out of here." The Chief frowned. "Aren't you supposed to be picking up some forensic reports in Augusta?"

"On my way in a minute, Chief." Finley turned and walked out. He could feel Corcoran's eyes on him every step of the way.

Finley picked up a squad car and started the trip to Augusta, another chickenshit errand the Chief dreamed up. The report could have been faxed or sent by email, but instead he'd have to drive two and a half hours there and two and a half hours back, effectively taking him out of play for the entire day.

But as he approached the spot where Rte. 15 crossed the small bridge between Holt Pond and the Inner Harbor, right where Chief Corcoran had killed the last smuggler, he slowed to a stop and looked around. Four houses overlooked the little beach where the drug smuggler's boat had put in. And while it was late at night when everything happened, somebody might have seen something. And he knew just who that somebody might be.

He made a note to look into it when he got home tonight.

———————

Finley was on the outskirts of Augusta when Honeycutt called.

"Where are you?" Honeycutt asked.

"Just arriving in Augusta. Another errand for Corcoran."

"Thought you might want to know that I sat in on the autopsy of the last smuggler, the guy Chief Corcoran and his men shot last light. Cause of death is pretty straight-forward: he was shot four times. There hits to the heart, one to the head."

"Okay," replied Finley. Everybody knew Chief Corcoran and his team had blown the smuggler away.

"So, here's the thing," Honeycutt says with relish. "The Pathologist , a Dr. Diana Chapman, she tells us the cause of death is gunfire and Corcoran thanks her and walks out. Because I like autopsies so much, I decide to stay. This guy, some cartel guy, he's got so many splinters in him that he looks, you know, like a goddamned porcupine.

"I haven't had lunch yet, Howard, can we dispense with the details?" Finley complained.

"Well, it gets better. Dr. Chapman, she's pulling out every splinter and examining him to see what the damage was. Well, she finds one, a big nasty one, imbedded in the base of his right thumb." Honeycutt paused.

Finley was cursed with a very visual imagination; he could picture a large shard driven into the man's hand in too much detail. "Howard, for Christ's sake, what's your point?"

"Your Police Chief told me in detail about the shooting. How the guy could barely stand upright, but he lifted his pistol to shoot, so they had no choice but to take him down. He was very clear about it."

"Yeah, okay," Finley encouraged.

"Corcoran specifically said the cartel guy was holding the gun in his right hand," Honeycutt said with satisfaction.

Finley abruptly pulled off into the breakdown lane and stopped. He held the phone tight against his ear. "I'm listening, Howard."

"Well, Dr. Chapman – a marvelous woman, by the way – she says that the shard I was telling you about drove right through the ball of the cartel guy's thumb and at a downward slant deep into his wrist. Frank, that splinter sliced right through the guy's wrist bones and nerves," Honeycutt said excitedly.

Finley's eyes widened. "You mean-"

"I mean the guy could not hold a gun in his right hand. His right hand couldn't be moved. He couldn't close his fingers or pull his trigger finger. He was not holding a gun because he couldn't even pick it up!"

Finley took a breath. "So Corcoran and his squad just murdered him," he said.

Honeycutt sighed. "Well...maybe. It was dark, it was raining, the poor bastard might have just held up his hand or something and spooked them and they blew him to shit. But the autopsy shows that whatever the hell happened out there, it wasn't the way Corcoran said it happened. Oh, and another thing-"

"Yeah?"

"The gun that Corcoran said they found on him, there were no fingerprints on it, there was no round in the chamber and the gun was dry."

"So they planted it," Finley said, stating the obvious.

"Well, I would have thought they'd at least wrap his fingers around it," Honeycutt said. "I think the ambulance showed up right after the shooting and they may have gotten distracted. Remember, these are not big-city cops. They don't deal with forensic niceties every day."

"Not as much to go on as I had hoped," Finley said. "Couldn't prove Corcoran's dirty just on that."

Honeycutt chuckled. "It's my business to collect bricks. Get enough bricks, you can make a wall. This is a brick. We'll find a few others and see where we are."

"Did Corcoran tell you how he happened to be waiting at Elm Tree Cove?" Finley asked.

"Said he had a hunch," Honeycutt replied. "Thought it would make a good drop-off location."

"That's bullshit, but we've still got nothing," Finley complained.

"We don't have enough to go to a jury, but it isn't nothing, either. I'm convinced that Corcoran is dirty. We keep looking, we'll find some dirt."

"Ah, Christ," Finley groaned. "It would have been so nice to catch them when they took the dope from the freighter. Now we've got dead witnesses and no good evidence."

Honeycutt chuckled. "We've got more than that. We know that the squeeze on I-95 North is working, forcing the cartel to look for alternative routes. Corcoran says the bag of dope he retrieved weighed fifty pounds. So, twenty-two kilos! What's that, street value of $10 or $11 Million? We're kicking their butts, my friend! And if we have to do that by blowing them out of the water one go-fast boat at a time, it works for me."

Ahead, Finley saw his exit. "Howard, I'm almost there, I've got to hang up. I'll call you later after I'm home. There's one more thing to check out."

Chapter 27
Saturday

What Honeycutt did not know was that Wallace Charles Moore III was a planner at heart. Above all, he believed in redundancy.

Saturday afternoon and early evening, two more freighters passed into the Gulf of Maine and then into the Bay of Fundy. Just two more freighters among many that went to Canada every week.

A man on the first freighter dropped a fifty-pound bag of heroin and ten pounds of fentanyl into the cold ocean waters at four o'clock. The second freighter reached the same position at eight o'clock. A man stepped out under the cover of darkness and dropped another fifty-pound bag into the water, then went back inside.

Neither man was on the open deck for more than two minutes. No one saw them.

Each bag sank to a depth of twenty feet, where it hovered until it was caught by the Eastern Maine Coastal Current and carried on its way.

A total of one hundred and fifty pounds of heroin and ten pounds of fentanyl, in three separate bags, were now drifting slowly towards the Maine coast. Their combined street value was in excess of $35 Million.

In Mexico, Wallace Moore sipped his gin and tonic and waited for the outcome to his experiment.

Chapter 28
Saturday Evening

It was almost suppertime before Finley made it back to Rte. 15 and followed it into North Harbor. As he approached the bridge bisecting Holt Pond and Elm Tree Cove, he pulled over and walked up to one of the small houses. This particular house had a splendid view of the Cove and the little sandy beach where the smuggler's boat had come in.

It was a simple two-story house, built plain and sturdy, with white clapboard siding and green shutters and a clear view over Elm Tree Cove to the Inner Harbor. Finley knew the old man who lived there, Ralph Cudworth. Used to be a commercial fisherman back in the day, but he was retired now and didn't get around as much as he used to.

Cudworth was sitting on the porch, a beer in his hand, smoking a cigar. He waved Finley over.

"Thought your doctor told you to stop smoking those damn things," Finley said mildly.

Cudworth snorted. "Doctors say a lot of things," he said, and blew a plume of smoke into the air. "Keeps the bugs away."

Finley sat down beside him in a wicker rocking chair that smelled vaguely of mildew, but rocked just fine. A breeze from the water fortunately dispelled both Cudworth's cigar smoke and the mosquitoes. From where he was sitting, Finley could see the little beach where the drug smuggler's go-fast boat landed.

"Seen a lot of pretty sunrises from this porch," Cudworth said.

"Quite the storm last night," Finley commented casually, not looking at Cudworth.

"Yup," Cudworth drawled.

Finley said nothing. The silence grew.

"You never could bullshit worth a damn," the older man chuckled. "Your old man always said he loved to play poker with you – it was a guaranteed payday."

Finley laughed, despite himself. His father and Ralph Cudworth had teased him as a boy because he could never tell a lie with a straight face. His dad would be astonished to hear his son was an undercover cop for the DEA.

"You want to know if I saw that boat come in," Cudworth declared with satisfaction. "Course I did! I may be old, but my eyes and ears still work pretty good. Storm had died down some and I heard an engine come around Whitmore Neck, into the Inner Harbor and the Cove. Guy had to be in trouble, seein' how nobody in their right mind would have been out on the water unless they were in trouble." The old man waved a liver-spotted hand towards the beach just a hundred feet away.

"No lights, no nothin'. Then he came right up onto the beach, just drove his boat up on the sand and some of them rocks. Fancy-assed boat, too." He shook his head at the foolishness of it all. "I came out here to the porch, that's when I saw the police cars. Three of 'em. Two men to a car. They all got out and walked closer to the boat. Then one of them called out to the guy in the boat, speakin' Spanish or Cuban or some such."

"Spanish?" Finley wasn't sure, but he didn't think Corcoran or any of the other cops on the beach that night could speak Spanish.

Cudworth shrugged elaborately. "One of them said, 'amigo.' Sounded like Spanish to me."

"Huh," Finley grunted. This didn't make any sense. "You're sure he was one of our cops?"

Cudworth absently scratched his chin. "Well, he got out of a cop car. Don't that make him a cop?"

Finley frowned. "Was he in uniform?"

"Nope," Cudworth said with certainty. "Them others were, all five of them, but this guy was wearing dark pants and a dark shirt. Carried a gun, though, I saw that much."

"You recognize him from around here?"

Cudworth shook his head. "Never seen him before. I recognized Corcoran, that asshole, and his four stooges, Wolf, Higgins, and Alisberg and that other asshole, Burrows. Burrows gave me a parking ticket last month."

"But you don't know the sixth man?" Finley pressed.

"Nope. Might be some State cop, maybe. But he was the one who almost shot the guy from the boat, but Corcoran beat him to it."

Finley digested this for a minute or so, taking another sip of beer. "Cuddy, the guy from the boat, did he shoot first?"

Cudworth snorted. "Poor fucker didn't shoot at all. He could barely stand up. He looked weird, Frank. I couldn't see him real good in the dark, but his chest and face looked like something was growing on him. But both his arms were down by his sides. I couldn't swear to it, but I certainly didn't see anything in his hands."

"So what happened, then?"

Another shrug. "The guy from the boat was talking to the guy dressed in civvies and Corcoran pulled out his gun and shot him. The guy from the boat, that is. The guy in civvies got real mad and I thought he was going to draw on Corcoran, but Corcoran said something to him and that seemed to calm him down. Then they searched the boat and took off some sort of bag." Cudworth looked at him shrewdly. "That was the drugs, right?"

Finley nodded.

"Well," Cudworth continued. "They put the bag into one of the police cars and about that time I decided that I would just sneak back inside and mind my own business. I couldn't tell what was going on, but I didn't want no part of it."

Finley sighed. "Cuddy, it might be best if we keep this between you and me. If anyone else comes asking around, tell them you were asleep."

Cudworth looked at him for a long moment, then nodded. "You be careful, Frank. These are not people you want to mess with. They shot that man like a dog."

"I will, Cuddy. Thanks for the beer." Finley stood up and walked back to his car, wondering just what the hell was going on.

Chapter 29
Saturday – Lunch

Jean-Philippe LeBlanc finally caught up with Banderas by telephone on Saturday. He had been busy with his family all morning in Bucksport and not heard about the police shootout at Elm Tree Cove. Banderas was eating lunch at a small Mexican eatery in Belfast, just off Rte. 1.

"I know where it is," LeBlanc said. "Stay there. I'll drive there, take me about half an hour."

"What's this about?" Banderas asked.

"Not on the phone. I'll see you soon." LeBlanc hung up.

The little restaurant was full and noisy when LeBlanc slid into the booth thirty minutes later. He tried to order a hamburger, but they didn't serve them.

"Try the chicken fajitas," Banderas suggested. "Nice and spicy!"

LeBlanc pushed the menu away and just ordered a beer. Once the waitress left, he looked hard at Banderas. "I heard Friday that one of the North Harbor cops, Frank Finley, found Henry Mitchell's body washed up on an island off of North Harbor."

Banderas put down his drink and stared at him.

"That means by now the cops know he was shot," LeBlanc continued.

Banderas wiped his mouth with a napkin and put it down slowly. "The police don't have his body," he said.

Now it was LeBlanc's turn to stare. "What do you mean?"

"I mean Finley didn't tell Corcoran."

That hung in the air between them for several seconds. If Finley didn't bring the body to the North Harbor police, then he took it somewhere else.

"Shit," LeBlanc cursed.

"You didn't know this because I didn't tell you," Banderas said. "Last night we took delivery of a shipment from a freighter near the Bay of Fundy." He paused. "Then the Coast Guard jumped us. They were waiting for us. They *knew*. We lost the boat, the shipment and the three-man crew."

"Ah, Christ," muttered LeBlanc. "Do you know who Finley works for?"

Banderas shrugged. "DEA, FBI, it doesn't matter. Whoever it is has enough clout to be able to call up a Coast Guard cutter, and enough juice to figure out which freighter was carrying the shipment." His voice hardened. "And they killed our men. They must answer for that."

LeBlanc suddenly looked nervous. "Hey, I didn't sign up for that, Bruno. Fuck with the Feds and the heat will be tremendous."

Banderas looked at him. *So weak.* "Do not worry, my friend." He thought for a moment, then asked, "Who told you Finley found Mitchell's body?"

LeBlanc smiled in satisfaction. "His older son, Jacob."

Chapter 30
The Inspection

On Sunday morning, Barbara Yancey, the drug technician from the Maine Drug Enforcement Agency, came to take custody of the fifty-pound bag of dope Chief Corcoran had seized from the smuggler's boat. As part of the process, she first took a sample of the product and put it through a chemical reactive to determine exactly what it was and its level of purity.

She viewed the results of the first test, then shook her head. She checked her equipment, ran a diagnostic test on the analyzer unit, then ran a second sample through the machine.

Same result.

Yancey had been with MDEA for fifteen years. She knew the score, knew there was always the possibility that someone in a police department might be crooked, but she also knew that sometimes equipment malfunctions gave bizarre results. She locked up the bag of dope, then walked casually out to her car, got in and locked the doors. Opening her glove compartment, she took out her service weapon, checked to make sure there was a round in the chamber, then put it on the seat next to her. Then she called her boss at home – it was Sunday for him, after all – told him the story and that she needed a backup analyzer unit right away.

She also told him there was no way in hell she was going back into the North Harbor Police Department without an armed guard accompanying her. When her boss hesitated, Yancey said, "Paul, that bag in there weighs fifty pounds. If it's dope, or if it *was* dope and somebody stole it, it's worth millions. Hear me, *millions.* Also, it is covered in salt spray and blood. *Blood,* Paul. And if my first test is right, then there is something seriously fucked up going on. I don't care how it looks, I am not waltzing back in there alone, do you hear me? I want at least two guys – big, *mean* motherfuckers carrying big, *mean* guns on their belts. I will not wake up dead in some shitty alleyway for the sake of not hurting anyone's feelings. Have you forgotten Miami?"

Of course her boss remembered Miami. A Federal DEA technician had gone in to inspect fifteen kilos of heroin captured in a raid, only to stumble upon three Miami vice detectives in the process of stealing half of it and replacing it with powdered baby food. If the unfortunate DEA technician had arrived an hour later, she would have just assumed the raid had netted some already-cut dope.

But she hadn't come an hour later. She arrived at the worst possible time. Caught in the act, the detectives had strangled her and dumped her body in an alley a few miles away, where she was discovered by a deliveryman.

The DEA had gone apeshit. The DEA and FBI descended on the Miami police station where the dope was being held and tore the place apart, finding enough DNA evidence and security camera footage to put the detectives in jail. But for the DEA and various State DEAs, it was a somber lesson: *You can never be sure who you are dealing with.*

An hour later a Maine DEA-issued sedan pulled up and Yancey's boss got out. Right behind him was a Maine State Police cruiser, carrying two of the largest State Troopers she had ever seen. Both of them wore dark glasses, bulletproof vests and black shooting gloves. They looked mean as hell.

Yancey was touched; her boss really did care.

Paul Abbott held up another analyzer unit in one hand and a double-shot espresso latte in the other.

Yancey had to smile. "Paul, you are the best!" she told him.

Paul Abbott snorted. "And you're a royal pain in the butt, but better safe than sorry." He took a deep breath. "Okay, let's do this. God, I hope you're wrong."

Yancey hoped she was wrong, too, but had a sinking feeling she wasn't.

The two Maine DEA agents, followed by the jumbo-sized State Troopers, walked back into the police station and down the corridor to the Evidence Room. No one tried to stop them. Yancey ran the tests for the third time, but this time using the new machine. She held up the unit for Abbott to read the finding.

He peered at it owlishly. "Shit," he muttered, then pulled out his cell phone. After it rang for a moment, a voice said hello. Abbott identified himself as the District 3 Supervisor for the Maine DEA. "I need to speak with Howard Honeycutt right away." He paused, listening, then said, "I'm sorry, but unless Mr. Honeycutt is meeting with the President of the United States, you'll have to get him out of that meeting." He listened again. "Yes, I'll hold."

Then he turned to the two State Troopers. "As of this moment, this room is a crime scene. No one comes in without my personal OK."

If the two State Troopers were nonplussed, they managed to hide it well. One simply turned around and walked to the hallway, where he stood, arms folded. The other simply stood in the doorway. They both managed to look intimidating and unmovable.

"Thank you, Paul," Yancey said.

"Don't thank me," he retorted. "You get to write up the report."

Then he held the phone up to his ear. "Mr. Honeycutt? I am Paul Abbott at the Maine DEA. I am at the North Harbor Police Station. We've taken a sample from that drug shipment seized last night." He took a deep breath, anticipating the shit storm that was coming.

"Mr. Honeycutt, there's a problem. You'd better get down here."

Chapter 31
Sunday Lunch Among Friends

Sunday afternoon Bruno Banderas got a visit from Chief of Police Corcoran.

And two of Corcoran's dirty cops.

Banderas was sitting at his favorite Mexican restaurant again – the only Mexican restaurant for thirty miles – when Corcoran slid into the booth across from him and one of his henchmen squeezed into the booth beside him. The other henchman stood beside the booth, effectively shielding them from other diners. All the cops were dressed in civilian clothes, but Banderas could tell in a glance they were all carrying guns under loose shirts.

"We need to talk," Corcoran said tersely. "Outside."

Banderas was pretty good at reading men and their intentions; he didn't think going outside with Corcoran and his thugs would contribute to a long and happy life. He had a gun, of course, but with three-to-one odds shooting his way out did not seem a constructive approach, either, so he held up his hands placatingly. "I can tell you are troubled by something, but I don't know what. Tell me," he said softly.

Corcoran leaned in, his voice pitched low. "They came and tested the dope we took off the go-fast boat Friday night," he said harshly. "And you know what, Bruno?"

Banderas pursed his lips. "Actually, Mike, I don't know what, but like I said, whatever it is that's bothering you, why don't you just tell me?"

"Imagine my surprise, Bruno, when the State Police and some guy from the MDEA show up and tells me that the dope isn't dope at all, it's baking powder."

Banderas sat back as if he had been struck. "*What?*" he asked, his voice rising.

"*Baking powder,*" Corcoran repeated, but he was taken aback at the clear shock on Banderas' face.

Banderas felt like he'd been kicked by a mule. He glanced at the tables near them, then blew out a breath. "Okay, let's go outside."

The four men walked to the far corner of the parking lot. When they were out of earshot of anyone, Banderas wheeled on Corcoran. "What the fuck are you talking about?" he demanded.

"The Maine DEA sent a tech in this morning to test the dope," Corcoran told him. "Well, she did, but it wasn't dope, it was fucking baking powder. Fifty pounds of *baking powder*. She assumed that one of us had stolen the drugs and replaced them, so she called her boss, who showed up with the State Police. They've already looked at the security cameras and didn't find anything, but they are still suspicious that we swapped the real dope for the baking powder before we checked it into the evidence locker. So, they're poking around. And the Coast Guard is apeshit. They got one guy killed and two others shot up and it turns out to be baking powder? And we shot a dangerous smuggler who pulled a gun on us, if you remember."

Corcoran poked a thick finger in Banderas' chest. "I want to know what the fuck is going on."

Banderas glared at him. The last time someone poked him in the chest, Banderas had cut off the offending finger. Now he stared at Chief of Police Michael Corcoran with such intensity that Corcoran took a step back and put his hand on the butt of his pistol. The moment stretched out. Corcoran's dirty cops sensed something was wrong and stepped in behind Banderas, fingers twitching near their guns.

Banderas was pissed off, but not suicidal. He took a deep breath. "Well, I don't know what the fuck is going on." He paused, considering, then grimaced. "But I know who might." He paused. "We've got another problem we need to take care of. And soon."

Now it was Corcoran's turn to look puzzled. "What are you talking about?" he asked suspiciously.

"Your man, Finley. He found something he shouldn't have." Banderas glanced meaningfully at the two other cops, not wanting to explain things in front of them if he didn't have to.

Corcoran jerked his head to them. "Guys, wait in the car. I'll be along in a minute."

Once they had gone, Banderas leaned in. "Your security is shit! You've got a fucking mole in your department. Finley found Mitchell's body washed up on some island, but he didn't take it to you, did he? No, he gave it to the DEA or the FBI or somebody. I think that's why the Coast Guard was able to jump us Friday night."

Corcoran wheeled around in a small circle, his face beet red. "Finley?" he grated. "Finley?"

Banderas poked him in the chest with a finger. "He's your mess. I want you to clean it up. Right away, you understand? I want him gone!"

Corcoran took several deep breaths, visibly calming himself down. "Won't be easy, Bruno. Like I said, this isn't Mexico, I can't just shoot him. He's a cop. Hell, he's probably fucking DEA. If I just kill him, there will be hell to pay. Questions. Investigations. They'll be watching us for months. If you want to keep using North Harbor for shipments, it would be better if your men handled it."

Banderas shook his head in disgust. "You guys kill me. You're happy to take the money, but you don't want to get your hands dirty."

Corcoran shrugged. "Just the way it is. I'd be lying to you if I told you otherwise. And as far as getting my hands dirty, I took care of your guy down on the beach Friday night. Don't forget that." He tried to smile reassuringly, but it fell flat. "Take him out and then plant some dope on him so that it looks like he was dirty."

Banderas stared at him. "This guy got three of my men killed. I grew up with them, you understand? I'm not just going to take *him* out. His entire family, all of them!"

Corcoran stared back. "Just do what you gotta do, Bruno. But while you're at it, find out why the fuck we just went to all of this trouble for a bag of baking powder."

————————

Banderas was driving to Lowell to recruit some men for the work that had to be done when his phone rang. It was the burner phone, not his regular phone. That meant the caller was from Sinaloa, Mexico. He quickly pulled to the side of the road and answered.

"I understand they tested the contents of the bag this morning," the familiar voice said.

Banderas scowled. "Yes."

"So they know about the baking powder?"

"Yes, it's causing problems for the locals. The Feds think they switched it for the real drugs."

In his office in Sinaloa, Wallace chuckled. "Tell them not to worry, I'll make it up to them. Right now we've got something more important to take care of."

"My men all got killed trying to get that baking powder to shore," Banderas blurted, then stopped, aghast at what he had said, and who he had said it to. There was a long silence on the phone, making Banderas wonder if he had just signed his own death warrant.

Wallace sighed. "Bruno, you know this is a tough business. There are risks, there are always risks. To test the safety of a new route, I sometimes must expose the men on the ground to more risk than I like. Sometimes it blows up in our faces." He paused again. "When it goes bad like this, I always take care of the families. Mateo's wife and children will get money and a new home. Pablo's mother will be taken care of. Arturo, well, Arturo was alone. From what I know of Arturo, he would have been happy that it ended like this."

Banderas said nothing, but gripped the phone very tightly. All this for a bag of baking powder? Just a test to see if a new route was safe?

"Bruno, I've sent some things to the warehouse in Lowell. There are written documents telling you how to use them. You still have access to several lobster boats, right?"

"Yes, of course."

"Good, very good." Then Wallace told him what had to be done.

At first, Banderas was speechless. Banderas was a hard man in a hard business, but he had never seen a plan this audacious, nor a man quite so ruthless. The American had not simply sacrificed the lives of three men simply to determine if a drug smuggling route would work, he had used them as decoys so that he could put another plan entirely into operation. It was brilliant, but it was terrifying. These were experienced, *loyal* men. But to the American, they were just pawns on his game board.

Banderas, a loyal and obedient soldier, choked back his doubts. "I will get on this right away, but first, I want permission to kill the cop who is working for the DEA."

The American was silent for a moment, then he sighed. "If you kill the police officer, it will create a lot of heat, Bruno. You know that."

"He is responsible for the deaths of my three men, *jefe*. He must be killed, as an example to the others".

And there it was, Wallace thought, the cardinal rule of Cartel operations – *Every threat must be destroyed*. Utterly destroyed., in order to make the next threat hesitate. A man is not just shot, he is tortured and shot. His wife and family are forfeit, the price he pays for his arrogance.

"I give you permission, Bruno, but on the condition that if your actions cause any interference with our operations, it will be up to you to make things right, at your own cost."

"Thank you, *jefe*." They hung up and Banderas immediately called Jean-Philippe LeBlanc.

When the lobsterman answered, Banderas said, "We've got to meet. Things have changed."

Chapter 32
Sunday Afternoon

On Sunday, Calvin took Gabrielle out with him to haul his traps.

The weather had turned after the storm, as it so often does, and the sun shone warmly in a sky of lazy cumulus clouds. Sea birds flew low over the ocean and the wind was as gentle as a mother's kiss. All in all, a beautiful day.

Gabrielle Poulin stood beside him in the boat, dressed in hiking shorts that flattered her long legs, sneakers and a long sleeve shirt she had tied at the waist. Her dark hair flowed to her shoulders and blew out behind her as Calvin accelerated towards Shingle Island, where he had put his twenty-two traps the day before. It was almost three miles offshore, but he took his time, enjoying the sight of Gabrielle and feeling the heat of the sun on his face.

Maybe if he had been paying more attention, he would have seen it sooner.

As it was, he rounded the rocky northern tip of the island, then turned due south and began to cruise along Shingle Island's long axis. It wasn't until he was halfway down that he realized something was missing: his marker buoys.

His buoys were colored with three bands of red, green and black. Easy to spot.

But they weren't there.

"Aw, crap," he muttered. His heart sank as he realized what had happened.

"What's is it?" Gabrielle asked.

"Remember I told you I had a run-in with Little Guy and his two cousins?"

"Yeah," she nodded.

"Well, I think he came out here and cut my trap lines. My buoys have floated away and my traps are down on the bottom." He shook his head in despair. "Gabs, the traps cost $100 each. I've been putting money away for a new boat, but this will put a pretty big dent in it." He looked up to the sky in frustration. "Those goddamned bastards!"

"Hang on, Calvin Finley," she said briskly. "Time to use that brain of yours again. How many traps do you have?"

"Twenty-two."

"Okay. Do you remember where you laid them down?"

Calvin though for a minute. He always started near some sort of landmark. He looked around and spotted two tall pine trees on Shingle Island, taller than the rest and close to a wall set back from the water about one hundred feet. He pointed to them. "I started right there. I dropped the first one about fifty yards offshore, then went straight south from there until they were all in the water."

Gabrielle pursed her lips in mock disapproval. "And knowing that you have very little imagination and do things in a rigid manner, Mr. Finley, how large was the space between the lobster traps?"

Calvin snorted in delight. "About thirty seconds apart, moving at low throttle."

"How deep is the water?" She looked like the cat that found the cream.

Calvin considered. "Hmmm...anywhere from fifteen to twenty-five feet."

"And do you have a wetsuit and snorkeling gear on board?"

He nodded appreciatively.

"And some rope and some sort of hook thingy to hook the traps?" she asked.

"Yes, I do. I certainly do." He smiled at her.

"Well, then," she said smugly, "while you are diving in this ice-cold water, I am going to eat some lunch and read a *delightful* book. Perhaps I'll even pour myself some hot cocoa from the thermos." She glanced at him. "Do *try* not to drip cold water on me when you are hoisting those heavy traps." I am very delicate and subject to a chill." She smiled at him. "Get me wet and I'll break your kneecaps"

Calvin found a 100-foot length of rope and tied a brass swivel snap hook to one end, then tied off the other end to a bracket on the skiff. He pulled on the wetsuit, flippers, mask and snorkel and unceremoniously flopped overboard. It took a while to find the first one — he had put it slightly further out than he remembered — but once they found the first one, the others fell into place. Ironically, most of the traps had lobsters in them, and some had two. As it turned out, Gabrielle had brought her wetsuit and snorkeling gear as well. He dove for the first few traps while she piloted the skiff. After the tenth trap was hoisted aboard and emptied, they switched places and Gabrielle dove for the traps, attaching the snap hook to the trap and swimming up to the surface to give Calvin a thumbs-up. He used the winch to pull the trap up, emptied it and stacked it in the skiff.

Two hours later, both of them seriously chilled, they were still unable to find the last trap. They spiraled out from the boat to a distance of about seventy yards, but there was no sign of it. At the surface, Gabrielle pulled her mask up and spat out the snorkel mouthpiece. "I'm done, Cal," she called, lips blue. "I'm freezing and have to get out."

"I think Little Guy took it as a souvenir," Calvin said, swimming along beside her as they made their way to the skiff. He hoisted himself out, then reached down a hand to pull her aboard. Gabrielle was so cold she could barely make it over the transom.

"Wetsuit or no, that water is cold!" she chattered, unzipping her suit and wrapping herself in a thick towel. Calvin opened the thermos of cocoa and poured her another cup. "Still hot," he warned. "Don't burn your tongue." He took a few minutes to tighten all the straps holding the stack of lobster traps to the deck, then ran a line through the uppermost trap to the bow and stern and made it tight.

"You take me on such interesting dates," Gabrielle said dryly. "Dead bodies, lost traps...what next? Getting run over by a freighter? Attacked by a vampire albatross?"

"No, no," Calvin protested. "The vampire albatross isn't until the fourth date."

Gabrielle looked at him, wrapped up in her towel and sipping hot cocoa, her eyes suddenly shiny with unshed tears. "I'm leaving in three months for Swarthmore," she whispered. "And it's already breaking my heart."

Calvin was caught flatfooted. "Aw, Gabs, c'mon. We've got the entire summer, and I'll figure out a way to visit you. You know that."

She turned away, staring out at the ocean. "I'm sorry, Calvin, that wasn't fair of me." But she couldn't tell him her real fear, that soon she would be immersed in new ideas and studying things she had only dreamed of, and surrounded by people doing the same, while he was going out onto the water every day to lay lobsters traps and collect old ones. Day after day. He would love it, but their worlds would diverge, highways traveling in different directions, never to converge again. It wouldn't happen at first, but it would happen. He could talk to her about the ocean and sunrises, but it wouldn't be enough, and after a time her tales about new studies would fall on deaf ears because he just wouldn't understand; not really. Even though she was young, she understood that love is not everything. She had observed her parents' marriage and those of parents of her friends. For many, there was a joyful, day-to-day playfulness mingled with constant conversation. They talked and argued about local politics, national politics, religion, books, the proper way to make coffee and whatever, just enjoying stuff with each other. Silly stuff, often. Their love was like a soft glow that infused it all and somehow made it more complete.

For others, there was affection, perhaps even respect, but so much distance. She played golf while he went fishing. But when they got home the questions were perfunctory and without any real interest. Talk at dinner was about family logistics, but it might as well have been a business meeting. They were respectful and faithful, but there was no sharing, no reading to each other some news story they wanted to share, and no joy. Two bodies pulled into the same bed by the gravity of everyone's expectations. Gabrielle had decided early she would never have a life like that. There has to be something more, something shared, some deep appreciation for what each other is going through and the simple desire to share all of the little things that make up a life.

But she didn't speak of this. Calvin had to make his own choices. She knew that, too.

She took a deep, shuddering breath. Men could be *so* stupid.

They got back to the dock in good time, unloaded the traps and locked them in a storage bin his Uncle Paul let him use. A subdued Gabrielle told him she was tired and drove home. Feeling that he had missed something, something important, Calvin walked to where his bicycle was chained to a post, then stopped and cursed.

Both tires had been slashed. And next to the bike was a pile of his lobster buoys. Calvin promised himself that when he next saw Little Guy, he would teach him a lesson he would never forget.

But he didn't see him again until it was too late.

Chapter 33
Monday Morning – Preparations

On Monday morning, Bruno Banderas returned to North Harbor with three large boxes and four experienced shooters – hard men who would do what they were told, without any inconvenient qualms.

The boxes were for installation on LeBlanc's lobster boats.

The shooters were for Frank Finley. And his family.

Banderas spent much of Monday afternoon and evening with Jean-Philippe LeBlanc, helping him install the gear on LeBlanc's lobster boat. The gear was clever. Each lobster boat would be equipped with a Benthos DRI-267 Dive Ranger, which emitted an interrogator pulse to a depth of 600 feet. Each of the drug packages they were looking for had an attached acoustic transponder. When the pulse from the Dive Ranger pinged the transponder, the transponder would reply with a ping of its own. That sound would be heard by a hydrophone towed behind each of the lobster boats, which would measure the acoustic range and bearing. The location of the package could often be determined with one ping by the transponder. If not, the lobster boat would turn ninety degrees to its present course and ping the transponder again within a few minutes. With two readings, the exact location of the package could be calculated.

At least, that was the theory.

"They tell me that this is good equipment," Banderas told LeBlanc. "High-end commercial quality. We don't have the licenses we need for military-grade stuff, but this is good. The man in Sinaloa, he tells me Benthos makes good shit. It should be, for what we paid."

They had enough Dive Rangers to equip three lobster boats.

"What's the effective range of these things?" Jean-Philippe LeBlanc wanted to know.

Banderas shrugged. "They tell me one hundred to five hundred meters, but that the packages are supposed to be floating only twenty feet below the surface."

LeBlanc looked disgusted. "Do these idiots have any idea how fuckin' *big* the ocean is? Even if we line up the three boats side-by-side, at most that will only cover fifteen hundred meters, a little less than a mile. Christ on a crutch, we got hundreds and hundreds of square miles of water and islands out here."

Banderas sighed. Killing people was so much easier than this. "Sinaloa tells me that you have something called the Eastern Maine Coastal

Current. It sweeps through this area, through all of these islands off of North Harbor and Stonington. The packages were dumped into the Current and should arrive somewhere in here most likely Wednesday or Thursday, but you'll start looking tomorrow just in case."

"And if the packages don't hang up on an island or somehow just pass through, then what?" demanded LeBlanc.

"Then we move the search south and west."

"And you don't think it will look funny when three of my boats are out doing sweeps instead of hauling lobster traps?"

"Nothing is perfect," Banderas said calmly. "I suggest that we don't use the same boats every day, but swap them onto your other boats. You have six boats. Three can hunt for the packages while the other three hunt your lobsters."

LeBlanc looked at him sourly. "Three days, maybe more? I'm gonna lose a lot of money chasing your dope around the ocean."

Banderas nodded. Wallace had anticipated this. "For each day you are searching, you will be paid fifty thousand American dollars, in cash. No taxes. Sinaloa told me to remind you that the Cartel is very generous with those who help them."

LeBlanc snorted. "Like I've got a choice, huh?"

Banderas said nothing. Nothing need be said.

LeBlanc was already thinking. The gear was easy to move, so he could swap the boats around without too much trouble. But he didn't trust all of the crews enough to let them see what they were doing. He could tell them it was some sort of high-tech bottom survey, but then they'd have to mark the place where they found a package and come back for it. He rubbed his chin. Scuba gear, wetsuits and all that shit. He'd have to have some on every boat, unless he used a fourth boat, something smaller, not a lobster boat. Send them the position and then move on, still pretending to do the "bottom survey." The small boat could run in and pick up the package. That would take care of the crew issue. He'd only need trusted men in the small boat, carrying the divers. Use one of his brothers. Have to think about that.

"All right, let's go test this equipment and make sure our end works." LeBlanc grinned savagely. "And aren't you fucked if the transponders don't work or the packages just sank when they got tossed into the ocean?"

Chapter 34
Monday Morning

On Monday morning, Calvin turned back from Sheep Island early and swam slowly back to shore. He couldn't get Gabrielle out of his mind and his arms and legs felt leaden. When he got back home he sat at the kitchen table, disconsolate, not even drinking his post-swim cocoa.

"What's the matter," his mother asked, "didn't the seals come out to play this morning?

"Aw, not that," he mumbled. "I told you about how Little Guy and his cousins cut my traps and then slashed my bike tires, right?"

Danielle nodded, not saying anything. Her sons were not usually forthcoming about what was bothering them, so when it happened, she just let them talk.

"Yeah, well, when I saw that the traps had been cut, I sorta thought they were gone for good. Lost, at a hundred bucks per pop! But Gabs got all Mr. Spock about it and made me realize I could find them and that getting them out of the water wouldn't be that hard. And she helped like a trooper. I mean, the water was *cold* and she's not used to it like I am, but she dove for the traps and hooked a bunch. We got out of the water and she wrapped up like a mummy in a big towel and we had hot tea and it was really nice." He paused, shaking his head.

"C'mon, don't leave me hanging. The suspense is killing me," his mother prodded.

Calvin sighed. "Then Gabs starts crying. She's going to college at the end of the summer and she's all upset and I tell her that I can plan on coming down to see her, but she just clams up, won't say another word." He threw up his hands. "I didn't know what to say!"

Danielle wondered if they were sleeping together yet, but decided that now was not the time to bring it up.

"So, Calvin, what do you think Gabrielle is worried about? Do you really think she's worried about you not getting to see her, or something else?"

"Is there any more bacon?" he asked.

Danielle snorted. "You answer the question and I might be willing to cook some bacon," she retorted. "You're smart, figure it out."

He blew out a breath. "Yeah, well I don't always feel so smart."

She smiled. "When it comes to emotions, particularly the emotions of an eighteen-year-old girl, you are just as dumb as anybody else in this family, male or female."

"Tell me something I don't know," Calvin muttered.

Danielle looked at him fondly, her very smart, very ignorant boy-man. "Well, answer me this, if you were in her shoes, what would worry you about leaving your boyfriend behind?"

He looked at her blankly, proving once again that even smart men could be incredibly dumb when it came to the life of emotions. "Okay, Calvin," she asked. "If you stay here and become a full-time lobsterman, what will you do every day?"

"Go out on the ocean and set my traps and harvest the old ones for lobsters," he answered, using the tone of voice that suggested this was rather obvious.

"Okay, and what will you do the next day?" she asked patiently.

"Why, pretty much the same thing," he said. "The only real variables are the weather, how big a catch I get and the market price for lobsters."

"And the next day?"

"Same thing as before."

"And meanwhile, what will Gabrielle be doing?"

He started to frown, but then realized that it was a question with serious consequences. While he was out on his beloved ocean, Gabrielle would be starting new classes each semester, meeting new people, talking about the same sort of things that fascinated him – ideas, issues, developing technology and what its impact might be – only she would be talking about it with other people, not him. Or at least, he admitted to himself, not in the same way she would talk about it with him.

Calvin closed his eyes for a minute, his thinking pose. His face went slack, what Danielle thought of as his 'Village Idiot' look. Then he opened his eyes and his face reanimated, startling her like it always did. One moment he was gone, the next he was back again, her Calvin.

"She wants me to go to school," he said evenly. "Because she's afraid that if I stay here and become a full-time fisherman, she'll lose me, that we'll be too different, maybe that she'll no longer really understand what makes me tick." He paused. "Or that I won't understand what makes her tick."

Danielle blinked. He got there much quicker than she had thought he would.

"Do you disagree?" she asked, putting some more bacon in front of him. How many households, she wondered, went through three pounds of bacon a week?

"I don't know," he said.

"Hmmm…"

"I mean–" but then he fell silent again.

Danielle poured herself another cup of coffee and sat down at the kitchen table. Didn't say a word, just sipped her coffee.

"Aw, there's nothing wrong with being a fisherman," he protested. "There are lots of lobsterman who have been trapping since they got out of high school. It's hard work, but they make a good living, have families."

"It's one way to make a living," Danielle said noncommittally.

"I can earn good money," he said stubbornly.

"Money is important."

He stared at her reproachfully. "I know what you're doing, Mom."

"I'm just sipping my coffee…and listening to my son work through a problem."

Calvin snorted and went back to pushing his cocoa mug around in small circles. "Duke is pretty far away. And expensive."

"It's the best marine biology program in the country, that's why you applied, Calvin. Duke is also offering you a very good financial package, even if you don't join the swim team. If you do, it's almost a free ride. And anyway, Durham has an airport."

Calvin looked morosely at the tabletop. Danielle went around the table and gave him a hug, more for her benefit than for his. "I know this sounds funny, but sometimes when you really get stuck on making a decision, you have to ask what is it that you are more afraid of: staying here in North Harbor, or going to college and finding that you like it?"

"What?" Calvin was confused.

She picked up his plate and took it to the sink. "Think about it, Calvin. You can work through it. And while you're at it, look up George Addair and his famous quote. Now hurry up or you'll be late for school." She smiled at him then, a mischievous, lilting smile, and walked out of the room.

Leaving her baffled son wondering how she had done whatever it was she had just done.

Gabrielle Poulin locked the Ford Focus in the parking lot behind the high school and began walking towards the rear entrance, near the gym. As usual, there were a bunch of boys, and some girls, catching a smoke before classes began. No one was supposed to smoke on school grounds, but the school turned a blind eye to seniors in their last quarter, as long as they were discreet.

On the way in she walked alongside Lois Lecompte, and they chatted about final exams and a new boy Lois was dating. As they neared the entrance, Gabrielle realized suddenly that one of the boys standing there was Martin LaPierre, Little Guy LeBlanc's follower. The other two were Juniors she recognized, but didn't know their names.

When he saw her, Martin pushed off the wall to block her way.

"I heard you've been goin' out with Finley," he said sullenly.

Lois Lecompte frowned at him. "Martin, don't be a jerk. Let us through or-"

"Or nothing, bitch," he said menacingly. "I wasn't talkin' to you, so shut up." He turned back to Gabrielle and poked her in the chest with two thick fingers. "Your boyfriend is a wiseass and a troublemaker. He's going to get what's coming to him, so you'd better watch who you pal around with."

Gabrielle's father had warned her about fighting. Before he had become a banker, he had served four years in the Marines. Once, at ten-years old, Gabrielle had gotten the worst of it in a fight with one of her brothers and had run crying to her father.

"Well, Gabs, it's like this," he'd said sternly. "Rule One, don't fight if you can talk your way out. Rule Two, if you can, stun your opponent and run to safety. I think you broke Rule One, don't you? You teased your brother until he got mad and hit you, so it's no use crying about it now, is there?"

But Gabrielle had already stopped crying. Her father had never spoken to her about anything like fighting before. She stood for a moment, replaying in her mind what he had said.

"But Daddy, what's Rule Three? What if you can't just hurt him and run away?"

And now her father looked a bit contrite, and...*sad*?

He sighed. "Rule Three, pumpkin, is that if you're forced to fight and there is little hope of running away, then you have to remember that it isn't always the strongest who wins, but the most ferocious. That's the fight where you have to accept that you're going to get hurt. Know it, but use it. Make them believe that you will take any pain, if you can at least hurt them. And if you get the chance, hurt your opponent so badly that neither he nor any others will bother you again." Then he had looked very sheepish and mumbled, "And for God's sake, don't tell your mother I told you any of this."

But Gabrielle remembered. In middle school she ran to build her stamina, climbed ropes to the gym ceiling to make her strong, skipped rope to make her quick and took dance to make her coordinated. When high school came she took the intro to martial arts course in gym – the only one they allowed girls to take – and pestered her brothers until they taught her the rudiments of boxing and wrestling. Wrestling, she soon realized, wasn't going to help her at all. She had to assume she would always be up against someone stronger and heavier than her. If she let them get close enough to wrestle, she was dead. No, her options were to talk her way out, run, or strike and run, or beat the crap out of them before they even realized they were in a fight.

Now Gabrielle looked hard at Martin LaPierre, then turned her gaze to the two boys behind him. "And you two?" she said in a strong voice. "You're *Juniors*, right? Of course you are, no one in the Senior class would suck up to Martin, so you must be Juniors." They looked at her blankly, confused that this slender girl was not showing any fear. Good, keep them off balance.

"I'm going to go into the school now," Gabrielle said evenly. "If Martin here plays the fool and tries to stop me, I'm going to hurt him. If you guys join in, three guys beating up one defenseless girl, you are going to get kicked out of school. Permanently. Your parents will have to send you to some other school, *after* you get out of jail."

Now they looked uncertain, which was right where Gabrielle wanted them. *Divide and conquer, that's the ticket.* Not that she thought they wouldn't jump in once the fight started. She just needed a moment of hesitation.

"Hey, shut the fuck up, dammit," Martin growled, leaning forward to push her hard in the chest. She staggered back three steps, almost losing her balance. Gabrielle used the motion to drop one sling of her knapsack off her shoulder and swing it in front of her, looking like she was trying to use it as a shield.

"You're so gross, Martin. Just because you're smaller than everybody doesn't mean you've got to pick on girls!"

Get the hook in his mouth.

Martin's face suddenly infused with red. "You shut up! You're just like Finley, all high and mighty, goin' to some fancy school next year. Think you're better than everybody else."

And give it a yank to set it.

"You're just a pussy, Martin," she said contemptuously. "You're mad because you tried to steal Calvin's lobsters and he threw you into the harbor! *Pussy!*" she hissed.

Martin's eyes narrowed to slits. He lifted his arms and screamed, "You deserve this, bitch." He took a single step forward.

Good.

Gabrielle threw the knapsack at him, square into his chest. He caught it in both hands, then laughed scornfully. "Not so smart now, huh? Think you're gonna knock me over with-"

With his hands occupied, Gabrielle stepped forward and smashed him in the nose with her elbow, feeling the cartilage collapse in a spray of blood that covered her face as well his. Her brother, Peter, had made her practice elbow strikes for what seemed like hours. "Never hit with your fist," he'd warned her. "All you'll do is break your hand and make 'em mad. God gave you elbows for a reason."

Martin staggered but didn't fall, so she swung a leg behind his ankle and pushed him hard. Off balance and still holding the knapsack, Martin toppled backwards onto the asphalt, nose gushing blood and his head smacking hard against the ground.

Out of it for a few seconds. Now the others.

Gabrielle turned to the two Juniors, who were wavering between jumping in to help their friend and shock at what they had just seen. If she tried to run, they would be all over her. Had she scared them enough to make them back off? Maybe, but as she looked, she could see resolve building on the face of one of them, so she turned and viciously kicked Martin in the side. "This is what happens to punks!" she screamed, then stepped over his body and kicked him again on the other side, not coincidentally putting Martin's prone form between her and the Junior she thought might jump her.

But the Junior made up his mind and sprang forward.

Oh, crap!

"Hurry!" Lois shouted into her phone.

Before she could duck away, the Junior grabbed Gabrielle by the hair and slapped her hard across the face. Once. Twice.

Then the gym door burst open and Vice Principal Nolan burst through. Without a word he tackled the Junior who was busy hitting Gabrielle, lifting him into the air and smashing him into the ground, a football tackle Gabrielle's brothers would have admired. The other Junior sized up the situation, sprinted around the corner of the building and was gone.

Meanwhile, Martin groaned and tried to sit up, but the pain in his ribs was excruciating, so he rolled onto his side and vomited.

Vice Principal Nolan stood up. When the Junior tried to get up, he stepped hard on the boy's chest and forced him back down. He looked at Gabrielle in alarm. "You okay?" he asked with real concern.

Gabrielle suddenly realized that her face was covered with Martin's blood, plus her cheek was cut open from when the Junior slapped her. Then Lois was there, gently taking Gabrielle's face in her hands.

"Oh, Gabs, your poor face," she wailed. "I'm so sorry, I called Mr. Nolan as soon as I could. Oh, you're going to have bruises, but I don't think you'll need stitches. Oh, I hope they're gone in time for the Prom!"

One of the local policemen came around the corner, taking in the scene at a glance.

Vice Principal Nolan pointed to Martin and the Junior. "Officer," he barked, "arrest these two for assault."

The officer nodded judiciously, then called on his walkie-talkie for backup. "Just what happened here?" he asked.

"I've got it all on my phone video!" Lois exclaimed. "They wouldn't let us through to go into school, then Martin attacked Gabrielle."

The police officer looked a little puzzled to see the attacker on the ground, looking the worse for wear, while his skinny female victim was still standing.

"You the victim?" he asked Gabrielle.

Gabrielle looked at him evenly. "I am not a victim," she said.

The officer looked startled, then pushed back his hat and laughed, a deep belly laugh that shook his entire torso and made him look surprisingly boyish. "No, Miss, I don't think you are," he wheezed through the laughter. "I really don't."

Later, after the two boys were taken to the Police Department and Lois and Gabrielle were walking to their class, Lois looked at her friend, a smile tugging her lips.

"The police asked for the video I shot on my cell phone. I gave it to them. But you know, Gabs, I think I screwed up the audio somehow. Most of it's gone." She shot a glance at Gabrielle. *Wouldn't do for the police to hear how Gabrielle baited Martin. Wouldn't do at all.*

Chapter 35
Monday Afternoon – Stanley's Secret

Every day before he went to Mr. Dumas' studio to work, Stanley peddled Big Moose to the dock in North Harbor. There were two docks actually, a large one for the commercial fishing and lobster boats, and a smaller one for the few pleasure boats that North Harbor lured away from Stonington by offering cheaper docking fees and, some would say, more bars.

Stanley liked to look at the boats and feed the seagulls. The seizures that had robbed him of much of his intelligence when he was an infant had left one little quirk that greatly enriched Stanley's life: Stanley had a deep appreciation of natural beauty. He didn't really understand that this wasn't the norm, or even particularly common, but a serene sunrise could bring him to tears and a sky rollicking with cumulus clouds would make him laugh and break into dance. The sea was endlessly fascinating to him. He would marvel for hours at the subtle colors and textures as the light shifted across its surface. He had no interest in painting the sea or even taking photographs; he just liked to look at it.

It gave him a sense of peace. It soothed him on those days when he couldn't get over the feeling that he was missing *something*, something others had that he did not. Everyone else seemed to know what it was, except Stanley, and try as he might, he couldn't put his finger on it.

But he had the ocean, and trees, and clouds and the birds and the whole sky and the flowers that just grew alongside the road that were so perfect in their color and shape it might have made his heart sing with joy, if hearts could sing. Which they couldn't. He knew that, but that was how he felt.

And oddly, no one else seemed to notice. Except Mr. Dumas, of course, because he could see really neat shapes in blocks of stone and carve them out. And maybe Calvin, who loved the ocean so much, but Stanley still doubted that they saw the incredible beauty all around them. As far as he knew, most people couldn't. It was all so *rich*, but they couldn't see it.

It made him feel sad for them. And made him giddy at his good fortune.

He knew who made these treasures for him – it was God. His mother used to tell him as a child that God did everything for a reason and that you had to put your faith in the Lord. Stanley believed that with all his heart. Sometimes it got confusing, like the time he heard his parents arguing about how to best care for him when they got old. His mother said

God would provide, but his father said God had abandoned them, or worse, played a cruel trick on them and then abandoned them. Stanley wasn't sure what he meant, but he knew that it was God who created all the incredibly beautiful things he saw, and that was good enough for him.

Today, he drank in the salt smell of the harbor and watched as the boats chugged in and out of the dock area. He knew all of the boats by name and could identify them as soon as they were in sight. When they tied up for fueling, he waved at the crew. Some of them waved back. It made him feel good.

And there were clouds today. Fluffy cumulus clouds sailed around the entrance to the harbor, while high, *high* overhead there were cirrus clouds that made great horse tails sweeping the sky. The cirrus clouds were made of tiny little pieces of ice. He couldn't remember who told him that, but someone did and it must be true. Little pieces of ice, way up in the sky. He didn't know why they looked like horse tails, but they did and it was beautiful. And there was a seal lying on a rock by the shore, sunning itself and looking all sleek and glossy. And best of all, there was an osprey nest with three chicks and a mother osprey that caught really big fish in the harbor and took them back to the nest for the babies to eat. It even carried the fish fore-and-aft to make it easier to fly. And he saw it all and—

Somebody smacked him on the side of his head.

"Hey, dummy, I'm talking to you!" Little Guy LeBlanc snarled. "Listen to me when I'm talking." His cousin, Paul LaPierre, stood just behind him, his face impassive.

Huckleberry stood up abruptly in his basket and growled menacingly at the intruder, baring his teeth. When Little Guy turned to look at him, Huckleberry lunged forward and snapped his teeth, causing Little Guy to flinch back, then flush with embarrassment at having been frightened by so small a dog.

Stanley chuckled – a mistake, although he did not appreciate it.

Little Guy flushed dark red. "Hey, you fuckin' retard, what are you laughing at?" He pushed Stanley in the chest hard enough to stagger him. "Huh? Somethin' funny? 'Cause you're the only thing funny on the dock right now, dummy." He pushed Stanley hard again and Stanley retreated a couple of more steps. Stanley had no idea how to fight, nor the temperament for it. He didn't have an aggressive bone in his body.

Little Guy knew this at some level and seized upon it. "I tell you what's funny, dummy. What's funny is that you think you're funny, but you're not. You are nothing but a dummy and you keep bad company. You hang out with the Finley kid, right? Calvin? You got bad choice in friends, but then, you're a fuckin' dummy. And you know what else, you're fuckin' weird. Who rides a tricycle for Christ's sake?"

Stanley was flustered and almost speechless. This was one of those times that *something* was happening, something, but he couldn't understand what. He wanted to sit on the pier and look at the water and feel calm, but he knew that turning his back on Little Guy LeBlanc was never a good idea.

"I– I can't drive a car, so I ride my bike," he explained reasonably, but there was sweat on his forehead and in his armpits.

Little Guy kicked the tricycle hard enough to make it skid sideways. "It's not a *bicycle*, you fuckin' dummy, it's a tricycle, like little kids ride. You're forty years old, you should be fuckin' ashamed to be riding this piece of crap!"

Now anger flared up. "Big Moose is not a piece of crap!" Stanley hollered, arms flapping. "Don't you go callin' Big Moose a piece of crap!"

And with that, Stanley sealed his fate.

Little Guy smiled, a perfectly vicious smile that slowly transformed into a knowing smirk. "Oh, it's Big Moose, is it? This piece of junk important to you, dummy? Think it's a pet or something? Huh? Cat got your tongue?" Little Guy was elated. This was going to be fun.

Stanley stared at him in horror, sensing that whatever it was that was happening, it had just gotten worse.

And he had no idea what to do.

"Well, I think Big Moose is a dirty piece of junk," Little Guy continued matter-of-factly. I think we would all be better off if your crappy tricycle took a bath." He picked up the tricycle. Huckleberry jumped from the basket and tried to bite him, but Little Guy gave him a kick that sent him sprawling.

"No!" Stanley screamed. He tried to grab Big Moose from Little Guy, but Paul LaPierre restrained him. Little Guy swung the tricycle around like a discus and threw it off the dock into the harbor, where it disappeared with a splash.

"No!" Stanley wailed, puling free of LaPierre and running to the edge of the pier. All he could see was the splash mark and some bubbles floating to the surface. "Big Moose!" he screamed again.

Then Stanley jumped into the water to save his treasured tricycle.

Not caring that he could not swim.

Huckleberry ran to the edge of the pier, barking furiously, then jumped in after Stanley.

Little Guy slapped his thigh and howled with laughter. "Jesus Fucking Christ, look at that dummy!" But it was Paul LaPierre who noticed that Stanley had not surfaced.

Oh, shit, he thought.

———————————

Calvin was spoiling for a fight. Not just with anyone, but with Little Guy LeBlanc. He'd heard about Gabrielle's run-in with Martin LaPierre at lunch, but there was no way in hell that Martin would initiate anything on his own – he was mean, but he was a follower, and he danced to Little Guy's tune.

Worse, he hadn't been able to talk to Gabrielle about it. She had left school early to have her face wound checked by a doctor. When the last bell rang, signaling the end of the day, Calvin decided to walk home, which would take him through the docks along the harbor.

You never knew who you might meet.

Maybe if he hadn't been so caught up in his own thoughts of revenge, he would have noticed the commotion at the end of the dock sooner. It wasn't until a kid he knew, Marc Gagne, the son of a lobsterman, came running up to him that he knew anything was wrong.

"Cal, c'mon, we've got to help Stanley!"

Calvin blinked in confusion. Stanley? What was Stanley doing down here?

Gagne grabbed him by the arm and began pulling him, and Calvin saw for the first time that there was a small crowd of people standing at the end of the dock, looking into the water. "They threw his bike into the water and Stanley jumped in after it, but the current's got him and I don't think he can swim," the boy gasped.

And then Cal heard barking. The unmistakable barking of a frantic beagle.

The two boys ran flat out to the edge of the dock, where Calvin could see Huckleberry frantically swimming in circles and barking to wake the dead.

There was no sign of Stanley.

"Where is he?" Calvin shouted.

Gagne shook his head. "He was right there, right where the dog is!" He clutched his head with both hands. "Oh, Christ, he's drowned! Oh, Christ!"

Gagne was on the swim team with Calvin. A strong swimmer. "Strip down," Calvin told him, pulling off his shoes and ripping his shirt over his head. Gagne followed suit. Out of the corner of his eye, Calvin spotted Little Guy and his cousin, Paul LaPierre. Little Guy was laughing and pointing at the dog. Paul just looked frightened, like a kid who has watched a joke get out of hand.

"The current will pull him out through the pier. Water's maybe ten or twelve feet deep, so we should be able to spot him. Take turns, but we've got to move fast," Calvin said, stepping to the edge of the dock.

"Water's going to be fucking cold," Gagne warned.

"We've got eight, maybe ten minutes, then we've got to get out." Calvin could hear a siren somewhere behind him, but they'd never arrive in time to help.

"Go!" he shouted, and they both dove into the harbor.

Without his thick wetsuit, the water was brutally cold. He came up gasping for air and spent a moment just treading water, hyperventilating. Gagne was beside him, doing the same. Calvin took a deep breath and swam under water, heading out along the pier pilings, but after a few seconds his lungs were burning and he surfaced, desperate for air. Gagne surfaced next to him, lips already blue, shaking his head to get the water out of his eyes. "Fuck, that is *cold!*"

Calvin felt breathless. The cold was like a living, malevolent thing that was sucking the life out of him. He was having trouble getting a good breath. He went under again, this time forcing himself to go a little deeper and stay under longer, but there was still no sign of Stanley. He swam under the pier, halfway around a piling and then towards the next piling, before sputtering to the surface, panting to get air. He could feel his heart race in his chest.

"Anything?" Gagne called from about ten feet away.

Calvin shook his head. For the first time he was aware that Huckleberry was swimming alongside of him, still barking his head off. He took a breath and went down again, making it to the next piling. In the shadows under the pier, the water seemed even colder, tightening his chest and making his movements sluggish. Couldn't take much more of this.

Gagne surfaced next to him, teeth chattering.

"Marc, you'd better get out," Calvin told him, pushing him toward one of the ladders. "If you stay you're going to cramp up and I might not be able to help you."

"Don't stay too much longer," Gagne panted. "Goddamn cold." He did an awkward breaststroke to the ladder and pulled himself clumsily out of the water.

Calvin took two deep breaths and held it, then dove under again. Shafts of light pierced the water here and there, creating an odd strobe-like image. Rather than just swim, he turned in a circle, looking carefully all around. Stanley was nowhere in sight. Calvin could feel the current pull him through the pier pilings and wondered bleakly if they would even be able to recover Stanley's body.

He surfaced, gasping through chattering teeth, feeling his leg muscles twitch with the cold. If he cramped up here, alone... It was time to go.

He had failed.

He was almost at the far end of the pier now. No one was out there and if he got into trouble, well, he didn't want to think of that. He swam slowly, economically, letting the current carry him to the next ladder. Grabbing it with one hand, he reached for the next rung, but there was something blocking the way.

"They threw Big Moose into the water, Calvin," Stanley said mournfully. He was crouching on the ladder, just above the water line, arms wrapped about a rung. He was sobbing.

"I tried to save him, but I couldn't find him and then I was under the pier and thought I was gonna end up in the harbor. He's gonna get all rusty and he doesn't like cold water. No sir, Big Moose *hates* cold water. How am I ever gonna find him, Cal?" He rubbed a wet hand across his runny nose, then repeated, "They threw Big Moose in the water."

Calvin Finley fought back tears. "Stanley, I was afraid you were going to get all rusty, too."

Stanley looked at him in confusion. "I can't get rusty, Calvin, I'm not a tricycle."

"Stanley, can you climb up the ladder a little? I'm freezing and I've got to get out of the water."

"Oh, oh, I can do that," Stanley said loudly, and climbed up the rungs to the pier. Behind him, groaning with the effort, Calvin gratefully climbed after him. Huckleberry swam up to him then, barking hoarsely. Calvin reached down and caught him under his chest, lifting him up to the pier, where the dog promptly shook himself dry in a spray of water, then lay down and went to sleep.

On top of the pier, Calvin waved to the people still standing at the beginning of the dock. "Hey, over here! I've got Stanley here. We need blankets and something hot to drink!"

Marc Gagne walked up, wrapped in a blanket, shivering and smiling. He took off his blanket and draped it around Stanley's scrawny shoulders. "So, Stanley, congratulations on rescuing Calvin," he said cheerfully. "I don't know what we would have done without you."

Stanley looked abashed. "I didn't really rescue him none."

Gagne clapped him on the shoulder. "Don't be modest, Stanley. I think you were great." He looked at Calvin, laughed and shook his head. "It's a great day, Stanley."

Stanley smiled and looked sheepish. "Aw, Calvin's my friend. I'd do anything to help him."

The three of them walked slowly back to the entrance to the pier, Gagne and Calvin still trying to warm up. "Stanley," Calvin asked quietly. "Who was it who threw Big Moose into the water?"

A hard look came into Stanley's face, all the more disconcerting because it was so out of character. His chin trembled. "Little Guy LeBlanc. I never did nothin' to him, but he picked up Big Moose and threw him in the water. Big Moose can't swim; he just sank. I had to save him, Calvin, so I jumped in, but I couldn't find him and then the water pushed me under the pier and I found the ladder."

Stanley looked up, grief stricken. "I've got to save him, Calvin. He's down there, all alone, and he *hates* cold water."

"We'll get him, Stanley, don't worry," Calvin reassured the man-child. "Once I warm up, I'll get my swim gear and we'll find him and clean him up."

Then the Fire and Rescue Squad reached them with warm blankets and hot, sweetened coffee thickened with condensed milk. Emergency medical technicians sat all three of them down and listened to their hearts and checked their body temperatures. One of them checking Calvin also gave him a piece of his mind.

"What the hell did you think you were doing?" he fumed. "This is *Maine* for Christ's sake. Fifteen minutes in that water, twenty max, and you will be unconscious and drown. You can't just go jumping into water this cold without a wetsuit. Christ, Calvin, you know that, what were you thinking?"

"Stanley could have died," Calvin protested.

"All *three* of you could have died," the EMT snapped. "Could have died really easily. Happens all the time. You've got to *think* before you act, dammit."

That's when Calvin saw Little Guy LeBlanc and Paul LaPierre standing at the entrance to the dock, enthralled by the mayhem they had caused. Calvin stood up abruptly, dropping his blanket. "Excuse me," he told the startled EMT, then strode to where Little Guy stood smirking.

"Hey, the hero of the day!" Little Guy crowed as Calvin approached. But LaPierre, seeing the look on Calvin's face, backed away several steps.

Calvin hit Little Guy square in the nose and felt the cartilage crunch under his fist. Little Guy collapsed to the dock, clutching his nose and screaming, blood seeping between his fingers.

"You sonofabitch!" Calvin screamed at him. "You almost killed Stanley!"

"You broke my nose!" Little Guy wailed. "Again!"

Calvin grabbed him by the shirt, getting ready to hit him again when the Fire Rescue guys swarmed over him. "Whoa! Whoa!" one of them hollered, pulling Calvin back. "Calm down!"

"He threw Stanley's bike into the water!" Calvin said loudly, struggling to get free and take another swing at Little Guy. "Stanley jumped in to try to save it. Stanley almost died in there!"

The burly fireman effortlessly picked Calvin up off his feet and held him suspended in midair. "If you don't settle down, I'm going to throw you in the harbor just to cool you off! Now cut it out!" the fireman told him.

"He also sent his cousin to beat up my girlfriend," Calvin said hotly. "Isn't that right, you little weasel?" he shouted at Little Guy.

"Ah, the plot thickens," the fireman said in resignation. "First things first, kid. We gotta finish checking you out and get a fix on your body temperature, and we really need to get Stanley to the hospital. He's built like a toothpick and for sure he's hypothermic. So all this drama will have to wait." He put Calvin on the ground, but firmly held onto his arm." Then he turned to Little Guy.

"Guy, if half the things he says are true, you are in deep shit. I suggest you get your ass to the hospital so they can pack your nose and tape it." He shifted to Paul LaPierre. "And you, I've known your family for years. You should know better than to follow this idiot. I don't know what the hell you guys thought you were doing, but Stanley could have died. If he had, you both would be in a world of hurt. Now get going."

He turned and dragged Calvin back to the ambulance. "And you, numbskull, you're supposed to be some sort of smart kid or something. Start acting like one." They reached the ambulance, where the EMT was loading Stanley and Marc Gagne into the back.

"Here, take this one, too. I'm sure he's got a touch of hypothermia because he was acting erratically and I had to restrain him."

The EMT's eyes shifted uncertainly back and forth between the fireman and Calvin.

The fireman sighed. "Just take him, okay? He needs to stay out of trouble for the next hour or so, and he should be checked out given how long he was in the water."

The fireman watched the ambulance pull away, lights flashing. "God save me from teenagers," he breathed.

Chapter 36
Monday Night – Lowell, Massachusetts

The thing about Monday nights, the truly blessed thing about Monday nights, was that nothing ever happened. People stayed home. They didn't go to bars and get into trouble, they weren't out late and getting into accidents. They stayed home and recuperated from whatever the hell they did over the weekend.

Officer Rob Cantarella loved it.

In fifteen years on the Lowell police, he'd seen it all. Stabbings, gunshots, people run down with cars, one beheading – one was more than enough – even one poor bastard garroted with a pink tutu – that one was sort of weird. Missing persons, domestics, a zillion or more drug busts, car accidents, missing children, children killed by their own parents – those were the worst, he decided – and more drunks than he would have thought possible.

But not much on Monday nights. Officer Cantarella *loved* Monday nights. Drive around, sip some coffee, listen to some Sixties Rock on his radio. Tranquil. Until…

"Unit 14, Dispatch. Report of suspicious activity near a dumpster behind Spinnato's Pizza on Elm Street."

Cantarella groaned and thumbed his mic. "Dispatch, Unit 14, any details on the 'suspicious activity'?"

"Unit 14, Dispatch. Patron reports blood near the dumpster."

Officer Cantarella sighed. His peaceful Monday night was slipping away. "Dispatch, Unit 14, on my way. Arrive in five minutes."

When he arrived, there was an adult and two teens standing several feet away from the dumpster. Cantarella swung out of the car and looked at them over the roof. "You the guys who called in something suspicious?"

The older man nodded. He seemed pale, though perhaps it was only the light. "My boy was throwin' an empty box into the dumpster, Officer, but the lid was stuck. He climbed up and opened it and…" He paused and took a breadth. "Well, he's pretty sure he saw a foot."

Aw, fuck, Cantarella thought wearily. *A body? On a Monday night?*

"I did see it!" the younger boy said hotly, and it was clear there had been some discussion as to whether he had really seen anything. "I can show it to you!" The boy had an unruly mop of black hair and sported a pair of thick glasses that made him look like a very young professor.

Cantarella nodded slowly. Something about this kid; he didn't look like the type to see things that weren't there. He touched his radio mic. "Dispatch, Unit 14. Request one backup unit to Spinnato's Pizza to assist in a search. Ask them to bring a good flashlight."

A moment later his radio gurgled: "Unit 14, Dispatch. Unit 6 is two minutes away."

He turned to the kid, who looked like he might be twelve or thirteen. "Okay, young sir, what's your name?"

The boy glanced at his father, then back to him. "Billy, Billy Shaw."

Cantarella smiled reassuringly. "Okay, Billy Shaw. Maybe you saw something, maybe you didn't, but you did the right thing calling the police. Can you show me where you think you saw the foot?"

Without a word, Billy walked to the edge of the dumpster, which was almost a foot taller than he was. He climbed up the edge, stepping first on a flange and then on the lip of the dumpster. Bending over, he pulled up the green lid and let it crash backwards.

He pointed inside. "See? It's right there."

Cantarella hoisted himself up and shined the flashlight on the cavernous interior. "Yep, that certainly is a foot." It was only a couple of feet away, lying on what was almost certainly a slice of pepperoni and mushroom pizza.

Billy was looking around the dumpster. "But where's the rest of the body?"

Cantarella slowly shined his light around the interior. It was a jumble of discarded pizza boxes, half-eaten pizzas and soda cans. Flies buzzed about industriously.

"There!" Billy shouted excitedly. "See it, near the box that's upside down!" He didn't sound horrified at all, just thrilled to be looking for body parts in a pizza dumpster.

Cantarella swung the light over to where the kid was pointing. Sure enough, there, sticking up between two sauce-smeared boxes, was an arm. A whole arm, severed messily above the elbow. He glanced at the kid to make sure he was okay.

Billy Shaw was beaming.

Cantarella shook his head. This kid was going to grow up to be either a cop or a serial killer, maybe both. "C'mon down, Billy. Good job, but now we've got to preserve the crime scene."

"Cool! Can I help?" Billy asked.

"Sure, why not?" Cantarella smiled. He fetched some crime scene tape from his car and gave one end to the boy. "See that tree by the building? I want you to walk this end over there and tie it around the tree, maybe four feet off the ground. Okay?"

While Billy Shaw was living out his fantasy of being a policeman, Unit 6 drove in, lights on, but no siren. Andy McGuire got out. "I'm here for the take-out pizza? Did you add the extra onions and mushrooms?"

Cantarella shook his head in dismay. "Cute, very cute. But I'd suggest you eat it first, because we've got a body in pieces in the dumpster. Gonna be a long night."

"Ah, Christ," McGuire muttered. "On a Monday?"

More radio calls. Soon a forensic team had assembled, all dressed in plastic overalls, gloves and biohazard helmets. Two of the forensic team climbed into the dumpster, now lit by four towering LED lights bright enough to guide small aircraft through a storm. Hundreds of pictures were taken. Then, slowly, meticulously, the pizza boxes and soda cans and everything else in the top layer were removed one by one and bagged and tagged. Including the foot. A man's foot, from the size and condition of it.

Then the arm was photographed in place again and then placed gingerly into an evidence bag.

Then the process was repeated for the next layer.

It was slow work, exacting work, but the Lowell forensic squad was experienced and patient. And, of course, little treasures were found along the way.

"Got a leg here!" one called up, which triggered another flurry of activity.

And twenty minutes later: "Ah, yeah. Got a head. Severed head here."

McGuire elbowed Cantarella in the ribs. "So, whatta you think? Drug gang killing or the guy refused to pay for his pizza?"

About two hundred photographs later, the head was safely bagged and they started on the next layer. The most important find came an hour after the head was discovered.

"Hey! Got a wallet here!" one of the techs called enthusiastically.

Heads were nice. Heads were sexy, but a wallet meant actual information. A wallet was gold.

More photographs, then the wallet was handed out in an evidence bag. The chief homicide detective on the scene carefully opened it. First, he glanced at the license and compared the picture to the face of the severed head. They matched, although the deceased had been smiling in the license photo. Not so much now.

Then he opened it to the smaller pockets where people normally kept credit cards and stuff.

And hit pay dirt.

He took out a slip of paper and saw a name and a phone number, then pursed his lips in a silent whistle. He took out his cell phone and dialed the number. After two rings it was answered.

"Honeycutt," the voice said.

Mr. Honeycutt, this is Detective Samuel Peterson of the Lowell Police. Am I correct that you are an Assistant Director with the DEA?"

"That's correct, Detective. What can I do for you?"

"Well, sir, I am standing by a dumpster in Lowell. We've just spent the past two hours removing the body of a man who was cut to pieces. Literally. We just found his wallet and there is a slip of paper in it with your name and number. I thought you might want to know about this in case the deceased is one of yours.

"Can you email me a picture of his license, Detective?"

"You bet. You'll have it in two minutes. Please call me when you get it."

"I will do that, Detective, thank you."

Two minutes later, Howard Honeycutt was staring at the license photo of his informant inside the Dominican gang in Lowell.

"Well, crap," Honeycutt said.

And then he thought about the last report he had received from the informant just a few hours earlier. And his heart sank. *Not that,* he thought in despair. *Please, not that.*

Chapter 37
Tuesday Morning – Searching

LeBlanc sat in the pilot's chair of the *Celeste,* moodily watching the water. The morning fog was finally starting to lift and he was tense, bored and antsy. It was only 6:30 a.m., but they had already been out for an hour, the *Celeste, Samantha* and *Rosie's Pride* running north in a line 1,500 meters across, each pinging the surrounding waters every fifteen seconds.

Next to LeBlanc, Banderas sat at the acoustic transponder console, wearing a pair of Bose headphones and watching the display screen carefully. He hadn't moved an inch since he sat down. LeBlanc had told his crews that Banderas was a researcher from the Maine Department of Fisheries, here on a project to map the bottom waters in the North Harbor and Stonington areas. Banderas even wore a fake ID badge on a lanyard around his neck, with a picture of him smiling at the camera.

Funny thing was, despite the ID and the fancy equipment, all the crew shied away from Banderas. They instinctively sensed danger. No matter how much Banderas might dress up, he looked like what he was, a killer.

LeBlanc's brother, Jacques, kept staring at the transponder's display screen. He leaned forward and tapped it. "If you're using sonar, why doesn't it show the bottom?"

Banderas shook his head in tired resignation. *Surrounded by imbeciles.* "It is not sonar, it is a transponder triggering a reply from a receiver. When the pulse from the transponder strikes the receiver, the receiver sends a tone, which we can hear."

Jacques looked confused. "Oh."

Jean-Philippe LeBlanc looked sourly at his brother. "It works the way it's supposed to, okay?" Then to Banderas: "Anything?"

Banderas shook his head.

There was a small chime from the equipment console. LeBlanc looked at it for a moment, reading text as it scrolled down the screen. He frowned. "National Weather Service alert. A storm is coming in this afternoon. High winds and rain from the northeast, shifting to the north, then northwest through tomorrow. Seas will be six to ten feet." He glanced at Banderas. "That will make a hash of this search. Lot of rocks in these waters. It will be noisy and dangerous. The receiver could sing the Star Spangled Banner and we might not hear it, plus there's a good chance we'll end up on a rock."

Banderas frowned. "Will other ships be out, or will everyone go to harbor?"

LeBlanc snorted. "Harbor for sure. Nobody risks his boat for a few more lobsters." He shrugged. "Anyway, with high winds and waves, it's damn hard to find your buoys, let alone haul them in. The decks will be rolling and the waves will be coming right over the rail. You just can't work in weather like that."

Banderas grimaced. The drug packages should be coming through the area sometime between Tuesday and Thursday. If they didn't find them today and they wouldn't be able to search Wednesday because of the storm, then everything depended on Thursday. And if they missed the packages Thursday... He ran a hand through his hair. By Friday the three bags could have passed through the cluster of islands off North Harbor and been swept out to the open ocean. Millions of dollars of drugs, just gone. And how would he explain *that* to his masters in Sinaloa?

"We search as much as we can today," he told LeBlanc. "As long as the weather holds, we search."

LeBlanc shrugged and turned back to the pilothouse. Banderas turned back to the transponder's display screen.

It was going to be a long day.

On the dock at North Harbor, Paul Dumas spied his nephew Jacob walking past with a brown grocery bag in his hands. Dumas' brow wrinkled. "Hey, Jacob!"

Jacob turned and grinned at his uncle. *"Oncle* Paul!"

Dumas reached him and the two men exchanged a hug. "What's this, a day off in the middle of the week?" he teased. "Why aren't you out getting covered in lobster slime and salt water?"

Jacob's grin broadened. "Actually, I do have the day off. Captain LeBlanc is out doing some sort of bottom mapping and doesn't need his regular crew for the next couple of days."

Dumas looked at the younger man quizzically. "Bottom mapping? What for?"

"Damned if I know. I just know no work today and probably tomorrow as well."

Dumas rubbed his chin. The storm Wednesday would keep all the boats in the harbor, but no need to tell Jacob that he was going to miss at least three days of work. He glanced at the bag Jacob was carrying. "That wouldn't be a six pack of beer, would it?"

Jacob grinned. "Just enjoying my day off, *Oncle* Paul."

"And would this day off include a certain dark-haired beauty that I've seen you hanging around with lately?"

Jacob laughed, but didn't answer.

Paul Dumas smiled back, but inwardly he cringed. He had known Katie Montgomery since she was a leggy ten-year-old following her daddy around the docks. He was pretty sure she was whoring to feed a drug addiction, which meant that one way or another, Jacob was in a world of hurt. He sighed – Jacob just couldn't seem to catch a break.

"Enjoy your day off," he told him, slapping the boy on the shoulder. "But be smart. I don't want to hear you were driving that motorcycle of yours after you've had a few beers, okay?"

"I'll be careful, *Oncle* Paul, don't worry," Jacob promised. But somehow Dumas was not reassured.

Paul Dumas watched his nephew put the beer into a pannier on his motorcycle, then drive off with a wave. He couldn't escape a nagging foreboding. Katie Montgomery. Shit, he was going to have to talk to his sister, Danielle, about it. And wouldn't that be fun?

———————

Jacob was fucking Katie Montgomery every chance he got. He couldn't get enough of her. Today he'd shown up with the beer and ten minutes later they had both chugged their second can and torn off their clothes.

The sex, as always, was frantic and greedy and mind-blowing.

But afterwards, as they lay next to each other, skin glistening with sweat, breath still rapid, Katie rolled over and reached under her side of the bed, coming up with a small glass pipe and what looked like a lump of white paste. Ignoring Jacob, she propped herself up against the pillows, tamped the paste into the bowl of the pipe and lit it slowly with a kitchen match. Once it was lit, she breathed in the pungent smoke and held her breath, closing her eyes and letting her head fall back.

"Christ, Katie, is that what I think it is?" Jacob blurted.

Katie blew out the smoke and sucked in another lungful. "I just use it to take the edge off," she said.

"I thought that was what we just did," Jacob said.

She just glanced at him noncommittally and went back to the pipe. "You know that nice feeling you get after *really* good sex, when you've come and you whole body feels all relaxed and tranquil?"

Jacob knew; he'd been experiencing it often since he and Katie had been having sex. "Post-coital lassitude," he said.

Katie giggled. "I love the words you know. That's what this is for me. It's like that feeling, but one hundred times stronger and it just lasts and lasts. Makes you feel so good that nothing else matters."

"Until it wears off and you come down," Jacob countered.

Katie shrugged and took another hit of the pipe. "Nothing in this world lasts forever." She took another lung full, then leaned close to Jacob and slowly blew the smoke into his face, until he was shrouded in it and couldn't help but breath some in. Then she leaned over and took him in her mouth. "This makes you feel good, doesn't it?" she asked softly. Jacob groaned under her ministrations. "It's just about pleasure, Jake," she whispered. "We all deserve pleasure in our lives. All of us." She sucked on him until he was fully erect, then she straddled him and lowered herself onto his penis. "See? Doesn't that feel good? Nothing wrong with that, is there?"

Then she sucked another lung full from the pipe, leaned so close that their noses touched, and slowly blew the smoke into his mouth and nostrils.

And Jacob felt himself swept away.

Hours later, Jacob stopped on the top of a hill and listened to the thunder of the ocean. The first winds from the storm whipped at his face.

The thought had been nagging at him for some time, but now it burst forth: Katie was as poor as a church mouse. Where did she get the money she needed to buy heroin?

Then the first fat rain droplets began to strike all around him, the forerunners to the impending storm. He started his bike and put it into gear.

The lowering black clouds chased him all the way home.

Chapter 38
Tuesday Afternoon – We Need to Talk

Howard Honeycutt pulled alongside of Frank Finley as he was walking back to the station from lunch. Finley was surprised to see him, usually Honeycutt only met in out-of-the-way places where the chance of them being seen together was small.

Honeycutt rolled down the window. "Hey, Frank, got a few minutes you can give me?"

Finley glanced up and down the street to see if anyone was paying attention to them. "Corcoran's out of the office most of the day. What do you need?"

"We need to talk," Honeycutt replied ambiguously. "Get in, Frank."

Alarm bells started ringing in Finley's mind. "What's going on, Howard?"

"Frank, I'm asking you to get in."

Then Finley noticed the two cars behind Honeycutt's, each with two men.

Staring rather intently at him.

Finley opened the door and slid inside. Almost immediately, the back door to Honeycutt's car opened and a man slid into the seat behind Finley's. Finley recognized him as one of the men who was at the scene when they brought in Henry Mitchell's body. Very slowly, Finley turned in the car seat so that he could face Honeycutt and see the DEA officer in the back seat out of the corner of his eye.

"Okay, Howard, you have my full, undivided attention," he said slowly. "What is going on?"

"Are you armed, Frank?" Honeycutt was as serious as a heart attack, and just as charming.

Finley gritted his teeth. Whatever the hell it was, he wasn't going to like it. "My service weapon in on my right hip. Safety strap is buckled and, I might add for the benefit of our friend in the back seat, my hands are in my lap, away from the gun."

"Frank, I am going to have Tommy remove your weapon, just so we can talk without me having to put you in cuffs. Okay?" Howard asked.

Finley stared at him in disbelief. At the same time, he knew objecting would get him nowhere...or maybe shot. "Okay, Howard, but tell your man Tommy that I am ticklish as hell and if he touches my side, I am going to twitch. Also tell Tommy that if he tickles me on purpose, I am going to break his nose. And then, Howard, I am going to break yours."

The corner of Howard's lips pulled in the slightest hint of a smile. "Tommy will exercise the utmost prudence," he assured Finley.

Tommy got out of the car and opened Finley's door, never taking his eyes off Finley's hands. There was the slightest of tugs as he undid the safety strap, then he slid the gun out and returned to the back seat. Honeycutt gave a wintery smile.

"Howard, for the love of God, what is going on?" Finley said in exasperation.

"You know we have a source in the Dominican gang?"

"Sure, you told me so just a few days ago."

Howard nodded. "Well, two things have happened, Frank. First, the source reported that he overheard a conversation between the Dominicans and somebody in the Sinaloa Cartel. He specifically heard the Dominican say that you, Frank, had reported to the Dominicans on the latest efforts the DEA is making to track down the smugglers."

Finley blinked, stunned at what Honeycutt had just said. Somehow he knew it was going to get worse. "You said there were two things, Howard. What's the second?"

"My source has gone dark," Honeycutt replied grimly. "He missed two scheduled calls. We left an emergency signal, but he hasn't responded."

In other words, the source had been murdered.

"And you think *I* told the Dominicans who your source was?" Finley asked conversationally.

"You know I have to check it out, Frank," Honeycutt replied.

Finley thought it through. Lie detector test. Had to be.

Finley snorted in something approaching amusement. "'Course you do, Howard, 'course you do." He clapped his hands together, inadvertently scaring the hell out of the DEA agent in the back seat, who fortunately did not have his finger on the trigger of his pistol.

"Knowing you, Howard, you've already got someplace set up to question me, right?"

Honeycutt gave the slightest of nods.

"Got a lie detector machine there, and somebody who knows how to use it?"

Another nod.

"Good, let's go!" Finley demanded. "I've got to be back at work within two hours, but it won't take that long, Howard, I promise you that."

Honeycutt opened his mouth to say something, but then just nodded and started the car.

———————

The someplace turned out to be a motel room on Rte. 1, just outside of Ellsworth. Honeycutt opened the door with a key and walked in, followed by Finley and three of the four men who had come with them. One of them shut the door and stood in front of it, arms folded, never taking his eyes from Finley.

The lie detector technician sat in one of the two chairs in the room. He was fifties, balding, and exuded that sense of quiet competence that highly technical people do when surrounded by technical illiterates.

"You the operator?" Finley asked brusquely.

The technician glanced at Honeycutt.

"You can tell him," Honeycutt said.

"Yeah," the man said.

"Police, FBI or DEA?"

"I was with the FBI for twenty-five years, retired and then went to work for Mr. Honeycutt."

"You already got your questions ready?"

The man nodded.

"Okay," Finley said, pulling off his jacket and unbuttoning his shirt. "You strap me up and we'll do it. But I'm telling you, I have sat through countless lie detector interrogations, so if I think you are screwing around, biasing the answers, I'm going to break your nose. Got that?"

The man bristled. "I do *not* bias answers," he said firmly.

"Good, good," Finley smiled. He believed him, sort of. He motioned for the man to get out of the chair, then he sat in it. "Wire me up and let's get this done." He turned to look at Honeycutt. "And Howard, you can ask me any fucking thing you want about your source. But I'm telling you now that you'd better start thinking about what it means that they've taken out your man and have tried to blame me, because the only reason I can think of is that they need you off-balance for the next couple of days. And that, my friend, means something is coming down real fast."

The technician finished attaching the necessary sensors and stepped back.

Honeycutt nodded to him.

The technician stood behind the monitor, flipped a switch, then said: "Please answer these questions with a 'yes' or a 'no.' Is your name Frank Finley?"

An hour later the technician stepped back and shook his head. "He's either been trained really well or he is being entirely truthful."

"I'm willing to take sodium pentothal or whatever new generation of truth serum that you've got," Finley told Honeycutt. "But the outcome is going to be the same, so let's stop wasting our time, Howard."

Honeycutt pursed his lips in thought, then motioned to the technician. "Get him out of the rig, John. Thank you for your work."

"Sure thing, Mr. Honeycutt." The man bent to free Finley from the sensors.

Honeycutt turned back to Finley. "I'm sorry to put you through this, Frank, but I had no choice."

Finley chuckled, but there was no mirth in it. "I'm just glad you prefer lie detectors to rubber hoses. I bruise easily." He got serious. "But I meant what I said – the only reason for them to take out your guy now and put me in hot water is because something is about to happen and they need you chasing your tail." He paused, then asked, "Are you sure they got your informant?"

Honeycutt nodded grimly. "I lied to you about him disappearing. Lowell police found him late last night in a dumpster. It wasn't pretty. His body showed signs of extensive torture." He paused, face twitching, obviously trying to keep a grip on himself. "The body was in pieces."

Finley shuddered. Every DEA agent lived in fear of being captured by one of the cartels or the gangs they worked with. Better to get killed in a gunfight.

"And Frank, if they are using you for bait," Honeycutt said, "then they probably know you work for me. Watch your back."

Chapter 39
Tuesday Evening and Wednesday Morning
The Lovers, and Those Who Would Kill Them

Tuesday night. Dumas stood in his studio, staring once again at the enormous block of marble that contained an Indian warrior riding into battle on his horse.

Try as he might, he still couldn't see it. The more he looked, the more opaque the walls of the marble became, until they shimmered with nothingness. Sighing, he tipped back the wine bottle and took a long swig. Dumas' mental image of despair was red-eyed crows perched on a white picket fence. His fence was *black* with the little bastards.

And his deadline with the casino crowded closer every day, until it threatened to suffocate him.

"Staring at it won't do you any good," his wife scolded.

Dumas grimaced. "Best I can do until I'm ready. I don't want to start cutting this thing only to find I've started wrong."

"There are other ways you can get what you need," she said tartly.

He scowled. "Céline, if you tell me one more time I should pray for guidance, so help me I'll scream."

She sniffed dismissively. "If you want to shake hands with the Lord, you first have to extend your hand in humility and gratitude. And you, Luc Dumas, are too damn stubborn to do that. Fifty-six years of marriage has taught me that much. Besides, you've got as much humility as a porn star running for President." She moved closer, rubbing the back of his neck and shoulders. "But even an old dog like you should know you need to relax now and then." She leaned over and kissed the back of his neck. "Don't tell me you're so old and cranky you don't remember how to relax," she whispered.

Dumas sat up in sudden interest. "Excuse me, my dear woman. I am in the midst of a serious artistic enterprise, requiring imagination, creativity, enormous skill and insight, painstaking attention to detail and perseverance of the highest order." He looked down his nose at her. "And you are trying to distract me with...with..."

"Sex," his wife murmured in his ear. "It's been a little while, lover boy, but you still remember how, don't you?"

He swiveled in his chair to face her. She sat on his lap and took his face in her two small hands. "I love you," she told him, managing to be serious and sultry at the same time. "And I seem to recall a few times when some good old-fashioned intimacy did wonders for your peace of mind."

Dumas slid his arms around his wife, marveling again at the delicate bones in her shoulders and the graceful curve of her neck. He still recalled the first day they'd met as fellow art students in Montreal. There had been some interest, some chemistry, but neither had made any moves. Then weeks later the class had been assigned the task of painting a nude, and Céline had offered to model for him if he would model for her. They agreed to switch roles – model and painter – every two hours. Céline had even agreed to pose first.

They used her apartment because the lighting was better, and he made a small platform out of a coffee table. She disrobed shyly and stood on the platform, turned three quarters away from him, glancing back over her shoulder. Dumas was utterly captivated. She was so petite, this lithe eighteen-year-old, with her slender body and smooth skin and flowing hair that reached to the tips of her breasts. So alluring. So...

He struggled mightily to concentrate on his painting, but the mischievous forest sprite on the platform kept looking at him through hooded eyelids and, adding to his growing discomfort, from time to time bit her lower lip. Luc stared at Céline Charbonneau, then wrenched his gaze back to his canvas, and was dismayed to find it was mostly empty. It had been almost an hour, hadn't he painted more than this?

Then he felt a warm hand on his. Céline, still naked, stood beside him. "I think it is your turn to disrobe, Luc," she said in a low voice, and he saw that her chest and forehead were damp with sweat.

She unbuttoned his shirt, one slow button at a time, pausing once to run her hand across his bare flesh and try, unsuccessfully, to stifle a moan of desire.

"*Mon Dieu!*" he croaked, and when her fingers reached his belt buckle, he swept her up in his arms and kissed her ardently, first her mouth, then her lovely throat and finally her small breasts. She bit his shoulder, marking him, *claiming* him, and he picked her up and carried her into the bedroom.

They were late for class. Very late.

"You know what I'm thinking of?" he asked his gray-haired wife of so many years.

She snorted. "Of course I do! I'd never tried to seduce a man before." She smiled wickedly. "I had no idea it would be so easy. Or so enjoyable."

"Lot of years," he murmured.

She touched his cheek.   "And two beautiful children, and grandchildren."

Dumas grinned. "Lots of fun making those children."

She stood up, taking his hand. "Come on, old man, let's see if you can show your gray-haired wife a good time. I just happen to have a bottle of *Chateauneuf-du-Pape* breathing in our room. Let's put it to good use."

"What?" he asked in mock horror. "No *Romanee-Conti Grand Cru Cote de Nuits*, 2015?"

She shot him a look. "I save that for my younger lovers. Much younger."

Chuckling, he picked her up and carried her to their bedroom.

Céline leaned her head against his chest.

And smiled.

The *Chateauneuf-du-Pape* was delicious.

Sex between older people is not quite the same as when they were young. Older bodies require more tenderness, more patience. Arousal is slower, but no less intense. Bodies are, perhaps, a bit more fragile, but no less needy, no less hungry. And if the physical act of love is somewhat less gymnastic than it used to be, it is no less satisfying.

And the emotional rivers and pools are much deeper, drawing on a wellspring of care and love crafted by decades of shared trials and joys. Old people make love to each other's minds as well as bodies.

Afterwards, Céline poured two more glasses of the excellent wine and carried them back to bed. Luc lay on his back, hands behind his head, looking happy and relaxed. She handed him his glass of wine. As she knew he would, he swallowed half the glass, then lay back with a sigh. She took a sip from her glass.

"That was lovely," she said.

"Very, very...adequate," he teased, which earned him an elbow in the ribs from Céline.

"Keep it up," she said, contentedly snuggling into his chest. "It will be a cold day in hell before you take advantage of this body again," she threatened cheerfully.

He reached over and gently stroked her back, which he knew she liked. "Do the kids think we still make love?" he asked.

Céline giggled. "I doubt it. Danielle probably thinks we're too old, and Paul probably never thinks about it at all. Anyway, children never like to think about their parents having sex. Too icky! Each generation likes to think they invented it. We certainly did."

"Hmmm," he said drowsily. "Maybe you're right. But maybe we should take a selfie and 'accidentally' send it to them."

"It would be the last thing you'd *ever* do," she warned.

He yawned, eyes drooping. "Be...worth...it." He yawned again. "Love...you."

His eyes closed and his breathing deepened as the Ambien she'd put into his wine took him in its embrace and carried him off to a dark night and a deep sleep.

She waited several minutes to be sure, then slid quietly from the bed, got dressed and went to the kitchen pantry. There, behind the jars of peaches she'd put up last fall, she withdrew the jar of wood ash and a fine haired, Number 6 paint brush.

Three minutes later, she was in her husband's art studio, standing beside the block of marble. Part of her wanted to rail against it, to curse it, to strike it. But in the end, it was just a piece of rock. Lifeless. Blameless. The flaw, if there was a flaw, lay within her husband. But in this he was as blameless as this chunk of stone. Blame was not the answer.

She turned to the work table, where Luc kept his notes and preliminary drawings. She riffled through the notes, seeking the critical measurements of how far from the top, front edge and center the location of the Indian's face was. Then she looked for notes on the location of the horse's head as well.

She knew what to look for. After all, she had done this five other times over the course of their marriage. Luc was a brilliant sculptor, but even brilliant artists get stuck sometimes.

Céline was simply helping him to get *un*stuck.

Moving quickly, she set the step ladder near the front of the marble block, then made three quick measurements to get the right location. She swapped the tape measure for the jar of ash and the Number 6 paintbrush. Dabbing into the jar, she located the right spot on the marble and was just about to make her first brush stroke when she heard a smothered giggle behind her.

Whirling around, she came face to face with Stanley. He stood there, holding a broom, his face blushing a deep red, his other hand covering his mouth to stifle his laughter. She had forgotten that he would be by to clean the studio.

"Stanley, what is it?" Céline asked tartly.

Stanley looked embarrassed. "Mrs. Céline, you're looking right at the horse's butt!" If anything, his blush grew more pronounced, and he was overcome with another fit of giggles.

Céline turned slowly and looked at the face of the marble block she had started to shadow. It was smooth and unmarked and looked nothing more than, well, a big chunk of marble. She turned back to Stanley, who was now hopping nervously from foot to foot and looking abashed.

"Stanley," she said slowly. "Show me where the horse's butt is."

Squirming with embarrassment, Stanley pointed to the spot she had begun to shadow. "Right there, where you were sticking your brush."

"Not a very good place to stick a paintbrush, is it?" she asked dryly.

"No." Stanley suppressed another fit of giggles with an effort.

"Okay, Stanley, and this is important. Do you know where the horse's head is?"

Stanley looked confused for a moment and Céline's heart sank.

"Well, yeah, Mrs. Céline, it's on the other end."

Céline nodded encouragingly. "Stanley, can you show me exactly where the horse's head is?"

Stanley, relieved to have something to do that would not embarrass him any further, walked around to the "back" of the marble block and pointed up. "The horse's head is right up there."

Céline dragged the ladder around, positioned it where Stanley had pointed and climbed up, awkwardly carrying the jar of ash and her artist's paintbrush. "Here?" she asked, pointing to a spot about two feet or more from the top of the block.

Stanley squinted, studying the expanse of marble, then pointed just to Céline's right. "Over there a little, Mrs. Céline." She moved the tip of the brush over several inches. Stanley nodded enthusiastically, and she carefully marked the spot.

"Thank you, Stanley," she said. "Now, can you show me exactly where the Indian's head will be?"

It took a bit longer, but finally Stanley nodded and she marked the second spot. "Stanley," she asked gently. "Why didn't you tell Mr. Dumas where the horse's head is?"

"Oh," said Stanley, abashed. "I wouldn't do that. Mr. Dumas, he knows. He knows, more than anybody. I think sometimes he just doesn't feel ready."

Grunting a little with the effort, she gingerly climbed down the ladder and, taking Stanley's face in her hands, kissed him on the cheek. "Stanley Curtis, you have helped me more than you will ever know."

"Mr. Dumas, he showed me the drawings," Stanley confided. "It's gonna be real pretty, Mrs. Céline."

Céline gave him a long, appraising look. "Stanley," she asked gently, and pointed to the spot he had showed her. "How did you know the horse's head is there?"

Stanley looked confused. "Because that's where it *is*, Mrs. Céline. Where else would it be?"

Céline tried a different tact. "Stanley, what if Mr. Dumas wanted to make a sculpture of a large deer with antlers? Where would the head be then?"

Stanley frowned in concentration, glancing once or twice at the block of marble. "Um," he said hesitantly. "Is it running or just standing there?"

Céline pursed her lips. "Running," she said. "And jumping over a log."

Stanley walked to the marble block, then ran his fingers over it. Finally, he pointed to an area on the narrow side of the marble. "There," he said. "Right there."

Céline smiled. "Stanley, you never cease to amaze me."

When Stanley had gone and she had regained her composure, Céline laboriously climbed the step ladder again and carefully, delicately shadowed the area of the horse's head and the Indian's head with the faintest touch of ash. She carefully climbed down to the floor and stepped back several feet. The shadow was almost imperceptible, not something consciously seen so much as a *suggestion* of something there.

Good. She knew her husband. It would suffice.

She collected the ladder, the jar of ash and the brush and left the studio, thinking about Stanley.

———————

Wednesday morning, with the soft sound of rain against the window. Danielle and Frank Finley were sharing that most precious of adult pleasures parents can share: privacy. Calvin was off at school and Jacob was...somewhere. Outside, rain beat on the windows, but they lay under a warm comforter, arms and legs entwined, bathed in the soft afterglow of lovemaking.

"My God," Danielle whispered. "The house all to ourselves. When's the last time this happened?"

"Making love, or being alone in the house together, with no rambunctious boys clomping about like wild elephants?" Finley replied.

Danielle stretched luxuriously, rolling one leg over his hip and running her hand across his chest. "Take your pick. Either way, I like it."

"Hmmm," Finley murmured, rubbing the palm of his hand across her stomach, then a bit lower. "Even though we've both got work this afternoon, I feel like we're playing hooky or something." His hand reached a sensitive spot and he very gently traced circles on it with the tip of his forefinger. "That good?" he asked softly.

"Delicious," his wife said, thrusting her hips forward onto his hand. But then she suddenly stopped. "Do you think my parents still have sex?"

"What? Céline and Luc?" he asked, confused by this abrupt change in course. "Heck, I don't know. How old is Luc, seventy-three? Seventy-four? I mean, they're both healthy. No reason why they couldn't still be sexually active."

"I can't imagine my mother still having sex," Danielle declared firmly.

Finley rubbed his chin and considered the mine field he had been thrust into. "You know, someday you and I are going to be in our seventies. Won't it be nice to still be able to make love with one another?"

"Not my parents," she repeated, then rolled out of bed and put on a bathrobe.

"Okay," her husband countered. "But-"

"Not having this conversation!" she said emphatically, heading for the bedroom door. "I'm going to go make breakfast."

"You brought it up!" he protested.

"No, I didn't!" she said emphatically.

Finley laughed. Danielle paused in the doorway. "What?" she demanded.

"I love you," he said. "Every once in a while I suddenly remember how precious all this is."

———————

Calvin had set out for school with nothing but good intentions. Then his phone rang.

"Did you know that school was just cancelled because of the storm?" Gabrielle asked him cheerfully.

Calvin stopped in his tracks. "Wait! Really? I'm not even there yet."

"Yes, really," she said. "But you know what? My mom and dad are both at work. Actually, Dad is on a business trip." She paused for a moment. Calvin did not say anything. "In case you haven't figured this out yet, it means that I am here all alone, by myself, for the next few hours. I figure Mom won't even check in with me until noon. S-o-o-o-o, I was wondering if you'd like to swing by? I mean," she added hastily, "if you aren't already doing something. You know, if you're free."

"Gabs, I just learned that school is closed, what else could I be doing?"

"So, you'll come, then?" He could hear the smile on her face.

"Well, I don't know, maybe today will be a good day to get my shoes shined. Or get a haircut. Or weed the garden. Or –

"Get your skinny butt over here, Finley," she said, and promptly hung up.

Gabrielle's home was only three blocks from downtown North Harbor, four blocks from the high school. Calvin trotted through the rain, but he still got drenched. He thought ruefully that for a bright kid, he still hadn't figured out when to take an umbrella with him. Gabrielle was waiting for him when he reached her house.

"Oh, Calvin, you're soaked!" she exclaimed.

"Well, you know, the rain."

She shook her head in dismay. "Okay, I'll get some of my brother's old clothes. Meanwhile, get out of that stuff and we'll run it through the dryer."

Calvin briefly experienced a hundred lurid fantasies, then shook them off. "Gabs, give me your brother's clothes and I'll change in the bathroom, then we can toss the wet stuff in the dryer."

Gabrielle headed to her brother's room. "I'm making tea. Want some?"

"Real tea, or that flowery, herbal stuff you usually drink?

She stuck her tongue out at him, then disappeared into her brother's room. "You might be able to fit into Peter's clothes," she called out. "You want a button shirt or a pull-over?"

"Doesn't matter, whatever is convenient."

She returned with a pair of jeans that had a hole in one knee and a flannel shirt.

"Thanks," Calvin said. And because he sort of thought where this might be going, he leaned over and kissed her. She put her arms around his neck and kissed him back, then pulled away.

"God, you *are* soaked," she said, wrinkling her nose. "Go change and I'll get your clothes into the dryer."

By the time Calvin had peeled off his wet clothes and squirmed into Peter's – they were a size too small for him – Gabrielle was knocking at the door and telling him the tea was ready. His wet clothes were dispatched to the dryer. But then Gabrielle took him by the hand and led him, not to the kitchen, but up the stairs to her bedroom.

"I've decided something," she said. She glanced at him and when he did not say anything, she blushed, but continued. "We've got a little more than three months before I go off to Swarthmore and you either go to school yourself or work full time as a fisherman. Even if we stay together, we won't be able to see each other every day like we do now." She reached over and touched his hand. "I want this summer to be about you and me. I want..." she took a deep breath and her eyes suddenly shone with unshed tears. "I want..."

"I know," Calvin said simply. He took her hands and very softly kissed her forehead, then her mouth. "Yes."

Gabrielle collapsed against him in a hug. Calvin suddenly felt embarrassed. "Ah, Gabs, listen, I don't pretend to be any great, you know. What I mean is..." His voice faltered and he stumbled into silence.

Gabrielle laughed nervously. "It's my first time, too." She leaned forward and began pulling his shirt over his head. They had fooled around quite a lot in the first weeks they had dated, but they had never seen each other totally naked. But when his shirt and pants had dropped to the floor, there he was, in the flesh, bursting with youth and health, and obviously aroused. Gabrielle took in a deep breath. "Oh, God, you're beautiful," she blurted and kissed him hard.

When they came up for air, it took them no more than three seconds to shed her clothes and she stood there: proud, blushing, lusting, and suddenly shy. She was the most beautiful thing Calvin had ever seen, and he wanted her with every fiber of his being.

Which raised another issue.

"Uh, Gabs, I didn't...I mean, I don't have a condom."

She giggled. "It's okay, I got some birth control. You know, just in case..."

"You did?" he asked in surprise.

A red flush of embarrassment colored her neck and chest. "I had an IUD put in. I was thinking about you and me, and this summer, and going away in the fall, and..."

"Oh hush," he said, kissing her, and they tumbled onto the bed. And it was fumbling and awkward...and utterly exquisite. And when they finished the first time, they took thirty seconds to recover, then did it again.

Afterwards, curled up against him with her head on his chest, she said shyly. "I'm so glad it was you."

And Calvin, mind awhirl with everything that had just happened, did not know what to say, so he pulled her close to him and held her as if he would never let her go. Tears of happiness ran down both their cheeks, making them both laugh.

And later still, Gabrielle sat up on one elbow, her face unaccountably serious. "Calvin, can I tell you something? I think my parents are going to get a divorce," she said miserably.

Calvin roused himself out of post-coital torpor. "Why do you think that?"

Gabrielle pulled the blanket up to her chin. "They used to make love. I could hear them, you know, at night. But I don't hear them anymore." She smiled ruefully. "It used to embarrass me, but now I sorta miss it."

"Gabs, it could be anything" Calvin tried to reassure her. "One of them might not feel well, or they might have had a fight, or, I don't know, maybe they're just getting older. Heck, your dad must be almost fifty. Do people that old even have sex?"

Gabrielle blinked in astonishment. "Of course people that old have sex! Don't your parents have sex? And they're older than mine. *Geez*, Calvin!"

Now it was Calvin's turn to blink. He tried to imagine his parents together, but his mind shied away from the thought. Mom and Dad have sex? They used to, of course – he was here, after all, and his brother. But still? At their age?

"And lately Dad has been taking all sorts of business trips, so he's gone a lot," she continued. "And when he comes home, Mom isn't overjoyed to see him. It's just so different from how they used to be."

"Have you asked your mom about it?"

She shook her head. "I'm afraid to," she confessed.

Calvin put his arms around her and she started crying. Not loudly, not big sobs, but he could feel her hot tears running down his bare chest and he tightened his arms around her to protect her from...he didn't know what.

Anything. Everything.

———————

While Frank and Danielle ate a late breakfast and Calvin and Gabrielle reveled in their newfound intimacy, Bruno Banderas met with the four killers in their hotel room.

He passed out several photographs. "This first one is Frank Finley. He's a cop with the North Harbor police, but he's also working with either the DEA or the Maine DEA. He's responsible for getting Mateo, Pablo and Arturo killed. He used to be a big-city cop, so don't underestimate him." Bruno pointed to two of the men. "You two are on Finley." He explained how the hit was going to work. "I don't care where you do it, but get it done." He glared at them. "And make sure he's fuckin' dead. No screwups, no mistakes."

He pointed to the other two killers. "You two are on the family." He gave them the address. "They usually eat supper together, so that's a good time." He pushed more photographs across the table. "That's the wife. She's a looker. Have fun with her if you want, but do not jeopardize the hit."

Another photo. "That's the younger son. He's in high school, some sort of jock, so take him out first if you can."

A third photo. "This is the older son, Jacob. If he's home with his mother, kill him, too. But if he's not there, that's okay, he gets a pass."

They talked at length on how the killers were to exit Maine and safely return to Lowell. Banderas took out a map and showed them the roads they'd have to deal with, then they all exchanged cell phone numbers and put them on speed dial.

"Be sure to be in position early for Frank Finley. You'll only get one shot at him. Remember, he's a cop. If you miss, he's going to call for help and fight back." He gave them a hard stare. "Don't miss."

———————

Jacob had hung around the docks for the morning, but when it was clear that the weather was not going to break and his boat was not leaving the dock, he called Katie. He arrived at her house in the early afternoon, but when he went to knock on her door, he hesitated. Something had changed. He couldn't say what, exactly, but something.

But then the door opened and there was Katie, wearing only a skimpy bath towel and a taunting smile, her hair cascading over her bare shoulders. His uncertainty vanished under an avalanche of lust.

An hour later, he collapsed back onto the bed, spent, covered in sweat, with a half-assed grin on his face. "Oh my God," he muttered.

Beside him, Katie reached under the bed and emerged with the glass pipe and a lump of heroin paste. He rolled over and caressed her cheek with the tip of his finger, tracing a line from her ear to her lips. She glanced at him quickly, then went back to tamping the pipe.

"Katie," he said softly. "I'm falling in love with you." She hesitated for a moment, but said nothing, then busied herself with the pipe again.

He put his hand on hers. "Katie, you don't have to do this," he pleaded.

She turned to him then, her eyes haunted and sad. "Yes, I *do*," she told him, then pulled her hand away and lit the pipe.

Chapter 40
Wednesday Afternoon – The Professor

The storm was pissing all over everything when Finley drove to the police station to report in for the afternoon shift, but he barely noticed. Something was going to happen, and happen soon. But he didn't know what or when or where. The Dominican distributors had come out of the shadows when they killed Honeycutt's informant. They knew it would bring heat, lots of heat, but they didn't care, which meant that either the informant was on to something and represented a huge danger to them, or they were creating a distraction to cover up something else entirely.

Finley was betting on a distraction. If the informant had suddenly become a serious danger, he would have just disappeared. The body would have been weighted down properly and dropped into the ocean. Instead, they left the body where it would be found. And tried to implicate Finley.

Stirring the pot. Waving a flag. Calling attention.

A distraction, something to keep them occupied while something else happened. But what?

He sighed. *Back to basics, Finley, my man.*

What do the Dominican drug gangs do? What is their primary reason for living?

Answer: they smuggle drugs for the Sinaloa Cartel. Whatever else was happening, it involved getting drugs into Maine and selling them.

Fact: Honeycutt has largely pinched off the I-95 access.

Fact: the Dominicans have been looking for another way to smuggle drugs into Maine.

Fact: they tried, and failed, to smuggle drugs into Maine by transferring them from freighters into go-fast boats. Only it wasn't really drugs, it was baking powder. In other words, a test run to see if that method was viable.

So if that didn't work, what would they try next? How do you safely get the drugs ashore when the customs agents in the US and Canada were on high alert and the Coast Guard was flying drones over passing freighters? How could another boat get out to the freighters and make it back to Maine unnoticed? It would be damn risky. Not impossible, but very, very risky. And the Cartel were businessmen. They liked profits, not risk. They might be able to buy off a random Customs agent, but they couldn't bribe the Coast Guard. So...if you can't get a boat out to the freighters to pick up the drugs, how do you get the drugs ashore?

Then Finley slapped his forehead. "You moron," he chided himself.

He needed an oceanographer. He pulled into the parking lot of the town's only Dunkin' Donuts and fired up his cell phone. First, he combed through colleges in Maine. Bowdoin College, the closest, was the obvious choice. There, after some poking around, he finally found Dr. Ron Klattenberg at Bowdoin's Department of Earth and Oceanographic Science. A few minutes later he had him on the line. He identified himself and plunged in.

"I'm with the North Harbor police, Professor. We have reason to believe that a fifty-pound bag of illegal drugs was dumped into the ocean just outside of the Bay of Fundy, right at the US-Canadian border. We think the drug smugglers hope that the drugs will be carried by ocean currents into Maine coastal waters, where another ship will pick it up. We need to know where and when those drugs might reach this area."

There was a long silence, followed by a sigh. "Well, I'm glad to help if I can Officer Finley, but some more details would help a lot."

Finley could almost see Klattenberg grimacing on the other end of the line. "What do you need, Professor?" he asked.

Another sigh. "Well, for starters, can you give me a better sense of where the drugs were dumped into the water? And when? And how they were packaged?"

Good questions, but it was information Finley didn't have. He thought frantically for a moment, trying to picture the map of the waters from North harbor to the Bay of Fundy. "Okay, Professor-"

"Officer, just call me Ron, it will be much easier. 'Professor' sounds like I have a pointed head, and I am nerdy enough already."

Finley chuckled. "Okay, Ron. I'm Frank. Let's assume that the package went into the water late Friday night or very early Saturday morning. Assume that the drop was about thirty miles south or southwest of Grand Manan Island."

"And how was it packaged?"

"Assume it was wrapped in heavy plastic to keep it waterproof."

"Hmmm...like a ball shape, or a lozenge?" Klattenberg queried.

"I'm just making guesses here," Finley confessed. "I doubt if it would be perfectly round."

A pause on the line. Finley could hear Klattenberg typing on his computer. "Okay, probably won't matter much anyway, unless... Is this thing going to be floating on the surface, where the wind can get it, or will it be underwater?"

Ah, Christ, more details he didn't know. "Does it matter?" he asked, buying time.

"Oh, yes," Professor Klattenberg said. "Definitely. In fact, it may be the most important part of the equation. You see, if it floats, and if part of it sticks up out of the water a little, then you get a sail effect. A wind from the north or northeast would push it along faster than the underlying current. On the other hand, if the wind is from the west or southwest, the wind will slow it down relevant to the current. Also, it could push it further to the east, into open water. If that happens, fat chance of finding it."

"Crap." Finley muttered.

Klattenberg chuckled. "Well, perhaps it's not that bad. Let's assume that the drug cartel has smart people doing this. Fifty pounds of drugs – I'm assuming either heroin or cocaine – that's a lot of money. Must be worth hundreds of thousands of dollars."

"Actually, Professor, closer to $11 Million, street value," Finley told him.

There was a stunned silence on the other end. "Well, Lord love a duck! I am in the wrong line of work! And dare I say, so are you, Officer Finley."

Finley laughed out loud. He was beginning to like this professor. "Not the first time I've wondered about that. But yeah, safe to assume they've put a lot of thought into this."

The professor took a deep breath. "And well they should! Eleven Million dollars in a fifty-pound bag. We can assume they have rigged this package so that it will hover below the surface, away from the wind. In fact, a storm like we're having today can churn the water for a few feet down, so I think we can safely assume the bag will be at least ten or fifteen feet below the surface, rigged to stay at that depth. With something this expensive, they will want to reduce as many variables as they can. Still, this is very, very risky."

"Walk me through it, but please use small words. I don't have my Ph.D. quite yet."

"Yes, of course," Klattenberg said. "I, on the other hand, have my Ph. D., but do not know the street value of heroin. Which one of is the less educated, Officer?"

It occurred to Finley that he knew a lot of stuff that he would rather not know, but kept it to himself. "Take me through it. How can we figure out when and where the drugs will turn up?"

There was the sound of a computer keyboard on the other end. "Well, there are several variables. First, if my computer is correct, it is roughly forty-five to fifty miles from the assumed drop point to the North

Harbor-Stonington area. Now, the Eastern Maine Coastal Current has a velocity of between .14 to .21 meters per second."

Finley groaned.

"Not to worry, I'll translate for you," Klattenberg said cheerfully. "At .14 meters per second, that works out to approximately 504 meters per hour, or .313 miles per hour. So, at the low end, the current should travel about 7.5 miles in a day. Anything carried by it will travel the same. With me so far?"

"Every step of the way," Finley said, and although there was a hint of sarcasm in his voice, the fact was he admired that Klattenberg had been able to pull this all together during a short telephone conversation.

"Good! Now, at the high end of the current's speed, it is moving at .21 meters per second, or 756 meters per hour. That's .470 miles per hour, or 11.28 miles per day. So –" the sound of more typing, and of Professor Klattenberg humming happily to himself – "that means if the parcel went into the water late Friday and was picked up by the Eastern Maine Coastal Current right away, it should arrive sometime today or tomorrow." He paused. "Barring mishaps, of course."

Today or tomorrow! Finley could feel his blood pressure abruptly skyrocket. But maybe there was something that could delay that schedule. "Mishaps?" he repeated hopefully.

"Well, yes," Klattenberg explained patiently. "You see, to hold fifty pounds of powdery material, you are looking for one parcel that might be twenty-four or thirty inches in diameter. Now just in the immediate area of North Harbor and Stonington, there are sixty or more islands of note and probably hundreds of rocks sticking out of the water, any one of which is big enough to snag the parcel if it washes up on it. You see the problem?"

"You're saying there is no way of predicting where the parcel will actually run aground."

"Well yes, but the problem is much worse than that."

Finley closed his eyes. "Explain it to me, Professor."

"Well, just look at a map of the area," Klattenberg said. "The parcel has to travel southwest for *days* to get to the North Harbor area. North Harbor is on the southwest corner of a fairly large archipelago, with dozens of islands and hundreds of rocks the parcel could snag on. And if it is rigged to hover beneath the surface of the ocean, then it will likely hit the ground and stop moving *underneath* the water. It won't just wash up on a beach where we can see it."

"But, that could mean..." Finley trailed off, feeling a little overwhelmed.

"You're looking for a pin in a football stadium. The parcel could hang up on a rock or island anywhere from Baker Island in the north, to Vinalhaven in the south, and everything in between," the professor said cheerfully.

Finley ground his teeth in frustration, but then listened more closely to the professor's tone. He was enjoying this.

"What aren't you telling me, Ron?" Finley asked warily.

Professor Klattenberg laughed. "I knew you'd catch on. Everything I've said is true, but it leaves out the drug cartel that is hunting for the parcel. If this parcel is worth $11 Million-"

"It is," Finley assured him.

"Well, then, the smugglers can't take a chance of losing the parcel, can they? I'll bet you a lobster dinner that they've got an oceanographer of their own. I'm sure of it. He would warn them of all these risks, so they would have to take steps to reduce the risk to something they could live with. I mean, this parcel is going to get snatched up by the Eastern Maine Coastal Current and carried right through the archipelago that starts at Acadia National Park and continues all the way to Stonington and beyond."

Finley was beginning to understand, but he needed the professor to spell it out in detail. "Keep talking, Professor," he said.

"Well," Klattenberg continued, "picture a pinball machine. The parcel of drugs is the pinball. Once it is carried along by the EMCC, it is on the board. As the current takes it to an island, for example, one of three things can happen: first, the current can carry it west around the island; second, the current can carry it east around the island; or third, the current can run the package onto the island, where it snags and just sits there.

"These options will present themselves with every island, rock and outcropping that the Current runs into," the professor explained, his voice rising with excitement. "Each time the package will move east, west or get snagged on the obstacle in question. The Current will brush past hundreds of obstacles. The variables are enormous, far too many to calculate, but the drug cartel has to have a way to find the $11 Million package no matter how the variables turn out!"

Finley was struggling to keep up. "Professor – Ron – what the hell are you trying to tell me?"

"Frank, there must be some sort of radio beacon attached to the package. Has to be. Because if there isn't, the chances of the smugglers finding the package are infinitesimally small, approaching zero."

And there it was, clear as day. But how did that help him? "Is there a way to hunt for the radio beacon frequency?" he asked.

"I don't know," Klattenberg admitted. "Probably, but you don't have much time. You're working with the Coast Guard on this?"

"Yes, they interrupted the first drop on Friday night, then we caught the smugglers in their go-fast boat when they limped to shore."

"Well, I'll bet the Coast Guard knows all about the electronics of radio beacons. If I were you, I'd ask them for the best bet way to either locate the parcels, or spot the people who are searching for them," Klattenberg told him.

"Huh," Finley said thoughtfully. He hadn't thought of that. Whoever was helping the Cartel locally, they'd have to be out there, sweeping the area, looking for the parcels. Would they be out in this weather?

"Thank you, Professor," he said. "I mean that. You've really helped a lot."

"Just remember, Frank, if there is a finder's fee for that drug parcel, say, ten percent or so, I would accept it with the greatest appreciation and humility. Cash or gold Krugerrands will be fine."

Finley laughed. "Would you settle for a pizza dinner at Pat's?"

"An admirable second choice," Klattenberg said.

After they hung up, Finley thought about radio beacons for a minute, then called Commander Mello at the Coast Guard Station. He found himself once again talking to Ensign Kauders, Mello's aide. He explained the issue.

"Glad to help you, sir," Kauders said. "My guess is that they are using a simple radio transponder system. The search boats would 'ping' for the packages; that is, send out a radio pulse through the water. If the package is nearby and its responder is hit by the ping, it activates a radio beacon that basically says, 'Here I am, come and get me.' The beacon might turn on and keep sending a signal until they find the package and turn off the signal, or it might send for just a minute or so, then go quiet unless it is pinged again. Either way works."

"Is there a way to hunt for the signal the searchers are sending?" Finley asked.

"I don't think that approach would be helpful, sir, mostly since the ping is being directed into the water. Even if you knew the frequency they're using, you wouldn't hear it much in the open air." Kauders paused, considering. "But there is another way."

"I'm all ears, Ensign."

"Well, you're talking about lobster boats or fishing boats searching the inshore waters. That's a lot of water to search, and you say the packages will probably arrive today or tomorrow. Chances are they are out there right now, with at least several boats, searching for the package and pinging away like mad. And if they don't find it today, they'll be out again tomorrow."

Finley frowned. "I hear what you're saying, Ensign, but I don't know how that helps."

"Well, sir," Kauders explained. "If the bad guys have thought this out, they will form a line with their search ships, spaced apart half a mile to a mile, in order to cover the maximum area as efficiently as they can. If they are using lobster boats, they won't be zig-zagging all over the place like lobster boasts do when they're hauling traps, they'll be moving in a straight line, with other lobster boats keeping formation. They'll stay in formation until they have to squeeze around an island or something. I'm making the assumption that they have enough transponder units to equip several boats, but I don't think that's too farfetched. This is a big operation and these guys have lots of money."

"So I'm looking for several lobster boats sailing a search grid instead of lobstering," Finley said.

"That's pretty much it," Kauders agreed.

Finley thought about it for another minute. "What I really need is aerial reconnaissance."

"Well, sir, we've got two helicopters," Kauders reminded him. "I can't speak for the Commander, of course, but if your Director Honeycutt were to make a request, Commander Mello might be favorably disposed."

"You are a prince among men, Ensign Kauders," Finley said fervently.

"Yes, sir, that was one of the qualifications to becoming Commander Mello's aide."

Finley's next call was to Howard Honeycutt, and he brought him up to speed on everything he'd learned from Professor Klattenberg and young Ensign Kauders.

"I like it," Honeycutt said, "but I'm going to have to scramble to get any assets out there today."

"Call Commander Mello at the Rockland Coast Guard Station," Finley suggested. "He may be able to help you."

"I'm on it. Can you get free tonight and give us a hand?" Honeycutt asked.

"I doubt it," Finley replied. "I'm late now for the second shift and won't get off until midnight."

All right, I'll keep you posted," Honeycutt promised.

Finley sat in his car, still thinking about the calls with Klattenberg and Ensign Kauders. One more call to make. He called his brother-in-law, the Harbor Master for North Harbor.

"Hey, Frank, what's up?" Paul Dumas asked.

"Paul, I've got an odd question for you," Finley began. "With the storm coming in, did most of the fishing and lobster boats stay in today?"

Dumas chuckled. "Quite a few of them went out early this morning, but all but a few are back now. The wind and waves have really picked up. Another hour or so and it's going to be really nasty out there. What's this about, Frank?"

"You say most of them are back. Anyone still out?"

"Oh, yeah, a few of the usual diehards."

"Paul, this could be important. Who's still out?" Finley pressed.

"Hmmm..." Dumas considered. "Well, Old Ben Weaver and his son, working the area from Russ Island to Devil Island, but he'll be in soon. His boat leaks and he won't be happy with these waves getting bigger."

Finley knew Ben Weaver; it wasn't him. "Who else, Paul? Anybody who surprised you?"

"W-e-e-l-l-l, Jean-Philippe LeBlanc's out there with his boat, and he's got his two brothers with him, but Jacob told me they aren't fishing, they're doing some sort of bottom mapping with some guy from the Maine Department of Fisheries."

"Bottom mapping, this close to shore?" Finley asked dubiously. The in-shore area was full of rocks, sandbars, old tires, lost traps, and old diesel engines that had been dropped overboard rather than paying the dump disposal fee.

"Do you know where they are or where they're going?" he asked.

"Well, you know, I actually went out in my boat to make sure everybody knew about the storm comin' in. You'd be surprised how many of them dumb bastards turn off their radios. I never caught up with the LeBlancs, but I could see them way up by Opechee Island, still moving north, all sailing in formation like toy soldiers."

Finley could feel his blood race. "What do you mean, in formation?"

"You know, spread out in a wide line so they can map a wide area at once," his brother-in-law said.

"Aw, Christ," Finley cursed.

As the storm got worse, Calvin knew he would have to get home, but he didn't want to leave Gabrielle. He called his mother at work. "Mom, I'm heading home soon. Gab's parents might be late getting home tonight. Okay if she comes for dinner?"

His mother thought through what was in the refrigerator, which was very little. "Sure, tell her she's more than welcome. I've got to stop at the store to get something anyway, I'll just get a little extra. You guys can help me cook dinner."

"Thanks, Mom."

"I'll be home just after four, so don't be late," his mother told him, then rang off.

Calvin turned to Gabrielle, who was sitting up in her bed, the sheets exposing the curve of her breasts, her hair, mussed and wild, hanging over her shoulders. "Mom says OK for you to come for dinner." He grinned. "But she won't be home until four."

Gabrielle smiled back. It was only 2:30 p.m. "Hmmm," she said. "What can we do with an hour and a half?"

———————

Once Finley finished his calls, he dashed through the rain to the rear door of the police department. But when Finley reached his desk, Chief Corcoran was waiting for him.

"Finley, the Bangor police have a report for me," the Chief said coldly. "It will be ready at 4:30 p.m. I want you to pick it up and bring it back here. I'll be here late, so bring it to me directly. Got that?"

Inwardly, Finley groaned. Another errand, and at the worst possible time. He would have to leave by 3 p.m. in order to make it to Bangor by 4:30 p.m., which mean that there was nothing he could accomplish before he had to go.

"Screw it," he muttered, then grabbed his raincoat and headed for the door. Outside, he dashed through the rain and the puddles to his service vehicle, one of the new Ford Interceptors. Inside he checked to make sure his car radio worked, that the computer was operating okay and that the AR-15 was clipped in its rack between the front seats. He was just turning away from the carbine when something caught his eye. At the base of the stand that held the AR-15, there were slots that could hold up to four 30-round magazines.

They were empty.

Finley frowned. That happened sometimes if one of the other cops who used this car went to the shooting range with the carbine and forgot to replace the spare magazines. Not often, but it happened. He unlocked the carbine and pulled it across his lap to inspect the magazine slot just forward of the trigger guard.

Also empty.

Now he was pissed. He would happily kick the ass of whoever had this car before. Fuming, he locked the carbine back in the rack, then stomped into the police building and went down to the basement to the armory. Martin Remy had pulled the duty for the day and was sitting at a small desk in the armory room, really nothing more than a large closet. Remy's face split into a wide grin when he saw him.

"There he is, the man who bested Ralph Harkins with a cheeseburger!" Remy chortled.

"Hey, Marty, how you doin'?" Finley greeted him.

"Every morning I wake up, it's a good day," Remy told him, only half kidding. "Hey, I got a joke for you! My grandson showed it to me on the Internet."

Finley groaned. Remy was notorious for his lousy jokes. "Remy, c'mon, give me a break here."

"No, no, you gonna love this. See, a cop on a horse said to a little girl on a bike, 'Did Santa get you that?' 'Yes, he did,' replied the little girl."

"'Well you should ask him to get you a reflector for it next year!'" the cop tells her and fines her five bucks for not having the proper safety gear on her bike."

"The little girl looked up at the cop and asked, 'That's a fine horse you've got there, officer. Did Santa bring you that?'"

"The cop laughed and said, 'He sure did!'"

"'Well,' the little girl says, "next year tell Santa that the dick goes *under* the horse, not on top of it!'"

Finley's lips twitched. Remy beamed. "See, I told ya!"

"Marty, I need five magazines, 5.56 mm, thirty rounds each. When I got in my car, there was no ammo at all for the carbine."

Remy clucked his tongue in disapproval. "Burrows had that car yesterday and this morning. He must have hit the rifle range."

Burrows was one of Chief Corcoran's fair-haired boys. He was also a bit of a thug. There were half a dozen complaints pending about him using too much force to resolve relatively mundane incidents, and one rumor that a sexual assault claim by a teenage girl stopped for a DUI had been withdrawn after Burrows had threatened harm to her younger brother. Finley hadn't had many dealings with him, in part because Burrows treated him with disdain, trending toward outright contempt.

In other words, Burrows was a prick...and a friend of the Chief of Police.

Finley mentally shrugged. Burrows would wait. He had bigger fish to fry today. "I've got to go to Bangor on another errand for the Chief. How about those magazines?"

Remy pursed his lips and nodded. He found the magazines, helped Finley load in the 5.56 mm rounds and handed them over. "Frank, even though this is just another one of the Chief's errands, you really ought to wear a vest," he said seriously, referring to a bulletproof vest.

"Yes, Mother," Finley said, but he put one on, waved to Remy and went back out to the car. He didn't bother with the GPS; Rte. 15 was pretty much the quickest way to Bangor, and he was already running a little late. But he took time to make one more phone call. Five minutes later he was through downtown North Harbor, such as it was, and on Rte. 15 North.

Chief Corcoran watched Finley leave from his office window. Once he was gone, he took out a burner phone he used sometimes, dialed a number and when the call was answered, said: "He just left. He'll arrive in Bangor about 5 p.m., then he'll turn around and come back. It's Rte. 15 all the way up to Bangor. He won't be there very long. I put the tracker in the car, so you can follow him no matter where he goes."

"What weapons does he have?" asked Banderas

Corcoran smiled. "He's got his service pistol. He's also got an AR-15 carbine, but what he doesn't know is that there is no ammo for it."

Banderas chuckled. "I like that."

"Don't underestimate him!" Corcoran snarled.

"We know how to do this, my friend," Banderas reassured him. "We have done it many times."

Corcoran didn't doubt it, but he said nothing.

Danielle Finley arrived home to find Calvin and Gabrielle in the kitchen, making an apple pie.

"It's really blowing out there!" she exclaimed and shook the rain off her umbrella. "I've got chicken, carrots, celery, peas and onions. It's a good night for chicken soup!"

"Hi, Mom," Calvin waved casually from across the kitchen. "This pie is just about to go into the oven, but I can't remember the right temperature."

"Um, 450 F for ten minutes, then 350 F for thirty-five minutes and we'll check it to see how it's doing," she replied absently, glancing discreetly from Calvin to Gabrielle and back again. Something different. What was it?

"Hi, Gabrielle," she said warmly, for she truly liked the girl, and knew her son was totally smitten.

"Hi, Mrs. Finley," Gabrielle replied. "Thanks for having me over to dinner." Then she flushed crimson and darted a glance towards Calvin, then looked at the floor.

Oh my God! Danielle thought, awareness blooming. *They're sleeping together! They've just made love. Today!* She leaned back against the kitchen counter, emotions swirling, words leaping to her lips and dying there, unspoken. Then she remembered her own mother's reaction to catching her and Frank, and what a gift her mother's simple acceptance had been. She took a deep breath to steady herself, then took off her coat and busied herself filling the kettle for tea.

Then, very casually, she said: "Listen, you two. I know what you mean to each other and I am happy that you have reached this point. I truly am." She looked at them earnestly. "Intimacy with someone you care for deeply is one of the great gifts the Lord gives us. But, please, tell me that you are using birth control."

"Mom!" Calvin protested, totally mortified to be having this conversation.

"Yes," Gabrielle said stoutly, but blushed furiously again. She stepped over and put her arm around Calvin. "I don't want anything to get in the way of both of us going to college."

Danielle looked at them tenderly. Two kids, just on the cusp of adulthood. And this tall, thin, brainy young woman, who just might be her daughter-in-law someday. She wanted to do something more, something to show that she blessed them both and wished them nothing but happiness, but she sensed that if she tried to give her son a hug right now, he would run screaming from the house. And if Gabrielle blushed any harder, she might spontaneously burst into flame.

"Good," she told them. "Someone very dear to me once told me that if you are old enough to be intimate, you are old enough to take precautions. I had to be told. It speaks well of you, Gabrielle, that you knew you had to be responsible for yourself."

The kettle whistled its readiness at that moment, saving them all from what was sure to be an awkward silence. Danielle smiled at her embarrassed son and his resolute lover. "So, who would like tea and who would like hot chocolate?" she asked brightly.

Chapter 41
Late Wednesday Afternoon – Early Wednesday Night
Without Pity or Regret

There were four of them: Hugo, Diego, Alejandro and Javier.

Hard men. Killers of men. And women...and in two cases, children. Remorseless men. Men without pity or regret.

They had known each other since childhood in the crime-infested streets of Los Guandules, one of the poorest neighborhoods of Santo Domingo. Each had seen brothers or fathers killed by rival gangs, each had been cold and hungry and afraid for his life. Each had struggled and fought and killed and killed again in order to stay alive. Each had robbed, beaten and raped.   And each had come to the dark realization that if God was not dead, He had at least turned his beneficent gaze away from them.

So be it.

They had no hope of ever growing old. They were to die by violence, for that is the fate of such men. But they could delay that reckoning by ruthlessly killing any and all who might harm them. This they were willing to do, for while none of them feared death, each of them secretly harbored a terror of what might come after.

Now they had another mission: kill a man and his wife and their two sons. They did not question the necessity of this, and certainly not the morality of it. It was their job, and they were professionals. Each carried an AK-47 with a 3X scope and extended magazine, plus a pistol, usually loaded with .45 caliber ammo.   They methodically inspected and readied their weapons. When they were ready, they placed them neatly on the table.

Then they sat down to wait for the phone call.

Chapter 42
Wednesday, in the Ocean off North Harbor

The three drug parcels each took a different path into the cluster of islands buffering North Harbor from the sea. The first swept along with the Eastern Maine Coastal Current and entered Jericho Bay. It drifted southwest, slipping through the shallows between Swans Island and Sunshine Point, only to run smack into a rock outcropping on the west side of Shabby Island. It bumped along the bottom, being pushed by the waves higher and higher up the rock incline, until finally one big wave picked it up and hurled it over the ledge into a tidal pool formed by four chunks of rock tall enough to break the surface.

And there it sat, in four feet of water, rocking back and forth as waves crested over the pool, only to settle back down again when they passed.

The second package also passed through Jericho Bay, but it missed Shabby Island by half a mile, then got pulled almost due west by the EMCC, threaded the needle between Phoebe Island and Enchanted Island, then swung south with the current and wedged firmly in the cleft of Gunning Rock, twenty feet beneath the surface of the ocean.

The third package slid along the eastern side of Swans Island and west of Frenchboro Island, then dutifully followed the current southwest again towards Isle Au Haut, unperturbed by the storm now raging twenty feet above it.

It would ground on an island or a rock, or it would not. If it did not, then it would collide with the Western Maine Coastal Current, which would push the package out past Georges Bank and into the open Atlantic Ocean. There it would be caught by other currents and move in a vast circle around the ocean until, years later, its wrapping rotted enough to allow water into the dry heroin within, it would sink.

But for the moment, its fate was undecided.

———

On board the *Celeste,* Jean-Philippe LeBlanc glanced sourly at the fading light and the rising waves. The ship's wind detector showed gusts up to forty miles per hour. In this weather he was an hour's hard sailing back to North Harbor, and the storm was getting worse by the minute.

So far, they had not caught any sign of the packages.

LeBlanc shook his head and turned to the others in the small cockpit. "We're shutting down. Radio the *Samantha* and *Rosie's Pride* and tell them to turn back for port."

"But we need to find the parcels!" Banderas growled. "They're coming through today or tomorrow."

"We can't find them if we get swamped by these waves!" LeBlanc snapped back. "I'm in charge and I'm telling you it ain't safe. We're going back to port. We'll go out first thing in the morning." He spun the wheel to bring the boat around, taking them southwest to the harbor's entrance.

"Listen, LeBlanc," Banderas began, his voice filled with menace.

"I've been sailing these waters for close to thirty years," LeBlanc said, cutting him off. "I know the islands, the rocks, the ledges and the currents. Most of the lobstermen know what I know. And you know what? We lose maybe three boats a year, all for the same fuckin' stupid reason: the captain stayed out just a little too late and the storm got him. Experienced captains who should have known better, but they screw up. One bad judgement, that's all, just one bad judgement."

LeBlanc looked at Banderas, who stared back defiantly. "So you're thinking maybe you should pull out that fancy gun of yours and take over the boat. Right? Or do something really fucking brilliant and shoot me. But before you do something you'll regret in about one flat minute, let me ask you a question: How many hours have you sailed these waters? At night, in a storm? How many minutes would it take for you to run up on a rock or an island and then capsize." He laughed shortly. "You even know how to swim?"

LeBlanc leaned out so he could see the other two boats and make sure they had turned for port, then turned back to Banderas. "So tell your bosses that tomorrow morning we'll go back out bright and early, and if your plan with these hi-tech transponders isn't total crap, maybe we'll find something. And tomorrow morning when you're eating breakfast, you can thank me for keeping you alive. Because, my friend, if we did what you want us to, we'd all be dead by morning."

Banderas said nothing, just leaned over and angrily slapped the power button on the transponder to 'off.'

Twenty minutes later they passed within two hundred yards of Shabby Island, well within the effective range of the *Celeste's* transponder. If it had been on.

Chapter 43
Wednesday/Wednesday Night
On Rte. 15 to Bangor

Hugo and Diego, being the more experienced, went after the cop. Hugo drove. Diego sat with a laptop open on his lap, watching the tracker dot as it moved north on Rte. 15. They had driven Rte. 15 half a dozen times now, taking notes on good ambush locations, noting where the rural highway was deserted and empty of houses. They had discussed waiting until full dark, but finally agreed that if they lost Finley in the dark, not knowing the back roads, he might evade them, tracker or no. No, it would be better to take him during daylight, if you call it daylight with all of this goddamn rain.

Finley was driving leisurely north on Rte. 15 and they followed, keeping far enough back so that they only caught occasional glimpses of the police cruiser, using the tracker to keep tabs on him. They drove past Ron's Auto and crossed Airport Road – although they did not know it, Jacob and Katie were together not more than a mile away from them – and then crossed over the Holt Pond Bridge, where the abortive effort by Mateo's go-fast boat had reached its bloody conclusion.

Finley sped up a bit and continued north on Deer Isle and Hugo increased speed to keep within the tracker's range. They followed Finley across Causeway Beach to Little Deer Isle, and less than a minute later crossed the bridge to the mainland and through Sargentville.

"About four miles to 175," Diego warned.

This was the first significant point. If Finley went straight on Rte. 15 towards Blue Hill, Hugo and Diego would turn left on 175 and race north, through the little town of Penobscot, then take Rte. 199 northeast until they rejoined Rte. 15. There they'd wait for Finley to come to them and ambush him on a long, lonely stretch of 15.

If instead Finley turned onto 175, they would accelerate to overtake him before he reached Penobscot and take him out there. That stretch of 175 was isolated; they could take care of Finley without serious risk of witnesses. Nice and tidy.

Diego watched the laptop screen intently as Finley approached the junction of routes 175 and 15.

———

In North Harbor, Alejandro and Javier carried their weapons out to the car in duffle bags and stowed them in the back seat. They drove to the harbor area, careful to stay within the speed limit, then parked alongside the road that led to the Finley home. Javier produced a pair of binoculars and scanned down the street, but could not quite see the house. They settled in to wait.

Thirty minutes later, Danielle Finley drove past them in her blue Toyota Prius, her lights on to pierce the gloom of the storm. Javier nodded. "That's the wife," he said in satisfaction. "Let's wait until the kid gets home from school, then go in."

Neither man had children. It never occurred to them that school had been cancelled due to the storm and that Calvin was already home.

They settled in to wait, chatting idly about what they'd like to do with the wife before they killed her. Banderas was right, she *was* a looker.

———————

Frank Finley decided that he would like nothing more than a good cup of coffee, and he knew just the place. When he reached the junction of 175 and 15, he stayed on Rte. 15 to the town of Blue Hill and the Bucklyn Coffee Shop, which served some of the best coffee in Downeast Maine.

The rain thickened and he put on his headlights, humming to himself. He checked the rearview mirror, but there was nothing to see. *Only fools and cops were out in weather like this,* he told himself. *And only God can tell them apart.*

———————

"He's turning toward Blue Hill," Diego said, an edge of excitement in his voice. Diego was the youngest of the four killers, but hardly the least experienced. Excitable, but good in a fight.

"*Bueno!*" Hugo said, and turned left onto Rte. 175 and pressed the gas pedal down hard.

Now it was a race to see who reached the killing zone first.

Hugo drove fast down the narrow country road, concentrating hard through the rain and enjoying himself immensely.

Five minutes later, near the edge of the tracker's range, Diego frowned. "He's stopping in Blue Hill."

"Note the location and look it up on Google maps," Hugo told him.

Diego typed in commands and then zoomed the screen in so he could see what businesses were in Blue Hill. "Looks like he's stopping for coffee at a café in Blue Hill," he muttered.

"Good," countered Hugo. "Gives us more time to get into position."
But he didn't slow down.

Finley glanced at his watch and decided he had time to stop at Bucklyn Coffee and enjoy it rather than just order it to go. He ordered a thick, rich Kenyan coffee and a delicious looking cream-filled pastry, then took a booth along the front wall. He mused for a bit about his career. No matter how this ended, he thought, it was time to talk to Honeycutt about a transfer. Get out of undercover work, get some time in as a regular field agent. He'd miss parts of it, and he was good at it, but it was time to move on.

He checked his watch again. Time to go. He drained the coffee cup and tossed out his napkin and plate, then strolled to his patrol car and hit the road, back tracking to Rte. 15 and heading north again. His fingers traced lightly over the AR-15, reassuring himself the ammo magazine was there.

He glanced once in his rearview mirror. Nothing.

Hugo and Diego sped through Penobscot, braked hard and took the right onto Rte. 199.

"I love this car!" Hugo said gleefully. He had never driven an Audi A6 before.

"We'll hit 15 in about two miles," Diego said. "The tracker's got him coming out of Blue Hill on 15, but he's going slow." He nodded to himself. "We'll be ahead of him. Plenty of time to get in position."

The plan was simple and lethal. Once the tracker showed Finley about half a mile away, they would pull out of Rte. 199, turning north on Rte. 15. They would drive slowly, much slower than Finley, forcing him to pass them. When Finley tried to pass, Diego – in the back seat with an AK-47 – would hose him down from ten feet away.

They had used this tactic many times before. It always worked.

Finley peered ahead through the rain, but couldn't see anything. He passed Range Road. Next "major" turnoff would be Merrill Turner Road. He was still miles from Orland, and a long way farther from Bangor.

And he still hadn't heard anything. He hesitated for a moment, then reached for his phone.

Forty miles away, Petty Officer First Class Nathan Johnson leaned forward to stare at the sensor reading from the LUNA drone he was flying. Gritting his teeth, he brought the LUNA around in a tight bank and swept up Rte. 199 again all the way to the Rte. 15 junction.

Nothing.

"Fuck!" he gritted.

Ensign Kauders was on him in a flash. "What is it, Johnson?" he demanded.

Johnson's shoulders slumped. "It's the goddam rain, sir. It's too heavy. I can't see a bloody thing."

Ensign Kauders blinked. "Wait, you mean you lost the other car?"

Johnson nodded glumly. "I think it's still there, sir, but I can't find it in this slop."

Ensign Kauders looked a little panicked. "What about infrared? Do you get any heat signatures?"

Johnson bit off a sarcastic reply. One might get away with sassing an Ensign, but then again, one might not. "Already tried that, sir. No joy. The rain is so heavy it is masking any hot source at ground level."

Ensign Kauders rocked back on his heels, thinking furiously.

"How high are you?" he asked the Petty Officer.

"One thousand feet, sir," Johnson replied, dreading what he knew was coming.

"If you took her lower, you'd have a better chance of picking up their heat source, right?"

"Yes, sir," Johnson replied. "But, sir, the winds are all over the place. If the LUNA gets hit with a wind buffet much lower than a thousand feet, I might not be able to save it." He paused. "Hell, sir, we don't even know for sure these are the right guys. This could be Tom and Jane on the way home from work."

Kauders quickly weighed the risks, but then stopped himself. *Screw it,* he thought. *I'm not going to be the guy who got Finley killed because I was nervous about crashing a LUNA.*

"Take her down to one hundred and fifty feet, Petty Officer. Go infrared, but keep your video camera going. Prowl Rte. 199 for half a mile back from 15, then go back to 15 and go south until you reach Finley's car. Once you see his car, turn around again and go north until a mile past the 199 junction. If it's them, they'll be skulking around there somewhere."

"Sir," Johnson protested half-heartedly. "The winds can –"

"Do it, Johnson!" Ensign Kauders said firmly, then he grabbed his phone and pressed speed dial.

———————

Every fiber of Finley's body was on high alert. The warning signs had been coming one after another. First Honeycutt's warning, then Police Chief Corcoran sending him on a last-minute errand to Bangor, and finally the empty rifle in the car he'd been assigned.

Finley pressed his speed dial. It rang once and Honeycutt answered.

"Hey, Howard," Finley said. "I'm getting kinda lonely out here without a regular drone report."

That had been the call he made just as he left North Harbor. Honeycutt had agreed to provide support in the form of two ground cars and the Coast Guard's lovely LUNA drone.

The Coast Guard had been tracking a car that had followed Finley out of North Harbor, but had split at the junction of Rtes. 175 and 15, when Finley had gone to Blue Hill. The last report that Finley had gotten was that the car was just passing through Penobscot.

"Frank, we lost them," Honeycutt said bluntly. "It's the damn storm – plays hell with the drone's sensors."

Finley took his foot off the gas pedal and let his car slow. "Tell me what you know, Howard."

"We lost them about four minutes ago, just as they approached the junction with Rte. 15. They can turn north or south there. If they turn south, they'll run right into you."

Finley swore under his breath and braked to a full stop, peering anxiously through the windshield. He couldn't see a damn thing through the pounding rain.

Then there was a loud buzzing sound that sounded like a cicada on steroids. It approached quickly and flashed past him. He didn't so much see it as have an impression of shadow and movement – fast movement – overhead.

"Howard!" he shouted into the phone. "Something just buzzed me! Tell me it's the Coast Guard drone, because if it's not, it means the Cartel is using some damn sophisticated surveillance and I'm going to turn around and run for it."

"Hold one, Frank." The phone went quiet and there was a moment's pause. But while the phone was dead, the giant cicada sound returned and sped away to the north.

"Crap!" Finley pulled the AR-15 from its rack and charged the action, then checked his service pistol to make sure there was a round in the chamber. He put the pistol on the seat beside him and set the rifle back in its rack, but left it unlocked.

His phone made a rasping sound. "Frank? Frank?"

"Yeah, Howard?"

"That was *our* drone," Honeycutt assured him. "Okay? The Coast Guard's drone just flew overhead your vehicle. Good news is that there is no vehicle – repeat, no vehicle – between you and the 199 junction. Can't see any heat signatures on Rte. 199 within half a mile of the 15 junction, so we think they've already turned north on Rte. 15. They are *ahead* of you, Frank. They've either pulled off and will wait for you to reach them, or they'll go slow and when you try to pass them, they'll ambush you then."

Finley frowned. "Howard, has the drone actually found them?"

"Negative," the older man said. "It is going down Rte. 15 now, flying low and trying to spot them using infrared."

Finley shook his head. "Tell them to abort! They're flying too low. If I could hear them, the bad guys certainly will. Abort!"

He could hear Honeycutt shout an order to someone, then: "Okay, Frank, the drone has pulled away and will circle about a mile out until you need it."

It occurred to Finley that controlling the drone through Honeycutt was not a great idea. He should have had a radio linked directly to the Coast Guard so he knew what the hell was going on. He looked at the cell phone in his hand. Or...

"Howard, can you patch the drone operator through your phone so that he's on with us in real time? Relaying orders through you is too slow."

Honeycutt blew out air. "Shit, should have thought of that. Hold on." There was another moment's pause, then a crackle and Honeycutt was back. "Frank, I've got Ensign Kauders on the line. He is supervising the drone operator. I believe you've met."

"Good to have you here, Ensign Kauders. Howard, where are the ground cars?" Finley asked.

"I've got one car about two miles behind you to the south and catching up. I've got another man in a car five miles to the north and coming towards you. The road is partially flooded up there, so they're moving slow."

Finley tried to picture it in his mind. The town of Orland was about four miles north of him, so the DEA car coming from the north had not yet reached the town. There was only one major turnoff between him and Orland that the hit men might take, but there were numerous, unmarked dirt roads that ran off for miles into the woods. Once back there, the drone would never find them in this storm.

Simple solution: he had to bring the bad guys to him.

"Howard, here's what I'm going to do." Even as he explained his plan, he dropped the car into gear and raced towards the Rte. 199 junction. He knew this road like the back of his hand. The junction sat at the top of a low rise. Going north, the ground sloped down for two miles, at least. If he could make it to the top of the rise and they saw him, he might be able to lure them back.

Flooring it, he sped as best he could through the rain until he reached the Rte. 199 junction, then braked hard, doused his headlights and turned on his emergency blinkers. Even in the storm, the blinkers would be visible for some distance. To his right, down a long driveway, was a trailer that had been mounted on a permanent foundation. Across the street to his left was an old vegetable stand, just as he recalled it, still boarded up, waiting for warmer weather. He got his hat and rain slicker, holstered his Glock and grabbed the rifle and the spare ammo magazines. He carefully turned off the interior lights, then opened the door and sprinted across the street and took position, crouching behind the vegetable stand.

And waited.

———————

Diego studied the tracking data on the laptop. Finley was finally moving faster, now. "Keep it slow," he cautioned Hugo. "We've got to make sure he overtakes us."

"You better get in back now," Hugo reminded him, eyes in his rearview mirror.

Diego nodded and moved agilely into the back seat, where he checked the AK-47 one last time, then reached in front and picked up the laptop. In the rearview mirror, Hugo spotted some headlights crest the rise a mile or so behind them.

Then the headlights went out. A moment later he could dimly make out emergency blinkers flashing wetly through the gloom.

Hugo frowned in confusion. "Diego, check the tracker," he ordered. "Where is the bastard?"

Diego hurriedly dropped the rifle and opened up the laptop. "He's stopped again." He turned around and looked through the rear window.

"Can't tell for sure, but I think that's him up on the hill there. Got his flashers on."

Hugo swore under his breath. Every minute they drove took them further and further away from their target.

"Do you think he just broke down?" Diego asked uncertainly.

Hugo had no idea, but he couldn't kill his target by driving away from it. He swung the wheel hard and turned around until the car was heading south on Rte. 15. "Get ready, if it's him, we are going to do it right now," he warned Diego.

He slowed the car to thirty miles per hour and they drove towards the flashing lights. In the back seat, Diego lowered the rear window and readied the AK-47.

From his vantage behind the vegetable stand, Finley watched as the suspect car made a U-turn and came towards him.

"Howard, did you see that? They made a U-turn! They're coming back," he shouted into the phone. His heart was racing now and his mouth was suddenly dry.

"Drone is over the car," Honeycutt assured him.

"Keep it high enough so that they can't hear it," Finley warned.

"It's almost one thousand feet," Ensign Kauders chimed in. "With all the rain, I don't think they can hear much of anything."

"Where are the backup cars?" Finley demanded.

"South car is about two minutes out," Honeycutt told him. "North car is about five minutes."

Not much help, Finley groused to himself. He peeked out again from behind the vegetable stand – the bad guys were only a couple of hundred yards away. "They're almost here!" he shouted into the phone. "About to engage!"

"Frank," Honeycutt said sternly. "We could be wrong about this car. Do not fire until they fire first! We can't risk killing some innocent civilians."

Great. Just great, Finley thought sourly. He stuffed the phone inside his jacket pocket and moved to the right-hand side of the vegetable stand, so he would have it between him and the approaching car. Within seconds he could hear it moving at slow speed and see the area brighten under its headlights. He dropped to one knee and brought the rifle to his shoulder, resting his elbow on his raised knee. His right knee was instantly soaked with cold water, but the ballcap kept the rain out of his eyes.

"Don't stop," he whispered to the strange car. "Just keep driving by."

In North Harbor, Alejandro and Javier waited at the entrance to the street Finley lived on. Rain beat steadily against the windshield, obscuring them from any passersby, but also making their surveillance more difficult.

"What time is it?" Alejandro asked irritably.

"Bit after five," Javier replied.

"Where is that fucking kid?" Alejandro was annoyed. They could have killed the woman twice over and be done with it if they weren't waiting for the son to come home from school.

Javier shrugged. "Maybe he belongs to a club at school or something. Give it another ten or fifteen minutes, then we'll go in and take care of the old lady. We can pop the woman and wait for the kid just as easy inside as here."

"Ten minutes," Alejandro said. "My ass hurts from all this sitting."

"*Claro, claro,*" Javier said. He hated it when Alejandro got into a bad mood. It was like being in a closet with a bad-tempered scorpion – no good could come of it.

As they approached the stopped police car, Hugo strained to see if anyone was inside, but the windows were slightly tinted and the rain covered them. He wasn't worried they had been spotted. They had trailed Finley mostly out of his sight, and now were coming from an entirely different direction than they had been traveling earlier. Plus, he wasn't getting any vibe from the car, nothing that suggested danger.

Still...

"This is the right car, yes?" he asked Diego.

Diego glanced at the laptop for confirmation. "Tracker says it is," he confirmed.

"Okay, I'm not stopping, but when we get there, I'll slow down a bit to give you a better shot."

"I'm ready," Diego said, rifle to his shoulder. He was calm now. It was one of the reasons he had been picked for the hit squad. He clicked off the safety. He had a banana clip feeding the rifle, so he could hose down the front compartment something fierce.

Hugo eased off on the gas pedal a bit.

Fifty yards.

Forty.

Thirty. He slowed down even more.

Twenty.

"Get ready!" he shouted to Diego, who had been ready since they made the U-turn.

Ten.

Hugo tapped the brake as they pulled abreast of the Ford Police Interceptor.

Diego opened fire on full automatic, emptying one clip and quickly replacing it with another. The Ford's driver window shattered with a dozen holes in it and fell into the car. The passenger side window blew out, then the rear left window disappeared. The car rocked with the impact of sixty high-velocity rounds. A small fire started under the dashboard, creating eerie, flickering shadows that gave the impression of movement.

The second magazine emptied and the bolt locked back.

Hugo brought the car to a complete stop. The two leaned out to look at the smoking ruin.

"*Madre de Dios!* I think he's still alive," Javier cursed as he saw a flickering shadow. He reached for another magazine.

From his kneeling position sixty feet south of the two hitmen, Finley opened up with his AR-15. It was not a fully automatic weapon, like the hitmen's AK-47, so it only fired one shot with every trigger pull. But it was fast enough.

The first twelve bullets riddled the back seat, where he had clearly seen the flash of the AK-47's firing. One of the rounds passed cleanly through Diego's neck, blowing out his carotid artery from back to front. Diego dropped the rifle and clawed at his throat with both hands, but it was already too late. A half inch of his artery had been shredded by the bullet and blood was pumping out faster than Diego could stop it. His brain reacted to the abrupt loss of blood pressure by promptly shutting down and he slumped forward, his head lolling out the window and blood splattering to the ground.

Finley emptied the first 30-round magazine in just under twenty seconds, dropped the magazine and slipped in the second one, then opened fire again.

In his excitement, he shot a little high. Hugo opened the car door and threw himself to the ground, safe for the moment from Finley's barrage.

He peered under the car trying to spot the bastard who ambushed them, and saw the rifle flashes near some sort of hut across the street. Holding his .45 caliber two inches off the road, he fired five times.

Finley heard the sickening *"zippppp!"* of the shots passing by on his left, and dove right, rolling and coming up on his stomach. His eyes were blinking stars from the muzzle flash of the .45, and shook his head in a vain effort to clear his vision. *Fuck it.* Aiming as best he could, he emptied his magazine at the space underneath the car, and was rewarded with a grunt of pain from the other side. There were two more shots from the Cartel hit man, neither close. Finley rolled two more times, managing to give himself vertigo, then crawled rapidly behind a pile of wooden pallets.

In the distance, the sound of a siren.

Hurry up, Finley pleaded. *Hurry up!*

The Cartel hitman fired four more shots at the spot where Finley had been until just a moment ago. Finley did not fire back, but kept his position behind the stack of wooden pallets, waiting for a clear shot. Then a State Police cruiser skidded to a stop fifty feet from the two cars involved in the firefight. Finley frowned; it wasn't Honeycutt's man, it was just a State cop responding to gunshots.

A young State Police officer leapt from the car, weapon drawn. His car blocked any clear shot from the Cartel gunman...hopefully.

"Get down!" Finley shouted. "He's between the two cars!"

The State cop dimly saw Finley in the dark shadows behind the pallets...and the unmistakable shape of a rifle. Instantly, he swiveled and pointed his weapon at Finley. "Drop your weapon! Drop your weapon or I will fire!" he screamed.

"I'm a cop!" Finley screamed back. "The gunman is between the two cars! Don't expose yourself!"

The young State Trooper, not to be tricked by something as simple as this, screamed, "Drop your weapon or I will shoot you!"

"Jesus God!" Finley snarled to himself. This was a nightmare. "Goddammit, I'm a cop with the North Harbor Police Department! I'm--," but he was suddenly interrupted by a voice from between the cars.

"Officer, watch out!" Hugo called in a deep, authoritative voice without any trace of a Dominican accent. "That man is a hitman for the mob. He tried to ambush me. My name is Frank Finley of the North Harbor police. I'm wounded or I could show you my badge. Be very careful; that man is dangerous!"

When he first heard the second voice, the State Trooper wheeled around to point his gun at the two cars, but he couldn't see Hugo. "Where are you? Show me your hands!" Then he swiveled desperately back to Finley, then back again in the direction of the new voice, then back to Finley.

It was a game he would have to lose and all three men there knew it.

"For the love of Christ," Finley shouted. "Stay behind your vehicle and call for backup!"

"Officer, don't let him get away!" Hugo shouted in return. "Call for your backup, but keep him pinned down!"

The young State Trooper pivoted back and forth between the two voices one more time. Had he been more experienced, he would have known to slide to the rear of his vehicle and call in reinforcements. But he was young and new at the job, and knowing that there was a man with a rifle out there in the gathering gloom spooked him.

Stepping to the right, the State Trooper slid into his vehicle, reaching for the radio with one hand and his Bushmaster XM15 with the other. The Bushmaster was an assault rifle that was almost a clone of the AR-15 Finley carried. Thus occupied, he never saw Hugo stand up and fire five .45 caliber rounds through his windshield. One struck him squarely in his vest, one blew away his lower jaw and one took him squarely in the throat. Hugo ducked back out of sight just as Finley got his rifle up and fired an angry fusillade, hitting nothing.

"Goddammit to hell!" Finley shouted, looking at the blood-splattered State Trooper.

"You're next," Hugo taunted.

More sirens. One from the north. One from the south.

One distant. One surprisingly close.

In North Harbor, Alejandro and Javier were growing inpatient.

"The fucking kid must be home already," Alejandro scowled. "Who stays at high school until five o'clock?"

Javier shrugged. He knew nothing about high school. He had dropped out in the sixth grade and learned his trade on the streets. "Maybe there's a shortcut or something. You know, walking. He doesn't have to drive." But he glanced out the window and thought the kid would have to be pretty stupid to walk home in this weather.

Alejandro grunted, then took out his pistol and pulled back on the slide until he saw brass, then released it. "Let's go," he said shortly. "I'm tired of waiting."

Javier nodded and checked his pistol. Alejandro started the car and turned into the long drive to Finley's house. They were both relieved to finally be doing something.

———————

Finley got on the phone and called Honeycutt. As soon as he answered, Finley said, "Howard, tell your man arriving at the shooting scene that I am hiding behind some wooden pallets to the left of the road. Got that, west side of the road. The asshole will call out to him and tell him that's he's me. Tell your man not to fall for it or he'll end up as dead as the State Trooper who fell for it five minutes ago."

"Frank?" Honeycutt said, trying to catch up.

"Just do it, Howard," Finley said urgently. "Your guy is coming from the south and will be here in a few seconds. Hurry!" He cut the connection. He paused, suddenly caught by the sensation that he was missing something. Something important.

Then the DEA agent arrived in a black SUV, at first parking close to the two bullet-ridden cars, but then abruptly reversing and backing up quickly to a distance of forty feet or so and turning so that the car would shield the driver when he got out. *Must have gotten the call from Howard*, Finley thought with satisfaction.

The other siren was still closing in.

Finley's phone rang. It was Honeycutt. "Frank, I've got you on a conference call with Michael London," Honeycutt said primly, as if this were a business conference and he was introducing Finley to a potential business partner.

"London, can you get over to the east side of the two cars and keep this guy from escaping that way?" Finley asked.

In response, the SUV backed up and straightened out, then moved closer to the cars and turned on its high beams. The two cars were lit up as if by floodlights. Finley could see the driver get out and, crouching, duck walk to the rear of the car and take up position.

"I've got a clear view of the east side of the police car," London said calmly. "The road's clear for about thirty feet on the east side, then there's some scrub brush. If he tries to get across, I'll nail him."

"Okay," Finley breathed, the knot in his gut relaxing just a little bit. "He's got a pistol, a .45 I think. They initially shot at me with some sort of assault rifle on full auto, but I must of hit the guy with the rifle, because this asshole has been shooting by himself."

"You want to rush him, or wait for Bobby?" London asked.

Honeycutt broke in. "That's Robert Lubik," he said. "The drone shows him about two minutes from you."

"Let's wait," Finley said. "This guy's good. He played the State Trooper, then nailed him. London, what are you using?"

London chuckled. "I've got an HK416 and the love of Baby Jesus right here in my pocket."

Finley shook his head at the old movie reference. The DEA agent was a film buff. "Auto or semi-auto?"

"Full auto."

"Okay, I've got a semi-auto AR-15 and two mags left. We outgun this guy, but I really want to take him alive."

"You really think this guy is going to surrender?" London asked skeptically.

Finley doubted it, but wanted to try. He needed information.

Hugo crept behind the police car to see if he could get away into the woods or something, only to discover there were no woods. Instead, there was a wide, sandy area that would leave him completely exposed, and after that some low scrub that wasn't much better. Then the next cop arrived and turned his headlights on his escape route.

"Fuck me," Hugo muttered. He crawled back to the rental car, ignoring the sight of Diego's bloody head sticking out of the window. For the first time he noticed that the barrel of the AK-47 was also protruding from the window. That might help. He glanced quickly through the window to where Finley was hiding, but couldn't see anything. Snatching the AK-47, he ducked back down and examined it. Seemed to be in working order. He popped out the magazine, but couldn't tell how many rounds were left. Snapped it back into place and holstered his pistol.

Hugo was resigned to the fact that he would probably die here. It was always going to be a day like this – rain and dark and what should have been a simple hit turned into a clusterfuck. It had to happen eventually. He shrugged. Fuck it. It was what it was. Now the thing was to go down fighting. He could hear the third car coming and knew he had to act while the odds were only two-to-one. Crossing the open space behind the police car was suicide, so he'd charge straight at Finley, and if Lady Luck threw him a bone, he just might take the bastard out before he died.

Deep breath, then he was up and running. Not yelling. Silent as an owl, the steady rain muffling the sound of his feet. Running, gun up, towards the wooden pallets where he last saw Finley. Just a little further.

Still nothing. Still nothing. Then he was around the side of the pallets, firing the AK-47 behind the pallets until the magazine ran dry, then drawing his pistol and–

————————

Later, Finley would never be able to recall what alerted him. He was watching the hitmen's car through an opening between two of the stacked pallets. It was getting dark fast. The only discernable noise was the steady drumbeat of the rain and the siren of the second DEA agent, less than a mile away. He was thinking what he would do if he were the hitman, hearing more reinforcements coming, knowing he was trapped.

Then, without any conscious thought, he scurried around the corner of the pallets so he was on the east side, not the south side where he had been hiding. While he was still wondering why he moved, a fusillade of bullets raked the ground where he had been.

Then, a pause as the hitman's assault rifle ran out of bullets.

Finley popped up, his AR-15 to his shoulder and the gunman was there, right there, five feet away, caught in the process of drawing his pistol out of his holster.

Finley instinctively fired, stitching three rounds into the man's chest, then watched in consternation as the man crumbled. Christ, no! Had to keep this guy alive. He scrambled back around the corner of the pallets and kicked the man's rifle and pistol away. Blood bubbled on the man's lips with each labored breath, but when he saw Finley, he spat.

"*Pinche culero!*" he coughed, spraying the air with blood. He smirked at Finley through bloody lips. "Too late for your family, *pendejo!*"

Finley stared at him, ice in his bowels. "What? What?" He shook the man. "What about my family?"

But the hitman was dead.

The DEA agents, London and Lubik, stood over him, weapons in hand, glancing around to make sure no one else was in play near them. "You okay?" London asked. Finley looked at him, stricken. Then he ran to the police car he had driven from North Harbor, stopping only when he saw the two flat tires and the numerous holes in the engine.

"They're trying to kill my family!" he shouted at the two astonished DEA agents. "I need you to drive me back!"

London didn't say anything, just ran to his car and turned it around. Finley piled into the passenger seat and they accelerated back towards North Harbor, siren blaring and lights flashing, going much too fast for safety. Finley dug out his phone again and called his wife.

No answer.

He cut the connection and tried his father-in-law, Luc Dumas. The phone rang and rang...but there was no answer.

"Call the North Harbor police?" Agent London suggested.

Finley shook his head. "For all I know, it *is* the North Harbor police at my house right now."

"Honeycutt?" London asked.

Finley called him and Honeycutt picked up on the first ring. "Frank!" Honeycutt was shouting. "I've sent a team, but they're coming from Ellsworth and won't get there until after you do. I also called the Coast Guard in Rockland. They're launching in a couple of minutes. It's only a five minute flight for them. Where are you?"

Finley realized he had no idea. He glanced at London.

"We're taking Hinkley Ridge Road to Rte. 177 south, bypassing Blue Hill," the DEA agent said crisply, driving way too fast for the poor conditions. "Tell him we're about three miles from turning south onto Rte. 176."

Finley relayed the information, but he fought back a scream of despair. They were still thirty minutes from North Harbor.

They were going to be too late.

———————

Danielle stepped out of the shower, toweling her hair dry. She slipped into some yoga pants and a fleece pullover. Calvin and Gabrielle were in the kitchen, hopefully starting dinner. Danielle was still musing over what it meant that her youngest child was old enough to be having sex, but she thanked her lucky stars that Gabrielle seemed to have a good head on her shoulders. Danielle was very sure of one thing: if women – or girls – relied on men to responsibly use birth control, the population of Maine would double within five years.

She was just putting on some sneakers when she distantly heard the sound of a car door closing. Not in the driveway, but nearby. Was Frank stopping by for a quick dinner? He did that sometimes, but usually told her in advance. She went to the window and peeked out. The driveway was empty. She glanced down at her parent's house, but their driveway was empty as well. Frowning a little, she leaned into the window and looked to the right, towards the main road. There was a dark car parked on the entrance road about fifty yards away. Two men were at the back of the car, taking something from the trunk. When they shut the trunk, each was holding something with the unmistakable long shape of a shotgun.

Danielle felt her heartbeat double in her chest. For a moment, she was absolutely paralyzed with fear. But Frank had warned her this day might come, and trained her for when it did. He had made her practice. Before the boys were born, he would walk into the living room, smile at her pleasantly, then bark, "Move your ass, Danni, there's a man with a gun coming up the walk!" And as she ran around the house, grabbing a weapon from the closet and fumbling with the magazine, he would chant, "Fast is slow, my love. Slow is fast. Ready your weapon! They've come to kill a mousy housewife, but instead Danielle Dumas Finley is waiting!"

Shaking off the paralysis, she went to the top of the stairs and urgently called down to Calvin and Gabrielle. "Calvin! Calvin! It's balloon time! No joke. Come upstairs now!" 'Balloon time' was the code word. If she or Frank ever used that phrase, the boys were to do exactly what she said. Immediately.

Praying that Calvin and Gabrielle hadn't snuck out for another bout of teenage sex, she retraced her steps to the bedroom and went to the closet. She pulled out the Sportical, then reached in and grabbed three 15-round magazines, dropping one in the process.

"Slow is fast," she muttered. "Slow is fast." She inserted the magazine the way Frank had taught her, then racked the slide to chamber a round and flipped off the safety.

She turned around to find Calvin gaping at her with wide eyes. "Two men are coming up the driveway with guns," she told him. "Get the pistol in the closet and load it. Take extra magazines. Hurry!" Calvin gulped, then did as he was told. The son of a policeman, he had been taught about guns at an early age.

Gabrielle, meanwhile, stared at her disbelievingly.

"Gabrielle," Danielle said briskly. "You get in the closet and shut the door. Don't come out unless I tell you it's okay. Do you understand?"

Pale and trembling, the girl nodded and went to the closet. Calvin was just coming out and they shared a quick, intense hug.

"You'll be okay," he whispered. "I'll come and get you when it's over."

Gabrielle almost asked him to promise, then decided that was pretty stupid. "I know you will," she whispered back, then turned quickly and went into the closet.

Where she saw that Calvin had left the gun safe open.

In the hallway Danielle told Calvin what she wanted him to do, then pulled out her phone again and hit speed dial. The phone on the other end rang three times and a deep voice answered. Danielle felt a wave of relief wash over her.

"Dad?" she said.

Ensign Kauders ran pell-mell for the Jayhawk helicopter, already spooling up on the takeoff pad. Close behind, Petty Officers First Class Josephs and Santana followed, dressed in ballistic vests and festooned with weapons and a predatory gleam in their eyes. The two of them and the flight crew were the only ones Ensign Kauders could round up on thirty seconds notice. He hadn't even been able to call Commander Mello.

It was the height of taking the initiative, or foolhardy recklessness, to commandeer a helicopter and a strike team, even a small one, with the intent of taking a flight to a civilian house in the middle of a city. Kauders wondered briefly if this was the end of his career.

He hoped not; he'd miss all these incredibly neat toys.

The pilot was Chief Warrant Officer Emily Waring, a no-nonsense woman who, truth be told, intimidated the hell out of Kauders.

Chief Warrant Officer Waring eyed the heavily-armed Santana and Josephs warily, then turned her gaze to Kauders. "Where are we going, Ensign, and what should I expect when we get there?"

Ensign Kauders took a deep breath. Waring was within her rights to refuse to take off without proper authorization from someone much more senior than a mere Ensign. "Chief, you know we've been working with the DEA and Maine to interdict heroin deliveries, right?"

Chief Warrant Officer Waring exchanged a glance with her co-pilot, and then nodded.

"One of the cops in the North Harbor police has been cooperating closely with us," Kauders explained. "The Sinaloa Cartel tried to kill him tonight, just a few minutes ago. I just got an emergency call from the DEA Regional Director that the Cartel has sent killers to the cop's house to kill his family."

Waring's eyes narrowed. "Why not call the local police?"

Ensign Kauders shook his head. "We think they're bought and paid for."

Chief Warrant Officer Emily Waring took a deep breath and blew it out. "Jesus H. Christ!" she muttered under her breath. Then, "Strap in everybody! Ensign Kauders, would you be so kind as to tell me where the fuck we're going?"

Kauders gave her the GPS coordinates.

"Joey, put it on the screen," Waring told her co-pilot, and then to her passengers: "Hold onto your balls, children! We'll be there in five minutes!" Then she pulled back hard on the collective and goosed the throttle. The Jayhawk leapt upwards. She adjusted the cyclic and the copter shot forward like a sprinter coming out of the blocks.

Behind her helmet visor, Chief Warrant Officer Waring sported a huge grin. *Yeah*, this was going to be a *good* night!

———

Calvin dragged the mattress to the top of the stairs, then pushed it down. It slid about halfway down, then wedged itself tight.

Good.

He ran back to his parent's bedroom and got the overstuffed easy chair, dragging it to the top of the stairs, then tumbled it down. It half-turned and bumped down several steps until it reached the top of the mattress, then stopped. Calvin stepped back as his mother stepped past him and threw a nightstand and a large laundry basket down the stairs, followed by a stand lamp.

"Let's get another mattress," she whispered urgently.

Then the doorbell rang.

———

Alejandro and Javier got the shotguns out of the car, checked the loads and walked quietly down the street. The house they were after was only fifty yards on the left. Two stories, with an attached garage on the side. Lights were burning in several windows. Further down on the right, there was a larger house, brightly lit. Neither of them knew who lived in that house, but it was understood that if they gave them any trouble, they would die as well.

They stepped over a small wooden fence and walked through the yard to the front door. Alejandro raised his foot to kick it in, but Javier touched him on the arm, then reached past him to ring the doorbell. Alejandro frowned, but Javier shrugged. "They come to the door and open it," he said reasonably. "If it's the boy, we kill him, then go get the mother. If it's the mother, we force her inside."

But there was no answer. Javier rang the bell a second time. Waited. Then stepped back.

Alejandro kicked the door in and they entered, moving fast and guns at the ready.

And found themselves facing a stairway, barricaded with a mattress and pieces of furniture, effectively blocking the way to the second floor. The two men exchanged a bewildered glance, then Alejandro gestured to Javier to check the rest of the bottom floor. Javier was back in a minute, signaling all was clear.

Alejandro sighed and looked at the blocked stairway. "Mrs. Finley," he called up. "I am Officer Nick Spears from the North Harbor police. We received a call from your husband that you were in danger and my partner and I have been sent here for your protection."

Upstairs, Calvin and Danielle looked at each other. Calvin raised his eyebrows in question, but Danielle shook her head and put a finger to her lips. Calvin dug out his phone. "Police?" he mouthed to his mother.

Danielle shook her head violently.

Calvin nodded, then dialed another number, cupped his hand over the phone and spoke quickly into it. Danielle could hear their address being given. "And send an ambulance!" Calvin concluded. "Hurry!" Then he hung up, looked at her and smiled, pleased with himself.

Downstairs, Alejandro and Javier could hear a footfall or so, but nothing else. They were up there, all right. Alejandro shook his head. This was taking too long. The bitch should be dead by now and he and Javier should be in the car and gone. "Cover me," he told Javier, then began pulling the mattress out of the way. He was a big bull of a man, and the mattress came easily. As it came, the easy chair on top of it shifted and then tumbled down, forcing Alejandro to skip to one side, exposing himself ever so slightly to anyone at the top of the stairs.

Danielle fired four quick shots, then ducked back as a shotgun boomed and an impressive amount of the ceiling plaster exploded above her.

"Mom!" Calvin cried.

Danielle waved a hand to show she was okay, and put a finger to her lips to keep him quiet. Calvin nodded.

More of the odds and ends blocking the stairs shifted and abruptly tumbled down to the bottom. Danielle ducked her head out, then pulled back. Now the bottom was clogged, but the rest of the stairway was clear. But the clogged bottom proved to be false security. Javier motioned to Alejandro, who fired three blasts from his shotgun up the staircase, splintering the wooden bannister near the top and suppressing any attempt at return fire.

Javier nimbly leapt over the nightstand and other crap at the bottom and quickly, quietly crept up the stairs, keeping the muzzle of his shotgun aimed at the bottom of the bannister, waiting for a shadow to signal that someone was moving in for a shot.

Something flew over the bannister and Javier reflexively shot it. The flower vase exploded in midair, but it was immediately followed by a lamp, a partially full humidifier and yet another nightstand. Javier shot once more before he got himself under control, but while the nightstand was crashing onto the stairs at his feet, Danielle leaned over the railing and shot him twice in the chest, then ducked back as Alejandro took a chunk out of the wall with two blasts of his shotgun.

"Por Dios!" Javier screamed, clutching his wounds. "Fuck!" Blood poured from between his fingers.

Luc Dumas stared disbelievingly at the phone. He struggled to focus on what his daughter was saying to him. When she hung up, he grunted as if he had been gut shot. Breathing hard, feeling the adrenalin pouring into his body, he ran to the closet where he kept the shotgun. He fumbled with the shells, dropping several in his haste to load the gun. Céline hovered nearby, concern distorting her face.

"Luc, what is it?" she cried.

"Danni's in trouble," he panted, his face flushed and his breath coming hard. "Two men with guns are walking up to the house."

Céline's hand flew to her mouth. "What are you doing? Why don't you call the police?"

"That's the problem," Dumas rasped. "It might be the police." He stood, trying to catch his breath. "Call Frank! Tell him what's happening."

Before she could reply, he ran out the door.

Enraged, Alejandro emptied his shotgun into the top of the stairs, climbing one step with each shot. He made it to the top just as he ran out of shells, dropped the shotgun and snatched his pistol out of his belt. Firing two more quick rounds through the bannister rails, he crouched at the top of the stairs.

The hallway was empty.

There were four doors, all closed.

Then the front door slammed open and a big man with a beard burst into the foyer. Without a moment's hesitation, Alejandro spun and shot four times. The man staggered back into the wall, then lurched out the front door into the yard.

Alejandro shook his head. Had he hit him? He was sure he had, could picture the wounds blossoming on the man's chest. Who the fuck was he? Where had he come from? He glanced back at Javier – his brother's oldest son – who was unconscious or dead, crumbled on the stairs like a discarded toy. He glanced back at the shotgun, but he knew he couldn't take the time to retrieve and load it. Hefting the pistol in his hand, he crouched low and inched along the corridor. The first two doors were directly across from each other. No matter what he did, he was going to have his back to one room or the other. He considered his next move, then took a second to drop his partially spent magazine and replace it with a fresh one.

Leaning against the left wall, he aimed at the door across the hall and rapidly fired four shots, the last one through the plaster wall to the right of the door. Then he wheeled around and kicked in the door on the left, ducking in fast and moving to the left, gun panning the room from right to left and back again.

Nothing.

Cautiously peeking out into the corridor, he thought he heard a muffled cough from one of the other rooms, but he couldn't tell which one. Aiming carefully, he fired four more rounds through the door at the very end of the corridor, then stepped across the hallway and kicked in the door there.

Nothing.

Frowning, he started to step back into the corridor...and froze. In the distance, he could hear sirens. A bunch of them, getting closer. Then another sound caught his attention, getting louder by the moment. A helicopter? Who in God's name had a helicopter?

Out of nowhere, three bullets shot through the door at the end of the corridor, whizzing just in front of him at head height with a "SNAAPPPP!!!" sound that told him he missed death by mere inches. Shifting his gun to his left hand, he sent two more rounds through the far door. But now the sounds of the sirens and the damn helicopter were roaring outside, obscuring any of the little sounds that might give away where the bitch and her son were hiding. Fighting off panic, Alejandro bolted to the stairs and ran down to the first floor, stepping over the body of Javier. He ran to the front door, paused to peer outside and saw an ambulance and a firetruck, where half a dozen firemen were milling about in confusion.

He ran past two medics treating the big man with the beard, pausing to shoot one of them. Chaos, he needed chaos if he was going to get out of this mess. Two firemen saw him and recoiled, shouting and pointing. He snapped off two shots at the men, sending one shrieking to the ground.

He needed a vehicle. No way he was going to steal the ambulance or the fire engine. His heart leapt. Yes! His car was still there. Turning to the right, he dropped a magazine and inserted a fresh one. His last one. He ran hard towards the car, glancing over his shoulder to see if anyone was pursuing. Then he looked forward.

And there were two men dressed as soldiers, not forty feet in front of him. Alejandro skidded to a stop, raising his pistol to fire.

And died.

There one moment, just a bag of meat and blood the next. Two 5.56 mm rounds took him just below the eye and in his forehead. No pain. No shock.

Just gone. Nothing.

———————

Upstairs, Danielle jerked opened the bedroom door and stepped quickly aside. Several feet behind her, half-hidden behind a dresser, Calvin kept his weapon trained on the doorway, listening intently for any footsteps that would reveal the gunman's position.

Shots rang outside, and the boy and his mother exchanged a glance. "He ran for it," Danielle said. Calvin stepped past her and then stopped, looking in horror at the holes through the bedroom door where Gabrielle was hiding.

"Gabs! Gabrielle? Are you okay?" he screamed.

The door opened and Gabrielle stood there, still holding the 9 mm pistol she'd found in the gun safe.

Her heart lurching, Danielle went to the slender girl, this woman-child who had captured her son's heart, and put her arms around her. Calvin joined them and the three of them hugged each in a tight embrace.

"We made it!" Danielle said. "We're alive!" She looked at each of them. "Remember what you learned today," she whispered forcefully. "Sometimes...sometimes you have to stand and fight. For yourselves and the ones you love. Never forget that." She pulled them in tight again, fierce and protective and ready to take on the whole damn world.

"I know you wanted me to hide," Gabrielle said apologetically. "But when I heard that guy in the hallway, I tried to get him by shooting through the door. Almost worked, too."

Calvin looked at her in astonishment.

"What?" Gabrielle demanded. "My brother Peter showed me how to use a gun." She glared at him.

"Jesus Christ!" Calvin said, half in awe and half something he couldn't put into words.

"My gun is safed," she retorted. "Is *yours*?"

Outside, Petty Officer First Class Josephs lowered his carbine. No doubt the man was dead, he'd seen the bullets strike him in the head.

Santana stood next to him, his carbine still up to his shoulder. "Sonofabitch, you beat me by no more than a second!"

Josephs grunted a laugh. "I always do."

Ensign Kauders stepped up next to them. "Nice shooting, Mr. Josephs. Please tell me you had your camera running."

Josephs pulled a face. "Always do, sir. Always do."

Ensign Kauders breathed out a sigh of relief. Men under his command had shot and killed someone, so his ass was on the line. There was a chance, a small chance, that since his men had been instrumental in stopping the dangerous criminal from escaping – he thought for a moment and decided that *"vicious killer"* was a more apt description – that he might survive this with his career intact. Having the video would be a plus.

At that point, one of the ambulance paramedics came running up to him. "You the guy who came in with that Jayhawk?" he asked breathlessly.

Kauders nodded.

The medic jerked his thumb over his shoulder. "I got an elderly man here with three bullet wounds and what looks to me like a heart attack," he explained. "Also, the fucking bastard you put down shot my partner. We need to load them in your helicopter and get 'em to Bangor if they're going to make it."

"Are they stable enough for the flight?"

"Shit, they're both dying!" the medic shouted. "I'll go with them and keep them alive, but we've got to move!"

They moved. Two minutes later, Chief Warrant Officer Emily Waring pulled back on the collector and they lifted off, bound for the Eastern Maine Medical Center, forty-five miles away as the Jayhawk flies. She carried one emergency paramedic, shot through the lung, and one elderly sculptor, shot in the hip, shoulder and left hand, and suffering from a stress-induced heart attack.

She hummed contentedly to herself as she accelerated to 160 knots.

On the ground, Danielle and her mother stood side-by-side, hugging each other, watching as the helicopter disappeared into the night sky.

Frank Finley arrived ten minutes later. Danielle fell into his arms and for a long minute they just held on and cried. Finally, she pulled back, wiping her tears with the back of her hands, then finding a handkerchief to blow her nose.

"It worked, Frank, everything you planned," she told him, half grinning, half sobbing. "It saved our lives."

He pulled her close again, hugging her as if afraid to let her go, which was exactly the case.

"You'd be proud of Calvin," she whispered in his ear. "When I told him it wasn't safe to call the police, he called the fire department and told them to send an engine and an ambulance. It was when the killer heard the sirens that he finally gave it up and ran."

Then, abruptly, she pulled away again. "But who called the helicopter? And who are they?" she demanded, pointing to Ensign Kauders and his two men.

Finley grinned. "The Coast Guard. Howard called them and they sent the cavalry."

Danielle sighed. "Okay...okay. Listen, I've got to take Mom to the Medical Center in Bangor to see about Dad. Will you stay here with Calvin and Gabrielle?"

"Yeah, of course," he said distractedly, his mind overloading with all that had happened.

"And Frank," she said softly. "Remind me to tell you about Calvin and Gabrielle, but in the meantime, you be real nice to her."

She kissed him softly on the mouth and then left to find her mother. Another crisis to face.

Finley stared after her. *Tell him what about Gabrielle and Calvin?*

———

The first police car from the North Harbor police arrived fifteen minutes after that. Officer Burrows, one of Chief Corcoran's bully boys, stepped out and carefully put on his hat and hitched up his pants. He spotted Finley and walked over to him, hands on his hips, then made a parody of looking around at the ambulance and the fire engine, their lights still flashing.

"Finley, you mind tellin' me what the fuck you are up to?" he scowled.

———

The police sealed off the house with crime tape, so Finley and Calvin trudged over to the grandparents' house. It was after midnight before Finley got to bed. Calvin had taken Gabrielle home and Finley heard him return a few minutes later.

Calvin stopped at his father's bedroom door.

"Your mom said you were great tonight. Calling the fire department was pretty clever," Finley said, studying his son closely. "You okay?"

Calvin took a deep breath and blew it out forcibly. "I guess. I'm not really sure. It doesn't seem real. I mean, Mom was incredible, but when the shooting started I-" He paused. "It just didn't seem real. It still doesn't."

Worried that his son was suffering slightly from shock, Finley swung out of bed and found a robe. But then another thought struck him. "Calvin, do you know where Jacob is?"

Calvin blinked for a moment. "Oh, geez, Dad, I forgot. Jacob called just before the men broke into the house. He said he was going to sleep over at a friend's tonight and go to work from there in the morning." Calvin looked embarrassed. "He'll call me on his way to work; he always does."

Finley looked at the clock on the nightstand. It was already 12:30 a.m. He would talk to Jacob in the morning. He turned his attention back to his younger son, who looked pale and wane in the hallway light. "Calvin, how about you and me have some hot cocoa with a shot of your Grandfather's best whiskey in it? I think we could both use it."

When Finley woke the next morning, Jacob had already left a message that he'd gone into work early and would call them when he got back to the dock that afternoon. Finley tried to reach him, but the call rolled over to Jacob's answering machine.

No matter, he'd talk to his son later in the day.

Sometimes it is the littlest things that make all the difference.

Chapter 44
Wednesday Night

At the docks, Paul Dumas sat in his office and watched as the *Celeste, Samantha* and *Rosie's Pride* steamed past the seawall and into the harbor, using spotlights to help them navigate the passage. The boats showed signs of the storm, with some torn lines and loose equipment sloshing around the deck. One cabin window was sporting a crack Dumas hadn't seen before. His office wall clock said 6:45 p.m., much too late for boats returning from an ordinary day's lobstering.

He watched as the crews tied up the boats and stumbled tiredly down the dock through the rain and the wind. There was one man he didn't recognize, not one of the locals who had sailed with LeBlanc for years. A hard-looking man who triggered a very instinctual fight-or-flight response in him. He watched them all as they made their way to the parking lot, then he picked up the phone and called his brother-in-law.

But there was no answer.

Paul Dumas sighed and looked at his watch. He needed to be home for something important soon. Someone important. He shook his head and decided he could tell Frank in the morning.

———————

Banderas got the phone call telling him about the disastrous attempted hits on Finley and his family. He in turn called LeBlanc.

"Jesus Christ! How'd that happen?" LeBlanc roared over the phone.

"Doesn't matter," Banderas said. "What's important is that the men I sent are all dead, so they can't tell the cops nothin'. But it also means that Finley and the DEA are going to be mad as shit, so we got to find the parcels tomorrow and get them delivered."

LeBlanc considered this for a moment, weighing the risks, but he knew he was already committed. The options were to pull it off under the nose of the cops, or risk jail. He sighed, wondering again how he had ever gotten into this mess.

"Okay," he said neutrally. "Okay."

"But we might want some extra insurance, you know?" Banderas continued. "We might want a little bargaining power, just in case."

LeBlanc frowned. "Like what?"

"The Finley kid," Banderas said patiently. "I want you to bring the Finley kid tomorrow, just in case we need him."

"For Christ's sake," LeBlanc said angrily. "If we bring him on board he'll see what we're doing. Hell, if we find a package, he'll know exactly what we're doing. If we manage to sneak the goods off to your people when we return, what's to keep him from going straight to his old man and spilling his guts?"

There was silence on the line for several long moments.

"Hey," Banderas said coldly. "I said I want him with us in case we need him. I never said he had to make it back."

"So when we make the delivery, we kill him," LeBlanc said coldly.

"You got a problem?" Banderas came back. "Maybe you think it's better if we let him go home and tell his fucking father all about this? Become the star witness at our trial?"

"No," LeBlanc said heavily. "No problem." He took a breath. There was no way out of this. And truth be told, he didn't really care anymore. "I'll call him and tell him to be at the docks by 5 a.m."

"You're a good man, Jean-Philippe," Banderas said sardonically. "I knew I could count on you."

Chapter 45
Thursday Morning – Final Search

The *Celeste* slipped its mooring forty minutes before dawn, followed minutes later by her two sister ships. It was the same crew as the day before, but with one addition: Jacob Finley. He had shown up right on time. Once he was on the ship, LeBlanc and Banderas took him to the small storage cabin at the stern of the ship and, before he realized what was happening, gagged him and tied his hands and feet with zip cords.

"Jake, you keep quiet here and don't make a fuss and everything will be okay," LeBlanc assured him. "This is just what we got to do for today." Then he left him and shut the door.

The three boats went out, sailing in an arrowhead formation towards the spot they left off at the day before. They passed Sheldrake Ledge and then Eastern Mark Island, then steered slightly north northeast to pass Shabby Island and give them a clear run for the western shoreline of Swans Island, which they would scour from north to south, then circle it pinging all the way. Swans Island and Isle Au Haut stood like two squat sentries, blocking the path of the Eastern Maine Coastal Current as it moved from northeast to southwest. If one of the drug parcels got that far, it would have to go east or west around them, or even better, ground on one of them. That was the hope at least.

Banderas had been quiet most of the ride, clutching his coffee mug to ward off the morning chill. The loss of his hit team had shaken him badly. He wasn't sure what had bothered him more, the fact that Finley had led one team into an ambush, or that the other team had been bested by a woman, a boy and a girl.

He put down his mug and asked LeBlanc, "Do you want me to fire up the transponder?"

LeBlanc was also in a foul mood. Yesterday's storm had seriously curtailed their search, and with the attempted assassination of Finley, the DEA was sure to be in a frenzy. "No," LeBlanc answered sarcastically. "We're just out here for a bit of fresh air. Of *course* I want you to fire up the transponder!" Banderas' face darkened and LeBlanc was once more reminded that this man was a killer, after all. He picked up his radio mic and called the other ships. "Start mapping now," he ordered.

When they pulled within a thousand meters of Shabby Island, the receiver unit suddenly registered a loud, crisp *"PING!"* It was so unexpected that no one said anything at first, then Banderas thumped his fist hard against the hull. Right on time the transponder sent out a second ping and the drug parcel's unit activated and sent out it's *ping* in reply.

"Where is it?" LeBlanc shouted, still not quite believing that they had located one of the parcels.

"Hold on, I've got a bearing," Banderas said, his earlier mood gone. "*Madre de Dios!* It's almost right in front of us!" He looked up, something approaching joy on his face. "Keep going for ten minutes and we'll get a cross-bearing."

And ten minutes later, they did. "It's right at that little island," Banderas said, pointing not half a mile away. "Has to be."

LeBlanc had sailed these waters since he was five years old. "That's Shabby Island. It's surrounded by a gentle ledge that stays pretty shallow for more than a hundred feet out. Storm could have driven one of the parcels right up onto it. Hell, it could be sitting on dry land by now."

He dispatched the *Samantha* and *Rosie's Pride* to search the rest of the island's coastline, and from there to head for Swans Island. Then he took the *Celeste* in closer to the west side of Shabby Island and pulled out a pair of binoculars.

"Anything?" Banderas asked impatiently.

LeBlanc ignored him, quartering the part of the island he could see with the binoculars and meticulously sweeping over the ground. The pinging from the receiver was getting louder and louder as the waves pushed them closer to shore. He was just beginning to think that it must have hung up under water somewhere...and there it was. Sitting high and mostly dry in a shallow tidal pool. Fifty pounds of some of the best heroin in the world, and perhaps some fentanyl as well. Worth somewhere around $10 to $13 Million.

"There it is," he said calmly. "Parcel Number One."

It took another fifteen minutes of maneuvering and some ballet moves with the throttle and rudder, but LeBlanc finally got the bow of the *Celeste* in about five feet of water. He left one of his brothers at the wheel to keep the boat from drifting onto the rocky ledge – the heroin might be worth $10 Million, but there was no way in hell he was going to scrape the bottom of *his* boat for it – while he and Banderas jumped overboard and waded into the tidal pool.

The package was about eighteen inches high and deep, and almost thirty inches wide. It was sealed in some heavy canvas sheeting that had been carefully stitched, then painted with waterproofing. Attached to the parcel by thick canvas straps was some sort of electrical unit, stored in a plexiglass container that also housed a lithium battery. This was the transponder, LeBlanc realized. This sent out a "ping" when triggered by the acoustic searcher on board the *Celeste*. Staring at the box, which looked for all the world like a delivery box from Amazon, LeBlanc wondered briefly how many people had already died because of the shipment of this one, single box.

He blew out a deep breath. "Give me a hand," he told Banderas.

Banderas snorted contemptuously, then bent over and picked up the fifty-pound box as if it were a box of Christmas chocolates and hoisted it to his shoulder. Together, they waded out to the *Celeste* and lifted the parcel on board, then hoisted themselves over the bow railing. Wordlessly, Banderas carried the parcel into the small pilot's cockpit and placed it on the map table, where he took out a flip knife and cut open the outer canvas layer. Inside was a layer of thick, clear plastic, which had been tightly wrapped around yet another layer, then sealed shut with a generous amount of duct tape.

Banderas cut through the plastic layer and peeled it back, exposing a layer of blue-tinted plastic that had also been duct-taped. He cut through that and ripped it away. He glanced over his shoulder then and saw three of the crew standing in the doorway, peering over his shoulder.

"Back to work!" he snarled, and hefted his pistol in one hand in emphasis. The men retreated hastily and he put the gun down and retrieved the knife. Beneath the blue layer were twenty-four brick-shaped bundles, all but one individually wrapped in two more layers of blue plastic, then carefully sealed with duct tape. The twenty-fourth was wrapped in pink-colored plastic and duct tape. Banderas knew that brick was the fentanyl. Carefully, he ran his hands over each brick, feeling for any break in the plastic water-proofing, then sank back in relief.

They were intact and dry. Unspoiled.

And worth a fortune.

LeBlanc radioed the other boats, who were almost finished with their circuit around Swan Island. Rather than go together, they had split up and circled the island in different directions at high speed, which LeBlanc grudgingly admitted he hadn't thought of. He ordered one boat to circle Long Island to the east and sent the other to Marshall Island to the southwest. "Pay particular attention to Popplestone Cove," he told the captain of the *Rosie's Pride*. "It hooks out into the water and usually catches a lot of crap floating in the Coastal Current as it sweeps in from the northeast.

Banderas, meanwhile, had locked the drugs in a utility locker just off the pilot's cockpit and was wiping his hands on his shirt. "Where next, Captain?" he asked.

Nothing like finding one of the parcels to put even him in a good mood.

LeBlanc unrolled the map and put it back on the map table. "We're here," he said, pointing a thick finger at Shabby Island. He moved his finger to the east. "The other boats covered Swans Island and now they're checking Marshall Island and Long Island, here and here." His finger moved over the map. "I propose that we move southwest into this cluster of islands immediately off of North Harbor and Stonington, then regroup after lunch to search the perimeter of Isle Au Haut using all three boats."

Banderas studied the map for several minutes, then nodded. "Let's do it." He stood up and stretched. In the east the sun was a little above the horizon, casting long shadows. The fact that they had found one of the parcels immediately gave him hope, but he knew that the other two could be anywhere among these islands, or nowhere. Part of him recognized there was a good chance one or both of the other parcels had simply drifted through the islands and back out to sea.

Nothing he could do about it, except search.

———————

Thursday morning, Paul Dumas' car wouldn't start. He fretted over it for an hour, but couldn't make it work. He borrowed a bicycle from the kid next door and pedaled ten miles, awkwardly, to the harbor, where he rubbed his sore backside and finally settled in behind his desk at 11 a.m. In the midst of catching up on his emails, he sat bolt upright. He hadn't called his brother-in-law. Muttering in French and English, he dialed up Frank's number.

No answer. He tried Frank's cell number and was rewarded with a tired, grumpy, "Hello?"

"You sound like shit," Paul Dumas said cheerfully.

On the other end of the line, Finley stared at the phone. He and Danielle had been unable to reach her brother last night. From the sounds of it, Paul still did not know about the gunfight or that his father was in the hospital, fighting for his life. He sighed. "Long night," he replied, but didn't explain.

"Yeah, listen, Frank," Dumas continued. "You asked about ships coming in late from the storm. Thought you ought to know three of LeBlanc's boats – *Celeste, Samantha* and *Rosie's Pride* – all came in just before seven o'clock last night. Everybody else either didn't go out 'cause of the storm, or came in early. These guys stayed out way too late, given the weather and all. All three of them had deck equipment kicked to shit when there was no need for it."

Finley wrestled with what to tell his brother-in-law, and when. Once he told him about it, he would not be able to get any decent information from him about what LeBlanc was up to. Feeling crappy about what he was doing, he asked: "Paul, did they go out again today?"

"Well, yeah. Don't know for sure what time they went out, but I got in late, about 11 a.m., and all three of them were already gone." Dumas sounded mildly apologetic.

Finley tiredly rubbed his hand over his face. "These are the guys you saw sailing in formation yesterday, right?"

"Yeah, same ships."

"Paul, any idea where they are now?"

Dumas shook his head, even though his brother-in-law couldn't see him. "Sorry, no. If I had to guess, I think they are still mostly in-shore. Weather report has another storm coming in tonight."

Finley blew out his breath. "Paul, I hate to tell you this, but you'd better call your sister. Your dad had a heart attack. He's up at Eastern Maine Medical Center."

Long silence. "Is he going to make it?" Paul finally asked, his voice shaky.

"The doctors think so, but, Paul, we had some trouble here last night. There was some shooting. Your dad tried to help, but he ended up shot in the shoulder and hip, so it's going to take a while before he's himself again."

"Jesus, Frank! Gunfight? What the fuck is going on?" Paul said angrily.

"Paul, we tried to reach you last night. I'm really sorry, but I think he'll pull through."

Paul Dumas took a deep, quivering breath. "Shit, I had my phone turned off. Ah, Christ…" His phone was off because he had company last night and neither one of them wanted to be interrupted. She was the wife of the pastor at the North Harbor Baptist Church. They had been seeing each other – if wild bouts of tempestuous sex in a clothes-strewn bedroom with the curtains down could be called 'seeing each other' – for almost a year now. If anyone found out, it would be the ruin of them both. She was married and had two teenage children. When he thought about that, he felt like shit. They both knew without a doubt that it had to end badly, but they wouldn't stop. Couldn't stop.

"Go see your dad," Finley urged kindly. "Danielle and Céline need your support, too."

Chapter 46
Thursday Afternoon – Countermoves

Lady Luck had embraced them early in the morning, but then she took a long coffee break. As the morning dragged on, the *Celeste* searched around Shingle Island, Clam Island, Bold Island, The Shivers, Hells Half Acre, Coot Island and Devil Island.

Nothing.   Just rocks, seaweed, mud flats, countless seagulls, cormorants, and egrets, but no parcels. They circled the two land masses called Coombs Island, then Bare Island and St. Helena Island.

The morning dragged on.   LeBlanc picked up the weather report that a squall was coming in late afternoon or evening. Squalls had a nasty habit of turning into something worse on the Maine coast. He chewed his lower lip and fretted over how much more they had to search. Accelerating, they quickly did Potato Island and little Sprout Island, and then steamed north to Russ Island and Scott Island, then turned back to pick up Green Island and Flea Island. He was skipping some of the smaller islands now, watching the clouds slowly thicken in the southwest. The other boats reported in that they had finished "mapping" Swan and Marshall Islands and he ordered them west to work on the eastern-most islands in the archipelago.

And the day wore on.

The meeting was at the Coast Guard Station in Rockland. Commander Mello, Ensign Kauders and Commander Diane O'Brien of the Coast Guard Cutter *Vigilant*, who was still wearing an arm sling from her earlier injury, were on one side of the table, and Frank Finley and Howard Honeycutt were on the other.

"We think they're out there right now, still searching for the drug packages," Honeycutt explained.

"You need the LUNA drone," Commander Mello said. "We can do that, particularly since you paid to replace the one we lost chasing the go-fast boat."

"I didn't want to bring that up," Honeycutt said. He wrinkled his face in a 'this is a touchy subject' expression. "Sort of awkward."

Mello shrugged. "Not really. Things worked out."

Commander O'Brien snorted. "With all respect, Commander, not that well. We lost Petty Officer First Class Sandy Elkin. He'd served with me in Miami and all through the Caribbean and was a damn good sailor. My crew and I would really appreciate the opportunity for a little payback."

Mello pursed his lips. The *Vigilant* was still under repair, but she was seaworthy. He studied Commander O'Brien carefully. Her eyes bore into him without flinching and she radiated a sense of iron determination.

"How long would it take you to put to sea?" he asked her.

"Ten minutes. I had the entire crew assembled as soon as I was invited to this meeting," she replied. "We have ammunition, the weapons are functioning, and the ship is seaworthy."

"Ten minutes?" Finley said skeptically.

O'Brien turned to him. "Yes, Mr. Finley, ten minutes," she said evenly. "That's how long it will take me to walk from this conference room to the ship." She pointed out the window, where they could see the *Vigilant* at the pier. "The engine is running. The crew is on board and all but the stern lines have been cast off."

Honeycutt nodded in approval. "If we can get the drone up, we'll be able to track the lobster boats anywhere near shore. The *Vigilant* will prevent them from running to sea. We should be able to intercept them regardless of the direction they go in."

There were nods all around. As everyone got up to leave, Finley touched Commander Mello on the arm. "Commander, I want to commend Ensign Kauders for his actions yesterday. If he hadn't acted so quickly and decisively, my family would be dead."

Commander Mello grunted. He had been more than a little peeved at learning about the incident only after it was over, but at the same time he couldn't fault how Kauders had carried out the mission. Part of the training program for young officers was to teach them to take initiative, but not *too much* initiative.

"I'm glad we were in a position to help," he said flatly, giving Kauders a hard look.

"Commander, seriously, he *saved* my family." Finley told him earnestly.

Mello softened a little. "Although I hope he will be mindful of the many *benefits* of keeping his superiors informed, I daresay that Ensign Kauders has a bright future with us."

Behind the Commander, Ensign Kauders mouthed the words *"Thank you"* to Finley.

"Now let's locate these wayward lobster boats and see what they are up to," Mello said.

Chapter 47
Thursday, Late Afternoon

Lady Luck finally returned from her long coffee break. The *Samantha* stumbled over the second parcel in route to Spruce Island. They were less than a mile away when the transponder pinged. It had never pinged before, and the Captain stared at it in bewilderment for a moment, unsure of its meaning.

Then it pinged a second time.

"Holy shit, I think we found something!" the man at the transponder shouted.

The captain of the *Samantha* was Robert St. Clair, one of Jean-Philippe LeBlanc's several nephews. A stolid man, not given to displays of emotion or flights of imagination, he powered down and listened intently as the transponder triggered several more pings.

"Note the bearing," he told the transponder operator, then he looked carefully at the chart. Enchanted Island was about a mile to his right, Southern Mark Island was over his right shoulder about half that distance, and No Mans Island was off his port bow. He looked at Gunning Rock and discounted it; it was too small. Having the drug parcel wash up on that would be like hitting a bullseye with a bow and arrow at a thousand yards. Not damn likely.

"Bob, if I'm reading this thing right," the transponder operator said, "whatever it is, it's on this course." He pointed straight along the bow of the ship. Then he drew a pencil line on the chart, showing a course that took them just past Gunning Rock and smack into Spruce Island.

"Okay," St. Clair said, seemingly unmoved. "How far?"

The operator shrugged eloquently. "Can't tell. That's what the spic was telling us yesterday, we got to get a cross bearing. You know, we have to go in a different-"

"I know what a cross bearing is," St. Clair said. He pursed his lips. "Okay, let's bear north forty-five degrees for a few minutes." That course coincidently took them five hundred yards due north of Gunning Rock. St. Clair didn't know it, but Lady Luck had just taken him in her hot embrace and was fumbling with his belt buckle.

Twelve minutes later they stopped and took another bearing on the sound.

"Which way?" St. Clair asked. For all the inflection in his voice, he could have been asking directions to the nearest church.

The operator did not point towards Spruce Island, but instead almost due south. Five hundred yards away, waves roiled over the top of Gunning Rock. St. Clair frowned. He knew he could trust the transponder and the signal strength indicator, but this somehow violated his sense of good order.

"Gunning Rock, really?" he asked doubtfully.

Another shrug. "That's what it says." The operator patted the top of the signal strength indicator.

St. Clair insisted on one more bearing, and turned southwest for several minutes, but the results were the same. They altered course directly for Gunning Rock, then slowed and dropped anchor about fifty feet from it. By then the signal strength indicator was jumping through the roof. They took the inflatable raft over to the rock, but there was no sign of the parcel. One of the crew had struggled into a wetsuit and he flopped overboard with a mask and snorkel and began swimming around the rock.

"Look on the north side first," St. Clair reminded him. After just a few minutes the man stopped and waved his arms to get their attention, even though they had been following his every move like hungry cats sitting under a bird feeder.

"Right below me," the swimmer shouted. "About fifteen feet down."

They threw him a length of rope. He took a deep breath and jackknifed down to the parcel, tied the end of the rope to it and came back up next to the raft. First they hauled him onto the dingy, then they hauled up the parcel. It was all brisk and efficient. They were sailors; they knew how to get things done with a minimum of fuss.

Back on the *Samantha,* St. Clair looked at the package and shook his head. He knew how much that package was worth. Another, more venal man might have entertained thoughts of taking the heroin and running for it, but St. Clair just shook his head at how much work had gone into finding that small package, and wondered what the odds were of finding the third one.

He radioed his uncle on the *Celeste* and told him that they hadn't seen anything except a broken trap. The "broken trap" was the code word for the successful recovery of a drug parcel. LeBlanc radioed back and suggested that all three boats meet off Pell Island, just north of Isle Au Haut and discuss how best to proceed from there. Three minutes later the *Celeste, Samantha* and *Rosie's Pride* were steaming towards Pell Island, while LeBlanc glared balefully at the clouds closing in.

In the aft storage cabin of the *Celeste,* Jacob Finley squirmed and twisted, trying to free his hands from the plastic zip ties, succeeding only in cutting his skin and bleeding all over the place. The storage area was unheated and he shivered in the damp cold. He couldn't understand why Jean-Philippe had done this. At one point he had to use the bathroom and kept calling out for someone to let him go to the head, but the gag muffled his cries and no one came. To his embarrassment and humiliation, he finally wet himself.

To make matters worse, he was ravenous. Usually they took quick breaks to eat, so he was used to several small meals a day. Now his stomach was empty and growling. They hadn't taken his watch, so he could tell it was approaching five o'clock in the afternoon when the door opened and Jean-Philippe LeBlanc walked in with a mug of steaming coffee and a sandwich. He yanked out the gag and handed the boy the food, which Jacob wolfed down. The coffee burned his tongue, but he hardly noticed.

"This is crazy! Why are you doing this?" he blurted to LeBlanc.

LeBlanc stared at him for a moment, then shook his head and left without a word, returning a minute later with a thick wool blanket, which he draped around Jacob's shoulders.

"Hang in there, kid," he said. "It won't be too much longer." He stood up to leave.

"I don't understand!" Jacob cried. "What's happening?"

"Not much longer," LeBlanc said. "Not much longer."

"From the air, these goddamn lobster boats all look the same," the pilot complained. Her name was Rachael Gardner. She was born and bred in Oklahoma and she knew how to make a drone do pirouettes, but didn't know diddly-squat about lobster boats. As she put it, lobster boats were a 'scarce commodity' in Weleetka, Oklahoma. "Do we have anybody who is familiar with the specific lobster boats we're searching for?" she asked for the third time. "Otherwise, we're just playing Pin the Tail on the Donkey."

Honeycutt glanced at Finley. "Your brother?" They were sitting in the Command trailer again, parked off Fire Lane 22 in North Harbor, right by the Settlement Quarry Preserve, an old, abandoned granite quarry that had provided the granite for hundreds of government buildings throughout New England.

"You mean Paul Dumas, my brother-in-law?" Finley considered it. As Harbor Master, Paul knew more about the various lobster boats in the North Harbor fleet than anyone except a lobster boat captain. He pulled out his smart phone and called him.

"Paul? Listen, we've got a bit of an emergency. Can you get to the Settlement Quarry Preserve right away, like *now?*"

"Sure, but what's this about?" His brother-in-law's bewilderment was obvious.

"Paul, I can't go into it on the phone, but it's important and we need you. Specifically, you. When you get here, you'll see a construction trailer parked on the east side of Fire Lane 22, in under the trees. Just knock."

"This is a cop thing, right?" Paul Dumas stated.

"We don't have much time, Paul." The *'get your ass in gear'* was implied, but not spoken.

Dumas chuckled. "Yeah, yeah, but I am counting on you to have coffee and donuts."

Chapter 48
Thursday, 5:30 p.m. Off Pell Island

Sometimes Lady Luck smiles at you, sometimes she touches your arm.

Sometimes she kisses you chastely on the cheek, and sometimes she rips off your clothes, throws you on the bed and ravishes you.

Today, she was a horny bitch.

Sunset was still more than an hour away when the *Celeste*, *Samantha* and *Rosie's Pride* met on the lee side of Pell Island. Clouds were scuttling in from the southwest and a warm, damp wind was blowing across the water. They pulled up alongside each other and idled their engines.

"You got it?" LeBlanc called over to St. Clair on the *Samantha.*

St. Clair grinned. "I most certainly do."

LeBlanc turned to Banderas. "You want both parcels on this boat, or keep them split up?"

Banderas scowled. It wasn't a simple question. He weighed the risk that one of the lobstermen might try to steal the drugs against the risk that the DEA might try to intercept the delivery. If all the drugs were on one boat, it made the DEA's job easier. If the parcels were split among two boats – or three if they found the third parcel, God, the Virgin Mother and Lady Luck willing – one or two of the boats might get away. At $11 Million per parcel, that would be important.

"Leave it where it is," he said. "Let's find the last one."

LeBlanc stepped closer, glancing up at the sky. "Sunset's a bit after 7 p.m., but the bigger problem is a squall is moving in. Weather forecast says it should reach us in a little more than an hour. Once that hits, our chances of finding the last parcel go to hell in a handbasket."

Banderas, also looking at the sky, nodded. "Maine has the worst fucking weather in the world," he declared.

"Part of its charm," LeBlanc said. "Crappy weather makes for good lobsters." He said it lightly, but he never took his eyes off Banderas.

Banderas shrugged. "We hunt for the last parcel as long as we possibly can, then we figure out someplace sheltered on the coast to deliver whatever we've got."

"I know a couple of places that should work, even if the squall is bad," LeBlanc said, relieved. Then, unable to stop himself, his eyes drifted to the aft storage cabin where Jake Finley was locked up. Poor stupid kid. He didn't even know why he had to die.

———————

Paul Dumas found the command trailer and stepped out of his car. As soon as he did, two very large men with assault rifles stepped from the trees, looking at him with hard eyes. Everything about them screamed 'soldier!', or perhaps 'Terminator!', and Dumas' mouth suddenly went dry.

"Excuse me, sir, but this area is off-limits to the public today," one of the soldiers said. The words were polite, but the rifle was held at the ready and his body language radiated threat.

Dumas took a deep breath to calm himself. "I was told to come here," he stammered. "Frank Finley...uh...Officer Frank Finley of the North Harbor police."

The door to the command trailer opened and his brother-in-law stood there. "He's okay," Finley told the soldier. Then, to Dumas, "Paul, give him your car keys so he can park your car up in the trees, out of sight."

Dumas handed over the keys. Finley nodded at the soldier. "Thank you, Petty Officer Josephs."

Josephs went to move the car and the second soldier melted back into the trees.

"Jesus, Frank," Dumas whispered. "Who are the Neanderthals?"

"Security," Finley said. "They are very serious guys, so don't be a dick or they might shoot you, and then Danielle would be mad at me. C'mon, I've got to introduce you to my boss and put you to work."

"I, for one, welcome our new Neanderthal overlords," Dumas deadpanned, glancing back over his shoulder to the men with the assault rifles standing amongst the trees. Then he swung back to Finley. "Frank, what are you doing here? Who's taking care of Danielle and the kids?"

"Three State Police are with Danni. Calvin's at Luc's and Jacob is working."

Paul Dumas nodded, then followed his brother-in-law into the trailer. The space inside was crammed with three radios, a large screen that showed a real-time map of the archipelago of islands off Stonington and North Harbor, and ships in the water with identifying names on some of them. The funny thing, though, was that the view on the map kept changing, as if the map was being dragged by a computer mouse. Then the perspective on the map zoomed in and Dumas realized he was looking at waves. Real waves, the kind that moved.

"Wait!" he exclaimed. "Is this some sort of live feed from a plane or helicopter?"

Everyone in the trailer – three radio operators, a woman holding onto what looked like a joystick and frowning at a video monitor in front of her, two guys wearing windbreakers that said "DEA" on the back, a young Coast Guard Ensign, who nodded politely to him, and an older man who looked like a balding accountant, all turned and stared at him at the same moment. Dumas felt like he had showed up at church with his fly open.

The older man stood up and extended his hand in greeting. Dumas automatically shook it.

"Mr. Dumas, I am very glad to meet you, and I hope you can help us out of a jam we're in," the man said.

Dumas glanced at his brother-in-law, his confusion evident.

Finley smiled thinly. "Paul, this is Howard Honeycutt, the United States Drug Enforcement Agency's Regional Director in charge of the New England Region. And, he's my boss."

Dumas' puzzlement grew in leaps and bounds. "Ah, I thought you already had a boss, Frank. You know, the Police Chief?"

Finley shifted uneasily. "Yeah, about that..."

Honeycutt stepped in. "Mr. Dumas-"

"I think you'd better call me Paul," Dumas said. "If we are all going to the insane asylum together, I think we should be on a first-name basis."

Honeycutt chuckled. "Okay, Paul, that's fair enough. Frank here is one of my agents. I'm not going to tell you what he's doing for us just yet, but I can tell you that what he is doing is dangerous and you should be proud of him."

Dumas shot Finley a look, and Finley could see pieces of the puzzle suddenly beginning to fall into place. He sighed. This could get ugly.

"And does this dangerous work explain why two men tried to kill my sister and father last night?" Dumas asked coldly.

"Yes, I'm afraid it does." Honeycutt nodded, then frowned, then sighed in resignation. "I'm going to tell you several things now, but you need to know they are highly confidential. If you mention them to anyone, you could be charged with obstruction of justice." This was said all matter-of-factly, but Finley knew his boss well enough to know that he was trying hard to keep tempers under control.

But Dumas was already hot under the collar. "Mr. Regional Director or whatever your title is, let's cut the crap. You need me to do something for you, but first I want to know how this involves the attack on my father and sister."

"Paul," Finley said softly. "The gunmen were from one of the Mexican drug cartels. They were going to make an example out of my family because they discovered that I am working undercover for the DEA." He paused. "At the same time they were breaking into our house, two other gunmen tried to kill me while I was driving to Bangor. All four of the gunmen are dead. Danni, God bless her, went all commando on them and protected Calvin and his girlfriend. She killed one of them and the Coast Guard arrived and killed the other. You dad got shot as he tried to help Danni."

"Fuck me," Dumas said shakily.

"For what's it's worth, I am very sorry," Finley said. "I never thought it would come to this. I'd never forgive myself if anything happened to Danni."

Dumas closed his eyes and blew out a deep breath. "Okay, but you and I are going to have a long talk about this." He shook his head, as if trying to shake away what Finley had just told him. "Now what?"

"We have a drone looking for three lobster boats," Finley explained. "But there are dozens of boats out there and none of us has the expertise to tell one from another. You know the fleet better than anyone, so we need your help."

Dumas blew out another breath. "Sure...sure, whose boats are you looking for?"

"Three boats belonging to the LeBlanc family," Finley told him.

Dumas recalled the "mapping" the LeBlanc boats were doing. "What are they doing?"

Honeycutt shifted forward just an inch, taking control of the conversation. "We think that the Mexican cartel dropped three large bags of drugs into the ocean north of here, near the entrance to the Bay of Fundy," he said. "Apparently the plan is that the bags will drift down into the island cluster off North Harbor and Stonington."

"The Eastern Maine Coastal Current," Dumas said.

Honeycutt looked impressed. "You know about it," he said approvingly.

Dumas snorted. "It's my backyard." He looked thoughtful. "You guys are the ones who caught that go-fast boat a few days ago. I assume that after the drug guys tried bringing in the dope above water, they decided to let it drift in with the current. Weighted down somehow, right?"

"Little more high-tech than that, but that's the gist of it," Finley said.

"Hell of a risk for them," Dumas said.

"Big rewards," Finley reminded him. "The lobster boats will find the parcels using some sort of radio transponder, then take them ashore. Once ashore, they'll be taken by the local gangs, cut up into little packets and sold. The cartel could make millions. Tens of millions."

"And this year several hundred Maine citizens will die because of it." Honeycutt was grim, his arms folded.

"Okay," Dumas said. "Show me the map and where the drone is."

As it happened, the drone was flying a circle over Spruce Island.

Paul Dumas rubbed his chin. "Is there a way to pull the camera out? You know, so it's not in so tight?"

"I can do that," Gardner said briskly, and the camera zoomed out until it showed a three-mile area around Spruce Island.

Dumas leaned forward, studying the screen. "I'm not seeing anything. From this height, should I be able to see a boat the size of a lobster boat?"

"Let me show you," Gardner said. She banked the drone and took it west, unknowingly away from the area where LeBlanc and his relatives were sailing. After a few minutes they could clearly see a small shape at the head of a long inverted "V" wake.

"Now we zoom in," she explained as the camera attached to the belly of the LUNA drone did just that. In a moment they had a picture of a small, red lobster boat, at a forty-five degree angle.

Dumas leaned forward a little further. "That's the *Witch Hunt!*" he exclaimed. "Sam Hutchinson's boat. I can even read her name on the bow. I'll be damned." He turned to Gardner. "Okay, I guess this height is just fine, at least until the storm comes in."

Gardner, Honeycutt and Finley looked at each other in consternation.

"You do know a squall is going to pass through here within an hour or two, right?" Dumas asked. "Only, now the weather forecast says it looks more like a gale mixed with some godawful rain, with winds up to forty-five knots and waves five to seven feet." He peered at them from the corner of his eye. "I mean, you *do* know this, right?"

Commander Mello and Honeycutt looked at each other, their expressions sour.

"Well, crap," Honeycutt muttered.

Gardner frowned. "Let's get to work, then. Mr. Dumas, tell me where I need to look."

Dumas blew out a breath. "You say some packages went into the water last Friday and the Eastern Maine Coastal Current is dragging them down here?"

Everyone nodded.

"And they went in near the Grand Manan Island?" Dumas pressed.

More nods, but noticeably more tentative.

Dumas ran his hands through his hair. "Well, I am no oceanographer, but from what I've seen over the years, you are looking too far north. Unless the packages have run aground somewhere and they found them, chances are good that they are further south-"" he pointed on the map, "near Isle Au Haut or, hell, even Matinicus. Remember, we had that storm last week that was pushing everything *to* the southwest or south. Now, this gale tonight will slow things up a bit, if – and it's a big if – the packages are near the surface, but by this time tomorrow, if they are around here at all, they will be moving east into open water."

"So, we find them tonight or they're gone?" Honeycutt asked.

Dumas grimaced. "Christ, they're probably gone already, but if you want to find the LeBlancs, I'd start south and work north. Frankly, if we don't find them at the Isle Au Haut or below, we probably won't find them."

Honeycutt nodded to the pilot. "Ms. Gardner, can you reposition the drone?"

"With alacrity, sir," she answered.

Ensign Kauders whistled. "*Alacrity,* is it? Pretty big word for a pilot."

"I am no less astonished that a mere ensign would know the meaning," she answered sweetly. "But then I've met so few. Most of them flunk out of pilot training very early."

They grinned at each other.

Commander Mello sighed. Young people were constantly distracted. "Do *try* to focus on the work at hand, people."

"Yes, sir," Kauders said, trying and failing to get the grin off his face. Finley glanced from Kauders to Gardner. *Huh,* he thought to himself. You could almost smell the hormones.

In the next fifteen minutes, the drone picked up three more boats. Two were lobster boats heading west towards Stonington Harbor, the third was a fishing boat heading towards Vinalhaven. Paul Dumas recognized all the boats and knew the captains. None of them were suspicious.

Then as the drone flew within visual range of the northern edge of Isle Au Haut, the camera caught three boats sailing in line, then dividing into two groups, with one going down the west side of the island and two going along the east.

"Lock in on those boats," Dumas told the pilot. Then, to the others, "See those boats? They ought to be running to a harbor, but they're not. Well, maybe this guy on the west is going to the Isle Au Haut Thorofare, down here where Kimball Island pinches in real close to Isle Au Haut. That's no more than seven hundred feet across at the widest point, maybe only three or four hundred at its narrowest. That would give them some shelter from a storm coming from the southwest. But that still doesn't explain what the other two are doing. No good harbor on the west side, and if the storm shifts around to blow from the south, those boats will be mighty unhappy."

"I can zoom in," Gardner reminded him.

"Sure, that would help," Dumas said. She zoomed in on one of the westward boats and Dumas leaned forward, rubbing his chin and peering at the monitor. "You're sure they can't see the drone? Or hear it?"

"Don't worry, sir," Gardner said, with only a hint of condescension.

"She knows what she's doing, Paul," Finley said. "Just tell us if these are the right boats."

Dumas peered at the boat again, but shook his head. "Can you take her in lower? I want to see the bow."

Gardner dropped the LUNA a thousand feet, got it stable and locked the camera on the bow of the little ship. Even for a working boat, she thought it was cute. "That better?" she asked.

"Much," Dumas grunted, standing up. "That, my friends, is the *Rosie's Pride,* out of North Harbor and skippered by Marc LeBlanc, one of the greatest weasels ever to skipper a lobster boat. Need a lobster buoy cut, a trawl line sunk or even a boat burned, he's your man. I'm not exactly sure what his relationship is to Jean-Philippe LeBlanc, maybe first cousins or something like that, but they're two peas in a pod. They're both greedy, ambitious, arrogant sons of bitches who never overlook the chance to make a crooked buck."

Finley looked thunderstruck. "Dammit, Paul, you never told me any of this!"

Dumas shrugged. "Can't prove anything, can I? Best to mind my own business."

"Ah, Christ," Finley muttered.

"Coming up on the two other ships," Gardner announced.

The two boats were rounding the top of Isle Au Haut and just beginning their turn to the south towards Old Cove. Gardner brought the drone across the island and circled over them at 10,000 feet, then killed the engine and let the drone lose altitude, traveling in a wide spiral around the lobster boats, but locking the drone's cameras on them so that they were always in the center of the picture.

Dumas snorted. "The first one is easy. That's the *Celeste,* Jean-Philippe's boat. See that equipment and storage shack he has on the stern of the boat? Lot of boats have them, but he painted his dark gray on top. Most captains in North Harbor paint the top of their storage shacks International Orange or fluorescent green or something bright like that." He wanted to say 'Screaming Yellow,' but he suddenly couldn't recall whether that was a color, an ice cream flavor or the name of a local rock band. "They know that little splash of bright color might make the difference if they're caught in a storm without power and need rescuing. Not LeBlanc. You might wonder why he doesn't want his boat easily recognized; I certainly do."

"And the second?" Honeycutt raised his eyebrows in question.

Dumas leaned in again for a better look. "That would be the *Samantha,* skippered by LeBlanc's nephew, Bobby St. Clair. Very bright young man, Bobby St. Clair. Ambitious, but not as...*overt* as Jean-Philippe and many of the others." He rocked back on his heels, pursing his lips. "But don't underestimate Bobby, he has big plans."

"Capable of smuggling drugs?" asked Honeycutt. "Capable of dealing with one of the cartels and not getting burnt?"

Dumas rolled his eyes. "Oh, Good Christ, I really have no idea! I don't know what it takes to deal with a drug Cartel and bring drugs in from the ocean. Hell, I sit in my office and make sure everybody pays their docking fees on time and don't cheat when they top off their gas tanks. I don't know about drug deals. This is *North Harbor,* not Portland, not Boston, not Providence and most certainly not New York City!"

Honeycutt nodded, accepting it for what it was. "How about this: Is LeBlanc capable of killing another lobster captain to protect an illegal racket he's running?"

Dumas considered this, but not for very long. "Yeah," he nodded. "Oh, yeah."

"They're changing course!" Gardner called out.

"Where to?" Dumas' face lit up. Finley and Honeycutt crowded closer to the view screen. The two boats had suddenly turned southeast, slowly pulling away from Isle Au Haut.

"I don't know, sir," Gardner answered. "I mean, east southeast, but there's nothing much out there."

"Remember," said Finley.   "They're looking for a fifty-pound package. Not very large in the scope of things. We don't need an island, it could get hung up on a rock."

"The other boat, the one on the west side, has turned around and is heading north again. From the wake, he's at full throttle," Gardner told them.

"LeBlanc is sniffing something and the other boat is coming to help, I'll bet." Finley turned to his brother-in-law. "What do you think, Paul?"

"Let me see the map again." He peered down at it, studying the area east of Isle Au Haut. There was York Island about halfway down, and Doliver Island, and the Rabbits Ear, but the boats would have to turn much further south to go there. He glanced again at the path of the *Celeste* and *Rosie's Pride*. Definitely not south.

"Pilot, can you take the drone along their present heading and pull the camera back a bit? I want to see what's out there."

"Certainly, sir," Gardner replied cheerfully.

"With as much *alacrity* as you can muster," Honeycutt added, a small smile tugging at the corners of his mouth. Ensign Kauders shot him a smile. Commander Mello shook his head.

"Do my best, sir," Gardner said, but even as the drone altered course, it was obvious that there was little to see except whitecaps and sea spray. The wind was picking up and roiling the surface of the ocean.

Paul Dumas stepped closer to the large viewing screen. He glanced at the others. "Do you see anything?"

"Do you see anything?" Jean-Philippe LeBlanc asked, peering through the pilothouse window.

"Water," Banderas answered sourly. "Lots and lots of water."

Beside them, the speaker on the searcher unit emitted another loud 'Ping,' making them both jump a little.

"It's close," LeBlanc said. "Very close."

PING

The radio crackled. Not the ship's radio, which could be heard for miles, but the small family-style walkie talkies intended for short-range work. These had a range of just over a mile, making them very hard to eavesdrop on.

"Can you see anything?" LeBlanc asked over the walkie talkie.

"Nah, water's too choppy," Bobby St. Claire answered from the *Samantha*. "But Richs Ledge is right in front of us, no more than two hundred feet. Can't see it, but with this wind, the water could be washing over it."

PING!

"I'll bet it's stuck on the north side of Richs Ledge," St. Clair mused. "Storm a couple of days ago could have driven it right up on it and wedged it in tight."

LeBlanc nodded. Good a bet as any. He turned to Banderas and his brother, Jacques. "I'm going in to look for it. You're in charge while I'm gone. Keep the radar on and tug on my safety line if there is anything I should know about."

Jacques LeBlanc nodded. "What about *Rosie's Pride*?"

"Call them, tell them to go to the north end of Isle Au Haut and call us again on the walkie talkie," LeBlanc said as he quickly stripped out of his clothes. With his brother's help, he struggled into the wetsuit, scuba tanks and regulator. He pulled on the hood and gloves – hypothermia would kill him as certain as a bullet in this water – and pulled on the various other pieces of gear: weight belt, flotation device, flippers, mask and 1,000 lumen waterproof flashlight. Jacques snapped a safety line to his harness and gave him the thumbs up.

Awkward in the flippers, LeBlanc walked to the stern of the *Celeste* and plunged into the water.

The rain started and visibility abruptly dropped to no more than a football field.

On the view screen, the image of the two lobster boats suddenly faded.

"Cloud burst," Finley muttered.

"Going to infrared," Gardner announced. The screen went blank, then came back with two bright patches where the boats were. She zoomed in and out to get the best perspective, but it soon became apparent that the boats were just sitting there, not moving.

Honeycutt pursed his lips. He thumbed another mic and spoke into it. "*Vigilant,* this is Gollum. Are you getting this?"

Eight miles to the south, plodding along at five knots, the Coast Guard Cutter *Vigilant* was doing its best to look like a very large fishing trawler headed for harbor before the storm hit. "Gollum, we see it," said Captain O'Brien. "Looks like they found something."

LeBlanc swam underwater towards the north edge of Richs Ledge. The percussive thrum of the waves enveloped him like a living thing, each large wave vibrating inside his chest. He moved carefully, playing the powerful flashlight along the rocky ledge, gradually rising along the incline as the ledge erupted toward the surface.

He would never admit it afterwards, but he was so preoccupied with searching the rocky bottom that he did not see the third package of heroin until he swam into it, banging his head. Startled, he backpedaled furiously, half expecting to see some sea creature from the Deep, all teeth and tentacles and ugly disposition. Instead, the third package floated placidly in front of him, twenty feet beneath the surface, just as it had been designed to. Strapped to its side was a transponder, dutifully replying with a 'PING' every time the search unit sent out its query.

For a moment, LeBlanc just hovered there, incredulous that he had actually found it. He reached out tentatively and touched it, just to confirm it was real. Then he unclipped the safety line from his harness and clipped it onto a loop on the package. With the package secure, he propelled himself to the surface with one powerful kick and waved to the ship.

Now came the hard part.

"Wind is getting worse. I have to get some altitude or I might lose the drone," Gardner warned.

The video screen showed little more than thick mist and water droplets on the camera housing. The infrared camera showed two indistinct red blobs, now moving north and gathering speed.

"Okay, take it up," Commander Mello said. "Three thousand feet. How is your fuel?"

"Good for two hours and change under present conditions," Gardner replied. "Getting worried about the wind, though."

On the screen, the two red shapes reached the top of Isle Au Haut and were joined by a third. They all turned to a northeast heading and sailed in formation.

Honeycutt studied the screen, then looked at a nautical chart pinned to a dry board. "Where the hell are they going now?" he muttered.

Finley and his brother-in-law crowded in for a better look.

"You know, better lighting in this trailer wouldn't hurt any," Dumas noted sourly. "Feels like a fucking church in here."

"Wait 'til we light the incense," Gardner smirked.

"They could be going just about anywhere north of here," Finley said. "Blue Hill, maybe even Mt. Desert Island. Hell, they could run north a bit then turn northwest into the Eggemoggin Reach, stop in at Brooklin, or go into Benjamin River up to Sedgwick. All sorts of roads run near the water up in the Reach, it'd be easy enough to get the drugs to shore anywhere in there."

"Fuck," Honeycutt swore. Finley glanced at him in surprise; Honeycutt rarely swore.

"Nah," Dumas said cheerfully. "LeBlanc and that whole crew are local boys. There's a storm outside and the weather forecast just said it's going to get worse before it gets better. LeBlanc will think about his three boats, want to keep 'em safe. He'll want three things: a sheltered spot, in local waters, and not too far away. If we can use that fancy drone of yours, we can follow him pretty well. As he gets closer, we can start making educated guesses about where he'll go."

"But what direction will he go?" Honeycutt demanded. There was uncharacteristic worry in his voice. Worry...and frustration. "The entire coastline around here is filled with little hideaway places he could use."

Dumas shook his head, smiling. "You're not thinking like a fisherman, Mr. Honeycutt. You work a desk. You don't worry about storms and wind and weather, or your very expensive boat sinking beneath you. LeBlanc does. LeBlanc is going home. He'll head for North Harbor."

Chapter 49
Thursday Night – Contemplations

Chief of Police Michael Corcoran sipped his coffee and pondered his situation.

He was on the take from a Mexican drug cartel.

He was an accessory to at least two murders.

The Coast Guard was now patrolling the waters off North Harbor.

The Federal Drug Enforcement Agency was investigating drug smuggling in the North Harbor-Stonington area.

The Maine State Police were looking into whether "heroin" seized from the go-fast boat had been replaced with baking powder, and the North Harbor police were suspect.

Tonight, he and his handpicked men were to provide security for the drug cartel and a bunch of lobstermen while they made a delivery of one hundred and fifty pounds of heroin.

The heroin was worth at least $30 Million.

In the darkness of his office, Corcoran grinned a predator's grin. Thanks to the money from the Cartel, he was wealthier than he ever had been, but it was peanuts compared to what was on those lobster boats. Meanwhile, at least two different enforcement agencies were sniffing around, and his luck couldn't hold forever. It was time to get out, but to get out, he needed money – a lot of money.

And tonight was his chance.

If he was ruthless enough.

Corcoran laughed, the deep, contented laugh of a man happy with the world and his role in it.

Life was so sweet.

Chapter 50
Thursday Night – Moving Pieces on the Board

Storms are noisy things. The wind howls, the ship's rigging thrums a deep harmonic, the rain pounds and pounds against the roof, the ship's engine screams. And the ocean, well, the ocean *roars* like a lion sitting at the foot of your bed, just letting you know it's there, and that now it is going to eat you.

On the *Celeste,* Bruno Banderas made his calls and lined up his men. Outside the pilothouse the rain lashed down and the wind snatched at the wave crests, flinging them like shards against the *Celeste's* windows. The wind was from behind, and the following seas swarmed over the open stern and flooded the work area, then poured back out into the ocean, and then crashed back in again.

Jean-Philippe LeBlanc stood at the wheel, his feet wide apart to brace himself. He had been in storms like this hundreds of times, and every time he wondered if this would be the one to kill him. He smiled grimly. "Can't have me today, you ugly bitch," he told the ocean. "Not today."

"What, boss?" one of the sternsmen asked, shouting over the cacophony.

"Nothing," LeBlanc said curtly. "Dial up the weather and see if they've changed the forecast."

Banderas leaned closer and spoke in his ear. "I've got to tell my men where we're putting in."

LeBlanc had already picked a location. It wasn't perfect because he could get bottled up there if the Coast Guard followed him in, but there was no sign of the Coast Guard and the weather would mask his movements. He checked his gauges and saw he was making six knots. His destination was a bit more than eight nautical miles.

"Tell them to meet us where Rte. 15 crosses over Holt Pond and separates Holt Pond from the Elm Tree Cove," he told Banderas. "We'll be there in an hour and a half. We're bringing in three boats, each carrying one of the parcels."

"That's where we met Mateo and the go-fast boat," Banderas said uneasily.

"Yep," LeBlanc agreed. "It's sheltered from this storm, got water deep enough for our boats, wide enough so we can bring all three boats in, it's right next to Rte. 15 so your boys can get the goodies and get out fast, and there's only one house that has a view of the beach where we'll land.

We'll go in dark, nose up to the beach, throw out the parcels and leave. The drop shouldn't take more than five or ten minutes, tops."

Bruno Banderas was many things, and one of them was superstitious. He had killed a man there, a man he had known all his life. Banderas didn't exactly believe in ghosts and supernatural vengeance...but he didn't exactly disbelieve, either.

"I don't like it," he said.

LeBlanc glanced at him, then returned his attention to not letting the boat breach in the storm. "Well, Bruno, that's too fuckin' bad. This storm was supposed to be a little squall, but it's gotten bigger than that and it is slowly coming around to the southeast. There are other places we can put in and meet your boys, but a lot of them aren't sheltered and there's a good chance we wouldn't be able to make the drop."

"What about the harbor?" Banderas demanded. He was not accustomed to having people argue back to him. Not infrequently, when someone argued back, he shot them.

LeBlanc snorted unpleasantly. "Well, see, you've only got two harbors to choose from. The first is Stonington Harbor, but it is full of rocks and, worse, it is exposed to the southeast, so the harbor will have more waves in it than usual. Worse yet, there are a bunch of warehouses, packing buildings and bars all throughout the harbor area. And restaurants for the tourists. Night like this, can't go for a pretty stroll along the harbor, so the bars and the restaurants will be full. Full of witnesses, Bruno. The odds of someone seeing us unload three parcels into a truck are pretty good."

LeBlanc's lip curled. "Oh, and did I mention that there is a police substation right in the harbor? And a harbormaster?"

Banderas could feel the heat rising in his face. He needed this man, needed him badly, but the time would come when he didn't need him, and then...

"What about the second harbor?" he reminded LeBlanc. "You said there are two harbors."

"Yeah," LeBlanc nodded agreeably, enjoying himself. "North Harbor. It's a bit more sheltered, but it has a lot of people in it. Not so many fancy restaurants, but my goodness we got a lot of bars in that harbor, and they'll be busy tonight. Plus, the harbormaster is the brother-in-law of Frank Finley, the guy you tried to kill, but didn't. And the harbormaster knows young Jacob Finley works on this boat, so you think he might notice when we all pull in and maybe, just maybe he might call his brother-in-law the cop?"

"Hijo de puta!" Banderas scowled.

"So my recommendation," LeBlanc continued pleasantly, "is that we go all the way around Coles Point and turn northwest, then slide down into the Inner Harbor and in towards Holts Pond. Once we round Coles Point the seas will be calmer and the peninsula will block the wind a bit. Won't be no problem putting into the beach by Rte. 15. We dump the goods, back off the beach and head out."

"I want to put all the parcels on one boat," Banderas abruptly demanded.

LeBlanc shook his head. "Too late for that. Next stop for us is the Rte. 15 overpass at Holts Pond. If we try to pull the boats in close together for a transfer in this shit, next thing you know is one boat will be sitting atop the other and they'll both sink. Nope, Bruno, we are all on the roller coaster now. Nothin' to do but enjoy the ride."

———————

In the stern of the *Celeste,* Jacob Finley stood knee deep in freezing water, hoping to hell that the little shack wouldn't rip off the boat and tumble into the ocean. As the *Celeste* rolled and wallowed in the waves, Jacob was hurled first against one wall of the shack, then another, like he was the pinball in a demonic pinball game.

Another wave slammed him into a wall, where he thudded head first. Exhausted, cold and bleeding and unable to help himself, he screamed.

And screamed.

No one heard him.

Chapter 51
Thursday Night – Convergence

On Little Deer Isle, five miles north of North Harbor, eight men carrying duffle bags got into three cars and began driving slowly towards Rte. 15. When they reached it, they turned south, towards North Harbor.

Each duffle bag contained a loaded pistol with extra ammo and an AK-47 with a collapsible stock. They didn't really expect trouble, but it was best to be prepared.

————————

At the Settlement Quarry Preserve in North Harbor, two cars pulled up. Six DEA agents got out, nodded to the two Coast Guard men guarding the command trailer and knocked on the door.

Howard Honeycutt opened the door and glanced at them. "Good. We've got two State Police Drug Task Force agents on call, once we know where we're going."

One of the DEA agents looked around. "Okay," he said slowly. "What about backup from the local cops? Or the State Police SWAT teams?"

Honeycutt frowned. "That would be problematic. I checked with the State Police in Portland and Bangor, but their SWAT teams are already committed to a raid on a white supremacist group today, so no help there. And it's not a good idea to involve the local police."

The DEA agents exchanged wary glances. "Are they dirty?"

"We think so, but we have no hard evidence," Honeycutt told them.

"And if they show up?" the agent pressed.

Honeycutt sighed. He had struggled with this. If the drugs landed in North Harbor territory, the local cops had every right to be involved. He could try to claim jurisdiction, but the fact was he would not be able to insist they leave.

"If they show up, we will have to be careful," he told the agents. It wasn't much of an answer, and from the sour looks on the agents' faces, they knew it.

"And the role of the Coast Guard?" one of them asked.

Now Honeycutt had something to smile about. "The Coast Guard is working closely with us. They give us one huge advantage."

One of the agents frowned. "You mean the drone?"

"No," Honeycutt replied. "The Coast Guard has really *big* guns. And knows how to use them."

Four miles behind the three lobster boats, the Coast Guard Cutter *Vigilant* slowly steamed northeast. Captain O'Brien kept her eyes on the video screen streaming the display from the LUNA drone. The three boats were making steady headway through the gale. She figured they were going to go around the little archipelago that stood off the Stonington and North Harbor coast, which was full of jagged rocks and sandbars and other things that can ruin a lobsterman's day. If she was right, they'd go north a bit, then turn west northwest. The big question was whether they would turn west at Lazygut Island, which would take them in towards the town of North Harbor and a twisting, turning set of coves, harbors, inlets and fuck all, or whether they would continue north, past Lazygut Island, which would take them up the Eggemoggin Reach. That way could take them a bunch of places, more than she cared to think about.

If they went into the North Harbor area, the bad news was that the *Vigilant* would not be able to follow them all the way in, not in this storm and at night. Too easy to run aground on a sandbar or, worse, a nice sharp rock. The good news was if they went into the North Harbor area, the lobster boats would have to pass by the *Vigilant* when they came out. If they went for Eggemoggin Reach, it was anybody's guess where the hell they'd end up, and in the cluttered waters of Eggemoggin Reach, she could lose them.

But these guys were local boys and knew the local waters. She was betting on North Harbor.

She opened a channel to the command trailer. "Pilot, this is Big Eyes, fuel status?"

In the command trailer, Rachael Gardner was fighting to pull the drone out of a nose dive. A wind gust had snapped the drone's twelve-foot wings over and it had tumbled a thousand feet before she had gotten control. Now it was under control, sort of, but pointed straight down. Gently, patiently, she eased it into horizontal flight and peeked at the altitude gauge. Nine hundred feet. Not bad, but not good, either. Another gauge showed wind gusts over forty miles per hour.

Definitely not good.

"Commander Mello," she called out. "Request permission to abort and return to base. The wind gusts are now significantly above my authorized flight parameters."

Mello stepped beside her. "How bad?"

"Like one more gust like the last one and she'll crash for sure," Gardner replied, tight lipped.

"Can you climb out of it?"

"No, sir. I had it up to the ceiling a few minutes ago and came down because it is too windy up there."

Mello leaned closer. "Gardner, with this storm, you are our only eyes. Can you keep it on station and follow the target, even if it means pushing the safety limits?"

"Sir," she said bluntly. "I am already exceeding the normal safety limits. I know this bird, I know what she can do. But this weather is just too damn much. She's not designed for it. I almost lost her a minute ago and the winds are getting worse, not better." She tore her eyes off the screen to look at him. "I'm going to lose her if I don't land soon. Very soon."

Mello sighed and straightened, looking at Honeycutt. "If we lose it, it's another $50,000," he said simply.

Honeycutt shook his head. He had already dipped into the agency's slush fund once to replace the first drone they'd lost. The auditors would raise holy hell if he did it twice within one week.

"Can't do it, sorry. Bring it home and get it on the ground," he said regretfully. Then, to Captain O'Brien: "Big Eyes, can you monitor them on radar?"

"Sure," she replied immediately, "as long as they stay in open water. But if they go into the archipelago, or into North Harbor, I'll lose them in the clutter of islands and crap."

Commander Mello spoke up. "What about visual? Can you close in on them enough to follow them visually?"

Captain O'Brien thought for a moment, weighing the risks. "I can close in, but will almost certainly get spotted by them in return. They'll just dump the goods and sail into harbor."

"Not an optimal solution," Honeycutt grumbled.

"I've got an idea," Finley said, "but it is going to stretch us out." He opened the map of the North Harbor-Stonington area on the small table. "We send the men out with binoculars. If they turn into the North Harbor area, they have to go past certain points. So," he pointed to a peninsula with his finger, "we put a guy here, at the end of Indian Point. He'll see anything that goes into Webb Cove, hopefully. And if he doesn't, we put a guy on the docks, just across the street from this trailer. He can see anything that gets past the first sentry and can tell us if it stays in Webb Cove or goes through the narrows towards Kiahs Island."

Honeycutt studied the map. "Okay," he said slowly.

"Then," Finley continued, "we send another guy to the very eastern edge of North Harbor, right here at the end of Fire Lane 32. There are some houses there, but chances are they won't be occupied this early in the season. He can spot anything that is rounding Coles Point and coming up into Southeast Harbor." He straightened. "If they see anything, they call us on their cell phones and we try to close the net."

"What if they go up Eggemoggin Reach?" Honeycutt asked.

Finley shrugged. "Harder, but still doable. And the *Vigilant* should be able to follow them better up there, more deep water."

"I agree," Captain O'Brien confirmed.

Honeycutt and Commander Mello exchanged a speculative look.

"Makes sense in terms of monitoring where they're going," Mello said thoughtfully. "The *Vigilant* can handle this storm okay."

"Unless we have to go up into the island archipelago," O'Brien broke in. "If we do, then all bets are off. Too many shallows and rocks up there for safe passage at night in this weather."

Honeycutt wagged his head back and forth. It meant sending out three of his men, and he didn't really have them to spare, but he could get them back fairly quickly if he needed to. And most importantly, they had to locate the drop point if this was going to work.

"Okay," he said briskly. "I agree." He pointed to three of the DEA agents. "You three are the chosen ones. Get binoculars and go where Frank Finley tells you." He rattled off his cell number. "I want reports every ten minutes, and immediately if you spot something. Go!"

Honeycutt looked around the command trailer sourly. From this command trailer he had access to ships, drones, helicopters and computer databases of every size and flavor, but he was reduced to sending men armed with binoculars out into a storm.

"Goddamned Maine weather," he muttered.

Chapter 52
Hide and Seek

Tommy Duffy was one of Chief Corcoran's favorite bully boys. He knocked on the Chief's door and then entered. Corcoran looked up in annoyance, but his expression changed to worry when he saw who it was.

"What did you see?"

"Well, I, uh, drove by the Holt Pond, the overpass, um, just like you asked. Didn't seen nothin' there. Um, then I drove around a bit. You know, over to the quarry."

Corcoran sighed inwardly, but then, he had not hired Duffy for his eloquence. Duffy's talent was that he followed orders. Any orders. Also, he could shoot the balls off a mosquito at two hundred yards.

"What did you see at the quarry, Tommy?" Corcoran prodded.

Duffy seemed startled by the question, then recovered. "Well, um, there was a trailer pulled up under the trees, and maybe five or six other cars parked off the road. I didn't stop, like you told me, but I took a picture with my phone."

Corcoran took the phone and looked at it. The trailer was in the shadow of some pine trees. It definitely was not a construction trailer, no construction trailer ever looked that clean. There were several other cars, also parked well off the road. At least two of them looked like government issue sedans.

As he was starting to hand the phone back to Duffy, something caught his eye. He wasn't even sure what it was. Holding the phone near his desk light, tilting it back and forth, he thought he could see the shape of a man in the trees, but the picture was just too damn small to be sure. Well, that could be fixed. He emailed the picture to his work address, then opened it on his computer and examined it on the larger screen. The picture was grainier than on the phone, but there was the picture of a man, wearing some sort of military uniform, standing between two trees.

Holding an assault rifle.

Corcoran leaned back into his chair, chewing through possibilities.

Duffy shuffled his feet nervously, worried that he might have done something wrong, but not sure what it could be.

Chief of Police Corcoran came back to himself and smiled reassuringly at him. "You did good, Duffy. Now I want you to call the others. Tell them to bring all their gear: rifles, vests, night scopes, the works. Got it? Oh, and at least three sniper rifles. Four, if you can find them."

"Sure thing," Duffy answered, relieved at having something to do. "What are we doin'?"

"We're going hunting, Tommy," Corcoran told him. "We're going hunting for big game."

———————

On the *Celeste,* Jean-Philippe LeBlanc frowned at the radar screen. The storm was making a hash of things, of course, but he could swear there was another ship out there, perhaps five miles behind them and keeping pace. The radar kept getting a faint, stuttering return, fading in and out. Whatever it was, it was not an immediate threat, but he didn't like it.

He looked at the GPS again. Another twenty minutes to Coles Point, then he'd start moving northwest, following the shore along the Oceanville section of North Harbor and towards the Inner Harbor. If it was the Coast Guard behind him, they'd hesitate to follow him past the turn.

Keeping a wary eye on his radar display, he continued plodding through the storm as the darkness deepened.

———————

While Honeycutt's men were fanning out with binoculars and Chief Corcoran was gathering his forces, the eight Dominican gunmen took Rte. 15 south until they crossed the bridge dividing Holt Pond from Elm Tree Cove. As soon as they were off the little bridge, they pulled the cars into the trees on the east side, retrieved their equipment and walked through the woods to where they had a clear view of the Cove and the beaches on the north and south sides. There was a small house on the north side – Ralph Cudworth's, although they had no reason to know that – but on the south side there was nothing but woods for a thousand feet.

The storm had pushed the tide into the Cove, flooding the outermost trees, so they set up a few feet back. When they were ready, the leader of the group spoke softly into his radio.

"In position," he reported.

In a moment, the voice of Bruno Banderas came back, "About forty minutes. Slow going out here."

The leader clicked the radio twice in reply.

Then the men settled in to wait, hunching in their ponchos against the downpour and the wind and trying to keep their weapons dry. One of the men lit a cigarette and inhaled greedily, anxious to smoke as much as he could before the rain put it out.

———————

On the north side of Elm Tree Cove, Ralph Cudworth stood inside his screened-in porch. When he saw the two cars drive slowly past his driveway, and then turn off just on the other side of the bridge, he'd walked to the porch with his binoculars and started watching. Wasn't long before he made out several shapes on the south side of Elm Tree Cove, standing just inside the tree line. Then one of the dumb bastards even lit a cigarette, giving off enough light so that Cudworth could see he was carrying a weapon.

Cudworth retreated slowly off the porch and into the house. He spent a minute finding Frank Finley's phone number, then picked up the phone.

———————

Calvin Finley sat at home alone and confused. Actually, he was not at his house – that was an active crime scene – he was at his grandparent's house. His mom and grandmother were still at the hospital, sitting with his wounded grandfather. And he was home, wondering where his dad was and what he could eat for supper.

Then the phone rang. Calvin could tell from the ring that it was a call to his house – his real house – that was being forwarded to the grandparents' house. He picked it up.

"Hello, is Frank Finley there, please." It was an older man's voice. Gravelly and bit rough.

"I'm sorry," Calvin told him. "He's not here right now and we don't expect him for some time."

The man on the phone grunted or muttered; Calvin couldn't tell which.

"Can you pass him a message?" he asked anxiously. "This is very important."

"I think so," Calvin replied, a little warily, wondering what this was about.

"Tell him that Ralph Cudworth called. Tell him that there are at least seven men with guns in the woods on the south side of Elm Tree Cove, and that it looks like they are waiting for something. Got that, the south side?"

Calvin was hastily scribbling notes. "Yes, sir, I've got it. He may want to talk to you. Can I have your number?" Cudworth gave it to him.

"And tell him that the men are *not* cops," Cudworth added. "Be sure to tell him that."

"Yes, sir, I will."

They cut the connection and Calvin dialed his father.

"The targets have just turned west and entered the radar shadow of North Harbor," Captain O'Brien reported. "Looks like they are going in now and not going to Eggemoggin Reach."

Honeycutt turned to Finley. "Frank, warn your lookouts to keep their eyes peeled."

Finley stepped outside to call the lookout when his phone rang. Glancing at the display, he saw it was Calvin, then declined the call, sending it to the answering service. He dialed the DEA agent who was watching from the end of Fire Lane 32.

Calvin heard the phone ring twice, then roll over to the answering service. He swore under his breath. His father had declined the call! He knew because he had helped his dad set up the call answering program, which normally required four rings before it activated.

Frustrated, with a knot in his stomach, he redialed.

DEA Agent Walter Mullins stood, cold and shivering, on the rocks at the end of Fire Lane 32. He'd been there for about thirty minutes, mostly crouched behind a pine tree, hiding from the ocean wind that howled up the inlet, lashing everything with stinging rain.

He hated Maine.

He hated the short, buggy summers, the voracious black flies and mosquitoes big enough to carry off small children, the grey skies, the constant fog, the goddamn wind, the lemming-like tourists, all of it.

He loathed the interminable winters that began in October and finally slunk away at the beginning of May. He hated the snow, the ice, and the bottomless slush that made Napoleon's retreat from Moscow look like a Sunday walk through the park.

On his honeymoon, he'd gone to Arizona. And fell in love. It was so hot and so dry that his eyeballs parched and his skin cracked. It was *wonderful*. He'd been looking at Arizona real estate advertisements ever since, but his wife wanted to stay in Maine because of her family.

It was worse than that Kafka play they'd made him read in high school.

His phone rang.

"Wally? This is Finley. Keep your eyes open; we got word three lobster boats passed Coles Point and are heading up the coast of North Harbor. They should be passing you any minute. Call me as soon as you see them."

He hated being called 'Wally.' Made him feel like a sniveling brat from *Leave it to Beaver*.

"Okay," he said, pulled out his binoculars and stepped forward from the lee of the tree so that he could scan the coastline.

Turned out he really didn't need the binoculars. There, no more than five hundred feet away, a white lobster boat loomed out of the storm, heading west. Three minutes later, a second lobster boat passed by, then a third. He could actually hear men talking on the boats, they were that close.

He fumbled with his phone and called Finley.

"Wally? What've you got?"

"They just came by my position," Mullins told him. "All three of them, in line. Not moving very fast."

On the other end of the line, Finley closed his eyes and sighed a deep sigh of relief. The boats were bottled up. Whatever else might happen tonight, the boats were bottled up.

"Wally? Listen carefully," Finley said slowly. "I want you to drive to the end of Fire Lane 37, right at the junction of Southeast Harbor and the Inner Harbor. Make sure they don't see you, but tell me when they reach you and what direction they're going in." Finley cut the connection.

The problem, Finley reflected, was that even though the boats were bottled up, there were still ten or more smaller inlets they could go to, beach the boats and escape overland. He called the other two DEA agents, redirecting one of them to Osprey Point Drive and the other to the bottom of Fire Road 506A. Both positions commanded a good view of the northern part of the large inlet the lobster boats were cruising through.

This way, he hoped, Agent Mullins could tell if the boats turned southwest into the Inner Harbor, or went north through Brays Narrows and toward the northernmost part of the large inlet. And if they did go north, then one of the agents he'd just sent up to the northern edge of the inlet would spot them.

Finley grinned ruefully. A dark and stormy night, ruthless drug smugglers, and only three scouts to watch the rough and ready Maine coast. What could go wrong?

———————

Agent Mullins jogged dispiritedly back to his car, located Fire Lane 37 on the GPS and headed out, windshield wipers on high. Under his slicker, he felt cold and clammy all over his body.

Tomorrow, he promised himself. Tomorrow he would apply for a transfer to the Arizona bureau of the Drug Enforcement Agency.

———————

As the lobster boats turned the corner northeast, they settled into a new line, with the *Samantha* in the lead. Bobby St. Clair kept a close eye on his fathometer and his radar display. There should be plenty of water under his hull, but it never paid to take chances. The waves were calmer now and the land blocked some of the wind. He picked up his radio handset.

"Increasing speed to eight knots," he told the other boats, and inched the throttle forward. He could feel the *Samantha* surge under his feet.

It was a good night.

———————

Finley put his phone away and stared at the map of North Harbor. Another half an hour or so and they'd know where the boats were going to make the drop. He turned to Commander Mello.

"Can your chopper fly in this weather?"

Commander Mello checked the weather readings. "Wind gusts are still a little high, but we can bring it on a course over land and then right to the inlet." He rubbed his chin in thought. "Let me check, but I think so."

"Good," Finley said. "We're going to need it soon. And, Commander, I think you'd better arm it."

His phone rang again. The readout showed it was his son, and that it was the fourth time he had called. He stepped outside the trailer.

"Cal?"

Chapter 53
Stars in the Sky

"Dad! Jesus, it's about time! I've been trying to reach you," Calvin shouted.

Finley sighed. "What is it, Calvin, we're sorta busy here."

"You got a call from an older guy, Ralph Cudworth."

Finley's eyebrows raised. "Ralph Cudworth?"

"Yeah, he said it was important that I give you this message: There are men with guns on the south side of Elm Tree Cove. And...and they're not cops. That's what he said." Calvin felt a little breathless, but he didn't know why.

Finley was quiet for a long moment. "Calvin, is your mother home yet from visiting grandpa at the hospital?"

"No, not yet. She called and said they would be pretty late."

"Son, are there any State Police at the house?"

"No, Dad, they went with Mom."

"Okay, listen, Cal, and do exactly what I tell you," Finley said sternly, trying to keep the panic at bay. "I want you and Jacob to go to Uncle Paul's house. Got that? The two of you-"

"Dad, Jacob isn't here," Calvin broke in. "He left a message last night that he wouldn't be home, then I got another message this morning saying he was on his way to work."

"Ah, Christ." Finley rubbed his face with his free hand. "Calvin, do you know which boat he was supposed to work on today?"

"Yeah, sure, the *Celeste*, one of the LeBlanc boats. He told me he got a call to report early. He was happy about it because he needs the money."

Finley stared at the phone in shock. "Jacob is on board the *Celeste?*" he asked, half incredulous, half resigned.

"Well, yeah, he is," Calvin said a little defensively. "Dad, what's going on?"

"Calvin, go to your uncle's," Finley said urgently. "The key is next to the sugar jar. Stay there, you understand. Stay there until I come get you." He paused. "I love you, son."

The connection broke.

Calvin stood there, staring at the phone. He had no idea what was going on, but he knew that his father could often be one of the most undemonstrative men he had ever seen. And yet his father just told him that he loved him.

A deep sense of dread stole over him.

––––––––––

"Move! Move!," Honeycutt shouted. "The drop is going to be at Elm Tree Cove, the same place the go-fast boat landed last week." He snatched up a ballistic vest and an assault rifle. "All your gear and as much ammo as you can carry."

Commander Mello stood beside him, speaking rapidly into his phone to someone at the Coast Guard Station. "Yes, yes, all the troops you can pull together, armed and in armor. And get the Jayhawk in the air. I want it in a circle pattern two miles inland, ready when we call it. I want the M24 on board with a gunner and a combat allocation of ammo. And the Barrett, with somebody who knows how to use it. Get Mayweather if he's on base, and check the bars if he's not." The Barrett M80 was a .50 caliber sniper rifle which could be mounted in a steel triangle hung from the doorway to keep it stable.

––––––––––

The Dominican team on the south side of Elm Tree Cove squatted beneath the pines and tried to stay dry. The wind was still strong, but the rain seemed to be lessening. The leader had walked about two hundred yards along the shore, carrying his night scope binoculars, but it was still quiet.

That would change. Or it wouldn't. He had been on so many operations for the Cartel, many successful, many not, that he had grown fatalistic about them. He would always try hard to make an operation succeed, of course, but on some level he felt it was fated, out of his control. It was as close as he could come to believing in a higher power. He lived with the ambivalence.

High above him a tiny opening appeared in the clouds. And, just for a moment, he saw stars.

––––––––––

Calvin tried to collect himself and think it through. It wasn't easy. He knew something was going to happen at Elm Tree Cove. He knew his dad was involved in trying to prevent it, and that his dad was hunting drug smugglers. And he knew his dad was upset that Jacob wasn't home.

And that his dad had been distraught when he learned that Jacob went to work this morning on the *Celeste.*

Calvin went to his grandfather's computer, booted it up, then put in a "Where is my phone?" search for Jacob's phone. The Apple map popped up with a bright dot on it, showing the phone was approaching the bend into the Inner Harbor. So, Jacob was still on a boat, probably the *Celeste.*

He couldn't believe that Jacob had gotten involved with drug smuggling. Pot, maybe, but pot was legal now in Maine, so there was no need to smuggle it. Jacob's other big vice was beer; plenty of that around.

Could Jacob not know what was going on? Calvin shook his head. The only thing he knew for sure was that Jacob was on the lobster boat and he was headed for trouble.

And Calvin was the one person who could get him out.

He spent five feverish minutes pulling together some hot coffee, a candy bar, and his cold-water swim gear, fished the car keys out of the drawer and headed for the car. But when he opened the door, he saw Stanley Curtis pedaling on the sidewalk on his beloved Big Moose. His dog, Huckleberry, sat in the basket, looking disgruntled in the rain, but wagging his tail in greeting nonetheless. Stanley saw him and waved. "Hi! Hi, Calvin!"

"Stan! Listen, I'd like to talk to you, but I've got to go help Jacob."

Stanley's forehead wrinkled in disappointment. "That's okay, Calvin, that's okay." Then he brightened. "My dad always told me that if someone needs help, you should always bring some rope. That's what he says. Rope's good. And a knife to cut it with." He frowned again. "I don't really know why, but that's what my dad says. Bye, Calvin!" He turned and pedaled his tricycle down the street through the rain.

Calvin stood for a long moment in the driveway, then sprinted to the basement where he kept his warmest wetsuit and gear. He added a five-inch knife on a belt and fifteen feet of rope. He paused then, weighing his next move, then walked to the bedroom he was using and fished under the bed for his 9mm and a spare clip of ammunition.

"Think!" he muttered. "Are you ready?" Abruptly, he realized he was going about it all wrong and tore off his shirt and pants, then pulled on the thick wetsuit, neoprene boots and hood and put on the knife belt. He got a ziplock bag and put the gun in it, then scrunched the top of the bag and tied it tight with a length of twine. The pair of neoprene gloves went under the belt, the rope went around his waist, and he grabbed the bag with his flippers, mask and food and ran for the door.

Three minutes later he was on Oceanville Road, driving too fast and headed north.

Agent Walter Mullins made it to the end of Fire Lane 37 in record time, doused his headlights and walked past the empty summer home to the shore. It looked like a nice house, the kind some rich doctor or lawyer from Bangor or Portland might own. Past the house the land jutted out into the estuary in two fingers, each the length of a football field. The one on the left was mostly bare, exposed rock, while the one on the right was covered with pines. He opted for the right and walked through the trees, stumbling constantly because he didn't dare use a light. At the end of the trees there was a rocky shelf about twenty feet wide, then the water. Waves curled over the rocks, the spray dampening everything as far as the tree line. The rain was lessening, thank God, but clouds still scudded across the night sky, racing with the wind like sailboats.

Mullins hefted the binoculars and trained them east southeast, but visibility was limited and his line of sight was cut off by a bulge in the Oceanville peninsula. He dialed Finley and when he answered, told him he was in position, but the boats were not yet in sight.

"Great," said Finley, obviously distracted by whatever he was doing. "Call back when you see them."

Mullins grimaced and raised his binoculars once more.

On the *Samantha,* Robert St. Clair motored northwest. He could see Cats Cove coming up on his port side. Just beyond that there were two fingers of land that stuck out into the water, and just beyond them he would turn southwest and head into the Inner Harbor, and then into Elm Tree Cove. The drop point was down there somewhere and, presumably, the guys waiting for them would make themselves known when he got there.

St. Clair hadn't even thought about being the lead boat, it had just sort of happened. His uncle was getting older and St. Clair thought he might be just sliding by on his reputation from his younger days. In any event, his uncle hadn't complained, and St. Clair sort of liked the idea that he would be the first boat in...and the first boat out.

The sailing was getting easier. The rain was noticeably lighter than it had been, though the wind was still strong. Water in the channel would stay plenty deep until he went into the Inner Harbor, then it would get patchy. Plus, there was a good-size rock ledge that stuck out of the water right in the middle of the entrance to Inner Harbor, but he'd been in the Inner Harbor before and he was confident he could pick his way past it without mishap. He hummed a popular tune, eyes roving left and right, taking in anything that might pose a threat.

The *Samantha* growled its way past Cats Cove, then past the two fingers of land and came up to the turn to Inner Harbor. St. Clair thumbed his radio mic. "Turning in now," he told the others.

Then he noticed the flashlight on the shoreline below the second finger. Taking his binoculars, he saw a man running by the shoreline, then stopping and looking toward the *Samantha* with binoculars of his own.

"Shit!" he cursed. "Davey, you got your rifle back there?"

One of the sternsmen straightened. "Yeah, I do!"

"You see that guy on the shore, about ninety degrees off the port bow?" St. Clair asked.

Davey squinted, then finally saw the guy a little over one hundred yards away. "Yeah, sure, I can see him."

"Can you kill him from here?" St. Clair cut back on the throttle, slowing the boat to a little over three knots. He'd need a steady platform for this.

Davey sucked in a deep breath. "Well, I, uh…"

"Yes or no, Davey, and make it quick!"

Davey sucked in another breath. In fact, he was a very good shot. At one hundred yards, with his 3-9x scope, it would be an easy shot. "Yeah, I'm good," he said. It never occurred to him that he was thinking only of the logistics, not of the morality. But that's who he was.

"Okay, get ready," St. Clair told him. "This guy's scoping us right now and I want him down before he can call in the cops."

Davey went to the side locker and pulled out his rifle, a bolt-action Winchester Model 70, .30-06. It had been his father's and he loved it. He slid the magazine into place and removed the protective hood from the scope. On the deck, he pulled over a lobster trap and sat on it, resting the barrel of the Winchester on a towel he'd thrown over the ship's railing. He scanned the shore left and right until he spotted him, then worked the bolt to chamber a round.

"Ready!" he called out, centering the scope on the man's head. On shore, the man turned off the flashlight. But it didn't matter, Davey had him.

As the three lobster boats sailed by him at the end of the finger of land, Walter Mullins realized he had made a serious error. He was on the right outcropping, but the left outcropping was a bit longer, and as the boats sailed further northwest, he wouldn't be able to see if they went straight into Brays Narrows or turned left into the Inner harbor.

Cursing his foolishness, he turned and ran as fast as he dared back through the woods. When he emerged near the summer house, he turned and ran southwest, gasping for air and deeply regretting the second slice of pizza he'd had at the trailer. He needed to intersect the shoreline below the second finger of land so that he would have an unobstructed view of which direction the boats were going.

Once he reached the shoreline, the ground changed abruptly from hard dirt and sand to bowling ball-size rocks that threatened to break his ankles. Mullins fished in his coat pocket for a flashlight and shone it on the ground, picking his way to the edge of the water.

There, just a bit more than one hundred yards away, the first lobster boat was rounding the second finger of land. Sighing with relief, he tucked the flash under his arm and pulled out his binoculars to get a better look.

It was them, all right. He turned off the flash and dug out his phone. Finley answered immediately.

"They're turning!" Mullins said excitedly.

"What?" Finley said. "Repeat that, Wally, I couldn't hear you."

"They're turning! Inner Harbor!" he shouted.

And then, oddly, he was lying on his back, on top of the uncomfortable rocks. His neck was wet and cold, and one foot seemed to be in the freezing water. The wind howled above him and he shivered violently.

"Wally? Wally? Was that a shot?" a distant voice called.

He hated the name Wally. Why didn't he ever tell people that? He should...he should... What?

There was something wrong with his neck. It felt wet and it stung. He tried to reach up and touch it, but his arms refused to move. That was odd, too.

Another violent spasm shook him. *Crap, this isn't good.* His eyelids fluttered; he had to concentrate to keep them open.

"Shit, I think that was a shot. The fuckers shot him!" the voice on his telephone said.

Lot of odd things, tonight, Walter Mullins thought distractedly. So hard to focus.

Far above him, the clouds swirled as if spun by a giant hand. An opening appeared and, through it, dozens of stars shone brightly.

Huh, stars, he mused. *Never thought I'd see stars tonight. Pretty.* His mind drifted away, then drifted back. The stars were still there, warm and almost...beckoning.

Then the stars seemed to reach down for him. Everything grew whiter and brighter. His neck suddenly stopped hurting and even the rocks felt softer. Walter Mullins felt himself rising up...and up. One last thought came to him, a little tongue-in-cheek, a little whimsical.

Are there mosquitoes in Heaven?

Chapter 54
A Meeting in Inner Harbor

Commander Mello was on the radio to the *Vigilant.*

"Captain, I want you to cork the bottle, do you understand? Come up the inlet enough so that they cannot sneak around you on the way out." All around him, men were grabbing guns and ammunition and running for the door, but the Commander spoke calmly and evenly. Finley, feeling his pulse race and the sweat under his armpits, could only envy the man's composure.

Honeycutt, meanwhile, was on the phone with his contact at the Maine State Police.

"No, an hour from now is too late," he barked into the phone. "We've already lost one man. Yes, I *know* your SWAT teams are tied up, but I need you to scrape together anybody you can and send them right now. I will grovel at your feet and beg forgiveness once this is over, but right now I need help and I need it now!" He paced the room like an angry lion and Finley, for his part, was happy to stay in the corner, out of the line of fire.

"No!" Honeycutt shouted. "I didn't alert the North Harbor police because we have reason to believe they're dirty. For Christ's sake, Bill, I'm not going to go into that now. I didn't call them and I stand by that. No, no, I would prefer you not call them either. What I would like is for you to send any available units you've got to the north side of Elm Tree Cove. Got that, the *north side* of Elm Tree Cove. As soon as they are there, they should call me at this cell phone number. Watch for my men; they'll be on the north side, too. And warn them there are armed men on the ground to the south and three lobster boats in the local waters, also with armed men."

He paced back again to stand in front of Finley and covered the phone with his hand. "Frank, take all the men you can and get over there. You're in tactical control until I can get there, but my best advice is to go in on the north side. You're going to be in a gunfight and you don't want to be mucking around in the woods on the south side. Stay on the north side and call in the Coast Guard helicopter if you have to."

Then he turned his attention back to the State Police. "Bill, for the love of God, send your men and *then* clear it up the ladder. If you dick around, I will have more dead agents and I will call a press conference to say that the State Police couldn't get off their asses to help us out!" He paused, listening. "Yes, I know I owe you big. Trust me, this is one night I will be *delighted* to owe you big. Just get your guys on the road."

Finley went out the door, signaling to the other agents to follow him.

In the woods on the south side of Elm Tree Cove, the leader of the Dominican squad cocked an ear. "Shit, was that a rifle shot?" The other men stopped whatever they were doing and listened intently, but whatever it was, it did not repeat.

The leader motioned to one of the men and handed him the binoculars. "Go over there and see if you can spot anything coming in. Hurry!"

The man scurried off, leaving the leader to listen intently for a noise that didn't come again.

Elm Tree Cove was only two miles from the command trailer. At first the driver of Finley's car floored the gas and sped down the highway, but Finley told him to slow down. "Hey, now, easy, easy. We're going to go right by them. If we go roaring by them, they're going to know we're cops and they're going to light us up. Understand? So instead, we are going to look like local traffic, like a couple of guys on the way home. Got that? Normal traffic, just goin' home." He turned around and faced the two men in the back seat. "You guys lie down on the seat. I don't want them spotting four men in a grey sedan, makes us look like Feds or some wannabe SWAT team. So get down, out of sight and stay there until I tell you."

Then he called the second car and told them to drive normally, but to wait for a few minutes before they crossed the bridge. "Once you're across the bridge, drive past the first righthand turn. That'll be Fire Road 498, but do not turn down it. Drive by for a couple of hundred feet and pull over on the grass and walk back. Bring *all* your gear; you're going to need it."

And that's what they did. As they approached the bridge, they saw some cars parked off the road, near the copse of trees that started fifty feet away. They kept driving, and Finley could feel eyes watching him from the woods.

Then they were on the bridge, then over it.

"See, nice and easy," Finley said to the driver, then wiped his sweaty hands on the knees of his pants.

Finley pulled his small band together and they walked in the dark to the other side of Ralph Cudworth's house. "Stay in the trees," he told them, his voice low and urgent. "Set up the floodlights and aim them across the Cove to the south shore, but don't turn them on until I tell you. No noise! I'll be back in five minutes."

Then he walked over to Cudworth's house and knocked softly on the door. He heard someone approaching the door. "Ralph, it's Frank. Don't turn on a light," he whispered. The door opened and Cudworth stood there, an old Army .45 pistol in his hand.

"Christ Almighty," Cudworth said with a sigh. "Am I glad it's you. I thought maybe some of those fellas from the south side of the Cove came over for a looksee." He smiled in the dim light. "I see you got my message."

"Ralph, is that thing loaded?" Finley asked nervously, gesturing to the pistol.

"Of course it's loaded!" Cudworth snorted contemptuously. "Wouldn't be much good to nobody if it weren't loaded, now would it?"

Finley sighed. Too many guns, too many guns in too small an area. "Ralph, we're set up just over there in the woods," Finley told him. "I think it would be smart for you to get in your car and get out of here for the next three hours or so. Whatever's happening should be over by then."

"And miss all the fun?" Cudworth grinned like a little boy with a new toy. "Not a chance, Frank."

Finley shook his head in exasperation. He didn't have time for this. "Then stay in the house and stay down. And for Christ's sake, be careful with that pistol."

———————

Calvin stopped short before the end of Oceanville Road, doused the lights and crept towards the water's edge, his waterproof carry bag in one hand and a pair of binoculars in the other. There were no streetlights at the end of the road, and no lights on the water, but he could faintly hear the rumble of diesel engines through the storm. He scanned the Inner Harbor with his binoculars, but while he could see the shadowy outline of three lobster boats a bit to the north of the rocky ledge that stuck out in Inner Harbor, he couldn't make out which one was the *Celeste.*

Leaving the binoculars on the rocky beach, he crawled to the water and slipped into it. Once he was deep enough, he slipped on his fins and swam out to the rocky ledge. The water was freezing, but he was used to that, and after several minutes he warmed up to the point where he was just uncomfortable, not hypothermic. The waves were high for swimming, two to three feet even in the shelter of Inner Harbor, so he kept his head up and hoped no one would notice him. The tide was also high – extra high with the storm surge – but was starting to drain out into the ocean. As he swam towards the ledge, he was being swept to the right with the current. Well, all right, when the time came, that would help him get closer to the *Celeste,* assuming he could find her.

He reached the rock ledge and crept out of the water. The wind caught at him and a chill ran through his body, making him shiver for a few moments. He crawled along the perimeter of the ledge until he had a view to the north, but while he caught a glimpse of three lobster boats, he couldn't tell for sure which was the *Celeste.* He slid backwards until he was mostly obscured by some of the protruding rock, then fished the thermos out of the carry bag and gulped some of the hot, sweet coffee. It felt like molten lava pouring into his stomach and he gasped with the pleasure of it.

A fresh spurt of rain splattered on him, but the wetsuit protected him from the worst of it. Lying there with his chin in the water, the question that had been snarling at him from the corner of his mind rose up: Was his brother safe?

Then a diesel engine growled loudly and Calvin peeked out to see one of the dark shapes moving towards him.

Crap, had they spotted him?

Jacob was hunched in the corner of the equipment locker, wrapped in the blanket LeBlanc had left and a scrap of canvas. He shivered from the cold. The *Celeste* had stopped and was now wallowing in the waves. There was no light coming under the shed door, so it must be night. His watch had stopped working, so he really had no idea what time it was. Rain beat sporadically against the roof of the shed.

He was very hungry.

It occurred to him that he was going to die tonight, but he didn't know which would be worse, to be shot to death by the hard-looking man or to die from cold and exposure. With that came another thought: did his parents and Calvin even realize he was missing and taken prisoner? If he died, would they even know?

Mostly, though, he was so confused. Why was LeBlanc doing this? What was going on?

Another gust of wind blew through the cracks and crevices of the shed and he pulled the sheet of canvas tighter around him. He leaned against the thin, plywood wall of the shed, his forehead rubbing against the cold, water-soaked grain of the wood.

He couldn't take this much longer.

Bobby St. Clair took one long, last look through his binoculars, but saw nothing amiss. Or more to the point, he really didn't see anything at all. Turning away from Elm Tree Cove, he blinked a flashlight at the two lobster boats behind him. Immediately, his phone chirped to signal an incoming call.

"See anything, Bobby?" LeBlanc asked him gruffly.

"All clear, as far as I can tell," his nephew replied, trying to sound nonchalant.

"Okay, I'm going to call them and tell them you're coming in. Keep a man on the radio in case I need to warn you off."

"Understood," St. Clair replied. "Walk in the park, Jean-Philippe."

"Don't get cocky," his uncle said sternly.

St. Clair grinned in the darkness. He stood to make $50,000 cash if this worked. He turned back to the pilothouse and nudged the throttle forward. Time to go make some money.

Chapter 55
Inner Harbor/Elm Tree Cove

Chief Corcoran and his five men drove slowly up Rte. 15 with all their car lights off. About a quarter mile from the little bridge that crossed by Elm Tree Cove, they pulled off and parked in an unused fire lane. Corcoran took a knee and his men huddled around him.

"Okay, keep your laser sights off until we are in position," he told them. "Safeties on until I say so. You know the drill. We are going to go through the woods until we are about a hundred feet from the south shore of Elm Tree Cove. The drug guys should be in position close to the water, but hidden in the trees." He looked around to each of them. "You've all got radios and ear buds." They quickly performed a radio check. "Nobody talks but me. Nobody! I don't care if you've got a snake biting your balls, you don't make a sound. We go in quiet. We mark their positions, then we wait until all three boats have dropped off their loads."

He grinned then, joyous and predatory. "Then we take out the fuckers. All of them! No witnesses. If we can, we take out the lobster boats as well."

The men nodded, but one asked, "What about the DEA guys on the north side?"

Corcoran nodded to Duffy, the group's best sniper. "That's his job. Once there is a firefight between the DEA squad and the druggies, Duffy will take out as many of them as he can with his sniper rifle. Most importantly, he keeps them on the north side of the Cove. Don't have to kill 'em all, but have to keep them on their side."

Duffy nodded, his earlier nervousness gone. He understood shooting.

Shooting was what he did.

On the north side of Elm Tree Cove, Frank Finley lay on the wet ground, covered with pine needles and mud, holding a pair of low-light binoculars and scanning the Cove and, just past it, Inner Harbor.

Or trying to. Between the intermittent rain and the damn humidity, his binoculars kept fogging up. He wiped them off with a handkerchief and tried again. He could make out the rock ledge that formed the rough boundary line between Southeast Harbor and Elm Tree Cove, and aways beyond it, three dark shapes. He lowered the binoculars and wiped a sweaty hand across his forehead.

Was Jacob on one of those boats?

One of the DEA agents crawled beside him. "Picking up movement on the south side," he whispered.

"What kind of movement?"

"Four guys with assault rifles have moved to the water's edge," the man said. "Looks like they're getting ready to receive a shipment."

The words were barely out of his mouth when the deep-throated rumbling sound of a ship's diesel engine came over the water.

It was starting.

"No one shoots!" he whispered into the radio. "If they're going to bring the packages in one at a time, we will wait for the third boat, got it?"

A series of clicks on the radio handset served as the reply.

"Stay down, out of sight. Agents Meacham and Sadler, you take as many pictures as you can. Try to get faces when possible and be sure to get the name of the boats." Finley looked up into the sky, wondering if the wind had dropped down enough yet for the drone. "Agent Cipollone, see if the Coast Guard can get the drone back into the air."

His cell phone vibrated in his pocket – Howard Honeycutt.

"Frank, I just pulled in and parked my car near yours," Honeycutt told him. "I've got the two Coast Guard shooters with me, but I left Ensign Kauders and Commander Mello to man the command trailer. Where are you?"

Finley gave him directions. "Stay low, no noise and call me again when you're close," he told Honeycutt. Then he radioed his men that friendlies were coming in behind them. "Resist the temptation to shoot them." He got answering clicks and a chuckle.

Honeycutt crawled up beside him several minutes later. "What's the status?" he asked, puffing a little. He was getting long in the tooth to be crawling around the woods in a storm.

"One boat coming in now. A bunch of bad guys, maybe six or more, on the other side of the Cove," Finley replied, still peering through the binoculars.

"Any hot coffee?"

Finley shot his boss a look. "Only if you brought it."

"Ah, well," Honeycutt sighed. He peered out into the darkness and recalled what the map looked like. "Josephs, Santana!" he called in a low voice. A moment later the two Coast Guard Petty Officers First Class appeared next to him, looking like a pair of mismatched, diabolical twins.

"You two have the best rifles," he told them. "Light-enhancing scopes, right?"

They both nodded solemnly.

"Good, find a position where you have a clear field of fire along the south bank. When the shooting starts, you are our big guns. You need to identify each enemy's location and take them out as quickly as you can, then move to the next one. Questions?"

Josephs and Santana looked at each other. "No, sir," Josephs said, "but we can't see shit in this weather. What's behind these guys? If we shoot and miss, are we shooting into a house or something behind them? Commander Mello will be pissed if I shoot up an orphanage or a convent or something."

Honeycutt started to answer, then realizing he had no idea, stopped and turned to Finley. "Frank, do you know?"

"Yeah," Finley said. "From the water's edge, the ground slopes up to a height of about eight feet. As long as you don't shoot high, you're okay. There is a house about one thousand feet back. Be careful if they retreat over the ridge line. Unless you have a really good shot, don't take it."

"Roger that," Josephs said. "Get your ass in gear, Santana, time to save the world." The two Coasties exchanged grins and crawled off into the darkness.

Finley stared after them a minute. "You know, they saved my family, but they're still two of the scariest guys I know."

"And more importantly," Honeycutt snorted, "they're on our side."

Finley looked out to the Cove. "First boat's here."

———

Petty Officers First Class Josephs and Santana crawled to the edge of the woods, found some cover behind a clump of gnarled pine trees and took a long look at the south side of Elm Tree Cove. Their binoculars were good in low light, but on the other hand they weren't high-tech night-vision binoculars, either. Not much to see, other than a shadow or two moving dimly in the woods on the other side.

Josephs gauged the width of the Cove at 400 feet, give or take. The wind was a bitch and almost directly in his face. "Wind is going to play hell with our shots," he murmured. He looked once more at the south shore. It was invitingly close.

"You know," he mused, "it's so narrow here we could swim across in no time. Once over there, we could have a lot of fun."

Santana gave him a scornful glance. "You think you're the only guy here with a low-light scope? Swim across there with our rifles held up to keep 'em dry? Shit, you'll stand out like a priest with an erection at church."

Josephs snorted. "Have I ever told you what an eloquent sonofabitch you are?"

Santana shrugged modestly.

In the end, they set up on either side of a stand of three pine trees, within whispering distance of each other. There was also a good-sized boulder sitting between two of the pines, so if things got really hot, they could get under cover. Each man set up a gun rest and cleared the ground behind it so that they could lie down without anything sharp distracting them. Each put five loaded magazines on the ground just to the right of their position. Then they slowly scanned the far bank with their magnified lenses, the low-light feature giving some definition and contrast to what they were looking at.

"See any assholes?" Josephs whispered.

"Couple of guys for sure, and maybe two more a few feet back in the trees. You can bet your ass there are more in the woods," Santana said confidently. "When the boat gets there to deliver its goodies, they'll come out of hiding."

Josephs grunted. "Shit, with the firepower we've got here, we might just want to ask them to surrender."

Santana grinned, his eyes alight with humor. "Where's the fun in that?"

Then they heard the sound of a diesel engine close by.

St. Clair brought the *Samantha* past the rock ledge and into Elm Tree Cove, keeping his eye on the depth finder. There was a very narrow channel running into the Cove, left over from the days when the Cove was used by fisherman to off-load their catch near Rte. 15. Fishermen stopped using it when the big docks were put in and the Cadot family built the fishery. The channel had silted in a lot over the years, but the depth finder still showed water five to seven feet deep. Not great, but good enough.

The channel slanted on a diagonal across the Cove to the southeast corner. St. Clair played the throttle like an orchestra conductor, keeping the *Samantha* moving at one to one and a half knots.

"Okay," he said to one of his men. "Give 'em the signal before they get nervous and shoot us."

His second-in-command lifted a flashlight with some red Saran Wrap taped over the lens and turned it on, then blinked it three times in the direction of the south side of the Cove. They waited for a long moment.

"Wonder how many rifles we got pointed at us right now?" St. Clair mused, which was, perhaps, more ironic than he intended. The *Samantha* reached the end of the channel and he pulled back on the throttle, giving it just enough power to prevent the wind and tide from pushing it backwards. He did it without thinking, muscle memory learned from thousands of hours at the helm.

One hundred feet away from him, the leader of the Dominican smugglers was studying every inch of the *Samantha* through his binoculars. To his left and right, seven men had their AK-47s aimed in, ready to fire. After scanning the boat, then sweeping the Cove and Inner Harbor once more, the leader raised his flashlight and blinked it twice, paused, then twice more. Beside him, his men relaxed and lowered their rifles. As one, they stood up and stepped forward to the water's edge.

Every man aboard the *Samantha* felt their balls shrivel when eight armed men suddenly appeared out of nowhere. Then there was a collective sucking in of air and nervous shifting of feet.

A voice from the shore called, "Can you come in any closer? Close enough to throw it to us?"

St. Clair checked his depth finder – four feet. Just enough, but no safety margin. But then, this really wasn't a night for safety margins.

"Maybe a little," he called back. "I can get the bow in the mud a little, but I can't risk getting it stuck."

"Okay," the voice called back. "Come in as much as you can."

St. Clair tweaked the throttle. Just a touch, and the forty-foot vessel crept towards shore. Five feet later, St. Clair could feel the bow begin to ground in the mud. Still too far from shore to throw the package, he pushed the boat into reverse and backed out.

"Hey!" the leader shouted. "Where the fuck are you going?" Beside him his men raised their rifles threateningly.

St. Clair killed the throttle and leaned out from the pilothouse. "My bow was grounding. You know what that means? You want this boat stuck here so the other two boats can't bring their packages in?" Even in the darkness he saw the doubt and annoyance on the Dominican's face. "I'm going to back out about fifteen feet and try coming in twenty yards or so to your right. I only need another foot or so of water under the bow and I should be able to get in closer to shore. You cool with that?"

The leader knew nothing about boats and channels, and he didn't like this man backing his boat further away before he delivered the package. "You try anything, *puta*, and I'll blow your fucking boat to matchsticks."

Fighting the urge to vomit, St. Clair smiled at the man. "Of course you will, and everyone within half a mile will hear your gunshots and call the police. Won't that be good? Now stop fucking around and let me do my job. Just be cool and you'll have the package in ten minutes."

"This goes wrong, you die first," the leader growled.

"Yeah, yeah," St. Clair shot back, then put the boat in reverse and backed out into the channel, spun the wheel to the port side and edged her forward. As he hoped, the water got a little deeper here as the Cove widened towards the Inner Harbor. Not much, but he didn't need much. After fifty feet or so, he brought the wheel over and turned the bow into shore again. The depth finder showed four and a half feet. He could see the Dominicans walking along the shore to where his bow was pointing.

"Jesus, Captain, don't beach us," one of his men muttered. "These guys give me the willies."

St. Clair took the boat in until the bow kissed the ground just ten feet from the bank. He flipped the throttle to idle and nodded at his second. "Throw it over to them, Leo."

Leo, a big man with a barrel chest, picked up the fifty-pound package and walked out onto the small bow, then knelt down and gently dropped it into the arms of two of the Dominicans. "And a very good night to you fine gentlemen," he said pleasantly.

The two Dominicans gave him a hard look, but said nothing, then waded ashore with $13 Million of heroin and Fentanyl. On shore, the leader waved the boat away. "Go! Send the next boat. Tell them to hurry."

———————————

From the north side of the Cove, Finley and Honeycutt watched the boat off-load the drugs, while other agents took still and video pictures of the incident.

The *Samantha* reversed back into the channel and turned north towards Inner Harbor.

The Dominicans dragged the parcel back into the woods and stashed it, then got ready for the second boat.

One hundred feet deeper in the woods, Police Chief Michael Corcoran and his crew silently watched, taking note of where the drug parcel was hidden.

Across the Cove, hidden in their sniping nests, Petty Officers First Class Josephs and Santana watched it all through their sniper scopes.

"Be nice if the rain stopped," Josephs muttered.

"Be nice if you stopped whining, too, but I ain't expecting either to change soon," Santana retorted.

Chapter 56
The Second Boat

The *Samantha* sailed right by him. Calvin lay very still, his face turned away, most of his body underwater. Once it was past, he confirmed that the other two boats were holding their positions, about eight hundred feet away, visible only as dark shapes.

One of them was the *Celeste,* with his brother on board.

Calvin was suddenly struck by the realization that he had no idea how he was actually going to free Jacob. What if he was wrong and Jacob wasn't being held captive by LeBlanc? What would happen if he somehow got on board and Jacob didn't want to go with him? What would happen if he got on board and Jacob wasn't there?

The *Samantha* chugged away, moving slowly. Calvin had no idea how deep the water was, but figured that was St. Clair's problem, not his. He had enough problems. He smiled, remembering the phrase his grandfather liked to use: "Sufficient unto the day is the evil thereof," or something like that. Yes, Calvin's problems were sufficient unto the day. He sure as hell didn't need any more of them.

Slipping again into the frigid water, Calvin let the current sweep him toward the remaining two ships. He was confident that they would not light up any search lights, even if they thought something was in the water, but just in case, he kept his head low and used a slow, steady breaststroke to guide him in the right direction.

Jacob would be there, or he wouldn't. But he had to try.

———————

"We'll wait until the *Samantha* is past us," Jean-Philippe LeBlanc said, "then we'll go down the channel to make the delivery." He had thought this through. If there were DEA stormtroopers out there, they would most likely wait until all three boats had delivered their packages, which meant that he did *not* want to be the third boat. No, he was going to drop the goods and then run for the sea. He was pretty sure that it was too windy for a police helicopter to hunt for him. And he'd let St. Clair be the first to head down the channel to the ocean. If there was a Coast Guard cutter waiting down there, LeBlanc would have enough warning so that he could go hide in one of the dozens of little coves and cubbyholes spread throughout the Inner Harbor.

Hard on St. Clair, but that's the way it was.

Banderas nodded. "I'll be getting off with the package." He gestured to the equipment shed at the stern of the boat. "What about the kid?"

LeBlanc shook his head. "He stays with me until I know we're out of here safe and sound."

Banderas shrugged, managing to convey both disagreement and disinterest at the same time. "Your problem, then. But remember, no loose ends."

"No loose ends," LeBlanc confirmed, and with that, sealed Jacob Finley's fate.

The water didn't so much embrace Calvin as assault him. The receding tide was pulling him out in one direction while the gusting wind was pushing the top layer of water in the other, with the result that the wavetops were constantly battering him about the face and head. The rain, which had seemed to be lessening just minutes ago, suddenly renewed with an almost tropical intensity, leaving the air for several inches above the water filled with a thick, choking miasma of water vapor. Could a man drown with his head out of water? He wondered grimly if he might find out.

Then, just to complicate things, another sound added to the mix, the guttural, throbbing sound of something large bearing down on him from behind.

The *Samantha* was returning, and he was right in its path.

Careful not to turn his head and show his white face in the darkness, Calvin began to swim diagonally towards the nearer of the two lobster boats.

Two hundred feet, one hundred feet, then fifty, then he was alongside the bow and letting himself be pulled toward the stern. Above him he could dimly hear voices.

"Relax, Bruno. Bobby is bringing his boat back now. Should be another ten or fifteen minutes, that's all. It's a narrow channel in there, so he's going slow."

It was hard to tell whose voice it was, but it sounded like Jean-Philippe LeBlanc. As he approached the stern, Calvin flattened his gloved hands against the hull to stop his forward momentum and peered owlishly at the name painted there.

Celeste.

Calvin let out a deep, shuddering breath – the first big hurdle completed. Pulling back his arms, he let the current take him the rest of the way to the stern, where he caught one of the service ropes and used it to swing around. And there, right above him, was the equipment shed, blocking the view of anyone looking this way from the pilothouse. Sliding along the stern, he reached the edge of the shed and cautiously did a chin-up on the protruding edge of the work deck, peeking over it towards the bow. He could dimly make out people standing near and in the pilothouse, but no one else.

Point of no return, he thought. Once he climbed up on the working deck, the chances of discovery skyrocketed. He got a good grip on the protruding lip of the work deck, said a quick, urgent prayer to the God who protected fools, then, in one fluid motion, pulled himself up onto the deck and stepped behind the shed. Out of sight of any prying eyes, he dug into his swim bag and pulled out the gun. Tearing off the plastic, he worked the action and checked that the safety was still on, but then was ambushed by a gut-wrenching sense of indecision and doubt that left him sweating and nauseous.

Could he actually shoot somebody? These guys weren't some Mexican Cartel thugs, they were fishermen from North Harbor. If one of them found him hiding, could he pull the trigger? Could he kill someone? A storm-driven wave caught the stern then, pitching Calvin forward into the back wall of the shed, smashing his head against the rough plywood. All the fear and rage that had been simmering inside him for the last hours threatened to burst forth. Calvin took a deep breath to steady himself, then tapped the butt of the pistol against the wall of the equipment shed. Just a light tap.

Trembling now with adrenalin, he shuffled to the left side of the shed and peered out at the pilothouse, but no one was looking in his direction. Sagging with relief, he crept back behind the shed, once again out of sight.

That's when someone tapped on the shed wall.

From the inside.

"Hello?" The voice was low and desperate...and wonderfully familiar.

———

On the *Celeste,* Jean-Philippe LeBlanc watched through binoculars as the *Samantha* laboriously made its way back out of the Cove.

Bruno Banderas came up to stand beside him. "What's taking so long?" he asked. He didn't like being on the water at night, didn't like the wind and the rain and how it made the lobster boat yaw back and forth like a child's toy. It all felt wrong, somehow, like the ocean was trying to seize the boat, and him, and suck them under the water. Worse yet, he was pretty sure LeBlanc could sense his discomfort.

"Relax, Bruno," LeBlanc chuckled, confirming Banderas' suspicion. "Bobby is bringing his boat back now. Should be another ten or fifteen minutes, that's all. It's a narrow channel in there, so he's going slow."

"No problems, then?"

LeBlanc shook his head. "Nah. Looked like Bobby had to maneuver around a bit to get close enough to shore to hand over the package. We might have to do the same. Just to be expected in tight quarters like this."

Neither man turned around to look at the stern of their boat. Had they, they might have noticed a figure in a black neoprene wetsuit pull himself out of the water and slip behind the equipment locker.

Chapter 57

Best Mom in the World

The house was empty and dark when Danielle Finley and her mother arrived home from the hospital around 8 p.m. Her father had been conscious, but fuzzy from the drugs and grumpy from the pain. Both women were exhausted and emotionally spent.

Once she had taken off her coat and put the kettle on, Danielle put in a call to her husband.

No answer.

She tried Jacob, figuring he had to be off the boat by now, given the hour and the weather.

No answer.

She tried Calvin. No luck there, either. Finally, she tried her brother, Paul Dumas. He picked up on the second ring.

"Paul, do you have any idea where Frank is?" she asked, a little snappish with fatigue and hunger.

Paul Dumas, sitting in the command trailer, surrounded by computer screens, maps, charts, people yelling into microphones, and at least three armed guards, found himself at a loss for words.

"Frank?" he repeated stupidly.

Danielle sighed. "Yes, Frank, my husband? Remember him? I can't find him or either of the boys."

Paul took a deep breath. Frank was out at Elm Tree Cove ready to go to war with some Mexican cartel. There was a chance – a very good chance – that Jacob was on the *Celeste* and about to drop off a shipment of heroin. And God only knew where Calvin was.

Standing next to him, Commander Mello bellowed into the phone: "I don't care if the crew is at dinner, I need that chopper in the air. Rearm the bird and get it up. Right now!"

"Listen, sis," Paul stammered. "I'm right in the middle of-"

"Paul, what the hell is all that noise? You sound like you are in the middle of a shopping mall or something."

For a long and awkward moment, he said nothing. "Danni, where are you now?"

"I'm with Mom, at her house," Danielle said. "We just got home from visiting Dad; who is in a lot of pain and would appreciate a visit from his son, by the way."

Paul looked around bleakly. He couldn't tell his sister what he and Frank were doing, that would send her up a wall, to say nothing of his mother. But there were a bunch of Cartel hitmen on the streets tonight and they might consider Danielle and his mother to be unfinished business. "Listen, Danni, I want you to turn on all of the outside lights, then lock all the doors and windows and stay there. I'll come over as soon as I can. Whatever you do, do not answer the door or go outside for any reason. Okay?"

Danielle stared at the phone. God in heaven, was she going to have to go through this again? "Paul, you are scaring the hell out of me."

"I know. I'm sorry," he apologized. "I'll be over as soon as I can. I'll call you when I'm in the driveway."

"Jesus, Paul, what's going on?"

"Hopefully only good stuff, Danni, but let's not take any chances," her brother told her. "Got to go." He cut the connection.

On her end, Danielle slowly dropped her cell phone back in her pocket.

"Danni?" her mother called. "What would you like for dinner? I can offer you tuna fish on wheat with a tomato...or tuna on wheat without a tomato." Then she walked into the kitchen and stopped when she saw the look on her daughter's face.

"Or perhaps," she amended, "a tall Scotch is in order. I could certainly use one."

Danielle looked at her, then shook her head as if to clear it out. "I have five men in my life who are more important to me than anyone except you. She held up a finger. "One is in the hospital with gunshot wounds and doesn't know yet if he'll ever be able to hold a stone chisel in his left hand. One just told me to lock all the doors and windows and I don't know why." She turned to her mother with tears in her eyes. "And I can't reach Frank or the boys and I'm getting scared, Mom, really scared that something is very, very wrong."

Her mother reached up to cup her daughter's face, the same gesture she had used to comfort her since Danielle was a little girl crying from a scraped knee. "When you were little, I used to be able to give you a hug and kiss the boo-boo and send you on your way with a smile, but I think this calls for a Scotch." She busied herself at the kitchen counter, dropping ice into two glasses and pouring a generous dollop of Scotch into each." They sat at the kitchen table, neither one saying anything for a few minutes.

"Do you think Dad will get better?" Danielle asked.

"Your father has a thoroughly mixed genetic heritage," Céline said disapprovingly. "I've been with him for almost fifty years and he has a knack for getting into trouble, sometimes violent trouble, but he always pulls through." She took an unladylike swallow of her drink. "I swear that man is half bull elephant, half mountain goat, half cockroach and half cat with a surfeit of lives. Things that would kill an ordinary man barely slow him down."

"You shouldn't drink, Mom," Danielle scolded in jest. "It trashes your math ability."

Céline put down her glass and looked her daughter full in the face. "Danielle, what's going on? Why were those men at your house with guns? Why did they attack you?"

Danielle sat back in her chair, putting a little distance between the two of them. "I can't tell you, Mom. I'm sorry, but I can't."

Her mother frowned, but nodded. "Okay, then, tell me this: Are those men coming back? Is that what Paul was warning you about?"

Danielle started to speak, to protest, to deny everything her mother said or implied, but in the end all she could manage was, "I don't know, Mom. I just don't know."

Céline stared at her for a long time, then nodded and walked downstairs to the basement. Danielle could hear her down there, but couldn't tell what she was doing. A few minutes went by, then she could hear Céline walking slowly up the stairs, something thumping on the stairs as she ascended. She emerged into the kitchen holding two shotguns.

"We often rely on our men to protect us," her mother said, smiling a little mischievously, "but there is no reason why we can't protect ourselves perfectly well." She handed one of the shotguns to Danielle. "Always best to be prepared," Céline told her daughter. "Just like when you were in Girl Scouts."

Danielle felt tears prick the corners of her eyes. She smiled tremulously. "Best Mom in the world," she said.

"No more Scotch for us, tonight," her mother said brightly. "Would you like a cup of tea?"

Chapter 58
Brothers' Reunion

Jean-Philippe LeBlanc started to push the throttle forward, but then thought better of it. He waited for the *Samantha* to pull alongside. "How did it go?" he called over to St. Clair.

"Well, the channel is pretty snarky," his nephew answered, a sailor first and foremost. "Kind of peters out and bends to the left. "You'll have to go in slow until you beach, then give them the package and back out until you can turn around." He shrugged his shoulders. "Not too bad."

LeBlanc nodded, accepting the information. "And what about our *friends* on shore?" he asked, giving the word 'friends' a heavy dose of irony.

St. Clair wrinkled his nose ruefully. "Ah, they are very nervous and they have very big guns. Lots of them. Best to go in slow and smile a lot." He nodded once to Bruno Banderas, standing beside LeBlanc. "No offense intended, but they seem rather touchy."

Banderas did not laugh or smile. "You're with me," he told LeBlanc. "There won't be any problems."

St. Clair waggled his eyebrows at his uncle, as if to say, '*What could possibly go wrong?*', then waved and sailed into the night.

As soon as the *Samantha* was past, two things happened: LeBlanc pushed his throttle forward and Calvin emerged from behind the shed, stepped around the front and unlatched the door, then stepped inside and closed the door behind him. It took no longer than two seconds. He was inside, and so was his brother.

Jacob looked like hell.

He was lying on the floor, with his back wedged into one corner of the shed, hands bound together with plastic ties, and some food smeared on the side of his mouth. The shed stank of urine, and a quick glance showed that Jacob had pissed himself sometime during the long day. His eyes were locked on Calvin's face.

"Cal? Jesus, Cal?" Tears streamed down Jacob's face. He closed his eyes for several heartbeats, then opened them again, as if trying to persuade himself it was real.

Calvin knelt down beside him, and only then realized that his brother was shaking with cold. Pulling out his knife, he quickly cut the plastic ties around his wrists, then dug into his waterproof carry bag and emerged with a thermos of hot, sweet coffee. He poured some into the screw-off cup and handed it to Jacob, who just stared at it. "Here you go, Jacob," he said softly, putting the cup into his brother's hands and wrapping his fingers around it. "Hold that tight and take some small sips. Warm you up in no time." He fished around in the carry bag and brought out an energy bar, tore off the wrapper and gave it to Jacob, who wolfed it down in three bites.

"Easy, not too fast," Calvin whispered. He stood and peered through a ventilation grid in the shed door towards the pilothouse. They were moving into Elm Tree Cove, but very slowly. He glanced at Jacob, who was now gulping down the hot, sugary coffee. How strong was he? Could he swim a couple of hundred yards in cold water? Heck, if he recalled correctly, the shoreline of the Cove pinched in as they moved deeper into it. If they could get into the water, he could pull Jacob to shore in just a few minutes.

"Jacob, can you stand? Can you swim?" he asked softly, pouring more coffee into the cup.

Jacob nodded. "I'm good," he croaked, his teeth still chattering. "More coffee will help."

"What I'm thinking is that once we're close to shore, we might just go over the side and swim like hell. I can help you if you need it," Calvin said. "Get to shore and get into the trees..."

Jacob's shook his head, his face pale. "Won't work! I've been listening to them – there are a bunch of drug guys on the beach with weapons. The Cove is narrow down there, they could shoot us clear from the other side."

Calvin considered, then put his eye to a small ventilation grid.

Then he abruptly stepped away.

"Wha-" Jacob began, but Calvin put his finger to his lips to quiet him, then flattened himself against the shed wall behind the door. Jacob's eyes widened and he thrust his hands together, then down between his legs, hopefully concealing the fact that the zip ties were gone.

The door swung open, hiding Calvin from immediate view. Tommy Burke, one of the two sternsmen, walked in, barely glancing at Jacob as he walked to the corner, picked up a coil of rope and walked out again. Calvin and Jacob both heard the "click" as Burke dropped the latch into place.

"Shit, we're locked in," Calvin said in a low voice, but Jacob shook his head.

"Not a strong latch," Jacob whispered back. "If we can't slip something under the latch and just lift it off, we can kick it open."

Calvin was going to suggest that kicking the door open would be damn noisy when his eye caught something. There, sitting at Jacob's feet, was the thermos of coffee Jacob had been drinking from, in plain view of Burke and the world. If Burke had noticed it, the entire escape would have been screwed.

"Jesus Christ, we were lucky," he breathed.

Jacob looked down and saw the thermos. "Ah, fuck me," he said, then he was laughing and crying all at the same time. Calvin knelt beside him, arms around his brother's shoulders. "Hey, we're doin' good, doin' good. You gotta eat now, Jacob, get your strength back. Eat and have more coffee. I'm going to keep my eye out and as soon as I think we've got a chance, we're outta here."

Jacob pulled back and wiped his nose. "I've been in here all day, Cal. Just thinkin'." He tried to smile. "I heard them talking about drugs and delivering them tonight. I think they're using me as a hostage to keep the cops from getting them. Dad, I guess. But, Cal, once they deliver whatever the hell this package is, I think they're going to kill me and dump my body in the water. They got no choice – I know who they are. They can't leave me alive, can't risk it."

Calvin leaned in, touching forehead to forehead. "Nobody's going to kill you, I promise. I've got a gun, if it comes to that."

Jacob shook his head. "No, you don't understand. I-I don't want you to die, too. I want you to sneak out and get to shore. With your black wetsuit, maybe they won't see you. You can get help, but I don't want you here when they come for me." He hung his head. "Ah, Christ, I've been so fucking stupid. I think they used me to get stuff about Dad and what he'd been up to." He rubbed his face with both hands, smearing snot and tears and dirt. "I couldn't bear it if something happened to you."

"You dumb shit," Calvin grinned. "Mom would kill me if I left you here. I'm a lot more afraid of her than anybody on this boat. When I go, you go with me."

———————

Bobby St. Clair navigated the *Samantha* back past the rocky ledge and further to Southeast Harbor. There, he cut the throttle and let the boat rock from the waves and the ebbing tide. If he turned right, to the east, he would head for open water and his home port. Of course, it hadn't escaped him that his Uncle Jean-Philippe had maneuvered to be the second one to make the delivery. That left the *Samantha* the first one to go down the channel to open ocean, which meant it would be the first ship to run smack into the Coast Guard if they had a cutter parked there. If it were him, he'd put the cutter just east of Toothacher Ledge, where the channel was narrow and there was nowhere to hide.

Uncle Jean-Philippe had been pretty slick. He'd made sure he wasn't the last boat in, nor the last boat out. If things went tits up, he'd be in the best position to run deeper into the maze of coves and inlets and try to hide, or abandon his boat and go ashore somewhere. St. Clair grinned ruefully – maybe his uncle wasn't going soft after all. Maybe he was sly as an old fox.

"Guys," he called back to his crew. "We're going to take a little detour. Instead of going home tonight, we're going west. We'll snug the boat up in some little cove and camouflage it as best we can, then see what's what in the morning."

One of his crew looked at him with concern. "Something wrong, Bobby? You know something?"

St. Clair spun the wheel and the *Samantha* turned west, slicing through the water towards Current Island and the Brays Narrows. "Nah, just being careful is all," he replied. "Just being careful." He whistled softly through his teeth. Uncle Jean-Philippe would be mad as hell when he found out what he'd done.

Tough shit, St. Clair thought.

LeBlanc guided the *Celeste* down the channel into Elm Tree Cove. It was very dark, in that oppressive, squinting way it gets when the clouds are low and the air is full of oily rain. Normally he'd have the floodlights on, but not tonight. Eyes on the depth finder, he took his boat in slow and careful. The *Celeste* was four feet longer than the *Samantha,* and a foot broader in the beam, so slow and easy was the name of the game. Banderas stood beside him, nervously shifting from foot to foot. LeBlanc was a little surprised; Banderas was such a hard-ass that he rarely displayed nervousness.

"Glad to be getting onto dry land, Bruno?" he asked.

"Glad to be finished," Bruno said shortly. "Most of my jobs are simple. Go to this place, do this thing, go home." He suppressed a shudder. "This job, nothing but problems, problems, problems. And your ocean, I do not like your ocean. Too...too-" he groped for the right word.

"Cold?" LeBlanc suggested.

"Mean," Banderas corrected him. "I think your ocean wants to kill me."

LeBlanc laughed, a deep, authentic belly laugh. "You got that right! Fucking meanest ocean in the world. And it doesn't just want to kill you, it wants to kill all of us. You can never take it for granted, that's for damn sure."

Bruno suppressed another shudder. "Dry land will be good."

The short trip down the channel into the Cove was uneventful, if wet. The rain picked up, lashing at the windows and reducing visibility to no more than fifty yards. LeBlanc followed the channel as it curved left, then Banderas stepped out and called softly in Spanish. An answering voice called from the beach and briefly shone a light. Banderas replied in Spanish and came back to the pilothouse.

"He says if you go further to the left, the water stays deep enough so you can throw the package to them in about thirty feet," he told LeBlanc.

LeBlanc checked his depth finder. He was right on the edge of running aground, but shrugged and nudged the boat forward at half a knot. Thirty feet later he felt the bow push gently into the rising bottom and he brought the throttle to idle. He stepped out of the pilothouse. Banderas handed him a thick envelope, then hefted the fifty-pound package to his shoulder.

LeBlanc was surprised to receive his payment before the third package was delivered, and said so.

Banderas smiled coldly, pausing at the rail. "It is a matter of risk, no? And with you there is no risk. I know where your family lives, where your children go to school, where you go to drink with your friends. You will never cheat us because there is nowhere you could hide. You know this."

LeBlanc did know it, but his blood ran cold and his bowels turned to water hearing Banderas say it. They dropped a small ladder off the starboard side and Banderas swung a leg over. "I'll contact you in two months about another shipment," he said, then he lowered himself into chest-high water and began wading ashore. Six men with rifles emerged from the trees and helped him out the water, two of them taking the package. One of the men waved to the *Celeste* and called out softly: "Send in the last boat!"

LeBlanc threw the engine into reverse and backed away, but at the first opportunity, he counted the money in the envelope. It was all there, and he breathed a sigh of relief. Hard to know what he would have done, or *could* have done, if Banderas had cheated him at the last minute.

After all, they knew where his children went to school.

"That's two. One more to go," said Finley. "Get ready, everyone. As soon as the next boat drops its package, we'll take them." He crawled over to Honeycutt. "Where are the State Police?" he whispered. "We need more men if we're going to send a team across the bridge to block their escape."

"If they don't come in time," Honeycutt answered, "I'll send you and the two Coast Guard guys across, then announce our presence from this side. You'll want to disable their cars first, then find a good shooting position."

Finley was appalled. "Christ, Howard, you call that a plan?"

Honeycutt grimaced. "If you've got something better, I'm all ears."

"What about the helicopter?"

Honeycutt looked grim. "I checked with Commander Mello a few minutes ago. The helicopter took off, then had to return to base because the winds were still too high. Weather might ease up in an hour or so, but that's probably too late to help us."

"Crap!" Finley muttered.

"The two Coast Guard guys are pretty damn good, Frank, you'll be fine," Honeycutt assured him, with the same blasé confidence of military leaders throughout history.

Finley was reminded of the old doctor joke, when the patient asks if the surgery is going to hurt and the doctor replies, "I won't feel a thing." It really wasn't very funny.

Back in his shooting position, he watched as the boat slowly backed up in the narrow channel, then turned around and picked up speed. His heart felt leaden and cold in his chest.

Was that the boat Jacob was on? Was his son really mixed up in this?

———————

LeBlanc waved to the *Rosie's Pride* as he passed it.

"Any problems?" called the captain, Marc LeBlanc. He was a short, squat man with a bushy beard and a chronically annoyed expression, a man who woke up every morning knowing that somehow the world was going to piss him off that day. He was rarely wrong.

"Channel's tight, but you can do it," Jean-Philippe LeBlanc called back. "When the depth finder hits four feet, turn to the left and you'll get another thirty or forty feet. You'll ground, so go slow. Mud bottom, no rocks. And don't be startled when the drug guys come out of the woods armed to the teeth."

Marc LeBlanc scowled. "Don't like the sound of that."

LeBlanc grinned. "For the money we're making tonight, I can put up with some guys with guns."

His cousin grunted sourly and pushed the throttle forward. "See you after, Jean-Philippe. You're buying the beer tonight!"

LeBlanc laughed. "No beer for us, cousin. Tonight, we drink Champagne!"

His cousin made a rude gesture and LeBlanc laughed again. Then he got on the radio and called Bobby St. Clair on the *Samantha*. "How's it going where you are?" he asked jovially, but he listened intently.

The *Samantha* was halfway through the Brays Narrows, heading northwest, *away* from the ocean. They were almost to Sawyers Island and Long Cove. There was a little inlet less than a mile away, a secluded spot surrounded by tall trees. A great place to hide for a few hours. In high school, St. Clair used to take willowy French girls there and go skinny dipping, and sometimes got lucky afterwards when they were drying each other with soft cotton towels. And sometimes not. He planned on holing up there for the night, then to return back through the maze and into open waters early in the morning. And then...just go lobstering. It wouldn't be the first time the *Samantha* had spent a night on the water.

St. Clair picked up his radio mic. "No problems. All clear where we are," he said truthfully.

———————

On the Coast Guard Cutter *Vigilant*, Captain O'Brien sat in the Combat Center, scanning the inlet to the northwest through a pair of low-light binoculars. Rain hammered at the windows and the cutter rolled queasily under her feet. Her bad shoulder throbbed.

"Anything on radar?" she asked the XO.

"No, Ma'am, but you could hide a goddamned armada behind these islands and headlands," Lt. Commander Hillson replied disgustedly.

Captain O'Brien studied the radar screen, then glanced once more at the charts of the area. The XO was right, there were islands, coves, inlets, peninsulas and all sorts of crap that conspired to make searching for a lobster boat much harder than it should have been. Night like this, a lobster boat could anchor right beside a finger of land or an island, power down and just sit there. For all practical purposes, they'd be invisible.

"What do you think, Mr. Hillson?" she asked mildly. "Should we put the small boat out to poke around and see what they scare up?" They had a twenty-foot inflatable with twin Yamaha 90 HP outboard engines and, more importantly, a mounted machine gun. It would be like a hunter sending out dogs to flush out pheasants. Or perhaps a bear.

Lt. Commander Hillson rubbed his chin in thought. "The small boat doesn't have any armor."

O'Brien nodded in agreement. "You're right, but it's got speed, a .30 caliber machine gun, a siren and a radio. I don't want them fighting a pitched battle, but they can poke around all the bolt holes a boat can hide behind or in. Meanwhile, we block the channel."

Hillson looked at her. They had served together a long time and she knew the look. She sighed. "I know, it's my decision. There's some danger we can't eliminate, but this is what we do, John. This is why we're here." Her shoulder throbbed again, making her yearn for a strong drink, a pain pill and a warm bed. She made up her mind. "Three-man crew. Make sure they wear full ballistic vests and helmets, and I want them to carry a ballistic shield with them so they can have some cover if it gets hot. Oh, and a transponder so we can track them in real time. Launch them as soon as they're ready."

"Yes, Captain," her XO said. She couldn't tell whether he agreed with her order or not, but it didn't matter now. There was another fight coming, she could feel it.

"Master Chief!" she called.

"Yes, Ma'am," Master Chief Petty Officer Ramirez responded.

"Get on the Bushmaster, Master Chief, things may get hot soon."

"Yes, Ma'am!"

Captain O'Brien had been appalled at the carnage they'd wracked on the drug smugglers go-fast boat, appalled and pleased. If she was going to be in a shooting engagement with a drug cartel, it was good to know that her weaponry was up to the task. If the crews on the lobster boats were stupid enough to fight, she intended to win.

As far as she was concerned, happiness was a Bushmaster autocannon.

Chapter 59
Choices

Calvin and Jacob watched through the ventilation grid as the men with rifles dragged the package ashore and carted it off into the woods.

"Who are they?" Calvin whispered.

"Not who, but what," Jacob said. "Drug smugglers, doesn't matter which ones." He turned his back to the grid and slid down the wall until he was sitting on the floor. "We'll go north to Southeast Harbor, then turn east for the ocean. And when we get to the ocean, they're going to throw me in."

Calvin moved to the side ventilation grid. "We're coming up on *Rosie's Pride.*"

"He's such a prick," Jacob said sourly. "I had to work on that damn boat one day, only one day, and I couldn't wait to get off."

"Who?" Calvin asked.

"Jean-Philippe's cousin. All he does is bitch about everything. Worst boss ever."

"Well, he's the last delivery tonight." Calvin wondered if his father was nearby, watching the deliveries and getting ready to pounce. He hoped so. "Anyway, you say Jean-Philippe is getting ready to kill you, so he can't be worse than that." Calvin moved to the front ventilation grid. "Jacob, once we reach Southeast Harbor and we start the turn east, you and I are busting out of here and swimming ashore."

Jacob stared at him. "How?"

Calvin held up the knife he had been carrying all night. "Slip this under the latch, then run to the side and jump. It's only three or four steps."

Jacob looked at him, white-faced and pinched. If they got caught, LeBlanc would kill them right away. If they made it, they'd be in the freezing water getting shot at. Hell, LeBlanc could just turn around and run over them. There were so many things that could go wrong he couldn't even count them.

"Okay," he said. "Sure."

———

Jena-Philippe LeBlanc increased speed when the depth finder showed twenty-one feet, marking the channel that would take him through

Southeast Harbor and into the long finger of water that would take them to the ocean. He chuckled to himself – he hadn't thought it was going to be this easy.

Only one more thing. "Jacques!" he called to his brother. "Get some chain from the locker, will you? We'll need it soon."

Too bad about the kid, he thought, but he was beyond the point of really caring about it. Jacob Finley was just another problem to be dealt with.

Then, from far behind him, the distinct stutter of automatic weapons.

Oh fuck! he thought.

On the *Vigilant,* the three men scampered on board the small boat and fired up the twin Yamahas. With a total of 180 horsepower, the little craft was seriously overpowered, not that Ensign Dunbar cared. Dunbar liked speed and he loved agility. The little boat offered plenty of both. He slipped on his radio headset and set the IFF transponder to "ON." He had no desire to be mistaken for a bad guy this night, not with the Master Chief on the autocannon.

Meanwhile, Seaman Levine was double-checking the .30 cal while Seaman Jankowski was warming up the radar and making sure his M4 was loaded, all the while humming a really stupid pop song.

Captain O'Brien leaned over the rail, wearing a small headset. "Mr. Dunbar, ready?"

"Other than Jankowski's really awful taste in music, we're ready, Captain."

"We all have our crosses to bear, Mr. Dunbar," she said dryly. "Launch your boat. Keep your radio channel open. And Dunbar, remember: you are a *scout*, not Patton attacking across the Rhine." Dunbar saluted smartly, turned the small boat away from *Vigilant*, and goosed the engines. Soon the boat was slamming through the waves and being pelted by wind-blown spray. Within five minutes all three of the young men were soaked and smiling and loving every minute of it, confirming the adage that you don't *have* to be crazy to join the Coast Guard, but it certainly helps.

They sped into the inlet, wind at their backs...armed to the teeth and hunting for bear. What better way to spend a Thursday night?

Chapter 60
Fireworks

Marc LeBlanc guided the *Rosie's Pride* down the channel into Elm Tree Cove without difficulty. His boat was a little shorter than his cousin's and handled well. When he came to shallow water, the Cartel gunmen emerged from the woods and waved him over to the spot where the water was deeper and closer to shore. LeBlanc spun the wheel smartly and soon had the boat nosed into the soft mud bank.

"Good to see you," Banderas said in accented English, his eyes scanning the crew members of the *Rosie's* Pride for anything suspicious. "Let's get the package off quickly."

"Fine by me," Marc LeBlanc said bluntly. He wanted to get out of the cramped Cove and into open water, the sooner the better. His crew was just in the process of dropping the fifty-pound package of heroin over the side when there was the crisp, unmistakable sound of gunfire from across the Cove.

Immediately, all of the gunmen pointed their rifles at the crew of the *Rosie's Pride.*

"*Bastardo!*" Banderas glared at LeBlanc. He gestured to his men.

"No! No!" Marc LeBlanc screamed.

Sometimes it is the littlest things. A cough on a quiet night, the unexpected sound of metal clinking against metal, an ill-thought cigarette in the dark...or an uncomfortable tree root.

DEA Agent Shawn Benson had been lying under a bushy pine tree for close to an hour, peering across Elm Tree Cove and trying to see something, anything. Visibility was tricky – one moment the rain was heavy, the clouds thick and the night black as a politician's heart, but then the rain paused, the clouds opened and thin shafts of light dappled the ground.

That was all very nice, but Benson's immediate problem was that a tree root was stabbing him painfully in the hip. The pain had slowly grown from being a minor annoyance to a sharp, throbbing agony. Although Finley had told them all to hunker down and not to move, the pain felt like he was lying on a fucking chisel and malicious little dwarfs were pounding the blade into his bones. Glancing about to make sure no one was looking at him, he shifted left, but there was another pine root that dug into his shin. No good.

If he crawled back, there was another goddamned root, and if he crawled back even further, his view to the Cove was blocked.

"Well, shit," he muttered. He decided to move forward. Getting awkwardly to his feet, he took one cautious step, then another, but on the third his foot caught on yet another root and he went sprawling. That wasn't so bad in and of itself, but Agent Benson had been carrying his rifle with his finger on the trigger, a bad habit he had been unable to break and usually didn't even think about. As he fell forward, he instinctively threw out his arms, and when he crashed into the ground, his trigger finger was jammed back against the trigger.

The rifle fired. Loudly. It was set to fire a three-round burst, and that is what it did.

On the other side of the Cove, all hell broke loose.

One of the Cartel gunmen had seen the flicker of light from the gunshots and turned his head. A sliver of starlight showed a dark form lying across some white, exposed rock. The Cartel gunman never hesitated. He lifted his rifle and shot a full magazine at the fallen figure.

"Game on," said Josephs. He centered his scope on the gook who'd just shot, and fired his M-16 in three-round bursts. The man crumbled to the ground and Josephs moved left to his other prepared position.

The Cartel gunmen by the lobster boat did what they had been trained to do in the opening moment of any gunfight – they killed everyone near them who might pose a threat. The crew on the *Rosie's Pride* were torn apart by the close-range fire of six AK-47s. Marc LeBlanc almost made it to the side rail on the far side of the boat, but four bullets took him in the back and blew out his chest. He died as he lived, sullen and resentful.

Two of the gunmen clambered on board to grab the package of heroin, then jumped back into the water and waded ashore.

Two more Cartel gunmen scrambled out of the trees, mistakenly thinking that one of the lobstermen had shot their comrade. They milled about, unsure of what to do.

Santana centered his scope on a man's chest and opened fire, then shifted to the man standing next to him. Both men went down. "Jesus, they're fighting dumb," Santana said, then rolled to the right and settled into his backup firing position.

Now they had the Cartel gunmen's attention, and the gunmen began to spray the northern bank of the Cove in earnest. Finley began firing his weapon, meanwhile shouting at his men. "Fire, for Christ's sake! Fire!"

Banderas ordered his men back into the tree line, but in the confusion, the last bundle of heroin was abandoned on the beach. Realizing what had happened, and unwilling to leave it behind, Banderas berated his men to fight harder. "Find a muzzle flash and concentrate fire on it," he yelled to them.

One of the DEA agents tried to move positions, was spotted and shot.

Josephs and Santana patiently waited for a clear shot, then picked off one gunman who rose to his knee and fired an entire magazine at them. Returning fire from the gunmen smacked into tree trunks all around them, and each man buried his face in the dirt.

On the south side of the Cove, Banderas grabbed two of his men. "Go through the woods to the bridge. Make sure no one is coming to flank us. If you don't see anyone, get across any way you can and flank them." He gave them a shove. "Go!"

In the woods behind the Cartel's gunmen, Chief Corcoran and his men watched through low-light scopes. Corcoran saw the two men break off from the main group and run toward the road. He snapped his fingers to get the attention of Duffy and Higgins.

"You two go straight out to the road. There are two of the Cartel guys moving that way now. You'll be behind them. As soon as you see them, take 'em out and come back. Move!"

Without a word, Duffy and Higgins ran through the woods. Duffy was smiling.

On the *Celeste,* Jean-Philippe LeBlanc blinked several times in rapid succession. What the hell happened? "Jacques! Guy!" he called for his brothers. "Go forward and aft and scan everything you can see. I need to know if there is another boat out there!"

The brothers ran to comply, with Jacques standing just inches away from the equipment shed, binoculars to his eyes, oblivious of the two boys crouched down inside. In a minute the two LeBlanc brothers were back at the pilothouse.

"Nothing I could see, but visibility is for crap out there," Guy reported. Jacques nodded in agreement.

They were in Southeast Harbor now, with deep water under the keel. To the left was the entrance to Brays Narrows, which would take them to Long Cove. There were places to hide in Long Cove, but there was no way out except back through Southeast Harbor and down the reach to Jericho Bay and then the open Atlantic. Jean-Philippe instinctively cringed at the idea of being trapped in Long Cove, with police boats and the Coast Guard coming in after him.

To the right, he'd have a straight run to open water, no more than a mile away. On a good day he could make that run in seven or eight minutes, and even with the storm and darkness he could do it in twenty, thirty at the very most. Twenty minutes to open water. He had an envelope with Three Hundred Thousand Dollars in it, plus the other money the Cartel had already paid him.

All he had to do is reach open water.

"Fuck it!" LeBlanc said. "We're going for it. Break out the rifles, then stand watch fore and aft. Keep your eyes peeled. First sign of anything, you tell me quick. And nobody fires a shot until I tell you!"

Jacques gave a whoop and the men scattered to their tasks. Within a minute each man was armed with a pistol and an assault rifle. Jacques' rifle had a 4X-8X scope on it and he held the rifle cradled in his arms. Guy and Doug Tynman, the sternsman, went up to the bow with binoculars and their rifles.

LeBlanc spun the wheel and the *Celeste* turned to the southeast. He pushed the throttle all the way forward and the propeller bit deeper into the water. He couldn't see shit, but there wouldn't be anybody else out on a night like this, except maybe the Coast Guard. There was deep water right up to the shore and the channel was about half a mile wide. There was a good chance he could sneak by the Coast Guard if they were there.

And if he couldn't, well then he had Jacob Finley as his "Get Out of Jail Free" card.

In Elm Tree Cove, the firefight was escalating.

One hundred feet behind the Dominican gunmen, Police Chief Corcoran watched with amusement. They sure were shooting the hell out of each other. He glanced at his watch – the shooting had been going on for almost ten minutes. He'd have to make his move soon, before the State Police showed up, but he really wanted to make sure Banderas was dead first. Nice if he could get Finley as well, but Banderas had to go.

Josephs and Santana had drawn too much attention to their position, so they'd moved behind the boulder to get some protection.

"Those fuckers know how to shoot," Santana said with a mix of admiration and disgust. At least two more DEA agents were down. Honeycutt was on the phone again, screaming for the helicopter, but the wind was still high and Santana wasn't holding his breath. And all around them, bullets slapped into tree trunks, whined off the rock they were hiding behind and clipped enough branches to cause a steady rain of pine boughs.

"We need to find new shooting positions," Josephs said. "They've got this one petty well zeroed in."

"Fuckin' right," Santana agreed cheerfully. "How about we crawl back a bit, then hoof it up to the road? If we can get up to the bridge, we'd have a good angle on them. Might take out a couple before they wised up."

"Sure," Josephs said. "We're not doin' squat here."

They crawled through the trees until they were behind Honeycutt and Finley. "Hey, Mr. Finley," Santana called softly. Finley was behind a tree, which was being peppered with bullets from the far side of the Cove. He looked at them and half smiled, half grimaced. "You boys having a good time?" he asked.

Josephs snorted down a laugh. "Fucking great, Mr. Finley. Fresh air, a gentle sea breeze, a pack of wild-ass assholes with AK-47s. Doesn't get better than this."

Santana spoke up. "We're going over to the road and see if we can't get a better angle on them. Unless you object."

"Go for it, but stay in touch," Finley said.

"What are the casualties?" Josephs asked.

"Three dead, two wounded," Finley answered grimly.

"Christ Jesus!" Santana muttered. "Is any help coming?"

"Well, some State cops are supposed to come, but they're already late. I don't know why the bad guys haven't taken the drugs and already beat feet out of here, but if I were them, I'd be gone as soon as I could." Finley paused for a moment, swung around the tree and fired off three quick shots, then hunkered down behind the tree again.

"You know," Josephs said, "I think they dropped the last package on that little beach there, and they don't want to leave until they get it."

"Really?" Finley brightened. "I didn't see that. Where is it, exactly?"

"'Bout ten feet to the right of the boat, and maybe five feet up from the water."

"Well, let's see if we can keep them from getting that, at least," Finley said. "It's been a piss-poor night so far."

"Mr. Finley," Santana said, examining the tree Finley was hiding behind. "You're gonna get your ass shot off if you stay behind that tree. Way they're shootin' it, bullets gonna start going right through and hit you in another minute or so."

Finley raised his eyebrows in alarm, then let his body slide down the tree. He rolled onto the ground, where he crawled over to a low rock and snuggled in behind it. "Thanks for the advice. You guys call me when you get to your new shooting position. I'll flip on the searchlights when you're ready. Might distract them a little, until they shoot them out."

"Yes, sir," Josephs said, and the two men crawled away from the water, deeper into the trees where they might get some cover. Five minutes later they were up and running.

Banderas peered north across the Cove. So far, he'd lost four men, but the volume of fire from the Yankees had dropped considerably. It was time to get the last package off the beach and get out of there. He gestured to two of his men.

"Crawl down to the beach and grab the last package, then drag it back here. We'll cover you."

The two men exchanged a glance, but got on their bellies and slithered down to the beach, using the lobster boat for cover as much as they could. They got to the end of the boat; the third package of heroin was only a few steps away, but it weighed fifty pounds and it would take the two of them to move it quickly off the beach into the trees.

"Go!" Banderas snarled, then he and his men emptied their weapons at the north side of the Cove.

The two men darted from behind the boat and reached the package in six quick steps. Each man grabbed one of the rope loops and they lifted it off the beach with strength born of desperation.

Then, from across the Cove, two bright searchlights flared to life and lit up the beach like it was high noon.

Chief Corcoran's two men reached the road just south of the bridge. Duffy signaled to Higgins to work his way up the east side of the road while Duffy started to cross to the west, but in the middle of the road, he stopped.

The two Cartel men were just reaching the far side of the bridge, moving slowly and cautiously, their backs to the cops.

Couldn't ask for an easier shot.

Grinning, Duffy lowered himself to one knee, raised his rifle and shot a burst into the man on the left, then smoothly shifted to the man on the right and fired a second burst. Both men crumpled to the ground like sacks of potatoes. Duffy fired two more bursts into them just to make sure, then signaled to Higgins and they melted back into the woods.

One hundred yards away, Josephs and Santana hit the dirt. "What the fuck was that?" Josephs whispered.

"Somebody just got whacked," Santana answered. "I think some of the drug guys were trying to cross the bridge and got caught in the open."

"Yeah, ok, but caught by *who?*"

"I dunno, but that sure as shit sounded like an M16 to me. Three-round bursts."

The two men cautiously crawled through the bushes to where the two bodies lay in pools of blood. Each man had an AK-47 beside him. They wore dark clothes and were dark complexioned.

"Assholes, all right," Josephs said, picking up the rifles and slinging them over his shoulder. "But who the fuck shot them?"

"And why the fuck haven't they shot the rest of them?" Santana wondered.

————————

"Shoot out the lights!" Banderas shouted, then emptied his magazine at one of them. There was the tinkle of glass and one light went dark. A fusillade of shots came back across the Cove, but within moments the other one was dark as well.

The two men on the beach bolted for the safety of the area behind the lobster boat, dragging the package with them.

"C'mon!" Banderas screamed. "Hurry!" The two men scrabbled up the sand and broken rock and reached the trees while bullets whistled around them. Banderas pushed one of them aside, took the rope handle and dragged the precious package deeper into the woods, the other gunmen following behind, all the while keeping up a steady fire against the DEA agents.

They reached the spot where the other two packages had been hidden. Everyone grabbed a handle and started half carrying, half dragging a package through the woods to their cars.

Banderas felt a flood of relief. It had been bloody, but they had done it!

———————

Police Chief Corcoran watched them come, five men carrying three packages worth more money than he had ever dreamed of in his life. They were less than a hundred feet away, barely visible in the gloom. But close enough.

"Okay," he said. "Light 'em up!"

Laser aiming dots suddenly appeared on the chest of each of the surviving Cartel gunmen.

Corcoran's men fired. One shot, then two, then a third.

All of the Cartel gunmen slumped to the ground. No theatrics. No screams. No return fire. They just got shot and fell down.

Keeping their guns aimed at the fallen men, the policemen quickly walked to where they lay in a sodden heap. One of the men was Bruno Banderas, lying on his back in the weeds, his chest covered with blood. Corcoran knelt beside him. Banderas blinked up at him with an expression of bewilderment, fear and hate. "Hey, Bruno," Chief Corcoran said, not unkindly. "Life's a bitch, isn't it?" Then he shot him through the head. Around him, his men were dispatching the others. There would be no witnesses.

"Okay," Corcoran ordered. "You know what to do. Get those packages into the trunk of the spare car and get them out of here. Rest of you, open my trunk and get what's in there. You two," he pointed at Duffy and Higgins, "put on some gloves, take an AK from each of these assholes and come with me. Move it!" he barked, and the men sprang into action.

Corcoran took Duffy and Higgins to the edge of the tree line, where he raised his binoculars and scanned the far bank.

Duffy and Higgins glanced at each other in confusion. "Uh, sir, what is it we're doing, exactly?" Duffy asked hesitantly.

"There's a man over there who is a threat to us," Corcoran said, eyes glued to the binoculars. "Once I spot him, I want you two to shoot him, then we'll join the others."

"Yes, sir," Duffy said.

———————

Frank Finley fired another burst into the south side of the Cove, but there was no return fire. He waited a moment, and when there was still no return fire, he cautiously stuck his head out and scanned the Cove with his binoculars. It was hard to see much, but as far as he could see, there was no one there.

"Christ Jesus, I think they're gone," he said loudly. He stood up from behind the rock that had been shielding him and stepped towards the water's edge. "Sing out!" he called to his men. "Anybody else hurt? Anybody missing?"

———

Across the Cove, Chief Corcoran saw a figure suddenly stand up and heard a voice call. He studied the shape of the man carefully through the binoculars, the way he moved and held himself, then smiled savagely. "Got you, you little weasel." He turned to Duffy and Higgins. "Guy who just stood up. Can you see him?"

Duffy was looking through his scope. He'd been more than a little surprised when the man had suddenly stood up. He'd had pretty good cover, so long as he stayed behind it. "I got him, Chief."

"Higgins, you got him?" Corcoran asked.

Higgins frowned, moving the scope slowly along the tree line. Then, "Got him!"

Corcoran nodded. "He's wearing a vest, so you're going to have to hit him hard, unless you think you can get a head shot."

Duffy calculated. "If we both hit him with a three-round burst in the chest, odds of causing internal damage are pretty good. Hard to guarantee a head shot in this light, though."

"Tell you what," Higgins said. "You go for the chest, I'll go for the head. Might get lucky."

"On 'one,' do it," Corcoran told them. "Three...two...one."

They fired simultaneously.

Chief Corcoran lowered the binoculars. "Shit, where'd he go?"

Duffy grinned. "Knocked him ass over teakettle into the trees."

"Did you get the headshot?"

Higgins shrugged. "We shot at the same time. I had a pretty good bead on him, but in this light I couldn't tell for sure if I got him or not."

"We fucked him up, for sure," Duffy laughed.

———

Finley never knew what hit him. One second he was getting reports from his men, then he felt/heard something *zip* the air on either side of his head. Then something pounded his chest with hammer blows and his body was jolted back and his feet tangled and over he went, cartwheeling to the ground so that most of his body was once again covered by the low boulder he'd been hiding behind. Now he was on his back, one leg snagged on top of the rock and a vicious, sharp pain in his chest. Bullets whined overhead. He coughed once and hot blood splashed on his chin and chest.

That can't be good, he thought distantly. Something shifted within him and the pain got weird. It seemed far away, hurting like hell and almost not at all.

Odd. Is this shock? He grinned inwardly, bemused. *Feels pretty good.* He opened his eyes and looked at the trees above him, birches and pines. *Why do they call this Elm Tree Cove? No elms in sight.* This was important, though he couldn't see why.

Honeycutt was standing over him, shouting his name. Finley wished he would just shut up.

And he'd never felt so tired in his life. So tired.

———————

Corcoran shook his head, frustrated. He wanted to know if Finley was dead, but in the distance there was the distinct wailing sound of sirens. Time to get out. "Leave the AKs, then come with me," he told Duffy and Higgins, "we've got more work to do."

In a few seconds they were out of sight of anyone on the north shore of the Cove. In five minutes, they were back at the cars, where Corcoran gave Duffy his orders again.

"You know what to do," he told him. "Go, and stay out of sight until I call you." As soon as Duffy had driven off, Corcoran turned to the rest of his crew. "Only two more things we have to do, guys. Let's get these packages to the bridge, then we meet up with the Feds. You guys just stand there and look like heroes, I'll do all the talking." Corcoran looked at them. "Got it?"

They all nodded.

"Good," Corcoran said. "Don't fuck it up now."

They picked up the three fifty-pound packages and carried them to bridge, just in time to watch four State Police cars pull up, sirens screaming and lights flashing. State Troopers leapt from the cars, guns drawn.

Much too late.

Chapter 61
Night Action

Calvin could feel the *Celeste* surge as it picked up speed. He searched through the equipment shed for an immersion suit that might protect Jacob from the cold, but found nothing except a flare, which he jammed under the rope Stanley had urged him to take. He looked around, and his eyes fell on a foul-weather jacket with a hood. Hmmm...could he do something with that? It was a size small, which was too small for Jacob, but a little tight might just be what he needed. Rummaging around, he found a roll of duct tape, the universal tool.

"Put this on," he told his brother, handing him the jacket. Jacob struggled to get into it. The sleeves didn't reach his wrists, and the hood went over his head with difficulty. Calvin struggled to get the zipper pulled up, but finally got it tight under Jacob's chin. Calvin stepped back and looked at him.

"Perfect!" he said. Then he ripped off a length of duct tape and circled each sleeve cuff, so it was taped tight against Jacob's skin, making it – hopefully – watertight. He ran a loop of tape around Jacob's waist, making the already tight jacket even tighter, then taped the bottom of the jacket to Jacob's pants. Lastly, he taped the opening of the hood to Jacob's forehead, cheeks and chin.

"There," he said, stepping back. "A poor man's wetsuit. That ought to minimize the flow of water around your chest and allow your body to warm it, just like my wetsuit does." He frowned. "One more thing, I think." He tore off another length of tape and put it firmly over the zipper seam, then added a layer to the left and right of the first one.

"Don't want water to leak in through the zipper," he said, nodding at his handiwork. "This won't make you warm, exactly, but it will buy you some time before hypothermia sets in."

Jacob held out his arms and looked at the duct tape. "I look like a dork," he complained.

His brother smothered a laugh. "I don't know, Jacob. With all that tape, you look like a 170-pound striped bass. Just hope there're no sharks out there tonight," he teased.

Jacob wandered to the vent and peered through. "Hey, Cal," he called softly. "Coming up on Cats Cove."

It was time. Calvin worked the action on his pistol to chamber a round. With his left hand he readied his knife, then looked at his brother.

"Out the door, turn right, two steps to the end of the shed, turn right and one or two steps off the back of the boat." He smiled, trying for reassurance. "Don't worry if you get cold, I'll get you to shore. Ready?"

Jacob nodded, his face pale. They stood looking at each other, then embraced, wrapping their arms around each other in a fierce hug.

"I'm sorry you had to come for me," Jacob said, meaning it.

"I'm not," Calvin said. They pulled apart, still looking at each other. "Hell, this story will get me laid at college parties for years to come," he said, cuffing his brother affectionately on the head. "I just wish it had happened earlier, so I could have used it in my college essay. Christ on a crutch, I'd be going to Harvard now."

Jacob tried to laugh, but he was trembling too much.

"Hey," Calvin said. "After everything else, this will be the easy part." He peeked through the ventilation grill in the door. No one was in sight. He slipped the knife blade under the latch and jerked it up, popping the latch. The door swung out.

Calvin stepped briskly through the doorway into the stern work area and immediately turned right.

And ran headlong into Jacques LeBlanc.

It was hard to know which one of them was more surprised. Jacques' eyes widened in shock and his mouth opened to yell, but Calvin swung the pistol butt up into his throat with a solid *thump* and the older man staggered back, both hands going to his neck, struggling to breath. Calvin rushed him, smashing him in the chest and forcing him back a step, then back another, until he abruptly tumbled backwards into the ocean.

"Jacques!" Out of nowhere Jean-Philippe LeBlanc was aiming a pistol at Calvin's head, but Jacob darted forward in a diving tackle, arms wrapped around Calvin's knees, feet churning. The impact carried them both off the boat and into the night water.

But not before Jean-Philippe LeBlanc shot Calvin in the chest.

———

In the small boat, Ensign Dunbar prowled up the north side of the inlet, searching in vain for any sign of another boat.

"Christ Almighty, it's black as an admiral's heart out here," he complained mildly.

Jankowski came back to the cockpit. "I got a suggestion, Mr. Dunbar, if that's all right?"

Dunbar was an ensign and Jankowski only a Seaman, but life on a small boat is pretty informal and Dunbar knew Jankowski had several years of experience with small boats and drug interdiction, while Dunbar had only graduated from the Academy a few months earlier.

"Any advice is fine with me, Mark." Dunbar throttled back a bit in order to be able to talk easier.

"Well, I used to hunt a lot at home in Wisconsin," Jankowski said, "and the thing my daddy taught me early is that in the woods, sometimes the best thing you can do is stay still, real quiet like, and listen. You might hear the buck you're after before you see it. But if you're movin' around, you can't hear nothin' over your own noise."

Dunbar resisted the impulse to remind him that there weren't too many trees about, but simply said, "Okay."

Jankowski was not deterred. "It's black as fuck out there tonight, sir. Storm is raising hell with the radar and there's lot of image noise from all the land around us. I'm not sure we're going to *see* anything, but we might hear them if we stop dead quiet and just listen."

"Huh," Dunbar grunted. He looked around at the inky darkness. Still a lot of wind and the waves were roiling the surface, but why not try it? He wondered briefly if he needed to inform the Captain, but decided not to quite yet. "Okay, Seaman, you've convinced me. Let's get into the middle of the channel and try it."

Ten minutes later, sitting in mid-channel, the engines off, they heard the sound of gunfire.

"Christ, was that a gunshot?" Dunbar asked.

"Sounded like one to me," Seaman Levine said.

Then, distinctly, there were several more "*pop! pop!*" sounds.

"It really works," Dunbar enthused. He flicked on the radio. "Big Eyes, this is SB One. We are stopped mid-channel, one mile northwest of your position. We have heard shots from our west. Repeat, shots from our west. Request permission to investigate."

Captain O'Brien's voice came back instantly. "SB One, Big Eyes. Permission granted. Report in if you have a contact."

"Big Eyes, SB One. Proceeding."

Dunbar couldn't hide his excitement. "Jankowski, make sure your rifle is handy! Levine, get the .30 cal ready. We're heading up the inlet to see what's going on. Keep your eyes peeled, gentlemen!"

The cold water felt like it was crushing Jacob's chest and squeezing the air from his lungs. Waves pummeled him no matter which way he turned. The *Celeste* was already pulling away, but there was a figure standing at the stern, firing a pistol at them. Jacob ducked underwater, but his oxygen starved body drove him to the surface within seconds. The figure on the boat fired another two shots, then seemed to run out of bullets. He turned and ran back to the pilothouse.

"Calvin! Calvin!" Jacob shouted. He turned around once, then again. "Calvin!" he shouted desperately. "Where are you?"

Another wave crashed over him, and this time something large struck him hard, pushing him under. Surfacing, he pushed the object away and realized it was Calvin, floating in his wetsuit, face up. Grabbing Calvin's arm, he pulled him closer. "Calvin! For God's sake, Calvin, wake up!" But Calvin gave no sign of hearing him.

Ensign Dunbar ran the boat for a thousand yards, then killed the engine and drifted. Everyone strained to hear anything in the darkness.

"Hear anything?" he asked the others. They both shook their heads.

He gave it another minute, then started the outboards and continued deeper into the inlet, but this time he kept the speed down, so that the engines were softly growling rather than howling. He remembered games of hide and seek on summer nights with his brothers when he was little, lying on the ground behind the big rhododendron bush as they prowled by in search of him, the coppery taste of excitement in his mouth.

Of course, his brothers didn't shoot at him.

"Guys, I am taking us to the south side of the channel," he called softly and got two nods in reply. Five minutes later he was one hundred yards off the south bank and cut the engine again.

In the front of the boat, Seaman Levine suddenly put up his hand in a clenched fist.

"What?" Dunbar demanded.

"Something out there! When the wind dropped I thought I heard it." Levine's voice was high with tension and excitement. He reached down and pulled up the clear ballistic shield and propped it beside him, ready to grab if he needed it.

Then Dunbar heard it, too. "Shit!" he muttered.

It was close.

On the *Celeste,* Jean-Philippe LeBlanc tried to quell the panic that was rising. *Who the fuck was that with Jake Finley?* It had all happened so fast. He had turned around to say something to Jacques, only to see someone pushing him overboard. Somehow he'd managed to get his gun up just in time and got a shot off. He'd hit the guy in the wetsuit; hell, he'd seen the blood splatter from the guy's chest.

But was he dead? When LeBlanc ran to the stern to shoot at them, he couldn't see anything in the darkness. Were they dead? Jacob was dead, or he would be in twenty minutes when the cold water killed him. But the other guy?

What a clusterfuck.

He went to the pilothouse, advanced the throttle to full and pushed the *Celeste* for all she was worth. Once he was out of this damned inlet, he would go into the maze of islands, work his way north and run for Canada. There were lots of places to hide in Canada. He hammered the ship's wheel with his fist. All he needed was a few goddamned minutes, that's all.

"Jean-Philippe!" His brother, Guy, calling him from the bow and urgently pointing. "Looks like a small boat out there, coming towards us fast!"

LeBlanc cursed. "Lay down on the work deck! Hide yourself as best you can, but be ready to fire! Hurry!" The two men hurried aft.

LeBlanc positioned his rifle in the pilothouse where he could reach it easily, fed a new clip into his pistol, then turned the wheel slightly to angle away from the small craft and into the mid-channel. He wanted room to maneuver, but also wanted to flush out these guys if they were really after the *Celeste* and this wasn't just some sort of stupid coincidence. Not that he believed in coincidence.

Sure enough, a light bar began flashing blue and red on the smaller boat and a loudspeaker boomed across the water. "Unidentified craft, this is Homeland Security! Kill your engine and prepare to be searched. This is Homeland Security, kill your engine! We are coming alongside."

"Get ready down there," LeBlanc called to his crew. "I'm going to stop and let them get close. Be ready to pop up and shoot when I tell you to. They'll have a machine gun mounted in the bow. Go for the gunner first, then the rest."

He picked up his mic and flipped on the loudspeaker. "What is this all about? I am taking my boat to North Harbor for repairs. Why are you stopping me?"

The loudspeaker from the other boat boomed back. "This is Homeland Security. You are ordered to kill your engines and we will come alongside. If you do not comply, you will be fired upon."

"Don't get your shorts in an uproar," LeBlanc replied, throttling back. "But I can't turn off my engines in this weather without risk to my boat. I need to maintain my orientation into the wind or I'll breach. You're supposed to be a fucking sailor, you should know that!" LeBlanc was trying for mildly aggrieved and thought he got it right.

───────────

Ensign Dunbar glanced at his men. Jankowski shrugged, but Levine nodded. "I wouldn't want to kill my engine in this wind. That lobster boat will slide sideways to the wind in no time."

Dunbar ground his teeth – he should have thought of that.

"Okay," he said through the loudspeaker, "maintain your head into the wind, but if you accelerate without our permission, we will consider it a hostile act."

"Yeah, yeah," the lobster boat's captain replied over his loudspeaker. He sounded annoyed. "I only need a couple of knots to maintain my heading. If you can hurry the hell up, I'd really appreciate it. The boatyard has men coming in early to work on my boat so I can get out fishing tomorrow."

The lobster boat slowed to a crawl, barely making headway against the wind. Dunbar flipped on the spotlight, which showed the captain standing in the pilothouse, shielding his eyes from the glare.

Dunbar turned to the radio setting. "Big Eyes, SB One. We are about to board and search a lobster boat. It is the only boat we have seen and it came from the direction of the gunshots we heard earlier."

On the *Vigilant,* Captain O'Brien turned to her XO. "How far away are they?"

Lt. Commander Hillson checked the radar return from the IFF. "Little more than a mile, Captain."

O'Brien nodded. "Pilot! Set a course to intercept. Military speed."

"Yes, Ma'am," Petty Officer First Class Cynthia Foster replied briskly, and the *Vigilant*'s engine roared to life.

"SB One, this is Big Eyes," O'Brien said into the mic. "We are coming to join you. Wait for us to arrive before you board. Confirm."

"Big Eyes, SB One confirms will wait for you before we board. ETA?"

"Five minutes, SB One." O'Brien cut the transmission. "Battle stations! I want everyone in vests and everyone armed. Radar, do you have them yet?"

"Not yet, Captain. I think they're behind that headland, about ten degrees off our port bow. Once we clear that, we should see them."

O'Brien nodded and settled in her chair, resisting the impulse to rub her injured shoulder, and nagged by the thought that there was something...something she forgot to do. It was right there, just out of her mind's reach. Dammit, she hated when she did that.

Ensign Dunbar turned to his crew. "We're waiting until Mother gets here before we board. Sit tight, keep your eyes open."

On the .30 caliber machine gun, Jankowski frowned. Their small boat was, well, *small*. And damn low in the water. They had already drifted so close to the lobster boat that he had to angle the gun barrel up to shoot over the side rail. If the lobster boat captain ducked down, he would be unable to hit him.

"Hey, Skipper," he said softly. "We're too close! Back us away so I can bring my gun to bear."

Dunbar frowned, looking first at Jankowski, then the lobster boat, then back to the machine gunner again. Suddenly the bad geometry fell into place and he hurriedly put the engines in reverse.

Unfortunately, he was not the only one who saw it. Jean-Philippe LeBlanc had been watching the small boat as it came closer and closer. The sailor at the wheel looked young, very young, and LeBlanc figured he might not have a lot of experience with small boats in rough weather. The small boat was being *pulled* by the tide, but *pushed* in the opposite direction by the wind. It was tricky to maintain your position in those conditions, and the Coast Guard sailor had overcompensated and given the little boat too much throttle.

And now the little craft was close to the *Celeste*. *Too* close.

LeBlanc turned in the pilothouse so his back was to the Coast Guard boat, calling to his brother and Doug Tynman. "Get ready, I'm going to shoot as soon as I turn!"

In the work area, Guy and Tynman glanced at each other, both swallowing nervously. Tynman blessed himself, making the sign of the cross. Guy settled for wiping cold sweat off his forehead. They both flicked the safeties off on their rifles. "Go for the machine gun first," Guy reminded them both. Tynman nodded stiffly, too nervous to speak.

In one quick motion, Jean-Philippe picked up his rifle and, crouching low and swinging around, brought the gun up to his shoulder in one smooth motion and panned across the Coast Guard small boat, which was located slightly below him. Jankowski saw him first, his eyes widening. He instinctively pulled the trigger on the machine gun, but the bullets shredded the superstructure above LeBlanc's head, accomplishing nothing other than annihilating part of the windscreen. Try as he might, Jankowski could not bring his weapon to bear.

LeBlanc shot him from less than twenty feet, catching him in the throat and blowing out his spinal cord.

Guy got off the second shot just as Levine was snatching up his rifle. At that distance, he couldn't miss. And didn't. A round smashed the Seaman's shoulder, spinning him part way around and dropping him to the deck. He wasn't dead yet, but was out of the fight.

Tynman fired just as Ensign Dunbar hit the throttle to full speed. The inflatable leapt forward, striking the lobster boat at an angle and bouncing off to end up parallel to the larger boat, pointing at the stern. The twin outboard engines roared and the boat shot forward with enough force that Dunbar would have fallen backwards if he hadn't been holding onto the wheel so tight. Bullets zipped past him left and right, one nicking the inflatable and puncturing one of the air cells. Dunbar wheeled left and right, forcing the boat to skid sideways first in one direction, then another. More fire came in and he suddenly realized that the police light bar was still on, making him an easy target. He flicked it off and the little craft plunged into darkness. Then he yanked the wheel to the right and went deeper into the inlet, putting as much distance as he could between himself and the lobster boat.

After about thirty seconds he stopped the boat dead in the water, then leaned over and violently threw up everything in his stomach. Spots swarmed in his eyes and he felt a rush of queasy lightheadedness sweep over him. There was a plastic bottle of water near him. Pulling it from its holder, he poured half of it over his face and drank the rest.

Jankowski was dead. His eyes were staring at nothing and the hole through his neck was large enough to drive a car through. He lay in a pool of his own blood, which rippled back and forth as the wind rocked the boat.

Levine was still alive and conscious, but bleeding profusely. "Did Jank get hit? I thought I saw him get hit." He moaned in pain. "Is all that my blood? Is it mine?"

Dunbar put an Israeli combat bandage on Levine's mangled shoulder and pressed it hard into the wound. Levine screamed, then his eyes rolled up into his head. Dunbar searched for a pulse and found it, but it was weak and uneven. Dunbar sank back on his haunches, emotionally drained and at a loss for what to do. Then he recalled one of his instructors telling him that the time would come when everything had gone to shit and his life and the life of his crew depended on what he would do next.

"And when you're standing there," the instructor had told them, *"stunned and bewildered and don't know what to do, do this: Stop! Take two deep breaths.   Look at your immediate options and then DO SOMETHING!"*

Numbly, Dunbar staggered back to the center console and picked up the radio mic.

"Big Eyes, they shot us," he croaked. "Jankowski's dead and Levine is hurt bad. I broke contact with the lobster boat. I am returning to your location, but if I see the lobster boat, I will engage."

On the *Vigilant*, Captain O'Brien touched her headset. "Small Boat One, negative! Do NOT go after the lobster boat. We are almost there. I repeat, do not go after the boat!"

There was no reply from the small boat.

"Shit," Lt. Commander Hillson said. "He's moving. The IFF is moving fast, headed back down the inlet towards us." Which meant that the lobster boat was between the IFF signal and the *Vigilant*.

O'Brien touched her headset.   "Master Chief, are you on the autocannon?"

"Here, Captain, and ready," he replied immediately.

"Keep your eyes peeled. We should be seeing the lobster boat any moment. Master Chief, they've already shot up the small boat and killed Jankowski. Ensign Dunbar may be trying to chase them down. I would like to neutralize the target before Dunbar gets into their range." She had just told him that it was okay to blow the lobster boat out of the water as soon as he saw it. Not exactly standard Coast Guard protocol.

Master Chief Ramirez's voice was calm and matter-of-fact. "Shouldn't be a problem, Skipper. If you give me a radar bearing and distance, I may be able to render them, uh, *harmless* before they even see us."

O'Brien glanced at Lt. Commander Hillson and raised a questioning eyebrow. Hillson nodded.

"Very good, Master Chief," she radioed. "Lt. Commander Hillson will keep you advised." She racked the microphone and peered through the windscreen. In the space of a few minutes she had one dead sailor, one critically injured sailor, and one very junior officer who might be in way over his head.

"Foster!" she snapped at the Pilot. "Can't you make this boat go faster?"

Jacob and Calvin were drifting down the center of the channel, pushed along by a six-knot storm tide that was swollen with rainwater and rushing eastward towards the ocean. Calvin's wetsuit gave him buoyancy and kept him from the worst effects of the frigid water, but Jacob's makeshift wetsuit was only delaying the inevitable hypothermia. How long that delay was might make all the difference, but in the meantime, Jacob was cold and getting colder.

Holding onto his brother with one hand, Jacob was doing the sidestroke with his other, gamely trying to move them closer to shore. The on-again, off-again rain was momentarily off again and he could actually see some lights on land a few hundred yards away. But they might as well have been on the far side of the moon. No matter how hard he tried to swim, he didn't seem to make any headway, and the effort was exhausting him. He was shivering and could barely feel his hands and feet. Finally, he just held onto his brother with both hands and let the current drag them relentlessly towards the sea.

At one point, a small motorboat of some kind went roaring past them, not more than one hundred feet away. Jacob croaked out a call for help, but the boat disappeared into the darkness. A few minutes later he heard it go back the other way, towards the ocean, but it was moving fast and Jacob was too cold and tired to even shout.

Then there was a searchlight in the distance, followed by the sound of shooting; not a rifle, but something big and noisy.

It didn't matter. They were too far away, and Jacob was resigned to the fact that he was going to die this night.

They drifted on, propelled by the outgoing tide, Jacob with his arms wrapped around Calvin's chest, holding him so his head was clear of the water. Calvin drifted to a muddy consciousness once, moaning with pain and thrashing about.

"Cal, it's okay. I've got you," Jacob said, trying to sooth his little brother.

"Wha-?" Calvin coughed, then took a deep breath. Jacob wondered how much water he might have swallowed. "Jacob? Jacob?" His voice was sluggish and weak.

"Cal, it's okay. I've got you, okay? Nothin' to worry about," Jacob crooned in his ear and tightened his grip.

"Where...where?" Calvin tried to ask, but had to cough again.

Jacob laughed at the ridiculousness of it all, immensely happy that he was no longer alone in the storm. "W – w– well," he managed through chattering teeth, "we're in the water. Fucking LeBlanc sh – sh – shot you, but I don't think it's bad," he lied. "Anyway, we're in the reach, off Cats Cove, I think. Or maybe we're past it." He paused for breath. "How are you feeling?"

Calvin coughed weakly, then groaned in pain. "Hurts like a bastard," he breathed. He turned his head to see his brother. "You?"

"Cold," Jacob said bluntly. "Really fu– fucking cold."

"Huh. Can we make it to shore?"

Jacob shook his head. "Tried. No good. Current's got us."

"Oh," Calvin said, then he fell silent.

Neither boy spoke for several minutes, just watched the lights go by on the shore. The rain held off, but the wind increased, making the surface choppy with the result that both of them were constantly slapped by waves and choking on salt water.

Jacob kept flexing his hands, trying to bring back some feeling in them. It wasn't working.

"Dad must be looking for us," Calvin said softly.

"I know," Jacob said.

Calvin laughed weakly. "Hope he finds us."

Then, Calvin suddenly stiffened in Jacob's grasp.

"What?" Jacob said, alarmed.

Calvin peered into the darkness. "Did you hear that?

Chapter 62
Brothers

LeBlanc pushed the *Celeste* as hard as he could, all the while keeping an eye out for the small Coast Guard boat in case it came at him from behind. They were so close to the ocean now, close to the maze of little islands and shoals that hugged the coastline. He knew them like the back of his hand, but he'd bet good money the Coast Guard didn't.

Guy stuck his head into the pilothouse. "See anything?"

"Nope," LeBlanc grunted.

Guy wiped the salt water and rainwater off his face. "Think Jacques made it okay?" He didn't ask if they were going to turn around and search for him. No need to ask.

Jean-Philippe glanced at him grimly, but said nothing. Jacques hadn't been wearing a life preserver when he went overboard. Worse, he had his thick-soled, heavy work boots on. They'd fill with water and drag him down within minutes, if not seconds. They'd been in thirty feet of water when Jacques went over. If he could kick off his boots right away, he might have made it to the surface. But if he didn't, well...

"Where are we going?" Guy asked.

"Canada," his brother said. "I know some folks up Nova Scotia way. We can hide there for a while. Got enough money to tide us over for a bit."

Guy chewed his lower lip. "They'll be lookin' for us."

LeBlanc shrugged. "No turning back now."

Guy had nothing to say to that. Shoulders slumped, he returned to the work area to keep a lookout.

Jean-Philippe LeBlanc turned his attention back to the dark water in front of him, and the salvation of open ocean creeping closer with every passing minute.

Five minutes later a powerful searchlight pinned the *Celeste* in its glare.

———————

"Captain, unidentified boat on radar!" Lt. Commander Hillson shouted. "Looks like she was hugging the shore and just moved into the central channel."

"Can you see it with the night glasses?" O'Brien asked.

"Not yet. Soon, I think."

"Position of the small boat?" she inquired.

Hillson checked his display. "IFF puts them on the other side of the unidentified boat, but moving fast. Also, looks like it's more on the north side of the channel."

O'Brien touched her headset. "Master Chief Ramirez, we have an unidentified boat coming up on the port beam. Can you see it through your targeting optics?"

At his station, Master Chief Ramirez fiddled with the settings to the virtual reality headset. As always, he was amazed at its versatility. At first he didn't see anything, so he switched to infrared and an image blossomed, just under a mile away. Marking that site, he switched back to enhanced night vision, but whatever it was, it was still out of sight.

"Captain, I can see it on infrared, but not yet on enhanced optics. Should be within optical range very soon. It is within range of the Bushmaster. Do you wish me to engage?"

"Not yet, Master Chief, but I want to know when you can see her with the optics. Let's make sure this is the right boat before we ruin their day," O'Brien said. "And Master Chief, Dunbar and his small boat are out there, probably on our starboard beam. Make sure you know what you're shooting at. Pilot, keep us on this course, but slow us down to ten knots. XO, please keep tabs on the unidentified boat by radar. Tell me if she changes course or speed."

Captain O'Brien changed frequency to talk to the Small Boat. "SB One, this is Big Eyes. Do you have a visual on the lobster boat?"

Dunbar came back immediately. "Big Eyes, SB One. No. Repeat, no."

"SB One, Big Eyes. We are slowing down and waiting in the center of the channel. Have an unidentified boat on radar a mile away. We are letting it come to us. Be advised that you are within range of our chain gun and should move your position to the northern side of the channel. North side. You should attempt to get behind us as soon as possible."

"Big Eyes, SB One. Confirm move to north side of channel and haul ass. Please be advised that Seaman Levine is still bleeding. Any chance of a helicopter pick-up?"

O'Brien looked at Lt. Commander Hillson, raising her eyes in question. He shrugged, then turned to the Comms Officer, who nodded and got on her radio to call the Coast Guard base.

"Mr. Dunbar," O'Brien said. "We'll check again on the 'copter. Just get back here as soon as you can so the Health Services Tech can stabilize him." She cut the connection.

Across the room the Comms Officer caught Captain O'Brien's eye and gave a thumbs down. The helicopter was still grounded due to wind. O'Brien frowned and shook her head. "XO, get the HS Tech up here. Tell him he's got a gunshot wound coming in with loss of blood." She wondered then if she should turn north and save a few minutes by intercepting Dunbar's small boat, but rejected it. If she turned away, the lobster boat might make it to open ocean. That was unacceptable; those bastards had killed too many Coasties to get away now. No, she would count on Dunbar to bring Levine to the *Vigilant*.

"Captain, I have a visual on the boat. It is a lobster boat," Master Chief Ramirez reported. "From this angle I cannot see its name."

O'Brien was in no mood for subtlety. "Put a spotlight on it and crank up the siren. All guns, report readiness."

The ten-million candlepower spotlights reached out through the evening gloom and pinned the lobster boat. The cutter's siren whooped.

"Unidentified craft, this is Homeland Security. Kill your engines and prepare to be boarded," O'Brien's voice boomed out over the ship's loudspeakers. "Do it now! This is not the night you want to try our patience!"

———————

LeBlanc felt something akin to raw panic. No way he was going to prison, no way at all. "Get your rifles ready," he barked to Guy and the sternsman. We'll let 'em get close, then let 'em have it and run like hell. Once we make it into the islands, they won't be able to follow us."

And when Guy looked doubtful, LeBlanc screamed, "You want them to stick a needle in you and kill you with rat poison? If they capture us, we will all be executed! Now get ready, dammit!" Guy and Tynman did what they were told, unable to break years of submission to Jean-Philippe's stronger will.

———————

The *Vigilant* came to a stop one hundred and fifty yards from the lobster boat, which was now being covered by two machine guns and the Bushmaster autocannon. As the lobster boat came to a dead stop, the Coast Guard cutter crept in a bit, shortening the distance and turning broadside so that each of its three guns had a clear line of fire.

"Unidentified craft," O'Brien bellowed through the loudspeakers. "I want the entire crew lined up on the rail, with both hands on the rail and visible at all times. If I see anyone with a weapon, we will open fire."

LeBlanc had Tynman crawl across the dark deck, dragging rifles for LeBlanc and Guy. Then Tynman stayed hidden below the rail as the LeBlanc brothers went to the rail and clutched it to keep their balance in the choppy water. The Coast Guard cutter was now only thirty yards away. Jean-Philippe LeBlanc kept an eye out as a small boat was launched from the Coast Guard cutter and motored towards them. He wished his brother Jacques was with them; he was the best shot in the family.

Without turning his head, LeBlanc said softly, "Wait until the small boat is right beside us, then we shoot them. The cutter won't fire on us for fear of hitting their own men."

The small boat came alongside and a young Coast Guard Seaman got ready to jump over the rail.

We can do this, LeBlanc thought. "Now!"

Tynman popped up like an evil Jack-in-the-Box and shot the Seaman in the chest. The Seaman tumbled backwards into the small boat. The two other Coast Guard Seamen opened fire with their assault rifles, hitting Tynman, but then LeBlanc and Guy were pouring fire into them at close range. One went down and the other hunched low behind the pilot console and goosed the engine. The little boat skittered past the *Celeste*.

Leaving it fully exposed to the tender mercies of the *Vigilant's* guns.

———

Captain O'Brien saw one of her men go down and heard the gunshot, then saw Petty Officer Hurland accelerate away from the lobster boat. An ice-cold spike of anger sliced through her.

Enough was enough, dammit. "All guns, fire!"

The two light machine guns opened fire, followed a fraction of a second later by the percussive drumbeat of the Bushmaster autocannon.

LeBlanc raced for the pilothouse, intending to somehow get by the Coast Guard cutter and run for the island maze.

He didn't make it.

Chapter 63
The No. 6 Bell

The sounds of the fighting receded as Jacob and Calvin floated past, dragged along by the ebbing tide. The channel widened and it got harder to see lights on shore.

Then Calvin stiffened in Jacob's hold. "Did you hear that?"

Jacob had heard nothing but wind and waves and the distant sound of gunfire. "What?"

Calvin was silent, then, "There! Did you hear?"

Jacob listened intently. Then, faintly, he heard it.

Bells. Or, rather, one bell.

Calvin coughed weakly. "No. 6 bell buoy. Near Toothacher Ledge."

Jacob saw countless buoys every day when he was on the water, but didn't pay any attention to them. "What? What are you talking about?"

"Toothacher Ledge. Two big rocks. Right in the middle of the channel." Calvin stopped for a moment, grimacing in pain. When he continued, his voice was thin. "There is a warning buoy anchored over another rock, about one hundred feet south of the Ledge. Rock's near the surface, so they put a buoy there." He paused again, panting breathlessly as the pain struck him. "Got a light, but because of the fog, they put a bell on it, too. I think that's what we're hearing. The buoy is rocking in the storm."

Jacob pictured one of the smooth red or green channel markers. "Yeah, so?"

"It's a platform buoy!" Calvin said urgently, then succumbed to more coughing.

And now Jacob understood. Platform buoys weren't like the smooth red or green buoys that marked the channel locations. This buoy had a small platform at the bottom that you could climb up to. You could sit on it, or stand on it if you wanted. Harbor seals basked on them all the time.

"Goddamn!" Jacob uttered. "Goddamn!"

He strained to listen, and when it rang again, it was close. Very close.

"One chance to grab it," Calvin said, craning his head around to look in front of them. "Watch for the light! If you miss, we're fucked." Then, seemingly exhausted from the effort of speaking, he went limp in Jacob's arms.

Jacob listened very carefully. The bell sounded like it was coming slightly from their left, but he couldn't see any light. Kicking his numb legs as hard as he could, he dragged them slightly left for a couple of minutes, then stopped to listen again. He turned his head left and right, trying to figure out where the buoy was.

And then the light on top of the buoy blinked not fifteen feet in front of him. And the bell rang cheerily.

Exhausted and half frozen, Jacob wasn't sure if he could move left or right if he needed to. But he didn't have to. The buoy was smack dab in front of him, getting closer at an alarming rate. He had the impression that he was standing still and the buoy was charging down on him. Closer...the bell rang...the light blinked...closer...

Jacob smashed into it. He squirmed around, making sure to protect Calvin's head, then felt a thrill of fear and adrenalin as the tide began to bump him around the bottom edge of the platform buoy, trying to suck him into the ocean beyond. Desperately holding onto Calvin with one hand, he reached as high as he could and grabbed one of the four metal struts that rose from the bottom of the platform to a point five feet above, curving to make a cage that housed the bell and the blinking light above it. The edge of the angle iron cut into his hand, but his hand was so cold he barely noticed it.

Two years hauling traps had built up his arms and shoulders, and now he held onto the platform with one hand, and lifted Calvin clear of the water with his other, sitting him on the edge of the platform, his head lolling onto his chest. Panting for breath, Jacob rested for a moment, one hand on the platform strut, the other on Calvin's chest so he wouldn't topple into the water. He couldn't seem to get enough air into his lungs, and he knew that if Calvin slid off the buoy into the water, he wouldn't have the strength to lift him back again.

Calvin, for his part, whimpered in pain, but said nothing.

Gulping air, Jacob let go of Calvin, grabbed a second strut and pulled himself onto the base of the platform, then grabbed the front of Calvin's wetsuit to keep him steady.

"Oh, fuck me!" Jacob groaned, panting for air again. His arms and shoulders felt like they'd been beaten with a baseball bat, and his hands were smeared with blood from grasping the sharp edges of the support struts. A large wave rolled over the buoy then, causing it to sway wildly and threatening to throw them both back into the water. Jacob hung onto the sharp-edged strut with one hand, and Calvin with the other, terrified that he might let go.

"Stop it!" he screamed at the storm, at the night. "For fuck's sake, stop it!" Sobs wracked his chest. After a few minutes, he recovered enough to look around. There were one or two lights far away, but whether they were ships or houses on shore, he couldn't say. Several smaller waves rocked the buoy, forcing him to hold on tight.

Dimly, he realized that he had to find something to tie Calvin to the metal struts so that he couldn't be thrown into the water. It was only when he realized that he was holding onto a piece of rope tied around Calvin's waist, that it occurred to him he had the means right in his hands.

"Idiot," he chided himself. It took a while for him to undo the knot that held the rope, but he finally shook it out. Something dropped to his feet then and rolled up against one of the struts. Jacob picked it up. A flare that had been held by the rope. He stuck it in his belt. With a tremendous effort, he pulled Calvin back until he was braced against the cage. "Putting you on a diet, Cal," he grunted to his brother. "Getting too damn fat to haul around." He ran the rope across Calvin's chest, then around two of the metal struts, pulled it tight and tied it off. There were still several feet left, so he looped that around Calvin's torso and tied it to the other struts for good measure. He examined his handiwork. Ugly, but serviceable. Calvin wasn't going anywhere.

Then he collapsed next to his brother, panting again for air and not being able to get enough.

Calvin moaned and tried to twist around, but the ropes held him fast. "Jacob? Jacob!"

Jacob leaned forward and touched his forehead against his brother's. "Right here, Cal," he panted. He grinned, a painful rictus of a grin. "We're on the No. 6 buoy. It's going to be all right. They'll find us soon."

Calvin sobbed softly. "Thought I'd lost you." He laughed, or sobbed; Jacob couldn't tell which. "Some rescue, huh? Wait 'til Mom hears, she's gonna kill me."

Jacob put his arms around him. After a while, Calvin fell asleep. A couple of larger waves smacked into the buoy, but the ropes held. The light blinked. The bell rang. Far off in the distance, he thought he could hear a motorboat, a high-pitched engine.

He fell asleep, then woke with a start when another wave almost pushed him off the platform. There was no longer any feeling in his legs, but his hands ached where they had been cut by the buoy's struts. Beside him, Calvin whimpered and groaned in his sleep, and when the light blinked on the buoy, Jacob could see a thin stream of bright red blood trickling down the front of Calvin's wetsuit.

On wobbly legs that threatened to buckle at any moment, Jacob stood up, reached to his belt and pulled out the flare. Careful not to drop it, he jammed the flare into the top of the cage made by the four struts, and with clumsy fingers pried off the metal starter cap. Holding onto the strut with one hand, he repeatedly struck at the open end of the flare with the starter cap. He feared his frozen hand would drop the cap, but was finally rewarded with a burst of light that nearly blinded him. With a groan he slumped down onto the platform. Another cold wave sloshed over him.

He touched his head against his little brother's, felt the warmth of his breath.

Calvin's eyes flickered, not quite opening. "Jacob?" he murmured.

Jacob leaned in, pressing his forehead to Calvin's.

"It's okay, Cal. You saved me," he said.

Chapter 64
Jacob

The buoy rocked and tilted in the rush of the outgoing tide. An occasional wave broke over the bottom of the platform, drenching him. Jacob's entire body shivered violently. The cold gnawed into his bones. He could no longer move his arms or legs. Head lolling, Calvin sat upright on the platform next to him, tied to the platform's four heavy metal struts.

Time sort of went away for a while, then Jacob's head snapped upright. In the distance he could see lights moving towards them, flashing blue and red, urgent and insistent. But his field of vision was contracting, getting smaller and smaller. He thought he heard Calvin groaning. "It's okay, Cal," he said, or thought he said.

Another wave tilted the buoy and Jacob, unable to hold on, felt himself silently slipping across the slick surface of the buoy and into the water. The water didn't feel so cold anymore. Somehow, he ended up floating on his back, watching the buoy recede into the distance. The flare burned with a brilliant bright light, illuminating Calvin, tied so securely that no wave could ever wash him off.

Somewhere inside of himself, Jacob smiled. All the mistakes of his life, all the regrets, fell away. They no longer mattered, had no hold over him. He stared fixedly at the glorious light of the flare, at his precious little brother, protected from harm.

He's safe, he thought with profound satisfaction. Despite the cold, a warm glow suffused him.

The frigid tide carried him on. His consciousness flickered like a candle guttering in a night breeze. The light of the flare filled his vision, then seemed to dim, then grew bright again. Then dimmed once more.

Jacob smiled.

The rushing tide took him around a bend, towards the ocean, and into forever.

Chapter 65
Aftermath

Captain O'Brien watched impassively as the *Celeste* burned to the waterline. Petty Officer First Class Foster had piloted the *Vigilant* in a circle around the lobster boat, looking for survivors, but none were found. No surprise. The autocannon had disintegrated the small pilothouse and most of the superstructure. The two light machine guns had swept the deck area. And the fire had done the rest.

No one expected survivors.

Ensign Dunbar had arrived in the small boat, carrying the body of Seaman Jankowski and the wounded Seaman Levine. Levine was carried off quickly, then Jankowski's body was placed in a body bag and tenderly brought on board the cutter. Ensign Dunbar struggled to not lose it completely, but could not staunch the tears that covered his cheeks. One of his men had died and he knew, irredeemably, that it was his fault.

Captain O'Brien studied him from the bridge. She had her work cut out for her if she was going to salvage him.

Then the XO was standing beside her, handing her a pair of binoculars. "Captain, the lookout just spotted a flare to the east of us. It looks like it's near one of the hazard buoys."

"A flare?" she repeated, raising the binoculars. *Yep, by golly, a flare.* Darn thing was so bright it blotted out any detail near it. It was above the waterline, but there was no sign of a boat. "Does the chart show a buoy there?" she asked.

Hillson nodded. "Isolated Danger Buoy, No. 6. Sits atop a rock that comes up to within two feet of the surface at low tide. Has a bell and a blinking light."

O'Brien frowned. "Well, it's a flare all right, but I can't see what else is going on." She tapped her headset. "Master Chief, can you put gun optics on the bright light to the south? We think it is a flare on a buoy, but can't make out much else. This is not a threat, Master Chief, so I would greatly appreciate it if you would not shoot anything."

Master Chief Ramirez turned his head to the south and the targeting system swiveled the Bushmaster in unison. He fiddled with the infrared, quickly discovered that was an utter waste of time, and switched to night optics. Not very good, either. He switched to daylight optics, electronically reduced the glare and zoomed in.

And caught his breath.

"Captain! Captain, there is a person sitting on that buoy, or tied to it, I can't tell which."

O'Brien blinked, then tapped her headset again. "Mr. Dunbar, we have need of your services! Grab two sailors and take the small boat out to the buoy about one thousand yards east of us. It has a flare burning on top and there is a person on the buoy who may need rescuing. Get going, Mr. Dunbar!"

Two minutes later, the small boat roared away from the cutter, a subdued but intent Ensign Dunbar at the wheel. There hadn't even been enough time to wash the blood out of the boat.

———————

Four minutes later.

"Big Eyes, SB One," Dunbar called in. "We've found a young man tied securely to the buoy. He's been shot in the chest and is unconscious. Wearing a wetsuit. He's breathing, but in bad shape."

"Bring him in, Mr. Dunbar," Captain O'Brien said. "As fast as you can."

There was a pause, then: "Captain, it looks like someone else tied this guy to the buoy. A second person, but there's no sign of him."

"I'll send the other boat out to search, you just bring the wounded man here."

"Yes, ma'am."

O'Brien wheeled to the Comms Officer. "Check again on the helicopter! We have two gunshot victims, one in critical condition. We need a medivac to EMMC now!" Then she tapped her headset again. "HS Tech to the deck! We have a gunshot to the chest arriving momentarily!" Then she rushed for the ladder to the main deck.

It was going to be a long night.

Chapter 66
Picking Up the Pieces

The storm turned away from land. The wind relented.

One Coast Guard helicopter landed on Rte. 15 and Frank Finley was hustled on board, along with the three most critically wounded DEA agents.

The second Coast Guard helicopter hovered above the *Vigilant* and winched aboard Seaman Levine, the other wounded sailor, and a young civilian whose ID said he was Calvin Finley of North Harbor, Maine. Once loaded, the copter roared away, headed at full military speed for Eastern Maine Medical Center in Bangor.

When she saw the name, Captain Diane O'Brien called Howard Honeycutt's cell phone. There was a long pause on the other end.

"Mr. Honeycutt?" O'Brien said tentatively. "I'm calling because we found a man in the water with a gunshot wound. His name is Calvin Finley and I am trying to ascertain if he is Mr. Finley's son.

"Ah, Christ," Honeycutt sighed. "We just put Frank on one of your choppers to go to EMMC. He was shot several times. He had a vest on, but the impact broke some ribs and punctured both his lungs." He blew out air. "And now Calvin, too? Is he going to make it?"

O'Brien recalled the image of the teen, ghost white except for a tinge of blue around his lips, and completely unresponsive. "I don't know, Mr. Honeycutt. I just don't know."

There was a long pause, then Honeycutt sighed once more. "Crap, I've got to tell Frank's wife."

"Mr. Honeycutt, please keep me informed," Captain O'Brien said, then cut the connection without even asking the outcome of the raid on shore.

It would take them an hour to get back to port. O'Brien went to her little cabin and called to have Ensign Dunbar meet her there. He arrived in a blood-stained shirt, expecting to be chewed out for making a hash of his mission to board the lobster boat. Instead, he found her sitting at a small table with a bottle of Scotch and two glasses.

"Sit down, Chris," she said, pouring them both a finger of Scotch. She pushed one of the glasses across to him. He picked it up. She studied him carefully.

"This can be a wonderful job, or a dirty fucking job, sometimes both at once," she said. "But it is a very necessary job, and we need good people to do it." She reached across the table and clinked glasses with him.

"Tonight, I welcome you to the Coast Guard, Ensign Christopher Dunbar. Drink up."

When Honeycutt told Paul Dumas about Calvin, Dumas shook his head. Danielle was going to be devastated, to say nothing of his parents. Then he looked at Honeycutt's face, and realized there was something more.

"What aren't you telling me?" he demanded.

Honeycutt grimaced, then sucked in a deep breath. "When they found Calvin, he was tied to a hazard buoy to keep his head out of the water."

Dumas stared at him.

"Paul, the way he was tied," he paused. "The thing is, Calvin had to have been with a second person, someone who tied him to the buoy, someone trying to take care of him."

Dumas visibly sagged, looking like he was going to collapse at any moment. "Jacob?"

Honeycutt nodded. "I think so, but Calvin was alone when the Coast Guard found him. They didn't see anyone else."

Now Dumas did collapse, half sitting, half crashing into a chair. "God help him," he said, weary to his soul. "No sign of him?"

"No," Honeycutt replied. "I'm sorry." He put his hand on Dumas' shoulder. "I'm sorry, Paul."

Dumas looked up, his eyes wet with tears. "How do I tell my sister? And my mother?"

"He saved his brother's life. The Coast Guard guys said that the storm was whipping the buoy back and forth like a pendulum. If Calvin hadn't been tied in, he would have been washed off the buoy into the water."

Dumas covered his face with his hands. "Oh, God, this is awful."

Chapter 67
Shell Game

The State Police were nonplussed to find Police Chief Corcoran and several of his men standing in the middle of Rte. 15, guarding three large, water-stained bags. The State Police cautiously lowered their weapons.

"Evening," Corcoran drawled. "'Bout time you fellas got here." He gestured to the woods that led to the south shore of Elm Tree Cove. "You'll find a bunch of bodies in there, drug cartel guys, I figure. We watched them take delivery of these packages from three lobster boats. They were shootin' at the DEA guys, and then resisted arrest, so we had to kill 'em." He nudged one of the packages with the toe of his boot. "Got these packages from them, and if you don't mind, I would be a lot more comfortable if you took possession of them. Haven't opened 'em yet, but I would guess that there's a shitload of drugs in there."

The State Police exchanged bewildered glances with each other. They all knew that the North Harbor police were under a cloud, so this was not what they had been expecting. One of the troopers stepped forward and touched the bags. They were still damp from the salt water.

"We can take these off your hands for you," he said politely.

Corcoran nodded, then gestured to the north shore of the Cove. "Quite a fight. Anybody hurt over there?"

Chapter 68
Friday. Hospital Visit

Danielle stood in the hospital corridor. In the room nearest her, her father was recovering from the bullet wounds he got during the Cartel's raid on her house. In the next room down the corridor, her husband was sedated and still attached to a ventilator, recovering from two punctured lungs and numerous broken ribs.

On the floor above them, her son, Calvin, was in the Intensive Care Unit, fighting for his life.

And Jacob. Jacob was gone. The Coast Guard was still searching, but there was no hope that he had survived all this time in the frigid water.

Jacob, her precious firstborn, was gone.

Weeping without a sound, she stood in the corridor, unable to take another step.

Céline Dumas put her arm around her daughter's shoulders, inwardly gritting her teeth and willing herself to be strong. Her family needed her. "Cry your tears, honey," she whispered to Danielle. "Then dry them. They're alive and they need us, especially you. And so long as they need us, we've got work to do. C'mon now, I can't do this without you."

———————

Calvin swam to the surface of consciousness like a man rising from a great depth, slowly and deliberately, mindful that there was an *up* and a *down* and it was important to know the difference, but when he surfaced, he had no idea of where he was. First, he was aware of the discordant background noise. Beeps, hisses, the sound of fluids moving, of air breathing with a steady, mechanical regularity, and the delicate clatter of computer keys.

Then he was aware of what he saw. His eyes fluttered open, then closed, then opened again. The room was dimly lit and at the foot of his bed was a large window that looked out on a small room. Three people sat there, two women and a big burly man with a large, white beard in a wheelchair. His eyes tracked left and right. Something was missing. Something...

One of the women looked up then and saw him. Her face lit up with delight, then closed down with concern. Then his mother stood up and walked into the ICU.

"Well hey there, sleepyhead," she said, brushing his hair back with a warm palm. "Welcome back to the land of the living." There were dark fatigue smudges under her eyes, which were bloodshot from crying. Calvin digested all of this slowly, his mind mired in molasses.

"I'm very glad to see you awake and doing well," his mother said softly. "Gabrielle was here for a while, but I sent her home so she could get some rest. She's a lovely girl, Calvin, you should count yourself lucky." She looked more closely at him. "Do you want some water?" He nodded silently and she fetched a plastic cup of ice water and held the straw to his mouth. The water was icy cold and he slurped it greedily.

The water was icy cold.

The wind howled and the waves washed over them.

Calvin's eyes widened in alarm as the memories crashed back into his consciousness. He struggled to sit up and pain lanced through his side. For the first time he was aware of a thick bandage wrapped around his left side, high up near his armpit.

"Stay still!" Danielle told him, putting one hand on his chest to keep him flat.

"Mom!" he cried. "Jacob? Jacob? He was with me. In the water. We got off the boat. Is he okay? Mom?"

"Shusssh," she said softly. "Hush now, it's okay." But the tears running down her face gave lie to her words.

Calvin felt his heart sink. "Did they find him?" He paused, not wanting to say the words. "Is he alive, Mom?" Is Jacob alive?" he asked imploringly, his eyes flooded with hot tears.

Mémè Céline came into the room, taking everything in at a glance. She took Calvin's hand, rubbing the back of it with the pad of her thumb. "Calvin, the State Police captured Jacques LeBlanc. He told them you somehow got on board the *Celeste* and freed Jacob from the equipment shed. He told them how you fought with him and threw him into the water as you and Jacob were escaping."

Calvin nodded. He was surprised that Jacques was alive. "But, Mémè, what about Jacob?"

Céline nodded. "I'm getting there, Calvin. Be patient. The Coast Guard said they found you tied to Buoy No. 6, down near Toothacher Ledge."

"The bell!" Calvin cried. "I heard the bell in the storm. I think I told Jacob, but I kept going in and out, I can't really remember."

"You must have heard it," Céline agreed. "The Coast Guard said that Jacob probably lifted you onto the platform of the buoy, then tied you to the bell tower so you wouldn't fall off." She frowned. "I certainly don't know where he would have found the rope, though."

"I had rope tied around my waist," he said. "Stanley suggested it."

Céline looked surprised. "Stanley?"

Calvin nodded weakly. "I was getting gear together to go find Jacob when Stanley came by on Big Moose. He told me to be sure to take a knife and some rope." His eyes widened. "Geez, I forgot. I used the knife to break us out of the shed, then I hit Jacques LeBlanc with the pommel to keep him from calling for help. But then—" He glanced at the bandage on his chest. "Then someone on the *Celeste* shot me. When I woke up, we were in the water and Jacob was holding my head up so I wouldn't drown."

Céline looked at Danielle, who had both hands over her face and was quietly sobbing. She stroked the back of her daughter's head. "Calvin, the Coast Guard thinks that Jacob tied you to the buoy, but that he must have fallen back into the water at some point."

Fresh tears pricked his eyes. "Did they find him, Mémè?"

She shook her head, face contorting with grief. "No, Calvin, I'm sorry. They couldn't find him anywhere. They think the storm tide swept him out to sea."

Calvin covered his face with his hands, sobbing unconsolably. "I'm sorry! I'm sorry, Mom, I'm sorry. I tried, but I couldn't, I couldn't..."

Danielle came back to the bedside and put her arms around him, and Céline embraced them both. A young nurse started into the room to see what all the fuss was about, then backed out hurriedly when she saw the family clutching each other in their grief and torment.

Chapter 69
Sunday Afternoon. Hospital Visit

Howard Honeycutt handed Frank Finley a Starbuck's coffee and a turkey club sandwich, then eased himself into the chair next to Finley's hospital bed. Finley was swathed in bandages all around his chest. His skin was grey, but a nurse's aide had shaved him, removing the three-day stubble from his cheeks.

"Last time I saw you, you were covered in blood and barely breathing," Honeycutt said. "Sort of gave you a macho look. Now you look like a newborn babe, all clean-shaven and pink faced. I'm not sure if that's a look I want on my tough, hardened agents."

"That's why you decided to poison me with this coffee?" Finley griped. "Enough acid in this to eat through a metal floor."

"What did the doctors tell you, Frank?" Honeycutt asked.

Finley shrugged. "The vest saved me. I got hit five times in the chest. Nothing got through the vest, but the impact broke three ribs and they punctured both my lungs." He smiled grimly. "Thought I was going to die, Howard. Couldn't breathe right, then felt myself losing consciousness and thought, '*Oh well, this is it.*'" He shook his head. "I still don't know who kept me alive until the helicopter arrived. They told me the helicopter EMT, or whatever the hell they call them in the Coast Guard, cut me open in three places, packed the wounds and reflated my left lung. Kept me going until I got here."

"They patched your lungs and put you on a ventilator," Honeycutt told him. "Gave your lungs a chance to rest a little while they healed. Your wife called to let me know that they took you off the ventilator yesterday. You've got the luck of the devil," Honeycutt added dryly. "Next time you get shot five times, you might not be so lucky."

"No next time," Finley said, shaking his head. "Not for me. Can't put my family through this again." He looked at his boss. "You understand?"

"How's your boy doing?" Honeycutt asked, and winced inwardly. He should have specified Calvin.

Finley grimaced. "Physically okay, but he's pretty broken up about Jacob."

Honeycutt sighed heavily. "Yeah. Christ, what a world. Frank, I want you to know that there is no evidence linking Jacob to any of the drug stuff. Jacques LeBlanc says that when Jacob went on board that day, Jean-

Philippe LeBlanc and a guy named Bruno Banderas grabbed him right away and locked him in the equipment shed. Jean-Philippe wanted to use him as a hostage in case we cornered him, a bargaining chip to give them time to get out into open water."

Finley nodded. "I sorta guessed that, but it's nice to hear it. What about Police Chief Corcoran?"

Honeycutt's face darkened. "Well, it seems that after you got shot, Corcoran and his crew tried to arrest the Dominican team the Cartel was using. When they resisted, Corcoran's men killed them all and seized three fifty-pound parcels they found on the beach. They met the State Police at the road and asked them to take possession of the parcels, which the State Police did. Corcoran and his men then helped the State Police do the initial forensic work-up of the firefight between the Dominicans and all of us on the north shore of the Cove."

Finley looked alarmed. "Wait, you mean Corcoran hasn't been arrested?"

Honeycutt shrugged. "No evidence against him. He and his crew were there because Corcoran got a tip there was going to be a drug delivery at the Cove. When they arrived, the firefight between us and the drug guys was underway, and they killed the drug guys. Might have saved our lives, for all I know."

"Jesus Christ," Finley muttered.

"It gets worse," Honeycutt said. "The State Police lab sampled the drugs from the three packages."

Finley stared at him uncomprehendingly, then blanched. "Oh, shit!"

Honeycutt nodded. "Each package contained fifty pounds of baking powder. No drugs, just baking powder."

"Ah, Christ," Finley seemed to sag right in front of him. "My son got killed over *baking powder?*"

Honeycutt grimaced. "It appears that way, yes. I'm sorry, Frank. I truly am."

There was a tentative knock at the door and Stanley Curtis stood there, smiling nervously. "Hi, hi, Mr. Finley."

"Stanley," Finley said slowly. He had only been off the ventilator for a day and was still getting used to talking again. "Come in, Stanley. Come in." He introduced Stanley and Honeycutt to each other.

Stanley shuffled his feet, uneasy in the presence of a stranger. "Mr. Finley, I just wanted to say that I'm sorry about Jacob, that's all." He hesitated. "And I wanted to ask if you ever found poor Mr. Mitchell. I know he went missing out there a couple of weeks ago."

Finley looked at Stanley curiously. "Henry Mitchell? You knew him, Stanley?"

Stanley smiled. "He was nice to me. He helped fix Big Moose when the chain got broke once. Made it good as new!"

Frank Finley thought about Henry Mitchell, whose clumsy lobster poaching started a chain of events that led to all of this, and realized with a start that there was one more thing he had to do. A very important thing.

After Stanley and Honeycutt left, Finley propped himself up on his pillows and, wincing with the effort, used his cell phone to dial the telephone number of Mrs. Henry Mitchell. As he had hoped, one of her children answered.

Finley explained who he was. "Would Chris Mitchell or one of his brothers happen to be there?" he asked.

There was a pause, then the man said, "This is Chris Mitchell, Officer Finley. What can I do for you?"

"Chris, are any of your brothers with you? I'd like them all to hear this, if possible."

Finley could hear an intake of breath over the line. "Well," Chris Mitchell said, "some of them are here. Hold on, we've got a speaker phone connection in the living room, I'll use that."

There were several crackles and bumps, then Mitchell's voice came back on, sounding a little distant. "Can you hear me, Officer Finley? I've got Billy, Peter and Hank on the line with me."

"Thank you, Chris." Finley took a breath. "I wanted to be the one to tell you that we recovered your father's body. It will be released to you after the coroner has examined it." From the other end of the line he heard muted crying. People always held out hope that somehow the lost person would miraculously appear, alive and well. Now he'd killed that hope.

"Also, I wanted to tell you that our investigation showed your father was not involved at all with any drug smuggling. He was– " Finley had been about to say 'just a poacher,' but caught himself – "just in the wrong place at the wrong time. You've probably all read about the big drug bust we made a couple of days ago. Your dad was not involved in any of that, but it was the investigation of his death that led to the smugglers."

For a moment none of the sons spoke. There was another muffled sob, then murmuring as the sons of Henry Mitchell comforted one another. Finally, Chris Mitchell came back on the line.

"Officer Finley, thank you for telling us," Mitchell said, his voice husky with emotion. "From all of my brothers, thank you. It...it makes a difference, you know. He's still gone, but it makes a difference."

Finley hung up and thought about Jacob, lost at sea, but only after he made sure his brother survived. Yes, he reflected, it made a difference.

Chapter 70
Monday Morning. Hospital Visit

Gabrielle skipped school and went back to the hospital. Calvin was sound asleep when she first got there, so she took a seat and read *The Guns of August* for her history class.

Or tried to. Calvin groaned in his sleep and called out. "Bell! The bell!" Once, still asleep, he started sobbing uncontrollably. Gabrielle sat on the edge of his hospital bed and put her arms gingerly around him, talking soothingly and stroking his face. This seemed to quiet him. When he began to shiver, murmuring, "Cold! Cold!" she went into the bathroom and ran the water until it was hot, then soaked a washcloth and wrung it out, then folded it and gently touched it to his forehead, cheeks and wrists. Then she put away the washcloth, returned to the bed and just sat beside him, holding his hand in both of hers.

"You're safe now, Calvin," she whispered. "You're safe and warm. You're safe and warm." Gradually, Calvin's breathing deepened and he seemed to relax.

"That was nicely done," a voice said softly from behind her.

Gabrielle looked over her shoulder to see a woman in a military uniform.

"I'm Diane O'Brien," the woman told her. "I'm a Commander in the Coast Guard. I was in charge of the cutter near Elm Tree Cove the night Calvin rescued his brother."

Gabrielle wasn't sure what to make of this, but had been raised to be polite. "I'm Gabrielle Poulin. I'm a friend of Calvin's."

O'Brien smiled warmly. "And a rather good one, I'd say." She came into Calvin's room and took off her overcoat and put it down, then sank into the only other chair in the room. "Not to be nosy, but are you two going together?"

Gabrielle flushed a little, but nodded.

"Good," O'Brien said. "He's been through a lot. It's likely to be tough for him the next few months, it's good that he has someone he's close to."

Still holding Cal's hand, Gabrielle frowned. "Do you know what happened that night? Nobody's told me and I don't want to ask Calvin's mother, she's already got enough on her plate."

O'Brien nodded slowly. "You seem like a fairly insightful young lady."

Gabrielle's lips thinned in annoyance. "Adults like to say that to teens when they don't want to answer their questions." She gestured to Calvin's unconscious form in the bed. "He's old enough to be in the military. So am I. We're old enough to fight for this country and get shot at, yet when I ask a simple, important question, no one will give me an answer because they don't think I'm old enough or tough enough or some other bull." A single tear crept down her cheek and she angrily brushed it away. "Tomorrow or the next day, Calvin is going to wake up and want to know what happened to his brother, and why. But his brother is dead. I know Cal well enough to know he's going to feel responsible for it. And guilty. And it's going to tear him apart." Her voice was rising now, her cheeks dotted with spots of color. "I'm going to do everything I can to help him through that, but I can't do much if I don't know any facts." She glowered at Commander O'Brien, United States Coast Guard. "And *no one* will tell me!"

"Jesus!" O'Brien said. "Does Calvin have any idea what type of woman he's got looking out for him?"

Gabrielle stared at her, not amused.

"Okay," O'Brien said slowly. "Okay, but it's not pretty. Heroic, but not pretty." She gestured to Calvin. "Your young man there took it upon himself to rescue his brother from a very dangerous drug cartel. Alone. At night. In a storm. He is either one of the bravest men I have come across, or the dumbest."

"He can be both," Gabrielle said, with mixed exasperation and pride.

"Well, whichever it is, he was also lucky. Once-in-a-lifetime lucky."

"Please," Gabrielle pleaded. "What did he do? What happened? And what about Jacob?"

So, Commander O'Brien told her. Some of it she knew, some she had been told by Jacques LeBlanc, some by Howard Honeycutt and Frank Finley, and the rest she could fill in. She told Gabrielle of Calvin swimming in the cove and sneaking aboard the *Celeste,* of freeing Jacob from the equipment shed and their desperate escape from the ship. Fighting with Jacques LeBlanc, getting shot and then drifting with the outgoing tide. The freezing water, the No. 6 Buoy. And of being found by Ensign Dunbar, tied to the buoy and alone. The frantic helicopter ride. Calvin's dangerously low body temperature and blood loss.

It took forty minutes, with one break to shoo away a nurse who came to tell them they needed to let Calvin rest. When she was done, Gabrielle sat very still, not bothering to wipe away her tears.

"Have they found Jacob's body?" she asked.

O'Brien shook her head. "I don't think they will. The North Atlantic rarely gives up the men it takes, and the storm tide would have carried him deep into the ocean."

"I don't know if I can help him," Gabrielle said quietly, gazing at Calvin. "The doctors told his mom that part of the reason he's sleeping so much is that he doesn't want to face what happened to Jacob."

"I know," O'Brien said softly. "But he'll come back soon. He's young, that helps. And when he's back, he's going to need some help."

"Calvin can be very stubborn," Gabrielle said hesitantly. "He might not let me help him."

O'Brien hid a smile. "Oh, I think there might be a little bit of stubbornness in you, too. You'll find a way."

Gabrielle looked at her, a hint of a smile tugging at her mouth. "Yes, I will."

Commander O'Brien would have bet money on it.

Chapter 71

Of Clam Chowder and an Unexpected Visit

They stood side-by-side at the kitchen counter, mother and daughter, losing themselves in the simple task of cooking. There was no need to talk; this was a meal they had made a thousand times and they each knew it by heart. They had made it in happy times and sad times, because people need good food to celebrate, and comfort food to weather the hard times.

And because they were both mothers, they made more than they alone could eat.

First, they put four dozen hard-shelled clams into a large enamel pot that had belonged to Céline's mother. Danielle added in the water and a pinch of sugar, her secret ingredient. They brought the water to a boil. In the best of worlds, they would have sent their menfolk out to dig up the clams, but the menfolk were in the hospital, or worse, so they had stopped on the way home and bought some fresh from a neighbor they saw carrying a clam rake and a heavy bucket.

When the shells opened, they took them out and set them aside to cool, then poured off the broth into a bowl, careful to avoid inadvertently contaminating it with sediment from the pot.

With the shells cooling, they took five slices of bacon – the recipe called for three, but Céline was partial to bacon – and cut them into small pieces, then put them in a pan over a low flame. When the shells were cool, they shucked the clams and separated them into two roughly equal piles. Then, side-by-side, they each minced the clams, hands and knives moving automatically from years of practice. Céline finished first, as she usually did, and turned her attention to chopping two large onions.

Danielle peeled the potatoes and cut them into chunks. Céline, who preferred neatly cut cubes, shook her head in disapproval and 'tsked' as she always did, but said nothing. Her daughter, who had been chunking the potatoes since she was twelve as a way to declare her independence, smiled and said nothing. It had become part of the way they cooked together, and neither of them would have it any other way.

When the bacon was ready, they added in the onion and sautéed it. Danielle began humming an old tune and, unconsciously, her mother joined in. Humming and stirring, the two women poured off some of the bacon fat, then added in the potatoes and the clam broth and stirred until the entire concoction was simmering, then added some black pepper. They left it to simmer until the potatoes were ready.

Danielle got a stick and a half of unsalted butter while Céline measured out three cups of evaporated milk and two cups of whole milk. Then, when the potatoes were fork-soft, they added the evaporated milk and whole milk, scraped the clams off the cutting board into the pot and dropped in the butter.

Céline added one more pinch of sugar and handed her daughter a cold glass of Chardonnay. Danielle sipped the wine and slowly stirred the chowder. When it looked like it might start to boil, she removed the pot from the stove and took a small sip from a spoon. She frowned and stirred in a slurry of cornstarch to thicken it.

"Cornstarch," Céline muttered in mock disdain. "Scandalous! Civilized people use crackers." She opened the oven and took out a pan of blueberry cornbread, still warm, then fished about in the refrigerator finding the butter dish. She smiled again at her precious daughter.

"There, I think we're ready," she said.

Céline ladled out two bowls and the women took their chowder and wine and cornbread to the dining room table. They sat across from each other, neither one touching their food.

"I'm not sure I can eat, Mom. I'm sorry." Danielle whispered, eyes brimming with unshed tears.

"I know, Danni. Try one spoonful and have a little more wine." Her mother stirred the chowder with her spoon and then blew on it to cool it. Raising it to her lips, she took her first taste and smiled. "Well," she said, as she always did, "not enough bacon, but not bad even so. Go ahead, try some."

Danielle forced a smile and brought the soup spoon to her lips. "Not as good as yours, but pretty good." In truth, she could not taste a thing. She might as well have been pouring warm sand into her mouth. She took another sip of Chardonnay.

Céline quietly cajoled her daughter to try some of the blueberry cornbread, buttering a slice and putting it on Danielle's plate.

"Gabrielle called and said that she went to see Calvin today," she said encouragingly.

But before Danielle could reply, there was a knock at the front door. The two women glanced at one another, then Danielle picked up her shotgun and moved to the door.

"Who is it?" she called pleasantly, bringing the shotgun up to shoulder and readying herself to fire if the front door was kicked in.

"Mrs. Finley, it's Petty Officers First Class Josephs and Santana," a voice called.

Danielle glanced out the window and saw the two Petty Officers standing there, in uniform. They stood right in the middle of the pool of light cast by the front door floodlight.

"Danni?" her mother asked uncertainly.

"It's okay, Mom," she replied. "I know them." But why they were here was a mystery. She opened the front door and stood back. The men saw her shotgun and glanced uneasily at each other.

"Ah, Mrs. Finley, if this is a bad time," Josephs said hesitantly, his eyes on her weapon.

"Sorry," she said, leaning the shotgun up against the wall. "Since the attack on our house, and then last Thursday, well-" She shrugged expressively. "We're just trying to be careful."

"Yes, ma'am, I can see that," Josephs said, not coming any closer.

Céline joined her daughter in the doorway. "Don't just stand there in the cold, boys. C'mon in, we don't bite."

"Uh, ma'am, it's not *biting* we're worried about," Santana said.

Unexpectedly, Danielle smiled. "Have you eaten? We're just sitting down to homemade clam chowder and blueberry cornbread. And there's beer in the fridge."

Both men brightened, exchanged another glance with each other, then walked briskly through the door.

Thirty minutes later, the two men pushed their empty bowls away and ate the last of their cornbread. "Oh, Mrs. Finley, that was great," Santana mumbled around some cornbread. Josephs nodded his agreement, still busy chewing.

Danielle looked at the two men, first Josephs, then Santana. Despite the warm welcome they had been shown, and the good food they had devoured, they were both so nervous they were vibrating. She glanced sideways at her mother, who met her eyes and nodded ever so slightly.

Danielle got up and went to the kitchen, emerging several moments later with a bottle of Glenfiddich Scotch, four glasses and a bowl of ice cubes. She set out a glass in front of each of the two men, gave one to her mother and kept one for herself. She held up the ice cubes. Josephs nodded and she dropped two into his glass. Santana declined. Céline accepted two and Danielle dropped one into her own glass.

She poured two fingers of Scotch into each glass. "This is some of my Dad's favorite Scotch," she said conversationally. "Even he can't drink wine all the time. I'm not much of a Scotch drinker myself, but I must admit, this is pretty nice." She raised her glass. "A week ago I didn't even know your names, but since then you've saved my life when those thugs attacked my house. You helped save my husband Thursday night, for which I can never thank you enough. I've seen you cool as cucumbers in a life and death situation, and yet tonight both of you are squirming like boys in church who really, *really* need to pee."

She glanced again at each man, locking eyes with them and nodding. "Now I want you to take a big slug of this Scotch and tell us whatever it is you've been wanting to tell us."

"Ah, man," Josephs said uneasily. "Mrs. Finley, we shouldn't even be here."

Céline reached over and patted his hand. "I understand, Mr. Josephs. So much has happened in the last few days, so many people have been lost or hurt. We'd appreciate anything you can share with us."

He sighed heavily. "Listen, this is confidential and all that crap. If Commander Mello ever found out, I mean, jeez-" He took a gulp of the Scotch. Danielle reached across the table and poured some more into his glass."

"I'm married to a cop," she said reassuringly. "I have to be discreet." She didn't add, 'Because if I'm not, bad guys might try to kill us,' but it was understood.

Josephs glanced at Santana, who shrugged eloquently. "When Tommy and I get involved in a shooting incident, we have to be debriefed by the Coast Guard afterwards to, you know, make sure we didn't screw up. So, right after a shooting, we have to write up a timeline of what happened and when." He rubbed his face, which was flushed from the Scotch. "They trained us to keep track of important stuff, like somebody getting killed, and to note what time it happened."

"We had this one teacher," Santana chimed in. "He was always yelling at us: 'Somebody gets shot, look at your watch!' Gets to be a habit after a while."

"The gunfight Thursday night was long and goddamn bloody. At one point, things weren't goin' all that good and your husband sent me and Santana to the road to try to flank the drug guys on the south bank of Elm Tree Cove."

"Okay," Danielle said encouragingly, wondering where this was going.

"Well, when we reached the road, we saw two assholes trying to do the same thing, creeping across the bridge going *north* and hoping to flank *us*," Josephs explained.

Danielle was startled; she hadn't heard of this. She looked at the two Petty Officers. "You guys shot them?"

"Nope," Josephs said bluntly. "But somebody else did. Real slick. Somebody shot the two assholes from behind, from the *south* side of the bridge. Took 'em down with a burst each, then fired a second burst into them to make sure."

"See, the thing is, we couldn't figure out who did it," Santana said, leaning forward. "It sure as hell wasn't the State Police, and Chief Corcoran said later that he and his men hadn't arrived yet."

Danielle looked at them expectantly.

"Me and Tommy," Josephs said, gesturing to Santana, "we heard the shots that killed those two assholes. Those were AR-15s, sure as shit. Or some AR-15 clone shooting 5.56mm. Very distinctive sound."

He let the words hang there.

Danielle chewed her lower lip. "Frank has told me that the North Harbor police use AR-15s, but only semi-automatic."

"Real simple to make them full auto," Santana said. "Any competent gunsmith can do it. Hell, anybody who knows his way around a workbench can do it. Find instructions right on the Internet."

"But there's more, isn't there?" Céline asked the Coast Guard men.

"Well," Josephs said. "When me and Tommy left Mr. Finley and started for the bridge, I looked at my watch, right? It was 7:20 p.m. We crawled some and ran some, then crawled again when we got closer to the bridge. When we saw the assholes get it, I checked the time again. 7:40 p.m. We waited a few minutes, then crawled to them to make sure they were dead. Right there, I looked at my watch again. 7:55 p.m., give or take a minute.

"We started back to the north side, because I was hoping to tell Mr. Finley what happened. There was still some shooting going on and we got pinned down for a bit, so it was slow going. We got there just as Mr. Finley got shot and, well, I looked at my watch again. 8:30 p.m. The thing is, once your husband got shot, there was no more shooting after that. None."

Beside him, Tommy Santana nodded in agreement.

"And you're sure about the time, Mr. Josephs?" Céline asked.

"He's right," Danielle said unexpectedly. "When Frank got shot, he fell down and broke his watch. He showed it to me; it said 8:33 p.m., but it runs a little fast." She turned back to Josephs. "But I'm not sure where you're going with this."

Josephs grimaced at the memory and shook his head. "See, the thing is, Police Chief Corcoran said he and his men arrived on the scene at 8:40 p.m. He was quite clear about it, but that is an hour *after* me and Tommy saw the two shooters with AR-15s blow away the drug guys."

"But if Corcoran was there all along, why didn't he-" Danielle's voice abruptly cut off. Understanding washed across her face. "Oh, that miserable bastard!"

Josephs nodded in sour agreement. "See, me and Tommy, we're thinking that maybe Corcoran and his men arrived earlier, killed the two assholes on the bridge, then watched the firefight for a while. You gotta remember, the drug guys, they fought until they got the last package off the beach. Maybe, just maybe, Corcoran and his men then killed all of the drug guys and took the three packages. A hundred and fifty pounds of heroin."

"It wouldn't be hard to kill them in the woods," Santana said. "Sneak up on them while they're busy shooting us, wait until they snatched the last package off the beach, then shoot them as soon as they pull back deeper into the woods. Classic ambush."

"But I doubt we could ever prove it," Josephs said.

"But why would they bother killing them? What do they get out of it?" Danielle demanded. "Chief Corcoran turned the three drug parcels over to the State Police."

Josephs looked startled and Santana sucked in a breath. "Oh, crap!" Josephs breathed.

Danielle looked first at Santana, then at Josephs. "Petty Officer First Class Josephs," Danielle said slowly, each word as crisp and sharp as cut glass. "Tell me what the hell is going on."

"I thought you knew," Josephs said weakly. "Those bags didn't contain drugs; they were full of baking powder. We think Corcoran switched the bags. I mean, he had all the time he needed. He took the real drugs and gave the phony bags to the State Police. The State cops had no idea what the real bags looked like, so how were they to know?"

With that, it all abruptly fell into place. Danielle finally understood, understood all of it.

And what she wanted to do.

She felt something awful and dark uncoil deep inside her and raise its head, knew that if she took this path some part of her humanity would die and that her soul would be scarred for the rest of her life.

Knew it for a certainty.

And embraced it.

She turned slowly to her mother, and saw her own resolve staring back at her.

"Yes," Céline Dumas said simply. "Yes."

Chapter 72
Dreams and Worries

A week passed. Luc Dumas came home from the hospital, but then went back when a blood clot formed in his hip. Frank Finley contracted a lung infection and the doctors kept him hospitalized so they could monitor him more closely. Calvin slept a lot and when he woke, he was listless. Dr. Goodwin, the staff psychiatrist, urged Danielle to keep him in the hospital for a few more days. Danielle could only agree – she could not risk losing her second child.

Police Chief Michael Corcoran was euphoric. The State Police had taken the three bags and discovered they held only baking powder. As far as he could tell, there was no investigation into him or the North Harbor police. Quite the contrary, they were being touted as heroes. Everyone who could identify him as being part of the drug smuggling was dead. The real drugs would stay hidden away for a while, but then he and his boys would quietly sell them to the biker gangs and have enough money to live anywhere they wanted. He worried from time to time that his men wouldn't be able to keep their mouths shut, but if he got wind of any problems, there was a fix for that, and Corcoran was the man to do it.

In the meantime, Corcoran had a police department to run. And at the end of the day, he would sit on his patio and stare across the bay, feel the warm wind on his face, sip his beer and dream of what was to come.

Life was good.

Chapter 73
A Long-Distance Phone Call

Danielle knew what she wanted to do, but not how to do it.

She spent two fruitless months searching the Internet, but if the answer was there, it eluded her. She drove to Portland and consulted a research librarian at the public library, but only succeeded in scaring the poor woman when she fully described just who she was trying to reach.

"I don't know how to find his phone number," she complained to her mother.

"Well, of course, dear," Céline replied. "If it were readily available, then everybody would be calling him. No, you have to ask yourself, who knows the number of a man who doesn't want his number known?"

She gave this some thought. Two days later, when the answer struck her, she kicked herself for not thinking of it earlier.

They met for coffee the following week, at a small coffee bar in Augusta, surrounded by college students and legislators.

Howard Honeycutt asked after Frank and lamented that he had left the DEA.

He hasn't left, not really," Danielle told him. "Give him another month and he'll get bored and antsy. There's nothing for him to do at home. He can't be a cop in North Harbor, not while Corcoran is still there. Be patient, Howard, he'll come back soon." She leaned forward. "Only this time, no more undercover work," she said intensely. "He's done his bit. Just let him be an agent, for God's sake. And whatever you do, don't send him to Mexico."

Honeycutt looked at her curiously. "Is that why we're having this coffee?" he asked kindly. "So you can negotiate the conditions of Frank's employment?"

"No, not that."

He gave her a long, studied look. "Then why?"

She told him what she needed.

His eyes widened and he sat back, gazing at her with a mix of astonishment and horror. "Why on earth would you want to talk to him?"

She stared back at him wordlessly.

Honeycutt shook his head. "Danielle, I can't-"

"Yes, you can, Howard," she said, steel in her voice. "And you will. You owe us that much."

"No, I can't," he said. "It's confidential information pertaining to ongoing investigations."

Then he got up and walked out.

Dispirited, Danielle drove home to North Harbor, unsure of what her next step would be. In the movies she would employ some super-secret computer hacker and have the phone number within a few hours, but she didn't know any super-secret computer hackers and had no idea how to find one.

She went home, had two glasses of wine and went to bed in a funk.

Two days later, the letter came. It was unmarked, with no return address. She opened it up and found a piece of cheap note paper, which contained a single name and a Massachusetts phone number. She thought for a long moment, then copied the name and number onto another piece of paper, which she put inside an old copy of *To Kill a Mockingbird*. She burned the original and sent a quiet prayer of thanks to Howard Honeycutt.

The next day, she kissed her husband on the cheek and told him she had to drive to Boston to see an old college friend. Instead, she drove to Worcester, Massachusetts, stopped in a discount electronics store and purchased a burner phone. She paid cash for the phone and wore a hat and thick-rimmed glasses to disguise herself, but knew she couldn't count on it. Then she drove to Greenfield, Massachusetts, staying off any toll roads. Once there, she found the town green and parked beside it. She opened the phone, made sure it was activated, and dialed the number she had been given.

———

Salvador Garcia was second in command to Bruno Banderas. The late, great Bruno Banderas. Salvador was now in charge of the biggest Dominican gang in Lawrence and Lowell, Massachusetts. His gang sold heroin throughout Massachusetts, New Hampshire, Vermont and Maine.

Or would, if they had enough to sell.

Two months earlier, a shipment of one hundred and fifty pounds of H had been seized by the cops and the DEA, and the cream of the crop of Salvador's gang had been killed. One rumor was that the cops actually captured the gang members, and then shot each one in the back of the head. Salvador didn't doubt it. The cops had also announced that the "drugs" they seized turned out to be nothing more than baking powder, but that was bullshit. That shootout had been like a fuckin' war, and nobody would go through that over some damn baking powder. Nah, the truth was the DEA or the cops took the drugs and sold it themselves.   Fuckin' government.

Salvador wanted payback. Somebody had to *suffer.*

And, maybe even more importantly, he needed a new shipment, because he was almost out. Running on empty. And if he couldn't supply the biker gangs in Maine and New Hampshire soon, real soon, someone else would, and that would be the end.

When the phone rang, he ignored it. It rang and rang and finally one of his boys picked it up. He listened for a moment, then said, in surprisingly good classroom English, "Never heard of him." But before he could hang up, the person on the other end said something that made his eyes widen. He turned to Salvador. "Boss, I think you want to take this. Some bitch says she knows where the missing Maine dope is."

"Are you the guy in charge?" A woman's voice. "The boss?" The voice was sorta sultry, sorta rough. It made Salvador feel a little tingle.

"Yeah, who is this?" he asked sharply.   Unlike many of his colleagues, Salvador had been born in the United States. His mother was a teacher and his father a dentist. Salvador was a good student and went through two years of college before dropping out due to boredom. He didn't take to crime because he was forced into it by poverty or coercion. He took up the life because he *liked* it. Liked the swagger, liked the thrill, liked the money, and liked the women. Within two years he went from a slightly geeky teen with acne to a street hood with lots of money and an endless supply of drugs. And suddenly, finding sexy young women was not a problem.

To his surprise, killing was not a problem, either. When he joined Bruno Banderas' gang, Salvador caught Banderas' eye when he nonchalantly walked up to a rival gang member who was selling drugs on Banderas' turf, and shot him twice in the head with a silenced .22. Salvador had expected to feel upset or agitated or something unpleasant at his first kill, but instead he had felt...horny.

Banderas took one look at him and laughed. "You be okay," he said proudly, and rewarded him with Alicia for the weekend. Alicia was fifteen and petite, with long dark hair and inviting brown eyes.

Now, while he found this mystery woman's voice attractive, he schooled himself to business.

"Who is this?" he repeated.

"I'm someone who can make you a lot of money," she said.

"I don't need no more girls, I got plenty," he said.

She chuckled. "Get your mind out of the gutter. I'm talking about *real* money."

"You said you know where the Maine dope is?" Salvador asked with surprising softness. He was re-evaluating this woman. She sounded confident, not like a crackpot or a doper. No bluster. Slight Maine accent. Spoke well. Educated. All in all, she sounded like someone who knew that *she* knew something he didn't.

Besides, he didn't waste bluster on someone he couldn't reach out and hurt.

"You wouldn't believe me if I told you I did, so I will tell you something better," she said.

Salvador snorted dismissively. "Sure, I'm all ears."

"I can give you the name of the man who stole the dope from Bruno Banderas," she told him. "I can give you the man who killed Banderas. Isn't that what you really want?"

Salvador sat up straighter. "And what you want?" he asked, consciously ratcheting down his syntax to remind this bitch that she was playing on his turf now.

"Me?" she laughed. "Oh, I want something you'll be eager to give me."

Now he was puzzled. "I'm getting impatient," he demanded, reverting back to the more refined language of his parents. "Talk sense."

"The man you are looking for is the Chief of Police of North Harbor, Maine. His name is Michael Corcoran." She rattled off his address. "You may have to persuade him to tell you where he's hiding the drugs he took after he shot Bruno in the head, but if I were you, I'd look around his yard. He's done a lot of landscaping recently."

Salvador looked at the phone in disbelief, then brought it back to his ear. "Lady, who *are* you."

"Oh, just a friendly lady who wants to help," she said. "Everybody needs friends, right?"

Salvador said nothing for a moment, still trying to figure out what was going on. The mystery woman spoke into the silence. "But there's one more thing; I don't want you selling that heroin in the State of Maine, got it? Enough good people have already died because of that crap. If you try to sell it in Maine, I'll make sure things go badly for you."

"Really, you think you can do that?" he replied sarcastically. "I think you may be in over your head."

"Oh, I don't think so, Salvador," she said matter-of-factly, using his Christian name for the first time. "After all, I found your number, didn't I? Makes you wonder whose other numbers I know, doesn't it? Like maybe *foreign* numbers."

"Hey, fuck you, lady! Try anything and-"

But she had hung up.

Salvador put the phone down, then sat there, thoughtfully staring into space.

———————

Danielle terminated the connection, put her car into gear and drove away. At the first bridge, she stopped and threw the burner phone into the Connecticut River.

She took the long way home, north on Rte. 91 to St. Johnsbury, then east on back roads to Augusta, then continuing east to Belfast and looping south around Penobscot Bay to North Harbor. When she needed gas, she paid cash and didn't speak to anyone. It was a long trip, just under eight hours, and when she got home she was exhausted.

Her mother was waiting for her. She handed Danielle a glass of red wine and raised her eyebrows in question.

"It's done," Danielle told her, then took a gulp of the wine. "God forgive me, it's done."

"God will forgive you," Céline said. "Or I'll give Him a piece of my mind."

Danielle looked across the harbor to the open ocean beyond. "He's out there, Mom. Somewhere. I'll never hold him again, never hear his voice, and it breaks my heart." She wiped away the tears with the back of her hand. "I wish to God we never came back here."

Céline stepped close to her daughter and put her arm around her. And tried, as best a mother could, to ease her pain.

And bleakly hoped that someday, somehow, she would be able to ease her own.

Chapter 74
A Reckoning

The next day Danielle and Céline took turns watching Corcoran's house from a vantage point on a hill four hundred yards away. They were dressed in brown and green clothes, and armed with a Roxant Authentic Blackbird 12-36X zoom spotting telescope, mosquito netting to keep away the black flies and give them some concealment, two bottles of water, four bananas, and two large coffees– Café Mocha for Danielle and Gingerbread Latte for Céline . And a burner cell phone.

Nothing much happened. They watched Corcoran leave his house and drive away to go to work, then come back at dinner time. He ate dinner on his patio, then went inside. The two women crept away, unseen.

They were back in position at dawn the following day. They watched Corcoran take his breakfast on his small patio, then drive off to work again. An hour after he disappeared, they watched as two men stepped from the woods and approached the house. They cautiously looked through the windows before bending to work on the lock on the front door. One man stayed outside while his companion went inside. After fifteen minutes, he emerged, carefully pulling the front door closed behind him. They walked into the woods and disappeared from view.

"Wait for Corcoran to come back, or go now?" Danielle asked her mother.

"I want to see it through," Céline replied.

At five o'clock, Corcoran's car came up the gravel road and he pulled into his small garage. He let himself in the side door and forty minutes later came out with a beer and a plate of food and took his customary position on the patio.

Danielle focused the spotting telescope on the far side of the house and watched as eight men emerged from the tree line, four carrying rifles of some sort and the rest pistols. Céline, too impatient to wait for her turn with the telescope, dug out a pair of Carson hunting binoculars from her knapsack and held them up to her eyes.

"Ahhh," she said. "The guests have arrived."

The eight men split up and went around the house from opposite directions, catching Corcoran by surprise as he ate his chicken cacciatore. He tried to fight, but one of the men struck him on the head with the butt of his rifle, then they dragged him inside.

The two women waited. They figured thirty minutes was about right. When it was time, Danielle sighed, looking sad, relieved, triumphant, and drained. She pulled out the burner phone, checked to make sure she had a signal, then called the administrative number of the State Police, not the emergency number.

"Hello? Yes, I'm calling because I just heard screams and gunshots from the little house at the end of Banner Road in North Harbor." She paused, turning her face to the sky and closing her eyes. "No, no, I didn't call the local police, I think this is a State Police matter. No, no, I won't give you my name, I really don't want to be involved."

She hung up.

Céline touched her on the shoulder. "Time to go, dear."

They packed their gear, scoured the ground to make sure they left nothing behind, and melted into the bushes behind them.

They were too far away to hear the screams.

Chapter 75
In Case There's Not a Hell

Howard Honeycutt stopped by the house two days later. It was a wet June day, with a cool offshore wind. He shook out his umbrella and left it standing in the front hallway after Frank and Danielle Finley welcomed him in.

"Would you like some hot coffee, Howard?" Danielle asked.

"Coffee would be great, particularly if you can put a little whiskey in it," he said, adding by way of explanation: "Need some warming up."

They sat down in the living room, with Honeycutt taking a grateful sip of the coffee. "Even summer can be cold in Maine," he said. "I've half a mind to put in for a transfer to Arizona."

Finley snickered. "You like being top dog, Howard. You're not going to give that up unless they promise you the Regional Directorship in Arizona, and that isn't going to happen anytime soon."

Honeycutt's mouth twitched in a smile. "Allow an old man his dreams, for Christ's sake." He peered at Finley. "You are looking positively rested, Frank. You let me know when you're ready to come back and do some work. You know you can pretty much pick your job."

Finley sighed, but he didn't say no. "Let me think on it, Howard."

"How's Calvin doing?" Honeycutt inquired.

Danielle spoke before her husband could. "Good days and bad, but the good days are gaining traction. He's decided to go to Duke University in the fall, wants to study oceanography."

"Ha! I met my wife at a mixer at Duke," Honeycutt said warmly. "Good school, I think he'll like it there. Durham is a great place to be a college student."

"Howard, I don't think you came out here to ask how Calvin is doing," Frank Finley said mildly.

Honeycutt nodded, his lips curled in a smile. "Well, yeah, there is something you should know about." He glanced at Danielle. "That is, if you don't know already."

Danielle linked arms with her husband. "What is it, Howard?"

Honeycutt pursed his lips. Two days ago, the State Police got a tip about a shooting in progress. They had a man in the area and he rushed to the scene, but he realized immediately that he was outmanned and called for backup. A SWAT team showed up, but by then it was a little late for the victim. The State Police called us."

Finley frowned. "Howard, who the hell was the victim?"

Honeycutt glanced at Danielle, who raised her eyebrows in question and smiled blandly.

"Frank, Chief of Police Michael Corcoran was tortured and killed at his home. The killers were captured; they're from one of the Dominican gangs in Massachusetts who distribute drugs in Maine, New Hampshire and Vermont for the Sinaloa Cartel." Honeycutt smiled sharkishly. "Among the guys we caught was Salvador Garcia, who became the top guy in the gang after Bruno Banderas got killed in the big shoot out."

"Jesus!" Finley breathed. "But why, exactly, did they go after Corcoran?"

Honeycutt's face hardened. "Because you were right all along: Corcoran was dirty. But not only was he dirty, he also double-crossed the Dominicans and stole the three bags of drugs from them that Thursday night. As far as we can determine, it was Corcoran and his men who killed the Dominicans on the south shore of the Cove. They swapped out the bags of drugs with bags containing baking powder, then walked out to the road and met the State Police and handed all of it over to them. The real drug bags were taken to Corcoran's house and buried."

"The Dominicans tortured him to learn where the drugs were buried?" asked Danielle.

Honeycutt turned to face her. "Yes, but given how brutal they were, they must have been very, very angry. I don't know how they figured out he killed Banderas and the others, but nobody could have withstood what they did to him. He was in pieces when we found him." He shuddered at the memory. "*Many* pieces."

"Such a shame," Danielle said sarcastically. "He was such a nice man."

"Did the State Police find all the drugs?" Finley asked.

Honeycutt frowned. "They found two bags, about one hundred pounds of heroin. One bag was missing, but we're going to bring in ground-searching radar and go over his entire property. We'll find it."

"How about the North Harbor police? Corcoran must have had people working with him," Finley said.

"Funny you should mention that" the older man replied. "Seems five of the North Harbor police have suddenly left town. Two even left their families behind and just ran for it." Honeycutt shrugged. "We've got a BOLO out for them. Only a matter of time." He stood up. "Time for me to go," he said genially. Then, to Frank: "Let's have lunch next week. I've got some projects you might be interested in. Thanks for the coffee."

Danielle stood with him. "I'll walk you out, Howard."

Outside, they paused on the porch.

"Did they really torture him, or are you saying that to make us feel like he got what he deserved?" she asked him.

"Danielle," he said somberly. "They carved him up like a Sunday turkey. Fingers, toes, ears, nose-" He sighed, not meeting her eyes. "And then a lot worse. When they were finally through with him, they beheaded him. It was...*medieval*."

"Good," Danielle Finley said firmly. "Just in case there's not a hell." Then she turned and went back into her house, smiling just a little.

Chapter 76
Healing

July came.

Frank Finley went back to work for the DEA as a Senior Supervisor, with twenty agents reporting to him. Danielle went back to work, carrying her son's death in her heart like a lump of frozen stone. But she understood grieving, and healing, and every day went through the motions of being caring and compassionate to the patients she worked with, and hoped there would come a time when her grief would lessen to something merely awful and heartrending. Not yet, but someday. She almost believed it.

About Police Chief Michael Corcoran, she had no regrets.

Her father, Luc Dumas, worked with the physical therapist and walked around the house squeezing a tennis ball in his left hand for hours at a time. He went to his studio often, staring at the unfinished statue of the Indian warrior. One day Stanley came in while he was studying it.

"Hi, hi, Mr. Dumas!" he shouted excitedly.

Luc Dumas stood up and formally shook Stanley's hand. "Stanley, thank God you're here. There is so much work to be done. But I can't work until this place is properly cleaned up."

Stanley laughed and nodded, his whole head bobbing up and down. "Oh, oh, I can help you, Mr. Dumas! Let me get started." And with that he walked to the little closet in the corner and took out a broom and dustpan and began to meticulously sweep the work area.

And when he was done, Luc looked at him fondly. "Thank you, Stanley. Now, could you please fetch me the chisel and mallet off the work bench?" He stood up, stretching. "I think it's time I got to work, don't you?"

Once Stanley brought him his tools, he stretched his shoulders and flexed his fingers, paying particular attention to his left hand, the hand that would position and hold the chisel. He walked around the block of marble, finally stopping at the place he had left off on the day he'd been shot. He'd been working on the warrior's face and had just another couple of strokes to finish it.

He positioned the chisel carefully, holding it tightly in his injured hand. If it slipped, the entire statue could be ruined.

Then he drew his right arm back and struck the chisel head with one strong, sure blow.

Stanley clapped excitedly.

Céline kept a watchful eye on her daughter and grandson. She had heard the story of how Chief Corcoran had died, nodded once to herself in satisfaction and then moved on. Corcoran was dead, the living needed caring for. She spent a lot of time taking walks along the shore with Danielle. Often, neither one of them said a word. Just walked. The sunsets were glorious and sad. There were meals to be prepared, house projects to consult on. Mother and daughter would sit on the porch and look out over the harbor and sip tea as the lobster boats came and went. And bit by bit, they could talk more about Jacob. The two of them often went to Luc's studio to see how the sculpture was progressing, teasing him about the many imagined imperfections they saw – the Indian's nose was too big, the horse's eyes too flirtatious, the whole statue was leaning to one side. Luc would scowl ferociously and stomp around the statue, pretending to examine it closely, while Stanley would giggle helplessly in the corner, then everyone would sit down and have a glass of wine. It was silly, but therapeutic.

Céline kept an eye on Stanley as well, but he was just Stanley – kind and sweet and forever a child.

Helping Calvin was another story altogether. She tried to talk to him about Jacob and survivor's guilt. He listened politely, but it was clear she made no headway. Gradually, she came to realize that she could no longer be the source of the healing he needed, that would come from another woman, a much younger woman, and though the realization plucked at her heart, she accepted it. Even grandmothers could not be the healer for everyone, all of the time. And when she saw Gabrielle and Calvin together, saw the tenderness and the teasing, the affection and the raw heat, she took comfort from the fact that he was in good hands and wished them well.

One evening, as they sat on the porch and Gabrielle and Calvin were getting ready to go out, Gabrielle came and knelt between Céline and Danielle, put her arms around each of them and whispered, "Thank you both for making Calvin such a wonderful man." And the two older women looked at each other with tears in their eyes.

Later, when the kids had gone, Danielle observed wryly, "I feel like a favorite old horse, put out to pasture."

Céline patted her hand. "Not to worry. Children go off, make their own families, then gradually come back again. Mine certainly did."

Chapter 77
Patience and Tenacity

In Mexico, Wallace Charles Moore III studied the report that he'd received from a police officer in Portland, who he bribed to keep abreast of what happened in North Harbor.

It was discouraging reading. There were several newspaper articles attached and even some copies of State Police files, but the short of it was everyone he had counted on in the North Harbor Police Department was gone, either dead or on the run. And the Dominican gang the Cartel had used in Lowell was in shambles, with most of its members arrested or in hiding. He sighed. North Harbor was no longer a viable route for smuggling drugs.

Well, if bringing in the drugs by sea wasn't viable, he'd simply find another way. If he hadn't learned anything else from smuggling, it was that there was always another way. Moore sat down at his desk and turned on his computer. He had faced setbacks before and always found a way around them. Patience and tenacity were the key. Old Hannibal said it best: "We will either find a way or make one."

He thought for a long while, then called up Google and typed in his search: *How to start a low-cost airline?*

He hit "enter" and smiled when Google told him there were 150,000,000 hits.

Patience and tenacity, that was the ticket. He nodded and got down to work.

Chapter 78
Calvin

July progressed and August beckoned. The Maine coast baked in glorious sunshine that chased away the black flies, but brought in the tourists.

Calvin's physical therapist released him to lift weights, swim and kayak in order to build up the chest muscles that had been injured when Jean-Philippe LeBlanc shot him. Weather permitting, Gabrielle would show up at the dock at 6 a.m. and they would kayak all through the maze of islands off of North Harbor, stopping at one or another for a mid-morning break of muffins and coffee or tea. They each grew obsessed with the many types of birds they saw, and tried to keep a list of what they identified on each trip: Red Knots, a Stilt Sandpiper, an Artic Tern, and once even a Red-necked Phalarope, which they both thought was pretty neat. And puffins, hundreds and hundreds of puffins, with their brightly colored beaks and funny waddle when they walked. Gabrielle used her father's camera and created a scrap book of the birds they'd seen.

Once they'd catalogued the birds, or scared them off, they'd push the boats out into the water and paddle further on. They would return to the dock by noon, drag the kayaks up on the bank and go to either Calvin's house or Gabrielle's. At that time of day, they usually had the house to themselves, so they would shower off the saltwater, and sometimes take advantage of their privacy. Or, sometimes, just be together and cuddle.

One of those times, Calvin surprised her by suddenly sobbing uncontrollably. She stroked his head and held him to her breast and said, "Shhsssh, shhsssh, it's okay, it's okay," and thought her heart would break.

"I tried," he said, his voice muffled against her body. "I tried. I swear to God, I tried, but I couldn't..."

"I know, Calvin," she whispered to him. "Sometimes our very best isn't enough. It's terrible, but it's true."

When he was ready, he began swimming again. The first morning he crept down to the kitchen at 5:30 a.m. and made his coffee and oatmeal. He assembled his gear, ate his hot breakfast and carefully put on his bright orange wetsuit. He walked slowly to the end of the dock and lowered himself into the water. There was still a visible notch in his muscle where the bullet had struck him, but it was smaller than it had been and the kayaking had helped to stretch it out and loosen the abused flesh. He kicked his feet and started towards Sheep Island.

The water was flat and golden with the sunrise. He fell into the rhythm of the breaststroke and sank into the swimmer's trance. And just swam.

When he neared Sheep Island, a pod of juvenile seals came darting around him, swimming alongside him and under him and even brushing up against the length of his body as they swam by. Soon there were six or more, all barking and jostling near him, swimming right up to his face and looking at him curiously, then barking and disappearing with a splash. He stopped for a moment and splashed water at some of them. The seals barked and twirled about, and one of them even managed to splash water back at him. Calvin laughed; the seals barked back. It was hard to tell which of them was enjoying it more.

When he got back to the house, his father was sitting at the kitchen table, wearing his old, worn bathrobe. "Heard you go out," he said. "Good swim?"

"Yeah," Calvin grinned. "Yeah, really good."

"Got some mail here from Duke," his father said. "Might be setting the date for freshman orientation."

So the summer went. Swimming, kayaking, lobstering on the *She's Mine,* and spending as much time with Gabrielle as he could.

Every few days a storm would sweep in, some large, some small. Calvin would sit on the porch and watch the lightning flashes chase each other in a game of celestial tag. But when the rain and wind came, it often made him feel uneasy and restless. He would retire to his bedroom, read late into the night, and finally go to bed.

And sometimes, just as he was drifting off, there would be the physical sensation of Jacob's forehead pressed against his, warm skin amidst the howling wind and frigid water, and he could hear his brother's voice.

"It's okay. You saved me."

And with that, came peace.

The End

Acknowledgements

So many people to thank. As some of you know, I write both science fiction and mysteries. One of the learning experiences has been how much more research is required to write a mystery novel set in the real world. In this case, the real world of Maine, lobster boats and the lobster industry, ocean currents, the Coast Guard, and, of course, drug smuggling. There were just so many things I didn't know, but, fortunately, so many people with expertise that I could call upon. My thanks to Joel Reich for his medical expertise regarding wounds; Craig and Michele Fontaine for tips about wetsuits, cold water swimming and for all things French Canadian; lobstermen David Cassoni and Matt Trundy for their enormous help in teaching me about the Maine and Massachusetts lobstering industries and what life is like aboard a lobster boat; Roy McKinney, Director of the Maine Drug Enforcement Agency, who took a cold call from me when he had much more important things to do and patiently educated me about drug smuggling in Maine (and a big thanks to his very pleasant receptionist, who listened to my story and put my call through to Director McKinney); my brother, Mike Hudner, who rarely reads fiction (and thinks it is sort of silly), but was happy to work through several time and distance issues between Mexico and the Bay of Fundy to help me avoid some glaring mistakes; and Sandy Phoenix and Phil Elkin for their interest in the story long before I began writing it, and their willingness to show me around Stonington, ME (and thanks for the map!). And a special thank you to Marcy and Ron Klattenberg for their enormous help in educating me about the intricacies of the Eastern Maine Coastal Current, which turned out to play a leading role in the story. Thank you for your time and enthusiasm.

There are also my early readers, people who read early drafts and told me what I did wrong so that I could get it right. Thank you to my sister, Nina Beitman, Beth Hillson, Bruce Hillson and his wife, Beth (the "other Beth"), Diane O'Brien, Nancy Goodwin, Michele Fontaine, and, in particular, my wife, Jennifer, who patiently read several drafts of key chapters and continues to argue character issues with me to this day. Each of these readers, together and individually, spent many hours reading the manuscript and making suggestions for changes. The resulting changes added polish and depth to the story (and gave Jacob the ending he deserved). I was very fortunate to find so many people willing to help. I can't thank you enough.

And my thanks to Don Kray, for patiently catching my many, many mistakes.

If I have inadvertently missed anyone, my apologies. But rest assured you are in my heart and your suggestions have made this a better story.

I received a lot of good advice in preparing this book, and any mistakes you might have found are mine and mine alone.

— Kennedy Hudner, June 25, 2019, Glastonbury, CT

Made in the USA
Columbia, SC
12 June 2020